ACCLAIM FOR COLLEEN COBLE

"Coble's atmospheric and suspenseful series launch should appeal to fans of Tracie Peterson and other authors of Christian romantic suspense."

—*LIBRARY JOURNAL*
REVIEW OF *TIDEWATER INN*

"Romantically tense, but with just the right touch of danger, this cowboy love story is surprisingly clever—and pleasingly sweet."

—USATODAY.COM REVIEW
OF *BLUE MOON PROMISE*

"Colleen Coble will keep you glued to each page as she shows you the beauty of God's most primitive land and the dangers it hides."

—WWW.ROMANCEJUNKIES.COM

"[An] outstanding, completely engaging tale that will have you on the edge of your seat . . . A must have for all fans of romantic suspense!"

—THEROMANCEREADERSCONNECTION.COM
REVIEW OF *ANATHEMA*

"Colleen Coble lays an intricate trail in *Without a Trace* and draws the reader on like a hound with a scent."

—*ROMANTIC TIMES*, 4 ½ STARS

"Coble's historical series just keeps getting better with each entry."

—*LIBRARY JOURNAL* STARRED
REVIEW OF *THE LIGHTKEEPER'S BALL*

"Don't ever mistake [Coble's] for the fluffy romances with a little bit of suspense. She writes solid suspense, and she ties it all together beautifully with a wonderful message."

"This book has everything I enjoy: mystery, romance, and suspense. The characters are likable, understandable, and I can relate to them."

"[M]ystery, danger and intrigue as well as romance, love and subtle inspiration. *The Lightkeeper's Daughter* is a 'keeper.'"

"Colleen is a master storyteller."

Rosemary Cottage

ALSO BY COLLEEN COBLE

HOPE BEACH NOVELS
Tidewater Inn

UNDER TEXAS STARS NOVELS
Blue Moon Promise
Safe in His Arms

THE MERCY FALLS SERIES
The Lightkeeper's Daughter
The Lightkeeper's Bride
The Lightkeeper's Ball

LONESTAR NOVELS
Lonestar Sanctuary
Lonestar Secrets
Lonestar Homecoming
Lonestar Angel

THE ROCK HARBOR SERIES
Without a Trace
Beyond a Doubt
Into the Deep
Cry in the Night
Silent Night: A Rock Harbor Christmas Novella (e-book only)

THE ALOHA REEF SERIES
Distant Echoes
Black Sands
Dangerous Depths
Midnight Sea

Alaska Twilight
Fire Dancer
Abomination
Anathema

NOVELLAS INCLUDED IN:
Smitten
Secretly Smitten

ROSEMARY COTTAGE

A
HOPE BEACH
NOVEL

By Colleen Coble

THOMAS NELSON
Since 1798

NASHVILLE   DALLAS   MEXICO CITY   RIO DE JANEIRO

Published in Nashville, Tennessee, by Thomas Nelson. Thomas Nelson is a registered trademark of Thomas Nelson, Inc.

Thomas Nelson, Inc., titles may be purchased in bulk for educational, business, fund-raising, or sales promotional use. For information, please e-mail SpecialMarkets@ThomasNelson.com.

Publisher's Note: This novel is a work of fiction. Names, characters, places, and incidents are either products of the author's imagination or used fictitiously. All characters are fictional, and any similarity to people living or dead is purely coincidental.

Unless otherwise noted, Scripture quotations are taken from the King James Version.

Library of Congress Cataloging-in-Publication Data

Coble, Colleen.
    Rosemary cottage : a Hope Beach novel / Colleen Coble.
        pages cm
    ISBN 978-1-59554-782-8 (trade paper)
    I. Title.
    PS3553.O2285R67 2013
    813'.54--dc23
                                            2013001541

Printed in the United States of America

13 14 15 16 17 RRD 6 5 4 3 2

For my aunt Edith Phillips.
While she doesn't surf cold water, every
child gravitates toward her.
You've always been my role model, Ede. Love you!

PROLOGUE

The Atlantic water rushed past her limbs in a silken caress. Gina Ireland loved the water, the busy fishermen boating to and fro, and the blue bowl of sky overhead. She was the first to hit the water every spring in her new bikini. This might be her last swim of the season, and she intended to milk every second from the October sun overhead.

She waved to her brother on the beach where he sat on the blanket with her tiny daughter. He was as crazy about their Outer Banks island as she was, and when he wasn't working on the water, he was plopped on the beach. Seven-month-old Raine squawked, objecting to being corralled off the sand. She already had her Uncle Curtis wrapped around her finger. Gina too, for that matter. The baby had changed everything.

Curtis waved in return, then squatted on the blanket with the baby. Other beachgoers splashed in the waves, and the distant roar of Jet Skis disrupted the serenity of her beloved Hope Island.

Gina flipped to her back and closed her eyes as the waves carried her on the whitecaps. She was different now, new and clean. The future looked bright. The water held no fear for her. Once she'd entertained dreams of winning an Olympic gold medal in swimming until life intervened, but contentment curled

1

along her spine. No need for a medal when she had everything right here.

The island had receded in the distance when she opened her eyes and turned to her stomach again. She started back toward the beach with long, sure strokes. When the shore was no nearer five minutes later, she paused and trod water in the riptide that had seized her. She experienced only a momentary stab of disquiet. The boating lane was near, and if the current didn't release her, she could hail a passing fishing boat. She swam parallel to the shore, then tried again, only to be thrust back by the strong tide.

The rumble of an approaching ski boat wasn't nearly as annoying as usual as it zoomed toward her. She waved and shouted. The man's eyes narrowed as he looked at her and nodded. Good, he'd seen her. She waved again so he didn't lose her in the waves.

The boat's engine roared to a higher pitch as the man aimed the craft toward her. The nose on the thing rose in the air as he forced it even faster. Sea spray foamed around the boat.

"Slow down!" She made a cutting motion with her hand, but the man merely smiled and stared at her.

When he grew closer, she frowned. What was *he* doing out here and why wasn't he pulling back on the throttle? She tried to dive to escape the big boat barreling down on her, but her head was only a foot under the waves when the great blades came at her. If only she'd had one last glimpse of her baby girl.

ONE

The distant sound of the sea blended with the hum of bees seeking the spring flowers. The clumps of blue-green vegetation gave off a spicy fragrance Amy Lang recognized as rosemary. *Rosemary for remembrance.* She stood on the stone walk beside her friend Libby and stared at the house with memories washing over her.

The old Hope Beach cottage in North Carolina's Outer Banks was just as beautiful as she remembered but sad somehow. As if the cottage knew Ben was gone and mourned with her. The two-story's soft gray siding blended with the slate roof, but the red door and shutters added a punch of welcoming color. The flower boxes at the windows held the dry remains of last year's annuals. The detached garage, in a carriage-house style, sat behind the house and off to one side.

Libby Bourne rested her hand on the belly that swelled her sundress. Her baby was due in two weeks. She wore her long brown hair in a ponytail, and her amber eyes smiled when she stared at the house. "I've always loved Rosemary Cottage. That circular porch is so unique. I did some research and discovered it was built in 1883, but I suppose you know that."

Libby was an architectural historian, and she knew more

about old buildings than most architects. The two had become acquainted last summer when Amy and Ben met for their annual vacation at the cottage. Both in their early thirties, the women became instant friends when Amy saw Libby trying to learn to surf and had shown her a few tips.

Libby shifted her purse to the other shoulder. "Earth to Amy. Where did you go?"

"Sorry, I was woolgathering." Amy recovered her composure. "Our ancestor, Oscar Lang, was a sea captain." The gray metal roof was new.

"It has so much character and detail," Libby said, pointing. "Look at the scrollwork under the eaves and the fretwork on the porch. No house has as much charm as a Victorian."

Rosemary Cottage had been passed down through the Lang family for generations, usually jointly owned by siblings. Now it was Amy's alone since her brother's death four months ago. She didn't know if she could open that door and step into the echoing silence of the house where she and Ben had spent so many happy summers. Her eyes stung, but she tipped her chin up.

Libby touched Amy's arm. "Is this all too upsetting? You can come back to Tidewater Inn if you'd rather ease into this whole thing."

Amy shook her head. She didn't want Libby, of all people, to see any weakness in her. "No, I'm going in. I'm just checking out what needs to be done. I really appreciate you coming with me."

Libby frowned at the yard. "It's a little overgrown. I should have gotten a gardener over here."

"Overgrown is an understatement." Amy forced levity into her voice. "The plants all need to be cut back, but I like doing it myself."

Roses rambled up the wall that surrounded the home, and wildflowers covered most of the front yard. Flyspecks marred the windows, and the clapboard siding needed to be spray washed, but the house called to her. If she opened the door, would she hear Ben's laughter, smell his cologne?

Amy pulled the key from her purse and marched up the three steps to the expansive porch. She stepped to the red door, then quickly inserted the key and twisted it. The door resisted her effort for a moment as if giving her time to change her mind. But she was determined to get past this, to get to the truth.

The stale scent of disuse rushed past her on its way to escape into the sea air. Inside the house, the sound of the waves faded and became a pleasant murmur. She shut the door behind them and glanced around. A layer of dust covered the hardwood floors in the entry. The pale yellow walls gave a sense of welcome. This was home. Just as much as it had ever been.

Libby followed her as she wandered through the living room, its furniture draped in sheets. "I wish I'd had a key. I would have made sure it was cleaned and ready. You should stay with me until we can get it spiffed up."

"It's only ten. I have all day to get it ready."

A photo arrested Amy's attention, and she picked it up. It was of her and Ben last summer. Surfboards in hand, they were coming up from a dip in the sea. Both looked immensely pleased with themselves. Amy put the photo back down. She had many more pictures of her brother that she'd brought with her, from babyhood to the last week of his life.

Amy moved toward the door. "Let's get the cleaning supplies."

Libby shook her head. "Let's hire it done."

"I want to do it myself. It will be part of the remembering."

Libby's expression was troubled. "Amy, don't get me wrong. I love having you here, but you said something on the phone about needing to know the truth. The truth about what?"

Amy held Libby's stare. "I need to find out what happened to Ben."

"I—I don't understand." Libby touched her arm. "He died surfing. The Coast Guard said the rip current dragged him out to sea."

"I don't believe it. Ben knew these waters, knew how to deal with currents. There has to be more." She turned away from the pity in Libby's face. Libby would understand when Amy let her read the e-mail that had come last week, but she wasn't ready to talk about it yet. Something had happened here four months ago, just offshore in those clear blue waters. And she intended to find out what it was. No matter what it took.

Amy moved toward the kitchen. "Let's get the bucket and cleaning supplies."

Libby gasped and pressed her belly. "Oh no."

Amy tensed. "The baby? Are you having contractions?"

"I think that's what it was." Libby's eyes widened, and she stared at the floor where a pool of water began to spread.

"I think your water just broke, Lib." Amy took her arm and led her to the sofa. She whisked the sheet off of it and sat Libby down on the leather. "Let me get my bag from the car."

Libby's amber eyes were panicked. "It's too soon!"

"Only a couple of weeks, and your baby will be fine. Relax, breathe. I'll be right back." Amy dashed out to the car and grabbed the suitcase that held her midwife instruments. Back inside, she unzipped the case and found her Pinard stethoscope, a trumpet-shaped device.

She hurried back to the living room and knelt beside Libby. "Doing okay?"

"I—I think so. Should I call Alec?"

"Hang on a minute. The baby is going to arrive today, but I want to see if we can safely transport you to the hospital or if I need to ready a bed here."

"Alec is going to freak! He wanted me to go to the mainland and stay until the baby was born, and I told him I was sure we had another week at least. I'd read that first babies are usually late."

Amy nodded. "It's common, but babies are unpredictable." She lifted Libby's top and pressed the stethoscope to her belly, then listened. The reassuring *thump, thump* made her smile. "The baby's heartbeat is strong." The skin of Libby's belly contracted, and Libby inhaled sharply. Amy patted her. "That was a strong one."

Libby bit her lip. "What should we do?"

"Without checking your cervix, I don't know how much time we have." She watched Libby's face contort again. "It's only been a minute. That was another contraction."

"I didn't want to say anything, but I've been feeling pressure in my back since about two this morning. Could it be labor?"

Amy didn't answer. She cupped Libby's stomach and waited for the next contraction. It showed up right on time about a minute after the last one. A small moan escaped Libby's lips.

Amy reached for her cell phone. "I think we'd better get Alec here."

———

It was Curtis Ireland's first day off in weeks, but he laid his Coast Guard pager on the beach towel beside his one-year-old niece, Raine. He prayed it wouldn't summon him to his duties. With any kind of luck, no boats would be in distress and no swimmers would need to be rescued. They would have a perfect day to themselves.

Raine had transferred enough sand to the towel to bury herself. He picked her up and tucked her under one arm, then snagged the towel with the other and shook it out.

She wiggled. "Down!"

"You're bossy." He deposited her by her bucket and shovel.

COLLEEN COBLE

"Do you want to get in the water?" The Atlantic waves were gentle swells. His aunt was out surfing those swells with his friend and coworker Sara Kavanagh. He itched to plunge into the refreshing water himself.

"Ga," Raine said.

He took that for agreement, so he shook the blanket more thoroughly, then spread it out. She lifted her arms, and he picked her up and carried her to the blue ocean. They wouldn't be able to go out too far, but a dip would feel great. He waded into the sea foam with Raine in his arms. She shrieked with delight and batted at the water. She'd been born a sea nymph and had never shown any fear of the ocean.

Edith waved at them, then let the surf carry her toward the shore. His mother's sister was a widow and had been quick to offer to move in with him to help care for Raine when Gina died four and a half months ago. Curtis didn't know what he would have done without her. Edith was fifty with merry hazel eyes and a constant smile. All children loved her on sight.

Raine saw her and squealed. She kicked her feet and reached for Edith. "Ede."

Her hair plastered down and her face pink from the cold water, Edith smiled as she came up out of the water. She scooped Raine out of his arms. "There's my little pint-sized general. I missed you." She gestured toward the water. "Go have some fun, Curtis. I'll watch her. There are some pretty girls on the beach."

Curtis grinned. His aunt was always trying to get him married. She thought Raine needed a mother, but he'd never met a woman who intrigued him enough to pursue. He wasn't into casual relationships either. He was an all-or-nothing sort of guy. "You're the prettiest girl here, Ede. I'd rather spend time with you."

She patted his arm with her free hand. "Save your flattery for one of those pretty girls on the pier."

8

Sara reached them too. She was about twenty-eight with honey-colored hair and eyes as gray as the sea in November. She was the medic with Curtis's helicopter team. They'd always been friends but nothing more. Sara only had eyes for Josh Holman, the team commander, though the idiot never seemed ready to make his move.

Sara shaded her eyes from the glaring sun and smiled. "I didn't think you'd be able to stay out of the water for long." She glanced at Edith. "Did you tell him?"

Edith shook her head. "Not yet."

"Tell me what?" Curtis didn't like the serious expressions on both women's faces.

"Amy Lang is living at Rosemary Cottage."

His stomach clenched. "So?"

"So she should know. Raine deserves some of that estate."

He set his jaw and looked away from Edith's pleading gaze. "Raine wants for nothing. I'll take care of her."

"What about Amy? Doesn't she deserve to know she has a niece? And her parents would love to know they have a grand-daughter. You should have contacted them when Gina died. It's not right."

It was a familiar argument, one he'd won only because it would take so much effort to find the phone number he needed. Edith had pushed him but hadn't insisted. Her entreaties were going to get fiercer with Amy on the island.

His aunt's eyes narrowed, and she pointed her finger at him. "I know that expression. You're mustering all the reasons why you should stay silent, but think, Curtis. What if the shoe were on the other foot and you didn't know Raine existed? Wouldn't you want to know?"

He couldn't deny it. Ben might be scum, but his family was one of the wealthiest on the Eastern Seaboard. They had a mansion in Newport, an expansive "cottage" on Cape Cod, and a family jet. Rosemary Cottage, cute as it was, was nothing to them. They could provide more for Raine than he could, but what if they tried to take her away from him? Curtis would never survive losing her. Her smile was the first thing he looked for every morning, and reading her a bedtime story was the nighttime ritual he most enjoyed.

"Curtis?" his aunt persisted.

"I'll think about it. That's all I can promise you." Like he would think of anything else.

He remembered Amy so well. The first time he'd seen her she'd been coming up out of the water with Ben. Curtis had come to the beach that day to confront Ben and tell him to leave his sister alone. Instead, Amy had asked him to take a picture of the two of them. She looked like a mermaid with her dark hair streaming down her back to her waist. Her eyes were an unusual color—part green and part golden—and they were full of love and laughter as she looked toward the camera.

It was because of her that he hadn't had the nerve to confront Ben. He didn't want to be the one to cause that expression of sisterly adoration to vanish. So he'd taken the picture, then gotten in his Jeep without a word.

A year later, when Gina was dead, he often thought about that moment and whether his sister would still be alive if he'd put an end to it then and there.

TWO

When she got off the ferry at Hope Beach, Hope Island's only town, Heather felt as though she'd stepped into another land. The sooner she accomplished her mission and got out of here, the better.

The sun beat down on her head as she walked along the pier to the quaint little town. Heather's first order of business was to find a job so she could fit in. A measly $532 nestled in the large Juicy Couture handbag slung over her shoulder, and it wouldn't last long—a few days at most. Grant could have been a little more generous, but he was a stickler for the little details being right in order to blend in.

Heather held up her head and ignored the friendly stares of the people she passed. There were several restaurants in town. Oyster Café was the first place she saw. Leaving her luggage on the porch, she tucked her long blond hair behind her ears, then pinned on a smile and approached the door.

The building was old outside with wooden siding that had been battered by the wind, rain, and sea. It was all Heather could do to keep her smile in place when she stepped inside. The floor was wooden with the finish worn off. Old tables and mismatched chairs crowded the three small dining rooms. Red-and-white-checkered tablecloths covered the tables, and the owner evidently thought the measly sprigs of flowers in jelly jars made up for the lacking decor.

It would be *so* humiliating to work here, and she nearly turned around. But no, she had no choice. Grant had tossed her out to sink or swim.

"By yourself today?" the server asked. She was in her forties with faded blond hair and tired brown eyes. She wore jeans and a red T-shirt with a huge oyster emblazoned across the chest.

"I was wondering if you're looking for any help?"

The woman looked her over. "How old are you, honey? Twelve?"

Heather tipped her chin up. "Eighteen." The lie was only six months off.

The woman smiled. "Sorry if I offended you. You look young. Can you prove your age?"

"Yes." She pulled out the ID, knowing it would take a person far more trained than someone in this backwater to realize it was fake.

The server stared at it, then back at Heather. "You ever worked before? That purse probably cost more than I make in a week." Her gaze swept over Heather's legs. "And you're wearing Joe's jeans. Though I don't recognize shoe brands, I can tell they were as expensive as your purse."

Heather tipped up her chin and stared her down. "You're judging me on my clothes? Would I be applying for this job if I had no experience?"

"You tell me."

She looked away from the woman's penetrating stare, then forced herself to look back and hold the woman's gaze. "I need the job. I'm a hard worker. Let me prove myself."

It took all her strength to humble herself with this woman. But she could do it.

Her smile seemed to sway the woman. "All right. There's an oyster festival going on all month, and I just lost my best server. I'll give you a try. Follow me to my office to fill out your paperwork. You can start tomorrow."

Heather bit back a jubilant giggle. "You're the owner?"

The woman nodded and thrust out a calloused hand. "Imogene Castor. And your name is?"

"Heather Granger." Just in time she changed the last name to match her ID.

Back in the office, she filled out the paperwork. She had to consult the fake Social Security card in her wallet, but she managed to hide the fact that it was the first time she'd ever seen employment paperwork. At least she had a job. She'd be able to melt into the residents and do what Grant wanted.

She tucked her pen away. "How do I get out to Tidewater Inn? I've heard that's a good place to stay. They have long-term rates."

"Oh, honey, if you don't have a reservation, forget it. Everything is booked for the festival. I guess you could ask though. The owner is a softie, and she might let you bed down on the sofa until a room opens up."

It was better than sleeping on the beach. "How do I get there?"

Imogene pointed down the main drag. "It's down Oyster Road just out of town. Big old mansion. You can't miss it. You have a car?" When Heather shook her head, Imogene gestured toward the phone. "Just call them then. They'll send a car for you."

"Thanks, but I think I might have more luck in person. I'll walk. Can I leave my luggage here until I find out if I can stay?"

"You can leave your luggage, but it's a long walk. Four miles."

Heather nearly winced at the thought of walking that far in these shoes. "I'll manage. Thanks again. I'll see you tomorrow. What time?"

"Five thirty."

"In the evening? I don't work the lunch shift?"

"In the morning. We open at six for breakfast."

Heather wanted to tell her to forget it, but she pressed her lips together and nodded. Only when she was back out in the sunshine did she exhale and mutter an expletive under her breath. She'd never gotten up that early in her life. This wasn't going to be as easy as she'd thought. Leaving her luggage on the porch, she trudged off down the narrow street.

It took over an hour to walk to the inn, and when she got there, she was informed that the owner was gone and not expected back tonight and that no rooms were available. The manager tried to call the owner, but voice mail picked up instead. The manager didn't have the authority to try to find a place for her.

Heather went back outside. Her feet hurt. She wasn't used to walking much of anywhere. The little Camaro her father had given her for her sixteenth birthday had never seemed so appealing. If only she could have brought it with her.

Her steps dragged as she walked back toward town. Her vision began to blur, and she was swaying by the time she could see the town in the distance. But she wasn't going to make it. She desperately needed water, food. Breakfast had been seven hours ago.

There was a cute cottage at the edge of the maritime forest. All kinds of flowers and weeds sprawled through the yard, and several vehicles were parked out front. Surely they could spare a drink. She headed toward it and noticed a sign in the yard that read Rosemary Cottage. Such a welcoming place might house friendly people.

Libby's smile beamed down at the tiny infant in her arms. "I don't know what I would have done without you, Amy." Her hair spread out on the pillow, and her smile was in contrast to the fatigue in her eyes. The baby yawned, his small mouth so perfect.

Amy poured her some water. "I'm glad I was able to experience the moment with you." No matter how many babies she delivered, the miracle of birth never ceased to amaze her. Meeting a new little life was an experience like none other.

Her gaze lingered on the mother and child. It was one she would never know any other way.

Brown hair askew, Alec knelt by the bed beside his wife and new son. His blue eyes were moist. "He's beautiful."

He still wore his Coast Guard uniform. When he touched Noah's hand, the infant gripped his finger. The baby's eyes fluttered and opened. He stared at his daddy with rapt attention.

Amy's eyes burned. Ben would never be a father, would never see a child's first smile or hear a little one call him Daddy. She'd thought she would feel closer to him here, but she hadn't realized how she would think of him with nearly every breath.

Alec stared up at her. "Thank you. I don't know what would have happened if you hadn't been here. There was no time to get her to the mainland. Good grief, I barely had time to get here before his head crowned."

Amy smiled. "You might have had to deliver him yourself."

He shuddered. "I would've been afraid I would drop him."

"You haven't held him yet. It's okay. He won't break." Amy leaned past him and lifted the infant from Libby's arms. She needed to clean him up better, but that could wait.

Alec's eyes widened as she laid the baby in his arms. "He doesn't weigh much." The infant appeared even smaller in his muscular arms. At six two he towered over Amy.

"A little over seven pounds. A good weight for two weeks early."

Alec glanced up. "You're sure he's fine?"

"Completely perfect. His lungs are strong, and he's nice and pink. You'll want to get the doctor to take a look at him, but I'm not concerned."

Alec's gaze went back to the baby. "His eyes are shaped like yours, Lib."

"He has your hairline." Libby winced as she scooted a little higher on the pillow. "You need to call your parents."

Alec nuzzled the baby's soft hair. "And Zach. He'll be bummed he missed the birth."

Amy hadn't met Alec's nephew Zach yet. She started for the door. "I'll leave the three of you alone to bond. My things are still in the car, and I need to get to cleaning."

"I'll help you get them out," Alec said.

"No, they aren't heavy. You need to get acquainted with your new son." Amy shut the door behind her. It was important for the new family to have alone time. She knew Libby and Alec would want to kiss all of Noah's fingers and toes and exclaim over every feature. It was a precious time, and she didn't want to intrude.

She lugged in boxes and luggage from the car and deposited them in the living room, then pulled all the sheets from the furniture. She got her cleaning supplies out of the car and dusted everything, including the wood floor. Once it was clean, she kicked off her shoes. The vacuum was in the hall closet so she cleaned the floors and furniture with it, then retrieved her most precious box—the one containing her pictures. She wiped off the frames before arranging them on every available table in her bedroom.

The last item in the box was her calendar. The date four days from now was circled with red. She needed to make an appointment here for that follow-up blood test. She hung the calendar on the refrigerator with a magnet.

She took a few minutes to wander through the house, pausing here and there to smooth the surface of a table or touch the plump

comforter on her bed. Rosemary Cottage was the same and yet—
different. While she recognized every item in the house, it felt odd
to be here without Ben.

The doorbell rang, and she looked out the front window onto
the porch. Pearl Chilton, Libby's aunt and the town postmis-
tress, stood at the door. She was about five feet tall and as round
as a beach ball with an enormous bosom. Her salt-and-pepper
hair was wrapped up in a French braid on the back of her head.
Surprisingly curvy legs extended below her skirt. Amy had always
liked Pearl. Everyone did. She knew everyone's business, but she
wasn't a gossip. People just gravitated to her warmth and uncon-
ditional love.

Amy threw open the door and hugged the older woman. "Did
Libby call you?"

Pearl's heavy brows winged up. "Why, no, honey. Was she
supposed to?"

Amy didn't want to spoil Libby's surprise. "I thought that's
why you came. Come on in." She stepped out of the way and let
Pearl enter.

"I saw Libby's SUV out front. Is she helping you?"

"Something like that." Amy nodded. "I was about to have
some coffee. Want to join me?"

"I'll take tea if you have any. And I brought you some cookies."

Only then did Amy notice the tin in her hand. "That's so
thoughtful." She accepted the tin and led the way to the kitchen.
"It's still a bit of a mess in here. I think the teakettle is in the cupboard over the stove." She opened the cabinet door and found the
battered metal kettle. Much of the red color had been rubbed off
over the years. She rinsed it and filled it with water, then set it on
the gas burner.

Pearl was already rummaging through the various boxes of
tea. "I think I'll have Earl Grey. You?"

"Coffee for me." She went back to the living room and carried her box of coffee supplies back to the kitchen. "I brought my own." She pulled out the cups she used. "Ben bought these for me." She held up the pottery mugs decorated with sea turtles.

Pearl's smile faded. "I was so sorry to hear about Ben, honey. I'm sure you're still grieving."

Amy's throat closed, and she swallowed hard. "I wanted to ask you about the accident. You were one of the first on the scene, weren't you?"

"I was on my way home and saw the Coast Guard cutter on its way in. I wanted to invite Alec to dinner so I went out to the pier when it docked."

"What did Alec say?"

"He told me that Ben was missing, presumed drowned. Then he showed me the surfboard with the shark bites on it."

"Did you see any blood?"

Pearl's forehead wrinkled. "No. I'm so sorry he drowned, honey. I know it has to be hard."

"I don't believe he drowned."

Pearl's wise eyes were studying her. "You have more information?"

Amy hesitated, then nodded. "His death was no accident."

THREE

The only way Amy would be able to erase the skepticism on Pearl's face was to show her the e-mail. She went to the living room, retrieved her purse, and extracted the paper. "I got this two weeks ago via e-mail."

Her expression troubled, Pearl unfolded the printout. "From someone named 'A Friend'? That person must have started an e-mail address especially to do this."

"I know." Amy watched while Pearl scanned the message.

Pearl laid the paper on the table. "It's pretty cryptic, Amy. It's likely a prank."

Amy snatched up the note. "A prank? Listen to this: 'Dear Amy, You might want to take a trip to Hope Beach. There is more to Ben's death than you realize. Your brother had secrets—secrets that led to his death. Hypocrisy is one of the worst sins a man can commit. I hate to say it, but he deserved what happened to him.'"

Pearl sipped her tea, then put the cup back in the saucer. "It sounds to me like someone disliked Ben. There's no mention of murder."

Would this be everyone's reaction? Amy held up the note. "Read between the lines! 'Secrets that led to his death.' Doesn't that sound like murder?"

Pearl held her gaze. "Honey, there are sick people in the world.

19

People who like to hurt others. This sounds to me like that kind of person. Did you show the police?"

Amy dropped the note to her lap and stared into her coffee. "Yes. They think it's a prank. They traced the IP address to a library in Richmond. They checked the log-ins, but the name used ended up being fake. I think that's suspicious all by itself. If someone had nothing to hide, why not use his real name?"

"Pranksters don't want to be caught." When Amy opened her mouth to protest, Pearl held up her hand. "I'm not saying you shouldn't investigate. I'll admit it's troubling. But it doesn't say someone killed him. Maybe Ben was involved in something that led to his death in another way. He may have been so distraught over it that he took his own life."

"He was surfing." Amy should have known better than to talk about it yet. Not until she had something concrete to go on.

The doorbell rang and Amy rose. "I'll be right back." When she threw open the door, she didn't recognize the young woman standing on the porch. She appeared to be in her late teens. Her long blond hair streamed over a white tank top that showed toned arms. There was a sullen slant to her full lips, but behind the insolent expression in her dark blue eyes, Amy saw desperation. "Can I help you?"

The girl swayed and put her hand on the door frame. Her color went to pasty. "I—I wondered if I might have some water?"

Before Amy could answer, the girl swayed again and Amy caught her and managed to break the girl's collapse to the porch floor. The girl's eyes were closed, and Amy checked the pulse in her throat. Rapid.

Pearl stepped into the entry. "What's wrong with her?"

"I think it's heat stroke or dehydration. Would you get a glass of water? I think she's coming around." Amy helped the girl into a half-seated position. "How do you feel?"

The girl's eyelids fluttered, then opened as she put her hand to her head. "Woozy. Did I pass out?"

"Don't get up yet," Amy commanded when the girl made a move to rise. She supported the young woman's shoulders with her arm, then took the glass of water Pearl handed her and put it to the girl's lips. "Slowly now."

The young woman drank a few sips. "I don't know what happened."

Amy saw no car parked outside. "Where did you come from?"

The girl waved vaguely. "I walked to Tidewater Inn and was on my way back when I started feeling funny. I saw your house and headed here."

"Come in out of the sun." Amy helped her to her feet and guided her inside. Pearl followed.

"Cute cottage." The girl's gaze took in the boxes and suitcases against the living room wall. "Looks like you're just moving in or out."

"I'm moving in."

"I'm looking for a room to rent." The young woman looked hopeful. "Any idea where I might find a place? I tried Tidewater Inn, but I was told they were full and the owner wouldn't be back for several days."

Pearl had started to sit down, but she immediately straightened. "Oh? I thought she was just upstairs." Her green eyes were avid.

Amy bit her lip and glanced toward the stairs. It wasn't her news to share. There had been no sound from the second floor since she'd come down, but she was tempted to make an excuse and slip up to the bedroom to tell Libby and Alec that Pearl was here.

Pearl frowned. "Amy? Where's Libby?"

"Upstairs. I'll let her know you'd like to see her. I'll be right back." Amy took the stairs two at a time. The door to her bedroom was open, and Libby sat up in the bed nursing the baby while Alec looked on. Amy paused and absorbed the heartwarming scene.

Libby looked up and smiled. "I can't get over how beautiful he is."

"Handsome," Alec corrected with a grin.

Amy hated to interrupt them. "Pearl is here. I didn't want to be the one to tell her about Noah's arrival if you wanted to."

Alec looked to Libby, who smiled again and nodded. "Send her up. She can meet our son."

"I thought you'd want to." The smile still lingered on her lips when Amy stepped into the living room and faced Pearl. "Libby is upstairs and would like to speak with you."

"I wondered why she hadn't come down." Pearl heaved herself off the sofa and moved fast for her size.

Amy turned back to her unexpected guest. "I should introduce myself. I'm Amy Lang." At the mention of her name, a strange expression flitted across the girl's face. Amy couldn't decide if it was fear or elation. Or maybe she was feeling faint again. "Are you all right?"

The teenager wetted her lips. "I'm fine. I—I'm Heather. Heather G-Granger. Could I have more of the water?"

"Of course." Amy retrieved the glass from the coffee table and handed it to her. "So you're feeling weak again?"

"A little." Heather sipped the water slowly. "You live here by yourself, or does the old lady live here too?"

Amy managed not to grin. Pearl wouldn't appreciate being called an old lady. "I live here alone."

"I don't suppose you'd consider renting out a room? I've been told there is *no* place to stay on the island because of the stupid festival. I've got to find somewhere to stay, or I'll be sleeping in a field or on a park bench."

Amy watched the girl pick at a piece of lint on her jeans. Panic lay just under the surface. There was much the girl wasn't saying. Where was her family? What had brought her here?

Amy studied her expression. "You don't live on Hope Island? How did you get here?"

She looked up again, her blue eyes hopeful. "I came by the ferry. I have a job and everything. Just no place to stay."

"You're too young to be out on your own."

"I'm eighteen."

When Amy lifted a brow, Heather grabbed her purse and dug out her driver's license. "See—eighteen! Please, I need a bed. Even the attic." Her eyes glistened with tears, and her soft mouth trembled.

The desperation in Heather's voice tugged at Amy's heartstrings. And she wasn't looking forward to listening for Ben's footsteps and hearing echoes of his voice in these empty rooms. What could it hurt to give the girl a place to stay, at least until the festival was over? "I've got a spare room."

———

Libby and little Noah were just down the hallway, but the cottage still felt empty. Amy sat on the edge of her bed and listened to the sea wind whistle through the eaves. Her eyes burned and her muscles ached as she pulled on her short nightgown. She pulled back the comforter and sheets, and the faint scent of rose petals wafted from the bed.

Tears moistened her eyes as she climbed onto the smooth cotton sheets. Closing her eyes, she inhaled the aroma of roses. Who knew it would be his last gift to her?

"Amy?" Libby's voice outside her door sounded panicked.

Amy threw back the covers and sprang to open the door. "What's wrong?"

Libby wore a blue nightgown and held her sleeping baby. Tears rolled down her face. "I—I'm scared, Amy. I don't know how to be a mother, and what if I hurt him?"

Amy drew her into the room and guided her to a seat on the

bed. "Oh, honey, you'll be fine. Babies aren't as fragile as they seem. All they need is lots of love. He'll let you know when he's hungry and needs to be changed."

Libby sniffled. "My mother was a drunk. What if I fail Noah somehow too?"

"Every parent makes mistakes, but kids survive. Look at you. Even with the problems in your family, you turned into a caring, wonderful person. Trust yourself, Libs. Noah is lucky to have you for a mommy."

Libby's smile came then. "You always know the right thing to say." Her eyes sobered. "You doing okay? It's your first night."

Amy blinked quickly but not soon enough to hold back the tear that escaped. "Smell the roses? Ben always put petals in the sheets when they were folded. Even when they're shaken before making the bed, the fragrance stays."

"I wish I'd known him better. You loved him very much."

Amy nodded. "He was eight years older than me and I idolized him. And he knew me better than anyone. He was the one who knew I'd never make a good lawyer. He saw my love of children and told me to follow my heart." She smiled and shook her head. "I don't think he realized I would take it quite this far. I'm sure I drove him crazy when I was small. I followed him around everywhere until he went to college when I was ten."

Libby brushed her lips across Noah's soft, dark hair. "Tell me more about him. I only met him a couple of times."

Amy loved nothing better than talking about Ben. "He was so smart. I don't even know how many things he had on his plate, but he knew so much about business. I think he would have ended up richer than Dad if he'd lived."

"He was engaged, wasn't he?"

Amy nodded. "Poor Elizabeth was devastated by his death. She still isn't dating."

"Such a tragedy. I'm so sorry, Amy. Did you get to see him a lot?"

"Not nearly enough. Mostly just the two weeks we spent here every summer." She fell silent. There had been plenty of times he'd begged off meeting for dinner or dessert, but she hadn't faulted him for that. He had a lot of friends and was always on the go.

And losing him wasn't something she'd ever dreamed would happen, or she would have pushed harder to spend every minute with him.

———

Curtis couldn't remember the last time he'd been to Rosemary Cottage. Probably last summer. Libby's family crowded around the rocker where she sat to meet little Noah. The rest of the Coasties team hadn't come by yet, but Alec had called him to ask him to bring by some things he'd left in his locker. Curtis suspected the small box in his pocket was a gift for the new mom.

Vanessa, Libby's younger sister, demanded to hold the baby, so while Libby was distracted, Curtis motioned for Alec to meet him in the kitchen. "Here's what you wanted. I think you should give it to her in front of everyone." He handed over the small white box.

Alec's eyes crinkled in a grin. "Want to see me embarrassed, is that it? Did you peek at it?"

Curtis shook his head. "It doesn't take a rocket scientist to figure out a jewelry box. What is it?"

"It's a mother's ring." Alec's gaze went over Curtis's shoulder. "Anything wrong, Amy?"

Curtis turned to see Amy standing in the doorway from the living room. Something about her always set him on edge. Guilt, maybe.

"I thought maybe you fellows needed something."

Alec grinned. "Nope, just some sneaky stuff going on."

He gave her the box Curtis had passed to him, and her smile

lit up the room. Or so it seemed to Curtis. She always seemed to be alight with an inner spirit that drew everyone to her.

She handed the box back to Alec. "When are you going to give it to her?"

"In a few minutes. Once Brent and Zach get here. Zach was out fishing, and I asked Brent to pick him up."

Amy was in no hurry to meet Libby's half brother. She'd heard how he treated his newfound sister at first. She moved toward the counter. "I think I'll make fresh coffee."

"Can I help?" Curtis followed her. "Alec needs to go back and worship at the shrine of mother and child." He nudged his friend and grinned.

Alec smiled back. "Says Uncle Curtis, who is curled around Raine's little finger."

Amy tilted a brow his way. "You have a niece? I didn't know."

Curtis's face heated, and he turned away to open cupboard doors in search of cups. "Yes, Gina's daughter. I'm raising her." He found the cups and pulled them out.

"I'm sorry about Gina."

"Me too. And sorry about Ben. We both had tragedy strike and not too far apart." When he glanced at her, her expression was hard to read.

She put coffee beans in the grinder and turned it on, then filled the carafe with water and poured it in the coffeemaker. "Gina was struck by a boat, is that right?"

"Yes. Idiot was going too fast."

"Did he stop after he struck her?"

"No. I turned the island upside down looking for him too. It's hard to believe he didn't realize he'd hit her. It was probably some young kid who panicked and rushed off without stopping."

"Um-hmm," she muttered under her breath.

He read the skepticism on her face. What was she getting at?

FOUR

The wind from the helicopter rotors kicked up the waves below them. Two women clinging to the swamped boat waved frantically. Curtis clipped Alec into the harness. "Clear!" He slapped Alec's shoulder and stepped back.

Alec dangled his legs out the chopper door and gave him a thumbs-up. Curtis returned the gesture, and Alec shoved away from the door and plummeted into the sea. Curtis returned to the door and readied the basket for retrieval while he watched the rescue unfold below.

With strong, sure strokes, Alec reached the first of the women. Curtis waited while Alec talked to them. When Alec held up his thumb, Curtis lowered the basket.

The rescue was as routine as facing the wind and weather ever was. Ten minutes later both shivering women were aboard the aircraft. Sara swaddled them in wool blankets and checked them out. Other than being cold and thirsty, they were both fine.

"That wave came out of nowhere," the older woman shouted above the roar of the rotors. She took a sip of the hot drink Sara had poured them. "One minute we were sailing along and making good time, and the next we were upside down." Her dark blond hair hung in wet strings down her neck.

The sea was capricious. Curtis had heard the same story so many times over the years that he'd lost count. He leaned in so they could hear him. "Where you headed?"

"Hope Beach." The younger woman studied him over the rim of her cup.

In her mid- to late twenties, she had long dark hair and eyes as deep blue as the waves she'd just been pulled from. She didn't wear a wedding ring, which was a good thing with the flirtatious glances she was throwing his way. He'd hate to think a married woman would be so blatant. He shifted away.

"We'll be landing on Hope Island." Alec pulled down the top of his wetsuit and pulled on a sweatshirt over his goose-pebbled skin.

Her teeth still chattered. "We're staying for a few weeks. Out at Tidewater Inn."

"That's my place," Alec said. "It's been in my wife's family for years."

She brightened and glanced at Curtis again. "That's great! We're here to help set up the campaign rally for Senator Kendrick."

"I like him," Curtis said. "I'm hoping to meet him when he comes for the rally. It's not often we get to participate like this in an election season."

The young woman tucked a strand of hair out of her eyes. "It will make for good media coverage."

Curtis supposed it would. The senator reaching out to the often-forgotten segment of his voter pool would be appealing to constituents. He suspected the senator hadn't thought about it like that though. It was clear these women considered every angle. "Are you his campaign manager?" he asked the older woman.

"Oh my, no," she said. "Dara here is his wife, Zoe's, best friend, and we're just here as a favor to the family. He tries not to spend much money on campaign expenses. He's very frugal."

"Too frugal sometimes," Dara put in. "But we were glad to

help." She stared at Alec. "But about the inn. We've heard so much about it. Would you mind if we went exploring in the attic?"

"Not at all. I'm sure Libby won't mind."

Sara refilled their hot chocolate. "Lieutenant Bourne here is a new daddy. His son was born two days ago."

The older woman lifted a brow. "And you're back at work already?"

"And it's good for you that he is," Sara countered. "Alec is the best swimmer we have."

"We're very thankful," the woman said. "I didn't mean to sound critical. I'm Winona Anderson, and this is my niece, Dara Anderson. Congratulations, Lieutenant. I hope we'll get a chance to take a peek at the new arrival."

"I'm sure you will," Alec said. "He's a keeper, nearly eight pounds."

Curtis grinned at the pride in his friend's voice. All babies looked alike to Curtis, and young Noah had the usual tiny red face and chubby cheeks. The night before, Alec hadn't even wanted to hand the little guy over when he squawked to be fed. The minute Libby had returned to the living room with Noah in her arms, Alec had demanded him back, though he'd had to do battle with Libby's siblings and his nephew. Alec was going to be a good daddy.

The village was still talking about how Amy had delivered the baby in her cottage. Scuttlebutt said she was thinking about staying permanently, and he wished he'd flat-out asked her last night. He hoped it was only a rumor. If she stayed, Raine's parentage was sure to come out. Not even his teammates knew who her father was. If they'd wondered, they hadn't been crass enough to ask.

He was sure Alec would urge him to tell Amy the full story as soon as possible, but the Lang family would want Raine, and it would be a battle to keep her. Edith meant well, but she didn't know the family like he did. Curtis would fight to his last breath to keep Raine.

———

Dressed in capris and a pink top, Amy rode her bike to downtown Hope Beach on Friday to meet Libby. The small shops had once been houses for fishermen, and their clapboard faces with their small porches looked out on the narrow village streets. She made a mental note to stop at the feed store later and look at the plants. Though she'd made inroads on the yard, the garden needed serious weeding.

She parked the bike in a rack as Libby pulled up in her SUV. Amy saw little Noah in the back and opened the door to get him out of his car seat. The plastic latch resisted her attempts to free the baby. "You have to be a physicist to figure this out."

"I practiced before he got here."

"Good decision." Amy gave up and stood back to let Libby unbuckle the little guy and lift him out.

"Amy," a woman exclaimed as Libby backed out with Noah in her arms.

Amy turned to see a young woman about eight months pregnant standing on the sidewalk. The top of her large purse was unzipped and bulged with romance novels. Amy struggled to remember the attractive redhead's name. She'd been the attorney's secretary.

The name came to her. "Mindy Jackson. It's been a long time."

"Mindy Stewart now." Mindy patted her bulging belly. "I'm so glad to see you! Are you staying awhile?"

"I am."

"Wonderful! I won't have to go to the mainland to deliver."

Mindy's enthusiasm warmed Amy's heart. She smiled at the young woman. "Actually, I'm not sure I'll be here *that* long. Looks like you have about a month to go?"

Mindy popped her bubble gum and nodded. "Stay permanently.

I'll be your first patient. I'm a sheriff's deputy now. When I lost my job as a receptionist, I decided to do something else with my life."

Libby moved in like a mama duck herding her young. "Amy will give you a call if she decides to start delivering babies. We'd better get going." They walked away and entered Hopeful Kids Shop. "I think it's a great idea to open your practice here. I don't know what I would have done without you when Noah was born. I was so scared, and you made everything calm." Libby smiled. "Well, as calm as childbirth can be. I was lucky you were on the island when my water broke."

What if she moved here? The thought tempted Amy. Living in this place was like going back in time to a happier, safer place. It would be a rewarding life. And she could get her overseeing physician on board. He'd told her for a long time that she should move to one of the places around the state that really needed her.

She glanced around the small shop. Children's clothing and necessities vied for space with boogie boards and souvenirs. Places like this didn't exist on the mainland, and she loved it. She pressed her hand to her stomach. Maybe it would be a place where she could forget the past.

She smiled. "Hope Beach is more than home. It's a haven. It always has been. And I see the need here. Most women have to go to Kill Devil Hills or the mainland in the last couple of weeks before giving birth. Taking the ferry once labor starts isn't a good option."

Libby shifted Noah to the other arm. "We *do* need you here. As a midwife and a healer."

Amy had heard this before, and she didn't deny it was true. Somehow she just knew what people needed. She could listen to a tale of pain and sickness and know what was wrong. And Libby had spoken the truth—it was a gift. No training or anything Amy could point to had given her the intuition she possessed.

"Maybe you're right."

Libby's brows rose. "You've decided to do it, just like that?"

"I've been thinking about it since I got here. I'm wondering why I didn't think of doing it sooner." It would take more than a couple of weeks to figure out what had happened to Ben. And she felt closer to him here, the memories precious.

Libby helped Noah find his thumb. "What do you need to get going? How can I help?"

"I just have to send for my things. I can use the downstairs study as an examination room so I won't need an office. I'll need to get my herb garden planted for my tinctures." She had to curb her excitement or she would turn around and head for the feed store right now to get that garden going.

A woman spoke behind them. "Good morning, Libby. Who's your friend?"

Amy turned to face a woman of about forty with tired brown hair, a turned-up nose, and thin lips. She wore a friendly smile. "I'm Amy Lang."

"Oh yes, you own Rosemary Cottage. And you delivered little Noah here. The village is buzzing about the news."

"Guilty as charged."

The woman held out her hand. "I'm Frannie Hurd, the owner of the shop. Women are always asking me if there are any midwives on the island. Think you might stay?"

The heat of a flush marched up Amy's neck. "I'm considering it."

"Let me know what you decide, and I'll send plenty of business your way," Frannie said. "What can I do for you today, Libby?"

Libby glanced around. "I need some clothes for Noah. He arrived a little too soon, and I wasn't quite ready. And I want to look at bedding. I don't think what I have in the room works."

"I just got in some catalogs you might find interesting. Come with me." Frannie led Libby off to her desk.

The door jingled behind her, and Amy turned to see a familiar face. Curtis entered the store with a small girl in his arms. Her pulse ratcheted up two notches as it always did when she spotted the handsome Coast Guard lieutenant. Not that he'd ever noticed her. His light brown hair had blond highlights put there by the sun, and his eyes were as gray as the sea on a stormy day. Her gaze wandered to the little one. Amy guessed the child to be about one. She had dark curls and dark eyes that tilted up at the corners.

Curtis froze when he saw her, and his smile was forced as she approached. "Amy. That must be your bike out there."

She nodded. "Who's this cutie?" Amy smiled at the child.

"My niece, Raine." He shifted as if he was uneasy. "I just popped in to get her some pajamas. Oh look, Raine, there they are. New pj's. Nice seeing you, Amy."

"You too." She watched him stride to the infant section. He hadn't been so uncomfortable at Rosemary Cottage. What had changed?

FIVE

The courtyard of the café held only a man and his teenage daughter eating soup. Amy kicked off her sandals under the table, then sipped her coffee and soaked in the island atmosphere. Her arm still ached from where the inexperienced nurse had poked her, but the pain was nothing compared to the fear tearing at her insides. What if she had to go back to treatment? She couldn't face it. She blinked back the moisture in her eyes. One day at a time. That's all she could get through.

The scent of the sea and the masses of roses growing along the edge of the sidewalk teased her nose with memories. The taste of the fish taco she'd had for lunch still lingered on her tongue. "I've missed this place."

"I'm so glad you're back." Libby glanced at Noah in his baby seat under the shade of a sycamore tree. He was fast asleep. Her expression was pensive when she looked back at the table.

"Is something wrong?" Amy asked. "I feel like there's something you aren't telling me."

Libby's smile seemed forced. "I'm trying to figure out what's going on and why you're here. Do you suspect Alec of lying about Ben's death?"

"Of course not!" Amy reached across the table and squeezed

her friend's hand. "I'd forgotten Alec saw him and found his board. You have to know how much I love you and Alec. I know the kind of man he is."

"Then why are you so sure Ben's death wasn't an accident?"

Amy reached for her large bag and dug out the e-mail she'd received. "Because of this." She handed it to her and watched Libby's face change as she read it.

"Secrets? Hypocrisy? It sounds like whoever wrote it disliked Ben." She looked down at her hands, then back at Amy. "There are stages of grief, Amy. One of those is denial."

Amy's cheeks heated. "It's not denial, Libs." She held up the paper. "I didn't make this up."

"Could it be a prank?"

"That's what the police think, but I don't believe it. I want to know what secrets the sender was talking about."

Libby handed back the paper. "Maybe there are none. If it's a prank, I mean."

"It just *feels* true. Don't you think?" Amy watched Libby's face until her friend nodded with obvious reluctance. "I showed it to Pearl. She thought it was a prank too, but I think no one wants to believe someone might have deliberately hurt Ben."

"You have to check it out. Where can we start?"

"You'll help?"

Libby adjusted the bonnet of the carrier so the breeze wasn't on the baby. "Of course. Alec too."

"I want to talk to the rescue team that looked for him. Alec, Josh, Curtis, Sara. I want to find out where they suspect he went in the water. And I want to talk to Tom and see if he did any kind of investigation and how quickly he decided to call it a drowning."

"I think everyone believes it was a simple drowning," Libby said. "And be careful with Tom. If you go in with both guns blazing, he's liable to be offended."

Amy smiled. "I do have a *little* diplomacy." She took another sip of her coffee. "I called him when I got the e-mail and sent it to him. He thinks I'm off base. So we've had our initial skirmish."

Libby smiled back, then nodded toward the doorway. "No time like the present to practice that skill." She rose and waved. "Tom, come join us. You haven't seen Noah yet."

The big sheriff, in his thirties, hiked his pants and came their way. His grin broadened when he saw the sleeping baby. "I stopped by this morning to make his acquaintance. I'm surprised you're out and about already." His brown hair was graying a bit at the temples.

"You sound like Alec." Libby leaned back in her chair. "I'm not one to lie around. I feel fine."

"You look good too." He bent over and touched Noah's soft hair. "He looks just like his daddy."

"I think so too. Alec just beams when people tell him that."

Heather appeared with her pad and pen. "Coffee, Sheriff?"

The apron was longer than the skirt she wore, and her feet were going to be killing her in those heels by the end of the day. Amy hadn't seen her get ready this morning or she would have advised her to wear something different.

Tom ordered coffee and a sandwich. "I heard you were in town, Amy. You here about that e-mail?"

Nothing like getting straight to the point, but Amy would rather have it that way. No beating around the bush. "I am."

His heavy brows came together. "I understand your concern, but there are some weird people in the world. I get the worst of them through my office."

"I don't think so. I would like to go over everything you did when you discovered Ben was missing."

Heather brought his coffee, and he took a swig of it before he answered. "Ben drowned, Amy. It was a sad day, but it's happened here more than we like to admit. The currents are strong, especially that time of year."

The man wasn't listening so she shifted gears. "That's another thing. Why was he even here in November? We always come in the summer."

"Not Ben," Tom said. "He came nearly every month, for at least a few days."

Amy caught her breath. Her chest hurt as though she'd been punched. Why wouldn't Ben tell her he was coming more often? She could have met him here. "For how long?"

"A good year."

Amy turned from the sympathy in Tom's eyes. "Did you know he was here too, Libby?"

Libby was quick to shake her head. "No, I didn't. He must have slipped in and out of town. Rosemary Cottage is pretty quiet. Maybe he needed some downtime. He had a stressful job."

"True." It hurt to think he hadn't wanted her company though. They'd shared everything. Or at least she'd thought so. His business was handling company mergers and making them profitable. There was always the stress of letting people go. He'd hated that part of the job.

"What do your parents say about this?" Libby asked.

Amy sipped her drink and wished she didn't have to answer. "They told me to let it alone, that Ben was gone and nothing could bring him back."

"Good advice." Tom nodded.

Noah began to fuss, and Libby rocked his infant carrier with her foot. "They believe it's a prank?"

"I think they don't care whether it is or isn't. Mom would rather bury her grief in her charity business and forget any unpleasantness, and Dad is too busy with golf to care."

Her family had always been different. That's why she and Ben had faced the world together. Without him, she might as well be alone.

⎯⎯

Amy walked barefoot through the emerging dawn toward the sound of the surf. The birds were beginning to awaken, and a blue jay squawked when she startled him. Amy's meeting with the Coast Guard team would be over dinner at Tidewater Inn tonight, so she had the entire Saturday free. The house was spotless, and the sea beckoned. There was a path through the maritime forest to the beach.

She crossed the narrow road and stood on the dunes. The sun hit the waves in a gorgeous display of color she'd seldom seen. Ben always wanted to wait until the sun warmed things up, so they never got here before the sun finished its climb out of the waves.

The waves were huge rollers today, surging up onto the sand to deposit shells before ebbing back to regain their fury. She pulled her sweater tighter around her to block out the chilly wind.

"Hello."

Amy turned at the pleasant female voice. A short woman of about fifty stood behind her with a surfboard in her hand. A Jack Russell terrier was by her feet. The woman's generous curves were stuffed into a wetsuit. She hadn't yet covered her short brown curls with the hoodie in her hand.

Amy smiled. "Good morning. You're surfing this early in the season? I bet the water is cold."

"I surf nearly year-round." The woman held out her hand. "I'm Edith Lowman."

Amy shook her hand. "Amy Lang."

Her blue eyes crinkled at the corners. "Ah, the miracle worker who delivered young Noah."

"I see the village drum has spread the word."

"A body can't pick a flower in Hope Beach without someone seeing it."

The woman's quip gave Amy hope. Whatever had happened to Ben, someone had seen something that would help her get at the truth. "I don't believe we've ever met. Did you move here recently?"

Edith tugged the neoprene hood over her head and began to tuck her curls into it. "I've only been here a few months. I came from Maine, so this water is warm compared to what I'm used to."

"You surfed in Maine?"

"Sure did. I've been surfing since I could stand on a board. I was about three, I think. The day I'm too old to surf is the day I'm ready to meet the Lord. Have you surfed here before?"

"When it's warm."

"Go get your gear, girl, and you'll see what surfing was meant to be. If you're brave enough." Edith lifted a challenging brow.

Amy opened her mouth to turn down the offer but instead found herself saying, "I'll be right back."

She raced to the cottage and found her surfboard in the shed. Her wetsuit was a 4 mil so that would help. And she had a hoodie. She pulled on her wetsuit and grabbed her surfboard, then jogged back to where Edith was waiting.

Edith slanted a smile toward Amy. "Oh my stars, you surprised me. I thought for sure you'd vamoose and I'd never see you again."

"I intended to, but I decided I'm up for an adventure." Amy stared at the whitecaps rolling to the thick dunes. "It looks cold." There was a light breeze that chilled her even more.

"Water temperature today is about sixty. It will be a shock at first, but you'll adjust quickly. Ready?" Edith asked. The dog barked in answer and ran toward the waves. Edith picked up her board and joined her pet.

It was always smarter to surf with a buddy in case you got conked on the head or rolled by a wave. Amy followed her into the water, gasping at the first shock of the waves on her feet and calves. She hadn't expected it to be quite this frigid.

She stopped. "I don't know about this."

"Wade in slowly to your waist and adjust, then plunge in." Edith was already to her waist. She flopped onto her board, then helped her dog onto the slick surface.

"Your dog surfs too?"

"Sheldon loves it. He puts me to shame." Edith straddled the board while she waited. "Come on, you can do it."

Amy wasn't so sure. She waded out a little deeper, wincing as the cold water touched her thighs. If she was going to do this, she'd better just take the plunge. She inhaled and dove under the large wave rolling toward her. The power and the cold squeezed her lungs, and even when her head popped above the water, she struggled to draw in enough oxygen. But she hadn't come this far to quit. Seizing her board with cold fingers, she heaved herself aboard and paddled to join Edith.

"Well done." Edith smiled. "Let's see what you're made of." She turned her board and paddled out to the breakwater.

Amy barely felt the cold now, only the exhilaration. She paddled out until she crested the surge, then waited for the right wave. There it was. Edith saw it too and paddled to meet it. Amy did the same. The curve of the wave lifted both boards. Amy found her feet and balanced on her board as the crest took aim at the shore. The warm air was in sharp contrast to the cold water spraying her legs and feet.

She spared a glance to see how Edith was doing and saw the dog straining at the front of the board with Edith balanced behind it. It was a picture Amy would never forget. This would be a keeper wave, one she would talk about for a long, long time. An exultant shout of laughter came from her throat, and she felt more alive than she had since receiving the news of Ben's death.

When the power of the wave left her in its choppy wake, she bobbed to the surface and laughed. "Let's do it again!"

Edith's grin stretched across her face. "I knew you'd love it. So did your brother."

Amy's smile faded. "You knew Ben?"

"I showed him how to cold surf too." Edith leaped onto her board and paddled out to catch another wave.

"I need to talk to you." Amy followed her.

Six

Curtis scanned the waves and saw his aunt's head bobbing in the water. Someone else was crazy enough to be out surfing in that cold water, but he couldn't make out who it was from this distance. He glanced in the rearview mirror to see Raine studying her book, a new Punky Grace book he'd just bought her.

She caught his gaze in the mirror. "Ede?"

"We're going to get her now." He pulled the car off the side of the road and parked, then tugged his Harley do-rag more tightly to his head and got out.

There was no parking lot along this stretch of beach, but Edith loved to surf here and usually walked the mile from their house. The waves were strong just off the point, and it was a beautiful spot with sea grass anchoring the thick dunes and the maritime forest struggling to survive the heat and salt. He often came here to listen to the waves himself.

He got Raine out of her car seat and grabbed a beach blanket. "Down," she commanded.

He grinned and put her on the sand until he spread out the blanket. The two of them sat on it and waited for Edith. There was no hurrying her. She went surfing every day it was safe. And that was most days. She even surfed in the rain. When Raine grew bored, he helped her build a sand castle, then glanced at his watch. Edith should be finished anytime.

He watched the two figures in the water. The slimmer one was a pretty good surfer, but his aunt put everyone to shame. She could balance on a roller in a hurricane, though as far as he knew she'd never attempted to surf in one. Edith might be nuts about surfing, but she wasn't crazy.

The wave deposited the surfers and receded. The two of them turned and started toward shore. Curtis brushed the sand from his hands and went toward the water to greet them. As they neared, he saw the other surfer was Amy. His gut tightened. Surely his aunt wouldn't betray him, but then, he knew her views on the topic.

Amy's eyes were shining as she came up out of the water. The wetsuit hugged every curve and her face was pink. "Curtis, what an incredible morning! Did you come to surf?" She pushed her hoodie off her dark hair and down around her neck. Her gaze went to Raine and she smiled again. "Hi, sweetheart."

"Dude." The child pointed at the water. "Swim." She stood and started toward the waves.

Curtis grabbed her. "No you don't."

His niece squawked and squirmed. "Down." Her small hand moved in emphasis of her order.

"Doodlebug, you are far too bossy." He set her back on the blanket. "You wouldn't catch me out there in April." He eyed Amy warily.

Amy lifted an eyebrow. "She calls you dude?"

He grinned. "I call her Doodlebug and it somehow evolved."

"Edith tells me that she got Ben hooked on winter surfing, but she hasn't managed the same thing with you."

"I'm immune to her wiles." He grinned.

He'd never been immune to Amy, though he wanted to be.

He'd met her exactly five times, and he could recount every word, every expression. The connection he felt with her was weird, and clearly one-sided. She'd cut her hair since he'd seen her last, and her dark curls just covered her ears and revealed the long column of her slender neck. But her eyes were still that funny color— green mixed with gold and brown—and topped with impossibly long, thick lashes. Her eyes seemed lit from within by her excitement for life. The eyes were supposedly windows to the soul, and he'd always been drawn to the soul he saw behind those eyes. The guys would laugh if they knew he had such crazy thoughts.

Her smile faded. "I need to talk to both of you about Ben."

She knows. His gaze flickered to Edith as she rubbed a towel on the dog. When she didn't meet his gaze, he looked back at Amy. "I thought we were talking later today at the inn."

"We are. But I know he spent a lot of time with your sister. I thought maybe you two might have seen or heard something."

"About what?"

"Did he seem afraid or concerned to you? Uneasy, maybe?"

He shrugged. "I didn't spend much time with him, Amy. He was Gina's friend, and I was working a lot of hours." That sounded just a little hostile, so he managed a smile. "You know how it is with siblings. They have their friends and you have yours."

She nodded. "Of course. Did you hear him talk about any enemies, anyone who disliked him?"

"Why are you asking about enemies? I have to tell you, we saw nothing to indicate foul play. And it *was* November. The water temp was pretty cold. I suspect he had a cramp and went down or else a shark really did get him, but I think the first scenario is more likely."

Her eyes filled with sorrow. "I know it looks that way, but I'm not convinced. I'll talk to you more about it tonight."

She took the hoodie off and ran her fingers through her curls, flipping him with water in the process. When she saw him flinch, she shook her head harder and laughed. "That's one way to make sure you join the fun."

Her dimples flashed in an adorable way that made it impossible for Curtis to look away. When her cheeks reddened, he directed his gaze at Raine. "Well, I guess I'd better get Edith home to get warmed up. You need to take a hot shower yourself. If I think of anything else, I'll let you know later tonight."

Amy grabbed his arm. "Wait! I didn't get a chance to talk to Edith."

His throat tightened at her touch. What an idiot he was. "You've been surfing with her."

Her dimples flashed again. "I can't talk and surf at the same time. Just a few questions." She looked at Edith. "You don't mind, do you?"

Edith glanced at Curtis and shook her head. "Not at all."

"If you surfed with Ben, surely you talked before and after you went out. Did he seem upset to you that week? Afraid?"

Edith pressed her lips together. "Now that you mention it, yes. He was quieter than usual, and he locked his car. He never locked his car."

"No, he hated locking things. It was almost a personal affront to him when he was in a big city and had to lock everything. He liked feeling safe here." She stared hard at Edith. "Except he wasn't safe." She swallowed. "Anything else you noticed?"

Edith squeezed the water from her hair. "He got a lot more phone calls than usual. He'd be tight-lipped and quiet when he got off." She stared at Amy again. "I don't like to speak ill of the dead, but I wondered if he was taking drugs, Amy."

Amy went white. "Drugs? Why would you say that?"

"His eyes were bloodshot a lot." She bit her lip. "I don't know, maybe I'm wrong. I shouldn't have said anything."

Curtis had to break this meeting up before Amy asked about Raine. "That's it, Ede?"

"I think so." Edith shot Curtis a warning glance. "For now."

———

Tidewater Inn sat on a hill overlooking the wide Atlantic. Sand dunes stretched as far as Amy could see, and man-made break-water sandbags attempted to keep beach erosion at bay. She parked her car outside the Georgian mansion beside several other vehicles. Her lungs tightened. Tonight she should find out *something*. Surely one of the Coasties would give her a clue that would lead her in the right direction.

Twilight haloed the beautiful old house in beams of color, and the yard shifted with shades of purple, orange, and pink as she went up the sweeping staircase to the grand porch. It never failed to impress her. Libby had done a lot of restoration work on the outside. She'd paid loving attention to every detail.

Her cell phone rang, and Amy glanced at the screen. Her steps slowed and her palms went slick. The doctor's office. "Amy Lang."

"Amy, this is Dr. Farmington's nurse. I wanted to let you know the blood draw from Friday was contaminated somehow. We'll need you to come in for another test. I'm so sorry."

Amy exhaled. "That's fine. I'll be in as soon as I can." She ended the call and dropped her phone back into her purse. She wanted to cry. Now she had to endure even more days of waiting, of not knowing.

Someone moved on the porch, then Pearl emerged from the shadows. Her purple dress made her green eyes glow in the last light of sunset. She hugged Amy, and the embrace brought back loving memories of being folded in her grandmother's arms as a child. She inhaled the scent of lavender.

She finally pulled away. "It's good to see you again, Pearl."

"You're sure pretty tonight, honey. Those single men are going to have their eyes popping out of their heads." The older woman tugged her toward the door. "Everyone is inside."

Amy glanced down at her red dress. It had seemed ordinary enough when she put it on. "Is it too short?"

"Girl, legs like those need showing off a little. In a tasteful way, of course. You look perfect."

"Am I late?"

"Not at all. Come along."

Amy followed her into the grand entry and down the hall to the parlor. Several people sprawled on the comfortable leather furniture. Her gaze landed on Curtis, who was smiling in a relaxed way. He held little Noah with a natural grip, and the infant slept contentedly. A woman with long dark hair sat beside him. Pretty and just a little proprietorial with the way she leaned toward him and looked down at the baby.

A shaft of jealousy rocked Amy on her heels. She didn't know if Curtis was dating anyone, and it wasn't her business if he was. He was an acquaintance, nothing more.

She averted her eyes and focused on Libby. "Hey, Libs, how are you feeling?"

Libby was dressed in a pretty white dress that showed off toned arms. Her little tummy pooch was already disappearing. "Pretty great. Noah had a checkup today, and he's in perfect health."

"I'm so glad to hear it." Amy approached Curtis and held out her hands. "May I?"

"I'll give him up but only under duress." He rose and transferred Noah to her arms.

She nuzzled the soft little head and inhaled the sweet scent of powder and new baby. When she glanced back at Curtis, he had an intense expression in his eyes as he watched her. She had no idea what he was thinking, but the warmth in his eyes made her shiver.

"Have you met everyone?" he asked.

When she shook her head, he introduced the pretty woman beside him as Dara Anderson, a guest at the inn. She rose after the introduction and excused herself. Amy tried to hide her relief.

The attractive woman in the chair by the fireplace was Sara Kavanagh. She was the medic on the team. Josh Holman was the captain and pilot of their helicopter.

Delilah Carter, the inn's manager and cook, poked her head in the door. "Dinner will be ready in about twenty minutes. There's coffee on the sideboard if anyone is interested. And shrimp cocktail."

Alec sprang up first. "You don't have to tell me twice."

The rest of them filed into the large dining room. The oak table dominating the room was massive and would easily seat twenty people. The deep red color of the walls reflected in the chandelier over the table. The sideboard held a spread of shrimp cocktail, homemade bread with butter, and a silver coffeepot with delicate blue-and-white cups.

Curtis poured a cup of coffee and added a heavy dollop of cream, then handed it to her. "You're a coffee drinker, right?"

She adjusted the baby to her left arm and accepted the coffee. "Thanks."

Sara carried a small plate of shrimp and cocktail sauce over to where Amy stood. "So you wanted to talk to us about your brother?" She motioned for Josh to join them.

With the three of them in front of her, Amy wasn't quite sure how to begin. She wet her lips. "Did you all see Ben on his surfboard out by the break?"

Josh shook his head. "I didn't see him. Just Curtis and Sara did. I brought the chopper down over the water, but he waved us on."

"You accepted that?" Aware her voice had risen, she made an effort to modulate it. "He was way past where it was usual to surf."

"Which was why we checked on him. But you can't make a surfer get in the chopper. He seemed in control of his situation and was paddling back toward the shore."

"And was never seen again." Her voice broke, and she cleared her throat. "His surfboard was found with a shark bite out of it, and his belongings were on the shore."

Sara set her plate on the sideboard. "I know it's hard to hear this, Amy, but we didn't do anything wrong. Your brother was an adult. We rescue people in danger. He was in no imminent danger. We saw no sharks cruising around him, and he was enjoying his day. We fully expected him to make it back to shore. He'd been out there before."

Little Noah yawned, and Amy concentrated on him for a moment to regain her composure. Of course they were right. "He was always a bit of a daredevil. Did he surf alone?" She hadn't thought to ask that before today.

Josh shook his head. "Ned Springall went out with him. But they split up when Ben wanted to go out farther. Ned said he was acting weird."

"Weird, how?" Amy asked.

"Nervous, jumpy. Whenever a boat would pass, he stared at it. Ned asked him what was wrong, but Ben put him off and said it was nothing."

She stared at Curtis, who stared back. This was further indication that someone had killed her brother and left his body to the sharks. Someone had been after him.

SEVEN

urtis walked Amy to her car in the moonlight and opened the car door for her. The rest of the guests had already left. The salt air was moist and he inhaled the fragrance of the sea. The surf roared off to their left, then ebbed like something alive. That was one thing he loved about living on an island— things could, and did, change moment by moment.

"Sorry we weren't more help about Ben," he said.

Holding her skirt in one hand, she slid into the seat. The light from the dash illuminated her face with its planes and angles. He could watch her for hours and never tire of it. She showed so many emotions—one moment pensive and the next glowing with the joy of life.

He squatted beside the open door and laid his hand on hers where it rested on the steering wheel. "I wanted to say that I understand how you feel, Amy. I lost Gina too, you know. Sometimes there's just no answer to the question of why."

Her lips flattened, and she moved her hand away. "It's not the same, Curtis. At least you had closure, and you know what happened to her. Ben's body was never recovered. You have her daughter too, and I—I have nothing left of Ben."

At her stiff tone, he stood. What a jerk he was. He was standing here denying her the one thing she needed—Ben's daughter. He wet his lips and tried to figure out how to tell her.

She put the key in the ignition, and the alert dinged until she shut the door and ran the window down. "I had hoped for some small piece of evidence that would help me figure out what happened."

He hesitated. "Edith mentioned the drug thing. That might be worth checking out." The tension eased from him at the change of subject. Now wasn't the time to tell her about Raine.

"I find it so hard to believe that he might get caught up in something like that."

"You've never known him to even try drugs?"

"Never. Did Gina?" Her chin lifted in a distinct challenge.

"Nope." He managed to keep his voice even. "If I think of anything else, I'll call you."

"Thanks." She gave a small wave through the opening, then ran the window up and backed way.

He watched her pull out of the drive before walking back to the house. When he reached the porch, someone moved from the shadows, and he paused when Dara emerged into the wash of light from the porch. "I thought you'd already gone up to bed."

"I came back down. It's too gorgeous of a night to sleep. Want to take a walk along the beach?"

He wasn't sure how to get out of it in a gentlemanly way. "I really should be getting home to put Raine to bed."

Her pout was meant to change his mind, but it steeled his resolve. Whatever she wanted from him wasn't something he was prepared to give. He didn't believe in holiday romances either. One of these days the right woman would settle here. He'd meet her and know she was the one. Amy's face flashed through his mind, but he pushed it away.

"I had some questions I wanted to ask you. Got time to chat at least?"

So she wasn't just flirting. Something was on her mind. He glanced at his watch. "I can spare a few minutes." He followed her to the row of white rockers on the porch.

Something about her manner put him on his guard. He pulled a rocker to him so it wasn't sitting so close to her, then dropped onto the seat. She nudged her chair a bit closer, then curled up on it with her knees to her chest.

"I love the sound of the sea," she said. "And it smells so good, don't you think?"

He took a whiff. "Kind of heavy with kelp tonight. And dead fish."

She grimaced. "Spoilsport."

She gazed over the railing. The moon glimmered on the whitecaps. She seemed in no hurry to talk to him about whatever problem she was having.

He waited for her to speak, then shifted when she didn't. "So what's this about?"

She sighed and turned to look at him. "You're Gina Ireland's brother, right?"

"Yes. Did you know Gina?"

She put her feet back on the porch floor, then shrugged. "Just superficially. She worked on the senator's last campaign."

"I know. She was a big fan of his."

"Yes, she was, and hey, I'm sorry for your loss." She played with her necklace. "Will you endorse the senator's campaign in her place? I know Gina's boyfriend had some issues with him and all, but I'd hoped you would follow your sister's lead."

Curtis straightened. "Ben had issues with the senator? What was it about?"

Dara shrugged. "I just know he came stomping into the office one day, shouting that the senator owed him money."

"Ben Lang?"

She nodded. "That was the name. Ben." Her eyes widened. "Hey, is that Amy's brother?"

"It was. He died a few weeks after Gina."

"Oh dear, I'm so sorry. How odd that they would both die."

"I'd rather not talk about it," he said.

"Of course, of course. So sorry." But she didn't sound sorry. Instead, she leaned toward him with her eyes shining.

"When did this happen?"

She paused a moment, a crease between her eyes. "The first week of November, I think."

Two weeks before Ben died and about the time of Gina's accident. "What else did he say?"

She rose and backed against the railing to face him. "I don't know. I think he was on drugs. His eyes were all bloodshot, and he was slurring his words. The senator was about to call security."

Drugs. Curtis didn't want to have to tell Amy about this conversation.

Dara's smile was self-satisfied. "So you'll vote for the senator?"

"I like Kendrick. I'll vote for him again."

Relief lit her face. "Good. Would you consider taking part in the rally we're having in a couple of weeks?"

"I don't think I'll have time." He rose, eager to end the discussion. "I'd better go. Raine will be wondering where I am."

———

How Amy had missed this church. Her church family in the city was nice enough, but talk went as far as "Hi, how are you?" before everyone wandered into their favorite pews. She probably knew the people in this church better than those she'd sat beside for fifteen years at her other church.

She sat in the third pew on the left beside Libby and Alec

and listened to the pastor bring the service to a close. Alec had reluctantly allowed Amy to hold little Noah, who was wrapped in a blue receiving blanket. His eyes were closed and his tiny mouth sucked at nothing.

The church had been built back in the eighteen hundreds, and while the solid oak pews had no padding, the seats had been worn comfortable by worshippers over the decades. A stained-glass window depicting Jesus in Gethsemane in rich tones of garnet, gold, and green was centered in the platform wall, and other beautiful windows lined the sides of the building.

At the final amen, Amy rose and handed over Noah to his daddy before she began to greet the friends she'd made over the years. Someone touched her arm, and the tingle that shot along her skin made her turn. Curtis and Edith stood waiting their turn to say hello. Curtis had little Raine in his arms, and her wide eyes took in everything.

"When you have a minute, I need to talk to you," Curtis said.

Amy glanced around. The church was clearing out. "Now is fine."

Curtis gave Raine to his aunt. "I'll be right back." He ignored Raine's shriek of "Stay!"

Amy frowned as she followed him to a quiet corner. "Is something wrong?"

His eyes were somber. "I wanted to tell you something Dara Anderson told me last night after you left."

"What did she say?"

"She works for Senator Kendrick."

"Oh? You'd think I'd know her, then. My family is good friends with the senator and his family."

Confusion clouded his eyes. "You are?"

She nodded. "He and Ben were good friends, and my father is a big supporter of his campaign."

Curtis rubbed his forehead. "This makes no sense, then. Dara said Ben and Kendrick had a big argument, and the senator was about to call security and have him thrown out."

"What?" Amy shook her head. "I seriously doubt that."

"Why would she lie? It came out in an innocent way. She wanted to know if she could count on my vote even though my sister's boyfriend had made a scene in the senator's office."

"Boyfriend? I thought they were just friends. Ben was engaged."

"They were more than friends." He hesitated, then touched her shoulder lightly before dropping his hand to his side again. "She said Ben appeared to be drunk or on drugs. His eyes were bloodshot and he slurred his words."

She exhaled. "Your aunt said the same thing. It would take something catastrophic for Ben to drown it with drugs or alcohol. Ben liked being in control."

He shrugged. "Well, I thought you'd want to know. This incident happened a couple of weeks before he died. Right about the time of Gina's death."

"Thanks. I'll see what I can find out." She followed him back to the group. This was not something she'd expected to hear about her brother. Could he have been involved in drugs somehow?

Josh and Alec were talking and they waylaid Curtis, so Amy stepped past them and rejoined Libby standing with Edith.

Edith smiled when Raine reached for Amy. "She likes you already."

Poor little motherless baby. Amy took the child. "You smell good, honey." She nuzzled the little one's smooth neck, sweet with the scent of baby wash.

"You should have a bunch of those babies yourself," Edith said.

Amy's heart squeezed, but she managed to keep her smile. Why did she do that? Hide the pain instead of being honest? It wasn't just here either. All around her she heard people asking,

"How are you?" and others answering, "Fine." They all wore masks. It hurt too much to lay all the pain out for someone to see. It was something she couldn't talk about yet.

"I'd love for you to come to dinner. How about Monday night? Curtis should be home by five. I make a killer enchilada."

Amy's heart stuttered. "I'd love to." She glanced toward Curtis from the corner of her eye as he stood next to Josh. "Can I bring anything?"

"Just your pretty face."

"How about dessert?"

"If you want. But don't go to any trouble. I thought it would be fun for Raine to get to know . . ." Edith went red, then cleared her throat. "Get to know you."

Amy eyed Edith's discomfiture. "I'd like that too." Was she playing matchmaker?

Edith cleared her throat again. "Wonderful. See you around five." She took Raine, then hurried off toward the exit while Raine called, "Stay."

Libby lifted a brow. "I think she's trying to match you up with Curtis."

Amy's cheeks heated. "I thought she might be."

"But you agreed to go. I think that says something. There's some kind of heat between you and Curtis. I can feel it every time he's around."

"Heat?" Amy laughed. "I wouldn't say that exactly."

Libby chuckled. "But you're interested."

"I'm interested in getting his help to figure out what happened to Ben. That's all."

Libby's smile widened. "And that's why your cheeks are so red, right? It's okay to admit he's quite a hottie."

Amy fixed her friend with a stern glance. "You're still a newlywed. You shouldn't be noticing such things."

"I'm happily married, but not dead," Libby said primly. She shifted Noah to the other shoulder.

Amy laughed, but her gaze went back to Curtis. Maybe she did like him, but it was just friendship. "Want to come back to the cottage for lunch?"

"Sure," Libby said. "It's Delilah's day off, so I'll take any excuse not to cook."

EIGHT

Amy threw together shrimp scampi and a salad for lunch. Alec ate his weight in shrimp, then he stretched out on the sofa with Noah asleep on his chest and took a nap. Heather was working.

Libby rose from the rocker by the fireplace and patted her tummy. "I'm fortified with food and ready to check out Ben's room with you if you're sure you want to."

"I'm sure." Amy led the way up the stairs to the first door on the right.

Ben's door had been shut ever since Amy had arrived. She steeled herself to turn the knob and step into the room. When she pushed open the door, the scent of Ben's cologne was almost a physical blow to her midsection. She paused in the hall and gulped in courage.

Libby touched her arm. "Are you okay?"

"I'm fine." She wasn't fine, but she hated to show weakness. It had always been her job to keep smiling and make sure everyone else was taken care of. Ben, her parents. They all looked to her to find the silver lining of any situation.

Amy forced herself to walk through the doorway. "Look for anything that will help us figure out why Ben seemed tense those last few weeks. Who might have been calling him. A-And if he might have been involved with drugs."

Libby glanced around the room. "Can you get his cell phone records?"

"I can try. The problem is, my parents don't want me stirring up anything. They might have to be the ones to request them."

"Unless Tom could do it."

"He thinks it's a prank too."

Libby pulled open the drawer in the bedside table. "I'll have Alec talk to him. It can't hurt to at least look into it." She riffled through the drawer. "Nothing much but pens, paper, a few clips, and a flashlight."

Amy eyed the dresser, then resolutely opened the top drawer. It held his underwear and socks as well as his swim trunks, but it was in disarray.

She frowned. "Ben was the neatest person I ever met. His clothes were always perfectly folded and arranged. This drawer looks like someone dumped everything in here without folding it."

Libby joined her at the dresser. "You think someone searched the room? Check the other drawers."

Amy pushed everything aside until she was sure nothing was there but clothing, then went to the next drawer of shorts and T-shirts. It was in the same condition. So were the other two drawers. "Someone has been here. Ben would never leave his things like this."

"Someone was looking for something. You need to make sure you tell Tom."

Amy nodded and moved to the closet. Clothing lay like confetti on the floor. "Look at this. Everything is off the hangers."

Libby joined her and murmured in dismay. "The question is, did they find what they were looking for? This proves something was amiss. Do you know where Ben might have hidden something important?"

Amy stilled. She knew exactly where her brother would have hidden something. But she wanted to be alone when she went there. Instead of answering, she stood on her tiptoes and ran her hand over the shelf. She couldn't quite reach to the back, but her fingers touched a hard rubber object. When she pulled it down, it was only one of his swim fins.

Little Noah began to fuss in the other room. "I'm going to have to go. He's hungry, and we've got our Bible study tonight. I'll come over tomorrow and help you look more."

Amy thanked her and walked her to the living room, then hugged them all good-bye. Once Alec's SUV pulled away, she dashed out the back door to the grove of trees at the rear of the property. The yard backed up to the state forest. The platform towered above her head in a live oak tree that had spread its branches in a canopy that shaded half the backyard. Their father had built it when he was twelve, and it had fallen into disrepair until she and Ben discovered it when they were about five and thirteen.

The pieces of wood that served as steps looked new. Ben must have replaced them. She planted her right foot on the first rail and climbed the tree. Her knee scraped the rough wood as she hiked her leg onto the platform. She lay panting on the rough boards for a moment, then sat up and looked around. The structure was eight feet square, big enough for the two of them to lie down and stare into the leafy roof over them. But the best thing about this place was no one looked up here, especially adults. It had been a secret haven she and Ben shared.

She got to her feet and found the rope ladder hidden in a tree hole. It had hooks on the top. This was always the tricky part, and Ben was much better at it than she was. She swung the hooks and aimed them at the large branch six feet above her head. The hooks scraped across the limb and fell. She tried again, and this time the hooks caught and held.

After testing the strength of the ladder, she climbed the rungs until she could peer into a hole in the tree that couldn't be seen from the platform. Whenever she stuck her hand inside, she cringed because she never knew what might be there. Once she'd stuck her hand in a spiderweb and had nearly fallen to the ground in her panic to get the sticky stuff off her fingers.

This time there were no spiders or anything else scary. Instead, there was a book. She pulled it out. It was a leather notebook about six by nine, maybe an address book. The cover was embossed with Ben's name, and she ran her fingers over it before stuffing it in her waistband and climbing back to the safety of the platform. She opened the book and blinked. It was all in gibberish. Was it some kind of code? She flipped through all the pages, but there was nothing on the few pages she could read.

Something in this book may have led to her brother's death, but what?

———

Heather's footfalls sounded impossibly loud when she stepped into Rosemary Cottage. "Hello?" she called, just to make sure she was alone.

Amy's car was in the driveway, but that didn't mean anything. The sea was just through the maritime forest, close enough to walk to the beach, and Amy seemed to spend a lot of time there. The house smelled of some kind of seafood, so Amy had been here.

Heather's cell phone rang, and she dug it out of her purse. When she saw the name on the caller ID, her heart leaped. "Hello, Grant."

"Heather, finally! Are you there?"

"Of course. I've been here for six days. I expected you to call sooner." She couldn't keep the whine out of her voice.

"I've been busy." He sounded impatient. "Did you get your room at Tidewater Inn?"

He might have told her he missed her before he launched into the inquisition. "No, they were full. I'm staying with a nice lady in a cottage a bit off the water. It's called Rosemary Cottage."

There was a pause. "You need to get to the inn. You'll have a better chance to get to know your target. The owners are friends of his."

"Well, you should have made my reservations so I could have gotten a room. I'm on a waiting list, but it's going to be at least three weeks before I can get moved over there. There's a month-long festival going on."

"I see." Grant's voice was tight. "Maybe it's just as well. You need to be part of village life so you're not a suspect, and that length of time will help establish you as more than a tourist."

"I've got a job serving at a local café. That should help make me a familiar face."

"Good. Have you met the family yet?"

"I met the old lady in the café. She was alone though."

"It's a start. Well, keep me posted. We need this done as soon as possible."

She gripped the phone and tried to think of a reason to keep him on the line. "You have everything ready for the pickup, right? I don't want to be left high and dry."

"You call the number I gave you, and I'll pick you up in a boat out at the old lighthouse. Take a walk out there so you know how to find it. It's remote, but that ensures no one will see you board the boat. Relax, I've got it all covered. And don't be so skittish. It will show in your actions. I appreciate you doing this. When it's all over, we'll take a nice trip to Jamaica, and I'll make it up to you."

His smooth voice always got past her defenses. She still remembered the first time she'd seen him. He was thirty-two, too old for her according to her dad, but that just made him more appealing. He reminded her of Ewan McGregor, and his blue eyes seemed to see the real person she was underneath. He'd flirted with her and bought her flowers that day in Atlantic City. They'd struck up an e-mail friendship that soon became more.

Was he ever going to marry her? She didn't know, but she'd do anything for him, and this trip was all about proving it. "I love you. I wish you could have come with me."

"I love you too, honey. We'll be together soon. Be careful and keep me posted."

Her lips curved. "I will."

Still smiling, she ended the call. He wouldn't have called to check on her if he didn't love her. And he wouldn't be attending to every detail if he didn't want to make sure she was safe. He might not be effusive with his words, but his actions showed he cared.

She dropped her phone back in her purse and went upstairs. Every time she'd been here, Amy was around. Heather liked digging into people's pasts, and Amy hadn't revealed much about herself. This was the perfect time to snoop. Looking around the spare bedroom that had belonged to Amy's dead brother hadn't revealed much of anything.

Heather pushed open the door to Amy's room and stepped inside. A quilt in blues and white covered the queen bed. The hardwood floors gleamed. The furniture was white too, and the pale blue walls and furnishings were welcoming.

There were pictures on the wall of her and a man. Heather froze when she recognized the man with his hand on Amy's shoulder. Ben. The picture showed a loving relationship between them. His fingers curled around the top of her arm, and he was smiling down at her with an indulgent expression. Amy was laughing as she shook water out of her hair.

Obviously they were close.

Heather moved from the pictures to the dresser and went through the drawers. She found nothing but clothing, so she moved to the closet. She'd begun to push aside the clothing when she heard a sound and whirled to see Amy standing in the doorway.

Amy looked more astonished than angry. "What are you doing?"

"I—I was chilly and didn't bring a sweater. I looked for you to ask if I could borrow one, but I couldn't find you." Heather kept a pleading expression on her face and hoped Amy would buy the explanation.

The question in Amy's eyes cleared. "I have several sweaters and zip-up sweatshirts." She went to the dresser and pulled out the bottom drawer. "I'm happy to loan you one. How about this one? It will look good with your hair and skin." She held up a pink cardigan.

Heather loathed the color pink, but she forced a smile to her face. "Perfect." Though she was anything but cold, she slipped it on. "I thought we were about the same size." She started for the door, then paused and glanced back at Amy. "Nice picture there on the wall. Who's the handsome guy?"

Amy's smile vanished. "My brother, Ben. He died several months ago."

Heather thought she managed to keep the shock out of her expression as she mumbled something about being sorry before escaping to the hall. The man she had known as Ben had a different last name. Maybe Grant could tell her what was going on.

NINE

"What do you mean you asked Amy to dinner?" Curtis wanted to bolt back to the Coast Guard cruiser in spite of the enticing aroma in the kitchen. He sniffed. "Beef enchiladas?" He'd know that scent anywhere.

"I thought I told you yesterday, Curtis." A huge red apron covered Edith's shorts and tank. She vigorously tossed the salad ingredients. "I like her."

He liked Amy too. That was the whole problem. His gaze landed on Raine, who was putting her doll in its little pink high chair. *Well, that isn't the whole problem.* There were pictures that needed putting away, and he had to guard every word while she was here. It would be better to be gone.

He pulled out his cell phone. "I think I'll see if Josh wants to meet for pizza."

"He's coming too. And Sara. Neither of them was about to turn down Mexican."

His gut churned. "Ede, this is not okay. You should have asked me before you did this."

A streak of red enchilada sauce marred her cheek when she turned and pointed her spoon at him. "You assured me when I first came that I was to treat this house as my own. I could

65

invite whomever I wanted whenever I wanted. Is that or is it not true?"

"Yes, but this is different." *Lame, lame.* "I mean, what if . . . ?" He shut up when he saw Raine's big blue eyes studying him.

His aunt put down the wooden spoon and sighed. "Curtis, you were brought up right. You know what you need to do."

His face heated. "It's not that easy." His gaze slid back to Raine. "Silence isn't wrong."

"It is when you're withholding the truth. A truth that's important to other people."

"I don't see it that way." The doorbell rang and he grimaced. "I'll get it." He saw Josh and Sara through the window in the door, and the tension eased out of his shoulders. He threw open the door. "Did you two come together?"

Sara shook her head and stepped past him into the entry. "No, we just happened to arrive at the same time."

Josh shrugged and rolled his eyes as he entered behind her. Curtis was beginning to think the guy was never going to ask Sara out. Josh was too skittish about relationships, though Curtis had never gotten to the bottom of why that was.

Sara sniffed. "Smells good. Your aunt makes the best Mexican food on the island." She headed toward the kitchen.

Curtis fell into step behind them. Sara's honey-colored hair was on her shoulders, and she wore makeup, not an everyday occurrence. *And* she wore a dress. Maybe she was trying to get Josh to notice, but if so, there was no sign that he was paying attention. Curtis could throttle him.

Edith had taken off the soiled apron and was setting the table when they entered the kitchen. Curtis left them to chat while he rushed to the living room and scooped up the photos on the tables. One was of Gina with Ben and Raine, a telltale picture that showed Ben holding Raine over his head and laughing. With them tucked safely away in his bedroom, he was headed down the stairs when the doorbell rang again. It could only be Amy, and his gut clenched when he saw her through the window.

It was going to be a tense evening. He inhaled and squared his shoulders before opening the door. "Welcome." He must have put more feeling in it than he intended because she blinked before returning his smile.

"I wasn't sure you'd be here."

The light scent of some flowery perfume trailed behind her as she stepped past him into the entry. She wore a navy dress that made her dark curls shine and brought color to her cheeks. Her legs looked impossibly long and sexy in the heels she wore. Not that he was looking.

He'd gotten the pictures put away in the nick of time. "Everyone is in the kitchen." He spied a carton in her hand. "Heavy whipping cream?"

"For coffee after dinner. I'm on a quest to inform people that fat is your friend. Once you have this in your coffee, you'll never go back." She peeked into the living room just off the foyer. "Darling house. I love the shingles on the outside and the porch. And the colors in here are very beachy."

The house was something he barely noticed any longer, but he glanced around with fresh eyes. The navy sofa blended with the lighter blue walls. Yellow curtains and pillows accented the blues, and the rug on the polished wood floors echoed the same colors. "Edith and I painted it last month. The white woodwork was her idea, and she had to talk me into the blue. I wanted beige."

Her lips twitched. "I think Edith has good taste."

He grinned. "You have something against beige?"

"It ought to be banned along with brown and orange."

"Orange too? I guess I shouldn't wear my Harley shirts when I'm around you." He touched her arm to steer her toward the kitchen.

The smile faded from her face at his touch, and their gazes locked. Did she feel the same jolt that tingled up his arm? "This way." His pulse beat ridiculously fast, but it was from worry of what she might find out tonight. That was all it was.

———

The scent of the sea blew through the gauzy yellow curtains in the living room and wafted across Amy's face where she sat on the plump navy sofa. Curtis was beside her, and she was acutely aware of the brush of his shoulder against hers. The hair on her arm stood at attention every time he moved. Ridiculous.

She sipped her coffee, strong and perfectly laced with the cream she'd brought. Josh and Sara sat in the navy armchairs, as far away from each other as possible. There was something brewing between those two, though she could only sense it.

With a shy smile, Raine brought a stuffed bear to her. "For me?" Amy took it when the toddler nodded. "I have one just like this. My brother bought it for me for my birthday a year ago."

Edith put a plate of fudge on the table. "A year ago?"

Amy nodded. "I've never grown up when it comes to stuffed animals. You should see my collection. Bears are my favorite, and there is nothing like a Steiff. Where did you get it, Raine? Uncle Curtis?"

The little girl looked at her with big eyes, and Edith answered for her. "Her daddy gave it to her. He went to heaven though, just like Mommy. But Jesus is watching over her, isn't he, honey?"

Edith's words brought tears to Amy's eyes. Life shouldn't be so hard for a little one. She almost asked Curtis who Raine's daddy was, but her thoughts were derailed when Curtis jumped to his feet.

"More coffee?"

She shook her head. "Not if I want to sleep tonight. One cup is my limit after four."

"I could make decaf." He shoved his hands in his pockets and shuffled a little as if he was eager to do something, anything.

She made a face. "The chemicals used to remove the caffeine are terrible for you."

"Mom?" Raine asked, still leaning on Amy's knee.

Poor little mite missed her mommy. Curtis's face went red, and he turned away.

Raine's pigtails bounced when she scrambled to her feet and turned to the coffee table. She stared at it, then at her uncle. "Mom?"

Curtis stared down at his small niece. "Uh, I was dusting the picture."

She stamped her small foot and began to wail. "Mom, mom, mom." She flopped onto her bottom and crawled toward the table.

Amy didn't understand the expression on Edith's face when she glanced at Curtis as Raine opened the door to the enclosed space in the end table.

She emerged with a five-by-seven frame in her hand and turned toward Amy with a proud smile. "Mom, mom."

Curtis sprang to his feet and reached for the little girl, but she evaded his rush with a giggle as if she thought he was playing. From his expression, Amy knew he was deadly serious. What was going on? Raine ran into her arms, and Amy lifted her onto her lap. Curtis stopped as his hands fell to his sides, then he exhaled heavily. "Have a look at the picture, Amy."

Edith pressed her hands together, almost a prayerful pose. "Yes, this needs to come out."

"Come out? I don't understand." Amy glanced from one to the other, then down at the photo.

A smiling Gina looked up at a tall, handsome man holding

little Raine on his shoulders. The little girl appeared to be about six months old at the time. Then Amy's gaze landed on the man's face, and she froze. She looked from the picture to Curtis and back again.

"Yes, it's Ben. Ben is Raine's father."

"That's impossible," she said, barely managing to whisper. "I would have known. He would have told me."

"Like he told you how often he was coming to the island?" Edith's words were soft but unyielding. "I think your brother kept a few secrets, Amy."

Amy couldn't breathe as she stared at the picture and back to the little girl. "You're sure?"

Curtis's lips flattened. "As sure as I can be. He claimed to be. His name is on the birth certificate."

Her chest squeezed and she hugged Raine to her chest. Ben still lived in this child. Her eyes burned, and she struggled not to let the tears fall. He wasn't gone, not completely. "Why didn't you tell me?"

"I almost did the other night at Tidewater Inn."

Josh got to his feet. "I think we'd better go."

Sara leaped up also. "Yes, it's getting late." Her cheeks were pink. She followed Josh out the door.

Edith rose and held out her hands for Raine. "It's time for your bath, honey."

Amy's arms tightened around the little girl, and she stared up at the older woman. "I'd like to keep her a little while."

Edith glanced at Curtis. "The two of you have things to discuss without little ears."

"Of course. I wasn't thinking." Amy brushed her lips across Raine's soft cheek and reluctantly let Edith lift her from her arms.

"I'll bring her back later." Edith carried a protesting Raine up the steps.

Amy finally exhaled. "You should have told me. And my parents. We had a right to know."

Curtis crossed his arms over his chest. "Your brother didn't marry her. I think he abdicated his rights."

"Ben would never—" But she couldn't complete her protest. A week ago she would have said no one knew Ben as well as she did, but she was wrong, oh so wrong. What else had he kept from her?

TEN

Lightning flickered out over the water, and Curtis got up to shut the window before the rain blew in through the curtains. Anything to avoid seeing Amy's crestfallen expression. Now that the moment of truth was here, he knew Edith had been right. He'd been wrong to keep this from Amy and her family.

When he returned to the seating area, he found Amy sitting with her hands clasped on her knee. Her expression was still stricken, and he wished he hadn't been the one to cause the pain on her face.

She straightened. "Do you know why they never married?"

He dropped into the armchair and shrugged. "He said his parents had plans for him."

She frowned. "It was always understood that he and Elizabeth Hawthorne would marry. She's the daughter of Dad's business partner. They were engaged and he seemed very attentive."

"He told Gina he was going to try to get out of the engagement, but that it would take awhile to accomplish." And look where her patience had gotten her. "She should have pushed him."

"Ben was never one to be pushed." She looked down at her hands. "But a child. It boggles my mind that he kept it secret. How could he think that was okay? He knew right from wrong."

"Knowing it and being willing to do something about it are

sometimes very different things." When her head turned sharply toward him, Curtis knew he had let his bitterness show. "Yeah, I didn't much like him. Gina was my baby sister, and I felt he was mistreating her."

She bristled a little. "There must have been some reason behind his decision. My brother was a good man." Her expression turned thoughtful. "Was he sure he was the father?"

Curtis clenched his jaw. "I know her reputation wasn't the best, but that was in the past. Ben never questioned it. He was even there when Raine was born."

She blinked and inhaled. "I didn't mean to offend you, but this is so unlike Ben."

Most people were defensive of their siblings. She clearly didn't know her brother as well as she thought she did. "You had no idea he was coming here so often?"

She tucked a curl behind her ear. "Not a clue. We always came here together in the summer. He visited once in a while without me, but not this often. And not for this reason." Her voice broke and she cleared her throat. "I'm not sure how to tell my parents. And Elizabeth." She clasped herself and rocked forward. "I still can't quite take it all in."

His fingers curled into his palms. Her parents would try to take Raine. From all he'd heard, it seemed they tried to manage their kids' lives. But looking at Amy, he knew she would be good to Raine. And did he have the right to deny the little girl he loved so much the love of more family? He'd thought he did.

Amy sat back against the sofa and studied him. "You still haven't answered my question. Why didn't you tell us?" Her soft words carried a steely undertone.

Thunder shook the house, and the rain began to beat against the roof and the windows. The din was so loud he had to raise his voice. "Ede wanted me to tell you. I was afraid of losing Raine."

"Losing her?" Then comprehension dawned. "You have custody."

He gave a slight nod. "I've started proceedings to formally adopt her."

"And my parents may have something to say about that."

"Gina left her in my care in her will. It's what she wanted. She would hate for your parents to have her." He held up his hand when she started to protest. "They ruled Ben. Maybe you were strong enough not to let them rule you, but I don't want Raine turned into some debutante who is expected to toe the line and make an advantageous marriage."

Amy didn't answer at first. She turned and stared out the window into the dark. "I need air."

He followed when she sprang to her feet and rushed for the door. The screen door banged behind her, and he hurried to catch up, praying all the while that she wasn't calling her parents and setting some legal action into motion. He was instantly soaking wet, then the scent of rain hit him. He couldn't see her with the wind blowing the downpour sideways into his face. Squinting, he glanced to the right where the chairs were but saw only the rockers swaying with the wind.

"I'm here."

He turned at the sound of her voice and found her leaning on the railing in a protected area of the porch. Her hair was wet and droplets of moisture trickled down her face. Her dress was drenched as well, but she was out of the main force of the storm.

He stepped to her side. "Sorry if what I said upset you."

She turned her wet face up toward him, and she seemed somehow tragically beautiful in the glow of the porch light. "I totally get how you feel. You've known Raine for a whole year. She's been part of your life. You love her and don't want to lose her. I'm sure I'd feel the same. But we've been deprived of that privilege."

"That's not entirely my fault. Only the last few months were my doing."

She sucked in her breath and rocked back on her heels. "You're right. Ben kept this from us first. And don't you find it strange Gina died so close to Ben's death?" Her eyes seemed to glow with intensity. "When did she die?"

"Two weeks before Ben drowned."

"So she died first. Did Ben come for Raine? I'm trying to make sense of how you ended up with custody if she died first."

He shook his head. "He stopped to see her, then told me he couldn't take her now but would make financial arrangements. I told him I wanted to adopt her. He didn't like it."

"I'm sure he didn't. So why couldn't he take her? Did he explain?"

Curtis shrugged. "He said his apartment wasn't big enough, and he had no one to care for her. Edith came at once, so she was here when he arrived. I guess he thought we had it covered."

She swiped a lock of wet hair out of her eyes. "Was that when he seemed distressed? Red eyes and all that? Maybe it was grief."

"Yeah, that was the time."

Her thoughtful gaze wandered back toward the sea. "So he was jumpy, nervous. Got a lot of phone calls." She gasped and turned to stare at him. "Did you ever think that maybe Gina was deliberately hit?"

Every time he remembered the way that boat had come out of nowhere and made a beeline for his sister, he'd wondered. "Sometimes. The guy never veered even though she yelled and waved her arms."

"What if they were both involved in something dangerous, Curtis? You know that I believe Ben was murdered."

"He went surfing and never came back. The most logical explanation is that he drowned."

"Ah, logic." She smiled and put her hand over her heart. "I know it here. But I also received an e-mail suggesting that Ben was murdered. I intend to find out the truth, and I'd like you to help me. We might find out who did this to your sister too."

"What about Raine? Are you telling your parents?"

"I have to think about how to do it. I don't want them to try to take her any more than you do."

He couldn't ignore the possibility that she was right. "Okay. I'm in. We'll see what we can find out together."

"One more thing." She smiled. "I've decided to move here permanently. I'm needed here."

He wasn't about to explain to himself why his heart had suddenly sped up.

⌣

Thunder rumbled the house in a morning storm, but it was nothing compared to the storm in Amy's soul. Ben lived in little Raine. Ben's room had been her haven all night, and she sat on his bed with her knees up to her chest. Sometime in the night she'd pulled on his favorite Harvard sweatshirt.

She buried her nose in the neck of the fleece. It still held a trace of his cologne. The room still held so many of his things, precious possessions she never wanted to release. But should she give some of these things to Raine someday? They were the child's birthright.

Her cell phone rang, and she snatched it from the table by the bed. Her supervising physician, Dr. Zellers, was on the other end. He was always up early, and answering it, she could see him in her mind's eye sitting in his sunroom with his morning smoothie. "Good morning, Doctor."

His deep voice rumbled in her ear. "I got your e-mail, Amy, and I wanted to talk to you about your plan."

At his reserved tone, her fingers tightened on the phone. "Of course."

"You say this place is only accessible by ferry? How easy is it going to be for us to meet? And I'm concerned I may get flack from the state board about how remote you are."

She straightened and swallowed. "We only meet twice a year for you to look at my records and assure yourself that I'm following your protocol. I'll travel to you. It will be my responsibility."

"I'm dubious, Amy. It's such a remote place."

She bit her lip. "You encouraged me to find a place that needed me. That's exactly what I've done. I can't think of an area in more dire need of my services." Silence echoed on the other end. "Doc, are you there?"

"I'm here." His voice was heavy. "I'll have to turn you down. I hate it, but I can't risk my license for you."

She swung her feet to the floor and leaped to her feet. "Please don't do that, Dr. Zellers! It's so hard to find a doctor willing to supervise. What about the women here?" *And what about my career?*

"I'm sorry, but that's my final decision. Let me know how you get along, Amy. You're bright enough—maybe you should go to medical school and become a doctor yourself. Have a good day. I need to get to the office."

She put down her phone and flung herself onto the pillow. Now what?

———

The festival was in full swing, and Heather had never seen so many people in her life. All in town for an *oyster* festival, of all things. There were more oyster dishes on the menu this week than she could count.

Heather's feet throbbed and her back ached from carrying the trays of heavy plates. And people were so demanding. They wanted their coffee just so and their sandwiches toasted to a certain degree. The sooner she was off this dead island, the better. Visions of her and Grant on a white-sand beach floated in her mind.

"Hey, watch what you're doing!"

The harsh male voice interrupted her pleasant daydream, and she looked at her customer's overflowing coffee cup. "Sorry." She grabbed a handful of napkins and mopped up the mess before moving on to the next table.

She froze when she saw the couple with the little girl, then managed a smile. "I wasn't expecting to see you here, Amy. What can I get you two?"

While Amy perused the menu a moment, Heather eyed Curtis and the child. She recognized him from the picture Grant had given her. The child too. The question was how to get close enough to him to gain better access. And what was Amy doing with him? That might complicate matters.

Amy handed her the menu. "Is there gluten in the lobster bisque?"

"Nope. It's cream only." Customers had only asked her that a million times.

"Wonderful. I'll have that."

Amy and her weird eating habits. The refrigerator back at the cottage was filled with nasty things like heavy whipping cream and real butter. Even the yogurt had fat in it. Amy had tried to get her to try them, but Heather stuck to her diet of Diet Coke and frozen dinners. She was into easy.

She smiled at Curtis. "And you, sir?"

He folded his menu and handed it to her. "I'll have a barbeque sandwich."

"With slaw on the side or on the sandwich?"

"On the sandwich. And coffee. Oh, and you can keep the pickle. I never eat it."

"Sweet potato fries okay with that?"

"Of course." He grinned and studied her face. "You're new here."

"She's boarding with me," Amy said. "Until the festival is over. There are no rooms in town."

"So this is Heather. I've heard about you. Libby and Alec hated to hear you'd been turned away from the inn, but it was a good thing Amy came to your rescue."

"Amy's been super to me." Heather scribbled down their order on her pad and stuck it in the pocket of her apron, then poured Curtis's coffee.

She had to figure out a way to stay longer. The rooms out at Tidewater Inn weren't cheap, and she didn't want to waste her hard-earned money on a room when there was all that space at Rosemary Cottage just sitting empty. Besides, if Amy and Curtis were friends, staying at the cottage might be beneficial in other ways. And she liked the little cottage.

Curtis took a sip of his coffee. "Where you from, Heather?"

"California." It was the first state that popped out of her mouth, one she'd always wanted to see.

Amy grinned. "You've gotten more information out of her in two minutes than I've gotten in a week. Until I met Heather, I thought all girls her age chattered a mile a minute."

Heather resisted the impulse to dump coffee on her head. Instead, she turned and smiled sweetly at Curtis. "Cute little girl you have there. She looks a bit like you."

"She's my niece, and she's the spitting image of her mommy at that age." He stopped Raine from pulling the sweetener packets out of the holder. "She'll have a grilled cheese sandwich and sweet potato fries. Chocolate milk. And applesauce."

"You take care of her?" Someone hailed her from across the room, but Heather ignored the summons. She took off her necklace and handed it to the little girl, who was immediately enthralled.

"Yes. She lives with me." His expression grew guarded.

"She's a cutie pie." Heather put more warmth into her voice than she felt. "I don't suppose you need a nanny for her, do you? Waiting tables is not for me, and I've worked in a day care center. I love kids. I miss being with them."

Pretty good, if she did say so herself. Her voice held just the right mix of pathos and wistfulness. She fastened her gaze on him and willed him to accept.

Raine started to put the necklace in her mouth, and Curtis stopped her. "My aunt takes care of her. She lives with us."

"What about time off for your aunt? I'd even be willing to do part-time. Give her a break once a week or something."

He studied her face, then nodded. "Come by one evening next week. Bring your résumé, and we'll talk. You can meet my aunt."

She wrote his address on the back of her pad, then went off to get the loudmouth at the corner table to shut up. Even the customer's demanding ways couldn't wipe the pleased smile from her face.

She'd accomplished the first part of her plan. Once she was in the house, the rest would be easy.

ELEVEN

The lobster bisque was every bit as good as she'd hoped, but Amy had struggled to force it down when she wanted to discuss what Curtis had just done. She simmered quietly through lunch until Edith stopped by to pick up Raine as they were finishing.

"Are you *crazy*?" Amy demanded when Edith left with Raine. She was ready to shake Curtis.

The hand carrying his coffee stopped halfway to his mouth. "What are you talking about?"

"You don't let a stranger watch Raine! If Edith needs a break, I'll take care of her. I like Heather well enough, but I still know very little about her—and certainly not enough to feel comfortable letting her babysit."

"Maybe she's just reserved. It's not like I was hiring her today. I just told her to bring me a résumé and we'd talk. She seems a nice enough girl. And Raine obviously liked her." He grinned. "You are still in big-city mode, Amy. This is Hope Island. Most of us don't even lock our doors."

"But she's not an islander! She's new here."

"Look who's talking. You're not an islander either. Not yet anyway."

That hurt. "I've been coming here since I was a little girl. I consider this place my home. And it's going to be my full-time home."

"But you've never lived here before now. And everyone who doesn't live here should be viewed with suspicion?"

She folded her arms across her chest. "Not suspicion, but at least some caution when we're talking about a little girl."

"Like I said, I wasn't hiring her on the spot." His voice held impatience. "I'm not an idiot, in spite of what you might think."

She leaned back in her chair and sighed. "I didn't mean to imply that. You're great with Raine."

At her softened tone, he exhaled. "I guess we both need to step back a second. You say to be cautious, and I'll agree to that. Okay?"

She nodded. "So does Edith need an occasional break? I'd be glad to help out. I want to get to know Raine better." When he didn't answer, she took a stab at what his problem was. "I'm not trying to take her away, okay? I just want to get to know her. And I want to tell her who I am." She folded her arms across her chest.

He put down his fork slowly. "I'm not sure that's wise."

"Why not? I think she could love me, and I already love her for Ben's sake. I want to love her for her own sake too, and I need to know her."

"Most anyone would love you, Amy."

The words, spoken in a low voice, took her aback. She didn't know how to respond, though she was probably taking the sentiment with more feeling than he meant. He was just being nice. "I don't know about that. So can I help? Can I tell her I'm her auntie?"

He sat staring for a long moment before he finally spoke. "I'll think about it."

"How long?" She knew she was being pushy, but Curtis struck her as one of those people who carefully thought out everything. That wasn't bad, but she had already lost a year. She didn't want to waste another moment of getting to know her niece.

"A few days."

Today was Saturday. "Monday then. You can prepare her if you like."

He looked at her. "You are basically saying you're going to tell her whether I agree or not."

She thrust out her chin. "I am. I've agreed not to tell my parents just yet until I think it through, but we are going to be a part of her life. There's no way you can stop that."

His jaw flexed. "This is happening so fast. I don't want her confused or upset."

"What can be upsetting to find out you have an aunt and grandparents? It's not like we'll be saying anything bad about Gina. I'll handle it gently. I know children."

"Looks like I don't have much choice."

When he put it that way, she felt bad about the corner she'd boxed him into. But none of them had chosen this situation. It wasn't something that was planned, but what a wonderful thing to realize she still had a piece of Ben. It was cause for rejoicing, not for sadness. But she couldn't tell Curtis all that was in her overflowing heart. He thought it was about control when it was all about love.

Why was it so hard to be herself, to be transparent? When she went to church, she put on a smile and never let anyone see her heartache. She was always "fine." It was the way she'd been brought up. Her parents had taught her to "buck up" and to look on the sunny side. And she did, for the most part, because she was naturally optimistic. But hiding her thoughts and who she really was had gotten to be a bad habit.

Curtis leaned back. "Let's call a truce, okay? It's too nice of a day to squabble."

She nodded and rose. They walked out together into the sunshine of the spring afternoon. The breeze brought the scent of saltwater and flowers to her nose.

"I know a great spot on the hillside to watch the kiteboarding. We can talk about what to investigate while we're watching them."

Amy nodded. Once they were out of the crowd, she would talk to him about what he'd just agreed to do. He led her along the crowded sidewalks to the edge of town. Dunes rolled along the edge of the maritime forest and made a grand seat for the show taking place offshore. Brightly colored kites rose on the breeze, lifting their riders high above the foaming sea. Sightseers with their striped beach chairs lined the water just beyond the tide line. The occasional cheer rose above the roar of the surf.

It was only when he rolled out a bright blue sheet from his backpack that she knew he'd planned this all along. Not that she minded leaning back on the sloping dune with him.

She would have to focus to keep her attention on the reason she was spending time with him.

———

Curtis was intensely conscious of how close Amy was to him where she lay stretched out on the sheet. He'd seen the way she glanced at him when he pulled out what they needed for the afternoon. Those green-gold eyes didn't miss much. If he'd thought he could hide the fact that he'd been looking forward to spending the day with her, he'd been mistaken.

The sun heated his arms, but that wasn't the reason he was warm. What was it about her anyway? He'd taken one look at her and had been instantly drawn to her. He wanted to know what she was thinking, what made her tick. What had her life been like growing up?

He cleared his throat. "So you and Ben were the only kids, right?"

She nodded. "He was eight years older."

He would have guessed she was older. Not because she looked

it, but because she was wise and smart. Ben had been brash and immature. "There was just Gina and me too. She was three years younger than me."

"You grew up here?"

He shook his head. "We summered here, though, until we were adults. When I signed on with the Coast Guard, I moved here. Gina followed a few years later. I grew up in Manhattan. Big old brownstone."

Her eyes widened. "That costs the earth. I'm surprised you made a comment about my parents and their money. You're from the same background."

"My dad was a self-made man, and he always expected us to do the same. There was no silver spoon in my mouth. He insisted I get my first job when I was twelve, delivering newspapers. Anything I wanted, I had to buy myself with money I earned."

Her gaze warmed. "Smart of them. Did they squawk when you joined the Coasties?"

"Nope. They are proud of me."

"You're lucky. My mother was scandalized when I told her I was going to be a midwife."

"You're a nurse too, right? They should be proud you want to help people."

She shook her head. "I was besmirching the Lang name. They wanted me to go into the family business of banking." She gave a mock shudder and laughed. "Numbers give me hives. Half the time I couldn't tell you if my patients pay me or not. As long as I have enough money to carry the mortgage and buy food, I'm happy. When I hold that newborn in my arms, I can feel God smiling at me."

He could barely take his eyes off her. The sunlight brought red lights out in her hair, and she glowed as she talked about her life's work. "And Ben? What did he think of your career?"

Animation surged to her face. "He hated coming to the clinic. All those mothers and babies gave him hives." She laughed. "But it was his fault. He told me to follow my dream and not let my dad's expectations get in my way."

"I think you're pretty special to do what you do. You get called out in the middle of the night and hold life in your hands."

"So do you. You and the rest of your team do some pretty heroic things."

His face heated at the admiration on her face. "It's just part of the job. What are you going to tell your parents about Raine?"

Her smile vanished. "I don't know. I fear your first assessment is right. They will want to take custody. And they have a lot of money."

He shrugged even though her comment made his gut tighten. "My family is wealthy too, and my parents will spend their last dime to keep her with us."

"And Raine will be caught in the middle." She rubbed her forehead. "It's a terrible tangle, Curtis."

He liked the sound of his name on her lips. Liked the almost confiding tone she used, as if they were on the same side. And really, weren't they? He had to believe she wanted what was best for Raine. "What about our investigation? I'm still not convinced anyone intended to hurt either of them."

"You said the boat seemed to head straight for Gina. Did she say anything in the days leading up to her death? Give you any indication she was worried?"

"No." The word slipped out before he allowed himself to think about it, and he knew it was because he didn't *want* to think that someone had killed her. "I mean, I don't know." He thought back to the last couple of weeks. "Wait a minute."

"What?"

"She drew up paperwork appointing me guardian. Gina had

never thought that far ahead before. I wondered why she was worrying about it. I mean, she had to know I'd take Raine without a formal will."

"When did she do the paperwork?"

He thought back to the day Gina had come to him to tell him what she was doing and to make sure he was cool with it. "Three days before she died. I thought she was just being careful, but maybe there was more to it than that."

"What did she do when Ben was here? Who did they see?"

He shrugged. "I hardly kept tabs on them."

Her eyes were intense with interest. "Did she live with you?"

"Nope. She and Raine lived in an upstairs condo out on the quay."

She straightened. "So people would have seen them. Could we go snoop around there? Ask her neighbors if they saw anything?"

"Sure thing. I think it's a good idea." The breeze whipped her curls as she turned to watch the kiteboarding, and he couldn't look away. There were six kites aloft, almost breathtaking in the sunlight, and he saw the interest on her face. "You ever been up on one?"

She shook her head. "I don't like high places."

He grinned. "I'll take you up, and I promise not to let you fall."

"You would be deafened by the screams by the time we got down."

He cupped his ear. "What was that?"

She laughed, a light melodic sound that made his smile widen. He wouldn't mind listening to that all day long.

TWELVE

Amy relished the warm sun on her skin and the sound of the surf. She kicked off her sandals and dug her toes into the sand at the edge of the sheet. Being on Hope Island was rejuvenating for her, and the frozen state she'd been in since Ben's death was beginning to thaw. Kites fluttered in the breeze against a backdrop of the surf's mesmerizing murmur. Boston's hustle-bustle was a million miles away. The island was a place apart, a Brigadoon. Different from any other spot, safer somehow.

Though it hadn't been safe for Ben. She still reeled from everything she'd learned since she'd arrived. Drugs. Was it possible? If so, she wanted to hide it from her parents.

She let sand trickle through her fingers. She still didn't see Curtis's broad-shouldered figure. He'd gone down the beach to a vendor to fetch water for them both. It had been a pleasant interlude, but they still had yet to decide on a course of action. The problem was that they had so little to go on. Her gut instinct was all they had. At least he believed enough to help her pursue it.

"Amy?"

Dara stood about five feet away with another woman with dishwater hair that was styled in a spiky cut that gave her a youthful flair. She appeared to be in her fifties.

Amy stood and brushed the sand from her hands. "Hi, Dara. Are you enjoying the show?"

"It's very thrilling. Are you going to compete?"

Amy shook her head. "Not hardly. You?"

"I wish I could! I love adventure. I've been trying to talk Aunt Winona here into learning." She glanced at the other woman. "I don't think you two have met. This is my aunt, Winona Anderson. We're here for a month."

"Pleased to meet you. Have you been here before?"

"This is our first time. I'm looking to buy a house next to the handsome Coast Guard officer who helped save us," Winona said. "So you might be seeing a lot of us. We wouldn't move here, of course. I have my constituents to take care of, and Dara has her modeling career to pursue. But I could see coming over in our boat every month."

Modeling? Amy thought Dara worked for Preston. "How nice. You're in politics, Winona?"

The older woman nodded. "I'm a North Carolina state senator."

"So I'm sure you know Preston Kendrick as well."

"Of course. That's how Dara here ended up helping on his campaign. She's hoping the visibility will help her modeling."

"You live here?" Dara frowned as though she didn't like her aunt talking about her.

Amy nodded. "I own Rosemary Cottage on the edge of town. You may have seen it? It's the one with the herb garden in the front yard."

"Cute place."

Her tone insinuated otherwise, but Amy refused to take offense. "You're a model, huh? How can you do that and work for Preston too?"

Dara colored a little. "Well, modeling is slow right now. It will pick up again soon. In the meantime, I'm doing good for the country. What do you do?"

"I'm a midwife." Amy smiled, knowing how that was likely to go over.

Winona had a bottle of water to her lips, and she choked. "A—A midwife? They're illegal in North Carolina."

"I'm a registered nurse midwife, and we can practice legally. We're working to change the status of all midwives in the state though." She smiled at Winona. "You could help."

"Oh dear, I'm quite opposed to the bill in the house right now. I'm afraid I can offer you no support."

Winona's warm manner had disappeared. Amy had gotten used to the prejudice she often encountered. Even people who should realize birth was a natural process and had taken place in homes for thousands of years sometimes gave her odd looks.

She saw Libby and Alec strolling on the beach with Noah in Alec's arms. She waved them over. At least they could help defuse the tension.

"Hey, Libs, you look a little pale. Sit down." Amy took her arm and helped her settle on the beach blanket.

"I think we came farther than I realized." Libby held out her arms for the baby, and Alec handed him to her. "Would you get me some water, honey?"

He gave her a worried look. "Sure. I'll be right back."

"You could try to call Curtis. That's where he is," Amy told him.

He grinned and shook his head. "Cell doesn't work here. I'll find him." He jogged off on tanned, muscular legs.

"You delivered Libby's baby, I hear?" Winona asked.

Amy nodded. "Noah was born at my cottage."

"Do you have a license to practice in your home, Amy?" Winona wasn't smiling.

What was her beef? Amy was beginning to wish she'd never brought up her profession. "Libby was visiting and her water broke. Noah came very quickly. I don't have a clinic set up at my house, but I have an overseeing physician. I'm perfectly legal." Well, she was. She *had* to find a new physician.

The woman shrugged and pursed her lips. "I hear your brother drowned surfing. I thought your last name was familiar. Ben Lang was your brother, heir to the Lang Banking services. It was all over the papers when it happened. He was killed by a shark. Or drowned and was eaten."

Amy hid her wince. "So they say." Everyone knew her family, and few people believed foul play was involved. "Do you know my parents?"

Winona nodded. "Your father is one of my biggest supporters. I attended the memorial service for your brother." Her demeanor softened, and she put her hand on Amy's arm. "He told me you have some crazy idea it was murder."

"I have reasons for doubting the official answer."

"I know it's hard to let go of a loved one, my dear, but chasing crazy ideas will lead you nowhere but into more pain. Let it go."

It was all Amy could do to stay still and not shake the woman's hand away. "Thank you for your concern."

The older woman released her. "We'd better go, Dara." The women walked off.

Would Winona call Amy's father and tell him about the lecture? Her parents would be sure to give her a call.

———

Amy pulled on a pink-and-white dress, then went to the kitchen and poured a cup of coffee. She held it up to Heather, who sat swaddled in a pink fuzzy robe at the table. "Want some?"

"Sure." Heather's voice was still sleepy, and her hair was tangled.

Amy didn't know what time the girl had come in last night.

She'd found some people to hang out with. Amy poured coffee into Heather's cup.

"Thanks." Heather cupped the coffee in her palms.

"Want to come to church with me this morning? You'll get a chance to meet more people."

"I don't thi—" A thoughtful expression crossed her face. "Wait a minute. Will Curtis be there with Raine?"

The girl sure wanted out of that restaurant. Amy nodded. "Probably. He usually goes."

"How long do I have to get ready?"

"Twenty-five minutes, thirty tops."

"I can make it." Carrying her coffee, Heather hurried from the kitchen.

The girl was going to hound Curtis about that job again. Amy carried her coffee to the back deck. The spring morning held a hint of moisture, and dew shimmered on the grass. The fence along the back of the property was falling over in one section, and she made a mental note to call a carpenter. Then she saw why it had been knocked over.

A banker pony stood munching her flowers. Its tail swished as it glanced up at her, then bent down to take another bite of her flowers. The small horses were total nuisances.

She set her coffee on the small table and leaped to her feet. "Shoo, go!" Waving her arms, she advanced on the animal.

The reddish horse snorted but didn't back away from her herbs. As she neared, still yelling and waving her arms, she saw a deep gash on the horse's flank. His foot was tangled in some calendula. The fight went out of her.

She held out her hand. "Oh, you poor thing. I'm glad you ate some calendula. It will help that wound heal." He quivered when she laid a gentle palm on his side. "You need some help. Wait right here."

She ran back to the house and grabbed her medical bag. When

she returned, the horse was still standing where she left him. He didn't try to bite her or kick when she sterilized the wound, then pulled the edges together and glued them in place. She smeared calendula ointment on the wound.

"You don't seem afraid of people, boy." She smoothed his flanks, then ran her hand along his neck. His coat was ragged. "You need a good currying. I'll have to get a brush."

The horse seemed to understand her intentions. He snorted and pawed the grass. His head dipped down to take a bite of her herbs. She didn't try to stop him. The damage to her garden was already done.

She was so intent on the horse that she didn't hear anyone approaching until he cleared his throat, and she turned to see Tom behind her. The sheriff stood watching her actions. His hat was pushed to the back of his head, and perspiration beaded his forehead. The hems of his pants were damp from dew. He wasn't bad looking, but she saw no ring on his left hand.

He didn't smile. "You're good at that."

She stepped away from the horse. "He got cut by the thorns."

The sheriff waved away some gnats. "Stupid animals are a nuisance. They should be herded up and corralled."

"I love seeing them roaming the island." She surveyed her mangled garden ruefully. "Though I wish he would have stayed out of my herbs. What can I do for you, Sheriff? Do you have news?"

He took out his notebook. "I've been going over the notes surrounding your brother's death, and I came on something I needed to talk to you about. You have a minute?"

She glanced at her watch. "A few. I could miss the singing, and the rest of the congregation will thank you." Ben used to say she sounded like a frog. "Want some coffee?"

"Wouldn't turn it down."

He followed her toward the house. As they entered the back

door, she glanced behind and saw that the horse had left, now that he'd inflicted all his damage. Heather still wasn't in the kitchen. Amy poured the sheriff a cup of coffee while he pulled out a chair at the kitchen table and sat down.

He palmed the cup. "Nice house. I've never been inside."

"Thanks." She sat at the table. "So what's this about?"

"The only evidence we have is your brother's wetsuit, the damaged surfboard, and his belongings left on the beach."

She winced but nodded. "Not much evidence since the sea consumed his remains."

Tom sipped his coffee, then put it back on the table. "His wallet is missing."

"Maybe he didn't have it with him when he went surfing. It might be here. Is it important?"

"He drove to this particular spot, so his keys were there. Seems odd he wouldn't have his driver's license. And there was a packed suitcase in the car, so it appeared he was leaving the island shortly. Ned Springall told me he thought Ben had brought clothes to change into, and then he was heading to the mainland. There's an outdoor shower at that beach."

Amy digested the information. On the surface, it didn't seem earth shattering. "Maybe he forgot it here."

"Would you mind looking for that wallet when you get a chance? I don't want to hold you up from church, but give me a call and let me know what you find. Even if it's nothing."

"I'll look after lunch." Her stomach plunged at the thought. Searching his room had been hard enough the first time, and she didn't really want to do it again. "One other thing. Have you requested my brother's cell phone records? I've heard he got more calls than usual and had been upset after them."

The sheriff nodded. "I put in a request for them. Don't have them yet." He took a last gulp of coffee, then stood.

"Is that all you've got?"

He shrugged. "I've sent the surfboard to an expert for evaluation on what kind of shark bit it."

"So you're trying to prove he drowned and the sharks disposed of his body."

His brows came together in a scowl. "I want to get at the truth for your peace of mind. And mine. I don't want to miss anything."

"I appreciate that, Sheriff." She rose and walked him to the front door. "I'll let you know if I find anything."

Were her suspicions all just wind in the trees?

THIRTEEN

Heather sat beside Amy next to Libby and Alec with their new baby. The singing swelled to the wood rafters of the small, quaint church. Hope Beach Community Church sat on a hillside overlooking the blue Atlantic, and the sea air blew in through the open windows on the sides. Prisms of color danced on the white walls as the sun shone through the stained-glass window behind the platform.

Heather craned her neck and saw Curtis with his aunt and Raine two pews ahead of her. She had to get a chance to talk to him about hiring her. Appearing here should allay any doubts he had. Maybe she'd suggest to Amy that they invite them back to the cottage for lunch.

Alec and Libby rose and went forward, and the pastor began a baby dedication service. Heather listened to them promise to raise their little boy in the ways of the Lord, and a surprising lump came to her throat. The way Libby and Alec looked at their baby brought a longing to her heart. She doubted her parents had ever had such love in their eyes. She'd been more of a nuisance than a treasured daughter. Anything she'd gotten in life so far she'd had to scrap and fight for. No one had given her a thing. That baby was going to have every advantage, including the security of love.

It didn't seem fair for some to have so much love and others, like her, to have so little.

She blinked back the sting in her eyes and glanced ahead at where Curtis was with Raine on his lap. Did he feel that kind of love for her? Raine was only his niece, not really his child. When he brushed a kiss across the little girl's soft hair, she averted her eyes. He probably did love her. Was she doing the right thing?

She remained lost in her thoughts through the rest of the service, struggling through how she felt about what she was about to do. By the time they rose for the final song, she was fixed on her course again. As Amy accepted the hugs and condolences of her friends, Heather slipped past her and stood at the end of Curtis's pew as he made his way to the aisle.

"Heather, hello." He shifted Raine to the other arm. "Say hello, Raine. You remember Heather."

"No." The little girl regarded her with a solemn gaze, then plopped her thumb into her mouth.

"She's a little shy," Curtis said. "This is my aunt Edith." He indicated the woman behind him.

His aunt smiled at her. She was in her fifties with a great tan and a bright smile. "You must be the young woman who has offered to spell me with Raine once in a while. That's very kind of you."

Amy's voice came from behind Heather. "I've explained to her that I'd like to do that myself." Her voice was a little stiff.

Heather's head jerked around. "You? Why would you want to do it?"

"Raine is my niece. I'd like to get to know her."

"Your niece?"

Amy smiled at Raine and held out her hands to the child. "I just recently found out." The little girl reached for her, and Amy took her. "Can you say 'auntie,' Raine?"

Raine grabbed at a lock of Amy's hair. "Mom."

Amy exchanged a glance with Curtis, and Heather thought her gaze held a challenge. Curtis shrugged and looked away. What was all that about?

Amy nuzzled Raine's neck and kept staring at Curtis. "Are we still on to go talk to the residents of the condos where Gina lived?"

"Yep. Lunch at the Oyster Café first? Ede, can you take Raine home for her nap?"

"I was planning on it," Edith said.

Heather interrupted, intent on her goal. "I'm sure there might be times you are all busy, so keep me in mind. I love kids." She held out her hand to Raine, but the little brat hid her face in Amy's blouse. "She'll warm up to me. All kids do."

Curtis nodded. "Thanks for your offer, Heather. Did you bring your résumé?"

"Got it right here." She dug for it in her purse and handed it to him. The résumé had been fluffed up a little, but she doubted he would actually call the day care where she'd worked. And even if he did, she hadn't done anything really wrong there.

Two women approached them, and Amy turned to speak to them. "Hello, Dara, Winona. Not too tired from your day in the sun yesterday to get up early this morning, I see."

Heather looked over her shoulder and froze. Luckily, the women hadn't seen her yet.

"Let me know what you think, will you?" she asked Curtis in a low voice. "I have to run." She had to get out of here before they saw her and gave her away. She couldn't be sure they wouldn't recognize her.

He looked startled but nodded. "Sure thing. Hope you'll come back to church."

Fat chance. All she wanted to do was forget this place and how it made her feel.

A few wispy clouds drifted lazily across the blue bowl of sky. Curtis and Amy had had a quick bite of lunch together at the café after church before heading to the harbor apartments. He stared at the apartment building. About ten years old, the building was in good repair. The yellow shutters contrasted with the gray shingle siding, an attractive combination. The two-story building held eight apartments. They all looked out on the harbor, a prime location. How had Gina been able to afford it? It was surely expensive. They hadn't shared financial details, but she'd worked at the fudge shop since she got out of high school. Maybe Ben had paid for it.

"Ready?" he asked.

Amy nodded. "I've got what I want to ask all mapped out."

"We might as well start with the residents across the hall from her." He held open the main door that led into the large entry where the stairs went to the second floor. "Her apartment was upstairs on the right."

The interior of the building smelled like fish stew. Someone must have cooked it for lunch, and the pungent odor invaded the enclosed space. Industrial gray carpeting covered the stairs, and the walls were painted a light aqua. Pictures of the island and the sea decorated the walls on the way up the stairs.

"Nice place," Amy said when they stopped on the second-floor landing.

"Very." He stepped to the door on their right and rapped on it.

A TV played inside, a comedy with canned laughter. A child squealed, then light footsteps came toward the door. A blond woman in her midthirties opened the door. She had a baby, maybe four or five months old, on her hip. He was chomping on a teething biscuit and had smears of cookie around his mouth.

The woman's eyes registered recognition. "You're Curtis Ireland. Gina's brother."

He nodded. "That's right. I think we met at a building garage sale. This is my friend Amy. Afraid I've forgotten your name."

She opened the door a little wider and shifted the baby to the other hip. "Leah Crook. I've been meaning to call you. Gina left something with me, and I think you should have it."

Curtis glanced at Amy, then back to Leah. "What is it?"

Leah stepped away from the door. "Come into the kitchen."

"Want me to hold the baby while you get it?" Amy asked. "He's a little cutie."

"That would be great if you don't mind." Leah passed over the child.

"Hey, little man." Amy took him and shuffled him to one arm. He grabbed a lock of her hair in a messy grip, but she didn't seem to mind.

Leah led them to the kitchen. "Coffee is fresh if you want some. I'll be right back."

"What could it be?" The baby started to fuss a bit, and Amy jiggled him until he quieted.

"She seemed pretty serious about it all." He tried to think of what Leah might have that would be important, but nothing had seemed to be missing from Gina's things.

She studied his face. "Are you okay?"

"It feels weird to be poking into Gina's privacy. I know we have to do it, but she was always a little reserved about sharing personal details. Even with me." He couldn't even remember how she and Ben had gotten hooked up. Likely she'd never told him.

"I understand. I hate poking through Ben's room too." She rubbed her forehead. "But we have to get to the truth."

"*If* someone harmed them. I'm still not convinced." He didn't want to believe it. The kind of hatred that would end in murder didn't seem to go with his smiling sister. She'd never hurt anyone in her life.

A shadow flitted across Amy's face, and she opened her mouth but closed it again when Leah came back into the room. The woman glanced at the baby, but Amy smiled and continued to sway. "He's fine."

"Here it is." Leah opened her fist and revealed a red flash drive.

"That's it?" Curtis reached for it. "Any idea what's on it?"

Leah nodded. "She said it was her banking information, and she wanted the backup in a safe place. I never looked at it, of course. In fact, I'd forgotten I had it until I was looking for a rubber band in the desk drawer last week."

Banking information. His fist closed around the drive. The contents might explain how she was able to afford this place. He held up his hand. "When did she give this to you?"

"Five days before she died."

He exchanged a glance with Amy, who was leaning over to brush her lips across the little guy's soft hair. "What did she say about it?"

Leah shrugged. "Just what I mentioned. That she wanted the backup in a safe place."

The baby nestled against Amy and put his thumb in his mouth. She shifted him a bit. "Did you see anything unusual going on at Gina's apartment?"

Leah tipped her head to one side. "Unusual?"

Amy nodded. "People you didn't recognize, arguments, anyone skulking around. That kind of thing. And did Gina seem upset in any way?"

Leah frowned. "She and Ben had a huge fight a few days before her death. I nearly called the sheriff."

"What happened? I'm Ben's sister, by the way."

"The midwife?" She nodded at her son. "No wonder you're good with kids. He's asleep."

Curtis looked down at the child and smiled. Amy had a special touch with children. She'd be a good mother someday. "Did Ben strike her or anything like that?"

Amy shot him an offended glare, and he looked away. Ben was no saint, no matter what she thought.

Leah shook her head. "I don't think so. There was a lot of shouting, and I heard things crashing like someone was throwing stuff. And there was some dude in a suit who came to see her the morning she died. She threw him out."

"Threw him out?" Curtis couldn't imagine his petite sister throwing anyone out.

"Well, not literally. She blocked the door and wouldn't let him in. I heard her say, 'You know better than to come here. What if someone saw you?'"

"You didn't recognize him?" Curtis asked.

"No, but his car was a big black Mercedes. You could tell he had money from that suit he wore."

Amy shifted the baby. "Any idea where he was from?"

Leah looked a little shamefaced. "I have to admit I looked at his car. I was taking the kids to the beach, and I took a peek at the license plate as I went past. It was a North Carolina plate."

That didn't tell them much. The flash drive bit into Curtis's palm. But the information on it might.

FOURTEEN

Curtis's office was through double French doors off the living room. Amy liked it from the first. Nautical books and Coast Guard manuals lined one wall. Several plaques showed off awards he'd won. She wanted to peruse them at leisure, but he gestured her to the desk where he'd booted up the flash drive on his MacBook.

"They're Quicken files. Like Leah said, it appears to be bank information." He opened the Quicken program, and numbers flashed onto the screen. He scrolled down to the bottom. "Holy cow, she had over two hundred thousand dollars in this account. It was opened with three hundred thousand."

Amy could see his shock, but surely that wasn't a lot of money to the Irelands. "You didn't know she had that kind of money?"

He leaned forward, still reading. "She never went to college and worked in a fudge shop all her adult life. Hardly the way to make that kind of money. Mom and Dad stopped giving her money years ago. She ran through it like a drunk on vodka." He whistled softly. "There's another account here too. It's got another hundred grand in it."

Amy hadn't gone through Ben's bank account, but her father had. "I'm not sure I could tell anything by looking at Ben's financials. He made good money."

"But he spent a lot too. That fancy convertible and his jewelry."

The comment felt a little accusatory to her, but she let it pass. It was Ben's money to spend. He didn't owe an explanation to anyone.

"Could you ask your father if he saw anything out of the ordinary?"

Amy could have shuddered at the request, but she nodded. "I could, but it won't be fun."

"I hardly think anything about this investigation is fun." He leaned back in the leather chair. "If you want privacy for the call, I can leave."

"Stay. I need the support." She sighed and pulled her cell phone from her purse. With each ring, the tension in her shoulders intensified. Her father would not be happy that she was poking into this.

Her father's deep voice answered with a trace of impatience. "Amy, hello. We haven't heard from you in a week. Your mom was getting worried."

Always start with the attack calculated to induce guilt. Guilt was her father's usual mode of control. And if her mother was truly worried, why hadn't she called? "Hi, Dad. I'm here in Hope Beach."

The long silence spoke of his disapproval. "I'd hoped you'd abandoned that idea."

She heard voices in the background. "Am I interrupting?"

"We're hosting a campaign party for Preston. He's facing quite a battle this election."

"Tell him I said hello. I met some ladies on his campaign out here. Listen, I have a quick question, and I'll let you go. You looked over Ben's financial statements. Did anything seem odd to you?"

"Odd in what way?" His voice grew even stiffer.

"Did he have a lot of money in different accounts?"

Her father was silent a minute. "I wouldn't call it a lot of money. A couple hundred thousand in different accounts. Why do you ask?"

She gave Curtis a thumbs-up. "Just trying to figure out who might have had something against Ben."

Her father's sigh was pronounced. "He drowned, honey. I wish you'd give up this obsession. It isn't healthy."

"I have to know for sure, Dad," she said softly. "I just have to."

"I know, I know. We worry about you, you know. Your mother and me. It's time you were settled. We'd like to see you happy with a good husband."

He used to say a baby or two, but the unspoken words hurt even more. It was a familiar lecture, one that usually produced the expected sense of failure. "I'm happy, Dad. In fact, I think I'm going to set up practice here and move to Hope Beach permanently." While her father might have been able to pull some strings and help find a supervising doctor for her, she closed her mouth. This was her problem to fix.

"That feels a little like a cop-out," her dad said. "Burying yourself on a primitive backwater island. It's a vacation spot, not a place to live full-time. They're hardly in the new century. I could help you set up in New York or somewhere that would appreciate your skills."

Her heart warmed at his concern. "Thanks, Dad, but I like it here. And I'm needed." She heard someone call his name in the background. "I'll let you go. Give Mom my love and tell her I'll call soon."

"Bye."

The phone clicked in her ear with the words *I love you* still on her lips. Closing her mouth, she put her phone way. "Ben had about the same amount of money tucked into his accounts. Dad didn't seem to find it unusual, and maybe it's not."

"But it might be. You have to admit it seems odd that the amount was the same."

"What does that tell us, though? We have no idea where the money came from. It might be that Ben had a profitable investment and decided to split it with Gina. He needed to pay support, after all."

His brows rose. "Amy, as far as I know, he never gave Gina a dime for Raine."

The condemnation in his tone stung. "I'm not sure she would have told you."

He winced, then nodded. "He never married her. That was bad enough as far as I was concerned."

"Maybe he wasn't sure Raine was his," she shot back. When she saw his stricken expression, she wanted to take back the words. "I'm sorry, Curtis."

"Apology accepted," he said in an even voice. "Gina never valued herself very highly. I never understood it. Our parents coddled her and doted on her every word. After her divorce from Travis, she changed."

"She was married?"

"It lasted all of nine months. Then she moved back here and told me she never wanted to hear Travis's name mentioned again. So I never asked what went wrong. I think she was trying to bury her pain with meaningless sex. It didn't work. Then there was a long spell where she didn't darken the door of the bar. She started helping out at the campaign headquarters when Tom was running for reelection and seemed to enjoy that and moved on to Preston's campaign."

That much made sense to Amy. "Which is where she met Ben, I bet. He was always interested in politics and liked getting involved in small-town races."

"I think you're right, now that you mention it." He rose and shut the lid of his laptop. "I'd better go relieve Ede."

His dismissive tone hurt more than it should have. She wanted to ask him about their next step, but she set her jaw and followed him from the office.

———

Curtis moved his chess piece. "Checkmate!"

"You're the man!" Josh leaned back in his chair and crossed his arms over his chest. "I thought I had you."

Curtis grinned, his gaze moving around the break room. A perfect blue sky out there today had left the shift quiet. No storms in the forecast, no distress calls.

An e-reader in her hand, Sara sat outside in a deck chair with her feet up. Alec was outside also, talking on his cell phone. Probably checking up on Libby and the baby.

Josh lifted a brow. "You look serious, buck. What's up? The pretty lady you've been hanging with?" His grin was cheeky.

"She *is* pretty," Curtis said. "But we're not really going out. She doesn't believe Ben and Gina's deaths were accidental."

Josh's grin faded. "I have to tell you, Curtis, I have always been a little suspicious of Gina's death. The fact that we could never find who did it, and we never found the boat that hit her. It has never set well with me."

"Me neither, but I tried to accept it as the accident it was called." He told Josh about the flash drive and the money. "So where did she get that kind of money when she told me Ben wasn't paying support? She sure didn't earn it making fudge."

Josh began to put the chess pieces back in the box. "Yeah, that's not likely."

His voice was carefully neutral, and Curtis gave him a quick stare. "You know something. What is it?"

Josh shrugged. "I saw her over on Ocean Street a couple of times when I was checking on a kid we fished out of the bay."

Ocean Street was a run-down area of the island, and several meth labs had been shut down there after an explosion. "You think she was involved in drugs?" Curtis shook his head. "I can't see her doing anything like that. She was crazy about Raine. I know there was a girl from church she was trying to help whose dad was arrested. Maybe Gina was trying to help her."

"Maybe. I wouldn't have said anything if you hadn't mentioned that kind of money."

"I appreciate the information, but I know my sister. She changed after Raine was born. I might have believed she'd do something like that a couple of years ago, but that old life was behind her."

"If you say so." Josh shrugged.

Curtis stared at him hard. "Is there something else you're not telling me?"

"I didn't care much for Ben. When I met him, I thought he was a great, upstanding guy. Then when I listened to him awhile, it was all about him and his plans. What if he had her doing something over there for him? He could be persuasive."

"You mean like being a courier for drugs?" Curtis thought about it a minute. Josh nodded. "That would explain why he came to the island at least once a month. But I'd like to think Gina had more sense than that."

"People in love can get sucked into things they never planned." Josh put the lid on the chess game. "Which is why I don't intend to ever let things get that far with a woman. Love 'em and leave 'em." He studied Curtis's face. "You might keep that pretty Amy at arm's length, buck. I see the danger signs all over you."

"We're just after the truth. So, seriously, you don't intend to ever get married? Why not? Raine is so much fun. You'd be missing out on a lot."

Josh turned away. "It rarely turns out great. My dad was

married five times after my mom died, each woman worse than the one before. And my mom wasn't so great either. My earliest memory is of her passed out on the bed. It's easy to be deceived by a pretty face."

It was the most Josh had ever said about his past. A lot of pain there. "Sorry, buddy. But don't shut the door to something God might have for you."

Josh put the game box back on the shelf with the others. "You're talking about Sara, aren't you? She looks a lot like my sister, did I ever tell you that? My sister has had three husbands so far, and she's only thirty-five. Her pretty face has sucked in lots of guys, but she can't stay true to any man. It's sad."

"Sara isn't your sister. You should know by working with her for three years that she's trustworthy."

Josh shrugged. "Really, buck, is anyone trustworthy?"

Curtis watched him walk out the back door and head to the hangar. Sara might as well give up. The man would never let down his defenses.

FIFTEEN

Amy stepped back and admired the soft yellow color of the walls that would be her new examining room. She'd ordered the sign for the yard first thing this morning, but only Curtis and Libby knew she'd made up her mind. Soon the entire island would know. *If* she could find a new supervising physician.

Her phone rang, and she saw it was one of the several doctors she'd called. "Dr. Hollensby, thanks for getting back to me. How's golf?" She'd always liked the middle-aged gynecologist. She'd worked for him right out of college.

His genial smile was in his voice. "Been too busy to get out so far this year, Amy, but I'm going this afternoon. What's this about you moving to some remote island in the Outer Banks?"

"It's true. And I need a supervising physician."

"You know I've never done that."

"I know. But this place needs me." She launched into a description of the island's location and the women living there. "And I'll even give you a vacation here whenever you want. I've got a great cottage on the island that's been in my family forever."

"Bribery?" His voice held laughter.

"If that's what it takes. I'm desperate, Doctor. I have to do this. I just have to." He went silent a few moments, and she held her peace, praying he'd understand.

He cleared his throat. "I'll think about it. Let me get back to you."

"Okay. I appreciate the fact you didn't say no right off. Can I send you some information about the island and the need?"

"Go ahead. I'll look at it. My next patient is here."

"When can I expect an answer?"

"Give me two days."

She sighed and put her phone away. Her head ached, and she rubbed her eyes before picking up the paintbrush again. She'd been feeling a little tired lately, but surely that meant nothing. She needed to get that blood test redone, but she'd put it off.

Her head thumped dully from the fumes so she stopped to make a kale smoothie after the last wall was done. She'd just poured her drink from the blender to her glass when the door-bell rang. Carrying her green smoothie, she hurried to the front door and saw Curtis through the glass. Ridiculous how her pulse jumped every time she saw him.

His tanned legs extended from his white shorts. He looked good in the red shirt. Too good.

His gray eyes looked her over. "You don't look so good. Are you sick?"

"I have a headache from the paint fumes."

"Take something for it."

She held up her drink. "I am. The green smoothie will help my liver detox the fumes. I don't like to take drugs. I just need fresh air."

He wrinkled his nose. "That looks nasty. Come with me and we'll blow the fumes out of your lungs." He pointed to a Dodge Viper behind him. "I thought we'd take the ferry to Kill Devil Hills. I got the summer car out of storage. It belonged to my friend Mike, and it's still a classic beauty."

The thought of getting out of the house, especially with Curtis, held appeal. "Why are we going there?"

"I want to talk to the attorney who drew up the guardianship papers."

She sipped her drink. "You didn't talk to him already?"

"I believed Gina's death was an accident, remember? There was nothing to talk about. And I don't want to just call him. It will be better face-to-face."

Her head pulsed hard, and she started to feel a little sick. "Can I ask you to do something for me?"

"Sure."

She held out her hand. "Squeeze the fleshy part between my thumb and forefinger as hard as you can. It will get rid of my headache."

"You're serious?" When she nodded, he grabbed her hand and squeezed where she indicated. "How's this work?"

"It's an acupressure point." The pain began to ebb almost instantly. It was like cold water running over the heat in her head and rinsing away the agony. She breathed deeply, in and out. "It's working. You have the touch." Not to mention the fact that his skin on hers made her stomach behave in funny ways.

The smile in his eyes changed to something else as he stood and looked down at her with their hands locked for several minutes. Almost as if he felt the same sense of connection she did.

The pain was gone, but she continued to leave her hand in his for a few more moments before she made herself smile and pull her hand away. "Thank you. It's gone."

"You're kidding."

"Nope. I told you—you have the touch. Do we have enough time for me to take a quick shower?"

"A beautiful woman is always worth waiting for."

It was more his expression than his words that brought her heart rate up. "I'll be right back."

She raced to her bedroom and tore off her shorts and paint-stained T-shirt. The warm shower washed away the last traces of the tension in her shoulders. She dried off and surveyed her closet. Shorts would work, but she'd rather feel feminine if they were going out in that car. The red sundress was festive yet casual. She yanked it over her head, then dusted a bit of powder over her face and added some blush and eye shadow.

With her wet hair twisted on top of her head, she slipped on sandals and grabbed a scarf from the drawer on her way out of the room.

Curtis wasn't in the living room when she entered. "Curtis?"

She heard a muffled shout from the backyard and rushed to the kitchen. Through the back door she saw him waving his arms and chasing the horse out of her herb garden.

Smiling, she pulled open the door. "It's a lost cause, Curtis. I'll have to fence my garden. He pretty much trampled it yesterday."

The horse snorted as if to say this was his domain and no one had better doubt it. Amy walked across the yard, and the horse approached her with his nose outstretched. She patted it. "Sorry, boy, I don't have an apple with me." The horse nudged her, then snorted and walked off toward the trees.

Curtis shook his head. "Sorry. I tried to save your herbs. The horses like them as much as you do." Then his eyes widened, and he gave a low whistle. "Glad I told you to take your time."

She couldn't look away from the admiration in his face. "You didn't. I thought I had fifteen minutes flat. Think what I could have done if you'd given me half an hour."

"I don't think my heart could stand it." His voice was almost too low for her to hear.

In fact, she thought maybe he hadn't intended for her to hear him because red crept up his neck.

She decided to spare him further embarrassment. "I'm starved. Do you mind if we stop for something at the café on our way to the ferry?"

"Fine by me. I haven't had lunch either. I'll buy."

Was this like a *date*? A silly thought because she was here to get to the bottom of her brother's death. It seemed somehow wrong to feel happy in Curtis's presence when her brother's body wasn't even resting in a grave.

———

Some residents hated the influx of tourists, but Curtis liked seeing people enjoying the sights and sounds of the Outer Banks. The traffic in Kill Devil Hills traveled bumper to bumper. New tourists had arrived over the weekend, and they were out in force driving slowly down the coast road and cruising the Croatan Highway in search of adventure. Hang gliders and people flying kites packed the dunes at Jockey's Ridge State Park. The miniature golf places were doing a brisk business.

Amy craned her neck out the open window to take in the activity. She looked stunning in that red dress, and it had pleased him more than he liked to admit that she dressed up for him.

He pulled into the Island Bookstore parking lot at the MP5 mile marker. His attorney was in the strip down toward the end. "This is it." The sign read Eric Bristow, Attorney-at-Law.

She was out of the car before he could go around to open her door. The wind blew her hair around her face. Wisps of dark curls had escaped the updo, but it was a charming look on her.

She fell into step beside him. "You think we can get in to see him without an appointment?"

He took her arm. "I hope so. If not, maybe the receptionist can provide some information."

The waiting area was empty when they entered. The receptionist, an attractive blonde in her thirties, looked up with a smile. "Mr. Ireland, good to see you again. I don't have you on the appointment calendar. Was Mr. Bristow expecting you?"

He shook his head and wished he could remember her name. "I just took a chance and stopped by to see if he had a minute."

The worry left her eyes. "I was afraid I'd messed up and didn't have you on the calendar. He left to go out of town a few minutes ago."

Curtis shook his head. "I should have called first. Maybe you could answer a quick question for me about the papers my sister signed. You probably drew them up, correct?"

"Yes, I did." Her expression was still open and helpful. "Is there a problem with them?"

"Not at all. I just wondered if you noticed anything unusual when she came in to explain what she wanted. When did she make the appointment, and did she say why she was doing it?"

The receptionist jiggled her mouse and squinted at her computer. "She called on October twelfth, and I had an opening the next day."

"Two weeks or so before her death."

She nodded. "As far as noticing anything, she seemed calm when she came in. The child's father was with her."

It struck him then—why it had seemed so odd. "There was no mention of Ben's rights at all?"

The receptionist raised a brow. "Every client is different, but I must admit it was a bit peculiar."

"Maybe Ben had existing rights to her as the father without it being spelled out in a will," Amy put in, her tone defensive.

The other woman nodded. "The baby has his name, so upon her death, he would naturally be allowed to assume custody."

But he didn't. The unspoken words hovered in the air between Amy and him. She had to be thinking the same thing. "So this arrangement was in the event of both their deaths. But why wouldn't she spell it out clearly in her will? Less hassle for Ben."

The receptionist nodded. "That's true. I don't know why they chose to do it this way. I'm sure they had no idea they would both die within a couple of weeks of each other."

"And Ben didn't make up a will detailing what would happen if he died after Gina."

Amy frowned. "When will Mr. Bristow be back? Maybe he will know why that wasn't done."

The receptionist shook her head and looked apologetic. "Not for two weeks, I'm afraid. He took his wife to Jamaica for their thirtieth wedding anniversary."

He hoped to have this figured out by then. "Thanks for your help. I appreciate it."

"Anytime. Sorry I didn't have more information for you." The receptionist reached for the phone when it rang.

Neither of them said anything until they stopped by the car. She had to be wondering about it as much as he was. He got her seated in the car, then went around to his side.

"It's very peculiar," Amy said when he slid under the wheel. "I mean, it wasn't a joint will, right?"

"No, it was only Gina's. She listed me as guardian, and the will stated all her possessions went to Raine. She appointed Edith executor, who would determine how much of the estate would go for Raine's maintenance." When she shot him a sharp glance, he added, "But I haven't taken any money out of the estate. I want to support Raine by myself, and I want her trust money kept intact."

"It's almost like they knew they both might die." Amy frowned. "Don't you think it feels that way? I mean, otherwise why wouldn't she have listed Ben as the executor or Raine's guardian or something? It's very strange."

"It doesn't feel that way to me. If they were afraid they both might die, why wouldn't he make a will too? Unless they both knew Ben wouldn't be in the picture any longer. There was that big fight her neighbor told us about."

She tied her scarf under her chin. "Ben wouldn't run out on his responsibilities. I just don't believe it."

Her brother was still on a pedestal in her eyes, and Curtis wasn't about to try to knock him off. He started the car. "How about some ice cream?"

Her smile extended to her eyes. "I never say no to ice cream."

"And here I thought you were a health nut."

Her eyes sparkled. "Ice cream has a special dispensation."

"How Sweet It Is is just down the road, and it's homemade so it's a little healthier." He pulled out onto the highway.

"As long as they have chocolate, we're good."

The rest of the day stretched out in front of them, and he had every intention of taking her to a nice restaurant for dinner. There was no need to hurry back to Hope Beach. He meant to enjoy his day off to the fullest.

His phone played "Gonna Fly Now," the theme from *Rocky*. Great. He pulled to the side of the road and looked at his phone. "It's Josh." He answered the call. "What's up?"

"We need you, buck. A fishing boat struck a rock and is going down. Stat."

Josh wouldn't ask if there was any other person to take his place. Curtis glanced at the clock on the dash. "I'm not on the island. It's going to take me several hours to get there."

There was a long pause. "We can come get you. That will be faster than waiting for the ferry. You can park your car at the airport."

"Amy can drive it home. I'll be ready." He ended the call. "Sorry, Amy, I have to go."

"An accident?"

He nodded. "Can you get my car home?"

"Of course. I'll be praying for you and the victims."

Her promise warmed his heart.

SIXTEEN

The helicopter rose into the air, carrying Curtis with it. Amy tried to tell herself she wasn't disappointed, but she recognized the lie. She hugged herself as the wind from the rotors hit, then walked slowly back to the convertible. It wouldn't be much fun tooling around in it without him. She could console herself with fudge, or she could simply head back to the ferry. Neither option held much appeal.

"Amy?"

She turned at the female voice and saw Dara leaning out of a sporty red Mercedes. The other woman's red top had sequins on it that glittered in the sunlight, and her hair looked freshly styled. The red in the car and in the blouse matched as if she'd planned it that way.

Her heart sinking, Amy smiled. "Hi. Are you taking in the sights?" It was clear the beautiful brunette was on a mission.

Dara shook her head. "I'm picking up Preston Kendrick. He's flying in on his private plane." Her voice was full of self-importance.

Amy approached the car and glanced at the passenger seat. Dara's aunt wasn't with her. "I thought the rally wasn't for another couple of weeks or so."

"Yes." Dara's voice was guarded, and she pressed her lips

together. "He and Zoe needed a little R & R." She studied Amy's face. "Your father wouldn't be *the* Oliver Lang, would he?"

Amy smiled. "Well, I'd hardly put it that way, but yes."

She was used to the awe and respect from people when they discovered who her father was. It wasn't his wealth that impressed people as much as the power he wielded with such care for others. While she would have preferred he was home more often when she was growing up, he had helped a lot of people over the years. And he'd put many politicians in office, including Preston.

"I'd never have put the last name together, especially with you out on Hope Island." Dara got out of the car. "There's Preston." She waved at the tall blond man striding their way.

Preston was a handsome man in his forties. He wore jeans and a light blue polo shirt today as if he didn't have to face voters. But then he had never been a man to put on airs, which was why Amy liked him so much. He never pulled any punches with what he believed about how to fix the problems facing the country either. Amy was as eager as her dad to see him reelected.

His smile widened when he drew near them. "Amy, I didn't expect to see you!" He nodded at Dara, then stepped past her with his arms outstretched.

Amy accepted his hug and brushed her lips across his smooth chin. "Dad should have let me know you were coming. Where are you staying?" She tried to ignore Dara's glower that Preston had greeted her first.

He released her. "At the Tidewater Inn. I'm just here for two days. Wish it could be longer."

"I arranged it," Dara put in.

What was with the woman and her jealousy? She seemed to think she deserved the attention of every man she was around. Amy wasn't interested in competing. Well, unless Dara started chasing Curtis.

Amy smiled and nodded as if it was fine with her. Which of course it was. "You'll like it. Some friends of mine own it, and they'll take very good care of you. Where's your entourage? And I thought Zoe was coming with you."

"My staff is coming. I like to get away sometimes without them, but you know how it is. And Zoe should be along momentarily. She stopped off at the restroom."

"You're here to relax?"

He nodded. "I'm going to try to get some surfing in. You game to go with me and show me the best spots?"

"The surfing is great right now. I have an extra board if you didn't bring yours. It was Ben's." Her brother's name hovered in the air between them, and Preston's smile faded.

"I'd be honored to use it."

She eyed him. "I want to open a midwife practice here, Preston, but I lost my supervising physician. You're friends with Dr. Hollensby. Any chance you could put in a good word for me with him? He's thinking about helping me."

Preston smiled. "He mentioned it to me on the phone when I bowed out of golf and told him I was coming here. I think he's going to do it. I told him you were the best out there."

"Preston!" She leaped to hug him. "Thank you, thank you!"

"My pleasure." He grinned.

Amy released him. "Well, I'll let you get to Hope Island. When would you like to go surfing?"

"Tomorrow morning?"

Dara guided him toward the car. "You're taking Zoe out on a yacht for the day. You won't be done until seven."

"How about dinner?" he called to Amy. "And I'll get up at dawn if you want to surf."

"You're on," she called back. She saw a familiar figure hurrying her way. Waving, she went to meet Preston's wife, Zoe.

Zoe's short brown hair was styled in a pert cut that suited her tiny face. Her face lit when she rushed to hug Amy. "I wasn't expecting to see you! What are you doing here?"

Amy had always felt a connection with Zoe. They were close to the same age and both loved children. "I'm living on Hope Island now." She brought Zoe up to speed.

Zoe's brown eyes were shadowed. "Oh, honey, I think you should let this stuff go. What good will it do to be obsessed like this? It won't bring Ben back."

Amy stepped back. "I owe it to Ben to get to the truth."

Zoe sighed. "You've always been a crusader." When Dara called to her from the car, she squeezed Amy's arm, then turned. "We'll talk later. Let me know if there's anything I can do. I'd like you to be at peace with this."

Preston and Zoe waved at her as they drove off, but Dara looked the other way. Amy figured it would be a miracle if the woman let Preston go surfing in the morning.

She started back toward the car and heard the *whup-whup* of a helicopter growing louder. She shaded her eyes and stared into the sky. A Coast Guard chopper was approaching. Was Curtis coming back? When the craft landed, she saw it was the same one.

Curtis motioned from the open door. "We need you! A woman is in labor on the boat, and we can't find Sara."

Amy gasped and ran for the helicopter.

———

The fishing boat pitched to one side, and the bow rode lower in the water than the stern. It was quickly taking on water. Curtis glanced at Amy, then focused on the task at hand. Two people were waving frantically from the rail. The woman was curled up on the deck, clutching her swollen belly.

Josh's voice spoke in Curtis's headset. "At the last radio contact, the husband said she was trying not to push."

They all had to speak by microphone to hear above the roar of the chopper's blades and engine.

Amy gestured. "I need to get down there!"

Curtis shook his head. "That boat is going down."

Amy leaned out the open window, and the wind made her hair fly around her head. "I don't think we can get her up here in the shape she's in."

Curtis took her arm and pulled her back inside. "You can't lean out, Amy, not without wearing a gunner's belt." Even he wouldn't lean out of the open door without a gunner's belt to keep him from falling.

Josh took his arm. "I think she's right, buck. We could lose the baby if it comes while she's in the water. We just have a few minutes. We can deploy the rubber raft and transfer her to it if necessary."

Curtis didn't want to run the risk of losing Amy, but he finally nodded. "You're a strong swimmer, I know. You're going to have to drop into the water and swim to the boat. Think you can do that?"

Her face was pale and set. "Of course. I'll need my instruments."

"We can put them in a dry pack and tie them to your waist." Josh pointed at the red jumpsuits. "You need a jelly fish too."

Curtis grabbed the jumpsuit and handed it to Amy. He held up a blanket and averted his gaze while she changed into it.

"I'm ready," Amy said from behind the blanket.

He turned and saw her zipped into the wetsuit. A hoodie covered her hair.

Amy grabbed her bag and handed it to him. "Let's get down there."

He prepared her bag for submersion in the sea. Attached to the gunner's belt, Alec sat on the edge of the doorway with his feet dangling over the edge. He adjusted his mask and pulled on his fins, then waited for the signal.

Curtis tapped him on the chest. Alec disengaged the gunner's belt and waited again. Curtis tapped him three times on the shoulder and Alec studied the water below, then dropped like a gull toward the waves.

When Alec's head popped up, Curtis sent the raft down to him too. As soon as the raft hit the water, Alec tugged the line on the bundle, and the raft inflated. Holding on to the raft's line, he swam to the boat, attached the line to the ladder, then clambered aboard.

Curtis took Amy by the arm. "We'll drop you as close to the boat as we safely can. When you know you're all right, raise your hand in the air to signal that you're all right before you start swimming for the boat. Got it?"

"Got it." She sounded a little breathless.

If he had any other options, he wouldn't send her down there. But the woman and her baby could die if they didn't get help. He attached the gunner's belt to her chest, then guided her into position. "Josh, get us down a little if you can."

Josh nodded and maneuvered the helicopter a little closer to the swamped boat. Curtis knelt beside Amy. "Keep one hand on your mask and the other across your chest so you don't hit it hard with the water. Stay in a slightly seated position with your fins pointing up. Give me a thumbs-up when you're ready. I'll tap you three times on the shoulder. That will be your signal to look for debris and, if it's all clear, to jump. Got it?"

"Got it." She swallowed, then adjusted her mask. Her eyes were wide behind the plastic. Her face was pale and set, but she jabbed her thumb up. "Ready."

He triple-tapped her shoulder, then disengaged the gunner's belt. "Look around below you. If it's all good, jump."

His throat tightened as she looked at the waves, then shoved herself off the floor of the helicopter and plummeted toward the water. Leaning out, he watched her hit the waves. He held his breath waiting until he could see her again. Where was she? It was dangerous for an untrained person to jump from this height, and he fully expected to get into trouble with his superiors for allowing her to do it. Her form had looked good as she'd gone into the water, but the force of hitting the waves had been known to knock someone out.

"I'm going down!" He sat in the doorway and inhaled. Then he saw her head pop up. "Wait, there she is."

She jabbed her thumb in the air, then began to swim toward the boat. Alec was leaning over the woman, but he turned to watch Amy's progress as well. He motioned with his arm as if she should hurry. Her strokes were long and sure, and she steadily neared the boat. Alec reached over the side and grabbed her arm as she started up the ladder. He hoisted her the rest of the way.

She knelt by the woman, then leaned around and grabbed her bag. Curtis couldn't see well with her and Alec blocking his view. He anxiously watched the boat pitch and yaw. The thing could take a nosedive and sink at any time. He began to pray and saw Josh's lips moving too. This was going to be close.

The boat wallowed low in the water. "That thing's going under any minute!" He attached the gunner's belt and sat in the doorway waving his arms at his friend. He gestured to the boat. "Get them off there!"

Alec looked back at the raft and made the gesture to back off. "He's not ready yet."

Come on, come on. There seemed to be a sudden flurry of movement, then Curtis caught a glimpse of something in Amy's arms. "She's delivered the baby!"

Time seemed to drag as Amy continued to kneel by the woman. She would need to clamp off the umbilical cord and deliver the placenta before they could get off. Praying, he waited.

Finally, Alec rushed to the ladder. He climbed down and seized the raft's line, then dragged the raft closer to the boat. Amy disappeared belowdecks. What was she doing? She needed to get out of there. Curtis could barely keep from going down himself. When she finally emerged, she had a bag in her hand. She pulled out a blanket and wrapped the baby in it. The husband helped his wife to her feet and half carried her to the ladder.

Alec climbed to the top of the ladder to assist while the husband helped the woman put one foot down onto the first rung. The woman swayed on the ladder, and Curtis held his breath, sure she was going to fall. She clung there for a long minute, then made it down another two rungs before she swayed again.

She lost her grip on the ladder. Amy made a grab for her but missed. The woman hurtled down, and the force of her fall knocked Alec from the ladder as well. They both plummeted into the water.

The husband shouted and leaped overboard after his wife. With the baby in one arm, Amy clambered down the ladder. She rushed to the side of the raft.

Alec's head popped up, and he had hold of the woman. The husband reached them as well and helped tow her to the raft. From here, it looked like her eyes were closed.

Moments later they were all in the raft, but the boat began to sink. If they didn't get away in time, it would drag the raft down with it. Curtis blew his whistle to attract Alec's attention, then waved his arms again, giving the sign to back away. Alec turned and grabbed the paddle. He paddled frantically away from the sinking boat.

The boat shuddered, then went under. The eddies caught the raft, and it began to rotate back toward the whirlpool, taking the craft to its grave.

"Please, God," Curtis whispered, clenching his fists. Alec paddled harder, and the eddy released the raft.

"They're free of it!" Josh yelled. "Deploy the rescue basket."

SEVENTEEN

Amy clutched the warming blanket around her. She couldn't stop shivering as she waited to disembark from the helicopter at the airport in Kitty Hawk. Evening shrouded the helicopter, and the interior lights lit it only with a dim glow. Her shudders were more a reaction to the stress than to the cold water, and her ears vibrated from the roar of the rotors. The woman and baby had been unloaded first and rushed to the hospital.

They were the last ones in the helicopter, and sitting in the tight space where she could hear Curtis's breathing and smell his cologne was such an intimate experience, one that made her wonder exactly what this emotion in her chest was. If she leaned over a bit, she would be able to touch him.

His face radiated approval. "You did great. Need another blanket?"

Her teeth were chattering, and she was cold clear to the bone. "I'm frozen. Glad they're okay."

He tucked another blanket around her, then wrapped his arm around her. "I hope you don't mind, but we have to get you warm."

"I don't mind." She relaxed against his warmth.

"If you were scared, you didn't show it."

"I was terrified. When she fell overboard, I couldn't believe it. I was sure she'd drown."

"The baby was early?"

Amy nodded. "About three weeks. She looked to be about six pounds though, so I think she'll be okay. This is one birth that her family will retell for years."

"I bet they name her after you."

Amy gave a weak chuckle. "So they said." The memory of holding that brand-new infant, literally snatched from the jaws of death, warmed her.

She clenched her hands in her lap. "I suppose we should get out ourselves."

"Yeah." But he made no move to release her and move toward the door. "Listen, Amy, I have to tell you that I don't know another person, male or female, who would have done what you did today. You're an amazing woman."

Heat scorched her cheeks, and she wanted to look away from the intensity in his eyes, but she didn't. "I'm glad I could help."

He covered her hands with his. "I think I owe you a special dinner as thanks."

"You don't have to."

"I want to. I think lobster is in order."

The heat of his hands warmed her better than the blanket. When he pulled his hands back, the coldness flooded back. "I'm famished, now that you mention it."

"No wonder. You've been in the frigid water, and it's getting late. We still need to get my car back too. You want to eat here in Kitty Hawk or somewhere else?"

"Let's eat here. I have a yen for the Black Pelican."

He rose and moved toward the door. "I think I have a banana in my jacket to hold you over."

She grabbed her discarded clothing and accepted the hand he

offered her. "I'll take it." He helped her down onto the pavement. The runway had emptied out as they walked toward the building. "Good thing my car is still here."

She glanced at her watch. It was after seven. They'd be lucky to eat by eight. "I'll take that banana now." He grinned and dug it out of his pocket. She peeled it and offered him half. "Can't have you keeling over on me. I'd never catch you."

He didn't turn it down, and they ate their snack in companionable silence. When they reached the building, the outside lights brightened the gloom. He grinned and reached toward her. His hand cupped her face, and he flicked his thumb over the corner of her mouth. "A fleck of banana."

"I was saving that for a snack." She pulled the hoodie from her head and shook out her wet hair. "I hope they seat us. I'm hardly dressed for a nice dinner out."

"You look beautiful."

The soft words turned her insides to mush. Where was this relationship going?

⁓

Curtis had parked the car under a light pole, and the bright light showed the Viper where he'd left it. The top was up.

Curtis frowned as he walked toward the vehicle. "I thought we left the top down." Amy and Josh followed him.

Amy stepped to his side as they approached his car. "We did."

From here, the car didn't appear to have been damaged, but no one could have put the hood up without a key. Curtis punched the key fob and heard the doors unlock. He yanked open the door and glanced inside. His jacket still draped the console. After rooting through the console, he saw nothing missing.

He exited the car and stared at Amy and Josh. "How did the top get up? I don't get it."

Josh reached past him and touched the button that operated the power top. It whirred and began to go down. "There's a key in the ignition."

Curtis leaned past Josh and looked at the steering column. "That's my extra set." He pulled the key free from the slot and stared at it.

"Where did you leave it?" Amy asked.

"It hangs on a ring by the back door at my house."

Amy pulled out her phone. "We need to make sure Edith and Raine are all right."

She placed the call, and he tensed until he heard her speak to Edith. When it was clear from Amy's end of the conversation that everything was all right, he stared at Josh. "What if someone has tampered with the car in other ways? It might not be safe to drive."

Josh looked uneasy too, and he nodded. "You might be right. You should probably have a mechanic go over it and make sure the brakes are okay."

Curtis stared at the car. "I don't like this. Someone was in my house." He pushed the button to pop his trunk. "I want to take a look around with my flashlight." He pulled it out but didn't slam the lid.

Amy ended the call. "Edith took Raine to the beach today. She was gone most of the day. The house wasn't locked."

"Most of us don't lock anything," Curtis said. "But someone had to know they were gone. And that I was on a mission and wasn't likely to walk in on them. What was the point?"

None of them had the answer to that. Curtis stared at his car again. "It's not like a good Samaritan decided to put the top up. It's just plain weird."

"You can have it towed to a mechanic," Josh said.

"Let me just have a look." Curtis dropped to the pavement and scooted under the car, then shone the flashlight around the undercarriage. "Brake lines are okay. Nothing unusual under here." Then the light landed on a small box. "Wait a minute." He moved closer and studied the box. It shouldn't be there. Wire ties strapped it to the exhaust pipe.

He shoved himself out from under the car, then jumped to his feet. "Run!" He grabbed Amy's arm and propelled her away from the vehicle. "I think there's a bomb under there!"

Josh leaped away from the car. Amy and Curtis raced after him. A *whump* sounded from the car, and a hot rush of air pushed him. Amy stumbled, and he seized her waist and half carried her away from the heat baking the pavement behind them. When he finally turned to look, he saw his car engulfed in flames.

"Holy moly," Josh said softly.

Curtis couldn't quite believe it. He stared at the flames. "Someone tried to kill me."

Josh glanced at Amy. "Or both of you. Whoever did this had to know the two of you were together, so it's hard to know who was the target."

Several men ran from the metal hangar with fire extinguishers in their hands. Curtis pulled out his phone and placed a call to the authorities. The dispatcher promised to send some officers and the bomb squad. The hot fire began to bubble the blacktop. If they'd been in that car, they would both be dead now.

Her face pale, Amy hugged herself. "Thank the good Lord that you decided to look under the car, Curtis. You saved our lives."

He didn't like to think about what might have happened to her. "You okay?"

She nodded. "Just shaken. Do you believe me now? That someone killed Gina and Ben?"

"You think this is related?"

"Don't you? It's the only explanation. Someone knows we're poking into their deaths, and whoever it is wants to stop us from getting to the bottom of it. But it makes me even more determined."

He absorbed her words and glanced back at the burning car. The fire extinguishers weren't making a dent in the ferocity of the flames. Whoever planted that bomb hadn't been messing around.

Curtis was ready to do just about anything to prevent another attack on Amy.

EIGHTEEN

Amy felt almost sick from hunger and fatigue by the time they settled at a table in Kitty Hawk. Their table at the Black Pelican faced the Atlantic, and watching the moonlight glimmer on the water eased the tension from her shoulders. It was almost nine, and the restaurant held only a few people.

Curtis glanced up over the top of the menu. "I promised you lobster, but I don't see it on the menu. Anything look good? And are you sure you're up to this? We could grab fast food and head for home."

"I wouldn't be able to sleep yet. I'm too keyed up. And hungry." She studied the selection. "Ooh, look at the Wanchese Fisherman's Risotto. 'Scallops, shrimp, jumbo lump crabmeat, and bacon sautéed with sweet corn, tomatoes, and baby spinach folded into creamy roasted garlic risotto topped with a crispy sweet potato nest.' I'll take it." She closed her menu and laid it aside.

The server placed a basket of hearth-baked pita bread and butter on the table. Curtis ordered for both of them and asked the server to bring an appetizer of seared ahi tuna.

She wrinkled her nose. "I still smell of smoke."

"We're lucky that's all we endured. I thought Edith was going to have a heart attack when I called her."

She squeezed lemon into her ice water. "We have to figure out what to do next."

"I know. I don't want anything to happen to you."

The intensity of his tone made her look up. He was staring at her with an expression that made her gulp. She was so unused to the dating scene. When should she tell him about her past? Now might be too soon. He could assume she thought there was more between them than he felt. It could scare him off.

She sipped her water. "About the investigation. Any ideas where to look next?"

"You said Tom mentioned he didn't find Ben's driver's license. Did you ever look for it?"

She choked on her water. "I completely forgot about that! What on earth is wrong with me? I intended to search for it yesterday after church."

"You went with me to talk to Gina's neighbors," he reminded her. "And we found that flash drive with all the money. So we had other leads to follow."

She nodded. "If I can find his log-in information for that bank account, I could track where the money came from."

"Would your father know?"

She shook her head. "Even if he knew, I don't think he'd tell me. He wants me to forget all about this."

"But someone tried to blow us up. He'd believe you now, wouldn't he? And wouldn't he want to know what really happened to his son?"

"I can tell him about it and see what he says." She studied Curtis's troubled face. "You know it wasn't an accident now, don't you?"

His jaw flexed. "I know someone tried to kill either you or me or both of us. I suspect it was both of us because we're in this together. What would he have to gain with us dead?"

"Whatever was covered up remains that way if we're dead."

The server brought their ahi tuna, and Curtis speared a piece of the rare tuna steak, then took a dab of wasabi and transferred them to his plate. "I'm going to go through Gina's things and see if I can find her log-in and password for her account too. I still have her laptop. It's stuck in my closet. The log-in and password might be on there."

At least he had a little more power than she did. "Edith is the administrator of her estate, right?"

He nodded. "I see where you're going. If we can't find a way to get to it online, I can get Edith to see if she can get the account number identified so we know what bank it's at. Then I can get access."

"Right. Unfortunately, I don't have that luxury. There's no way my father will help me get into Ben's. If I can't find his information, I'm sunk." She was *not* looking forward to another conversation with her father about this.

"Maybe it's in his wallet, if you can find it. I'll help you look if you'd like."

"That would be great. I hate prying through his things." She took a sip of water and tried not to notice the intent expression on his face. What was he thinking? She suspected it had nothing to do with bank accounts.

Curtis leaned forward, his gaze never leaving her face. "I want to get to know the real Amy behind that beautiful face. The one who cares for other people. The woman who risks her life for a stranger."

She took another sip of water to cool the heat in her head. "I'm like most women, Curtis. There's nothing special about me."

He gave an emphatic shake of his head. "Oh, but there is. You jumped out of a helicopter into the ocean. Without training. Who else has done that? You kept your cool when my car exploded right in front of you. And what other sister would drop everything and try to track down what really happened to her brother? You left a thriving practice to come here, didn't you?"

She looked down at her hands. "Yes." Such praise was foreign to her. Her parents expected great things from their children. The only choice she'd had was to strive to make something worthwhile of her life, even if it was in a direction they disliked.

"So tell me how you got started with your career," he said.

She took a helping of ahi tuna and wasabi. It might be the opportunity to tell him the truth, if she could get the courage. "It's a boring story."

He grinned. "I doubt that."

"My parents wanted me to be a doctor. I went to Harvard, but while I was there, I met a nurse midwife and went on a delivery with her. When I held that new life, something shifted inside of me. I knew I wanted to do more than sit across a room and listen to patients list their symptoms. I wanted to be involved in turning life back into the miracle it truly is. I wanted to see women give birth in their homes instead of an antiseptic hospital. I wanted to have the entire family involved in greeting the new life."

"You're passionate about it."

"I guess I am. Sorry if I sound like a zealot. I get a little carried away when I talk about it."

"I like your commitment. It's the same way I feel about my work. I could go to work in an office, but I wouldn't be doing anything worthwhile with my life. What I do *matters* out there."

She nodded. "People would die without you. Even today."

"I think we're two of a kind, Amy."

He stretched his hand across the table, and she took it. When she'd decided to come here, she had no idea God might have some kind of turn in the road for her. She pulled her hand away and excused herself to go to the ladies' room. She'd told Curtis the truth, but not all of it. Was she even ready for a relationship?

⌣

The night air was moist and fragrant with spring flowers as Curtis parked the rental car in her driveway and they got out. He couldn't remember the last time he'd enjoyed someone's company so much. Amy had a quiet strength about her that drew him.

"Want to sit in the swing a few minutes?" she asked. "Or do you need to leave?"

He took her hand and walked to the swing with her. "I have no idea what time it is, but I'm not tired. I suppose we both should be exhausted with the day we've had."

The seat was comfortable for two, and it swung gently when they settled into it. The scent of the sea mingled with the roses rambling up the railing behind them.

She leaned her head back. "I love this place. The smells, the vegetation, the colors of the sky and sea. I'm glad I decided to move here."

"When does the rest of your stuff arrive?"

"It should be here tomorrow. I think around three."

"You need help unloading?"

Her hair grazed his arm as she leaned back in the swing. "I could use the help. I've got some heavy stuff. My desk, my dining room table. And the bed of course."

"I could get the Coasties to come help."

"That'd be great! I love being around them. How did you decide to get into the Coast Guard?"

Her eyes glimmered in the porch light, and he knew she was truly interested. Such rapt attention made him look down at his hands in his lap. "I'm no hero. I like being outside testing my mettle against the elements." He shrugged. "Sounds dumb when I put it like that, but I feel like I'm using all the talents God has given me when I'm using every bit of my strength against the fury of the sea. We are out there racing against time, and we are all that stands between life and death."

"Sounds like a hero to me." Her voice was soft.

"Or stupid." He grinned. "And when it's all over, I sometimes want to shake the boat captain who ignored a hurricane warning or who didn't check his boat before he went out." His smile faded. "And when we lose one of our own, we're all really mad at the idiots."

"I can imagine."

He shifted a little closer. "I guess I have to admit the basic reason I joined. Mike, one of my best friends from high school, dared me to do it. He said I didn't have the guts to go up against drug runners or go out in a hurricane."

She lifted a teasing grin toward him. "Ah, the truth comes out. A dare. Somehow I didn't take you for the kind to listen to taunts."

"I'm not anymore." He went quiet as he remembered. "Mike died in Katrina. I was there and couldn't do a thing when his chopper went down. No one survived the crash."

She gripped his hand. "Oh, Curtis, I'm so sorry." Scooting closer, she hugged him.

He let his arm drift down around her shoulders and pulled her tight against him. Tight enough he could rest his chin on the top of her head. Close enough that he could drink in the scent of her, the press of her against his side. It was almost enough to make him forget the night Mike died. Almost.

"I was ready to get out after that. Mike was like my brother. Hearing the whine of the helicopter going down over the howl of the wind was something I've worked hard to forget. Every time I pull someone from the ocean still alive, I chalk one up for the home team. But no matter how many home runs I get, none of them will bring back Mike." He tugged on the edge of his Harley do-rag. "The hat was his."

Her eyes grew wide at his admission. "Thanks for telling me."

"I should put it up on a shelf with his picture, but as long as I'm wearing it, it's like Mike is helping me. Like he's still rescuing people too." He shrugged. "I'm getting downright maudlin tonight. We need to lighten things up. So tell me, what was your funniest delivery?"

She rested her head on his shoulder in companionable silence a moment. "Childbirth is so special, so fun. My first home birth was hilarious because my supervising physician was called away on an emergency C-section, and the mother, who had already delivered four babies, had to tell me what to do. I'd been fully trained, of course, but I just froze. The head crowned, and I stood there gaping like some kind of idiot. The mom yelled, 'Hold out your hands, it's coming!'" Amy giggled. "So I did what she told me, and that baby just plopped right into my hands."

He liked watching the light in her eyes. "Boy or girl?"

"Baby girl. They named her after me. I hardly earned it." She laughed again.

"You love children. So do I. I want a houseful someday."

The light in her eyes faded as she nodded. "I started babysitting when I was eleven. I told my mom I was going to have ten kids when I grew up." Her lips flattened and she looked down.

"What's wrong?"

She sat up and pulled away a bit. "Nothing. Tired, I guess."

"I should say good night, then." He knew he should release her, but his fingers tightened around her shoulders, and he pulled her close again. His lips brushed hers gently, and he inhaled the sweet scent of her breath before deepening the kiss.

She didn't pull away, but her response was less than he'd hoped so he let her go. "What an amazing rescue delivery. I'll never forget it, Amy. We had a fun, though eventful, day. Let's do it again soon. Only this time without the car blowing up."

She nodded and rose. "Good night, Curtis." In a flash she was across the porch and inside the house.

He smacked his forehead and stood. They'd been having such a great time, and he'd moved too fast. What had he said wrong?

NINETEEN

Amy took her boards and exited Rosemary Cottage in the dim glow of the rising sun. Yesterday's events had left her muscles aching. If she hadn't promised Preston she would meet him for surfing, she would have slept in instead.

The air held a hint of early morning moisture as she walked the mulched path to the beach. The shredded bark crunched under her reef shoes, and birds sang from the fragrant bushes crowding the path. When she stepped out of the maritime forest, she saw a sleek Mercedes parked along the side of the road, and her heart sank. It was Dara's car, so she must have come with Preston. Sure enough, two figures were standing on the sand dunes.

Preston wore a black wetsuit that showed off his muscular physique. Dara was in slacks and a blazer.

Her gaze flicked over Amy, and her smile was tight. "There you are. I thought maybe you stood us up."

Amy refrained from mentioning that there had been no *us* in the invitation. "I wouldn't dream of it." She pointed at the pinkening sky. "It's not quite dawn, so I'm actually a little early. No Zoe this morning?"

Preston shook his head. "She's still curled up in bed. Surfing's

139

not her thing." He took the board she'd brought. "I'm ready though. I rented a heavy wetsuit. That water is cold."

"Refreshing," she corrected with a smile. "The waves are cooking out there this morning too. Beat you in!" Sand kicked from under her feet as she raced toward the foaming waves. The strong scent of the sea enveloped her. She gasped when the cold water soaked her thighs, then dove into the waves and came up sputtering and licking the salt from her lips.

Preston was right behind her, and she laughed when he shouted at the water's temperature. "Weakling!" She splashed him, then leaped onto her board and paddled out to the break. She duck dove to reach the lineup, then paddled faster as the wave started to lift her.

In moments she was riding the pocket. Preston yelled behind her, and she knew he'd caught his own wave. The foam deposited her in flatter water, and sitting astride her board, she turned to watch him finish his ride.

He was grinning when he paddled over to join her. "Awesome! That was worth getting up for." His smile faded. "Who's that?"

She squinted toward the shore. "Edith Lowman. She's an avid surfer and comes out here year-round."

"She looks familiar."

"She is Curtis's aunt and is helping him take care of his niece. She's a really great person. She talked me into surfing in the cold water."

"Curtis? The Coast Guard guy you had dinner with?"

"How'd you know we had dinner?"

His eyes were smiling. "Your dad wanted me to keep an eye on you. One of my staff members mentioned they saw you at the Black Pelican last night. He's raising a niece?"

She nodded, suddenly self-conscious and protective of Raine. "His sister, Gina, died a few months ago."

"That's too bad."

She veered back to the subject that had tightened her stomach. "My father asked you to keep an eye on me?"

Preston shrugged. "You know your dad. You'll always be a kid to him."

She studied Preston's face. Maybe he could help her. "You knew Ben well. Did you ever know him to use a code?"

Preston laughed. "You mean like a spy sort of thing? Ben was hardly a cloak-and-dagger sort of guy. Why would you ask that?"

"I found a book in his handwriting. It was all in some kind of code."

"Sleuthing, are you? Your dad says you think Ben was murdered. If someone hurt Ben, I intend to make sure he's very sorry." His lips tightened.

Her feet were getting cold in the water, and she flexed them. "I'd thought about calling you from the first, but I didn't want to cause any division between you and Dad."

His eyes softened. "You let me worry about your father. I want to help if I can."

Her burden lifted with the realization that she had an ally, someone who knew and loved Ben. She told him about the e-mail she'd gotten and about Gina's death. "Ben is Raine's father."

His eyes widened, and he said nothing for several long moments. "Your parents need to know about the little girl. You haven't told them?"

She shook her head. "They're coming for the weekend, and I thought it best to tell them in person. I want to protect Raine if I can. I love them, but you know how my parents are. They'll want custody, Preston, you know they will. And she doesn't know them. She loves Curtis and Edith. It would be cruel to yank her away from everything she's known. She's already lost her parents."

He winced. "It's a hard situation, but we're talking about their grandchild. They'll want to be involved in her life."

"I want that too. But my parents can swoop in and not even see the damage they're causing. I don't know how to tell them to back off and be gentle."

"Maybe by telling them just that. Be blunt. Sometimes that's the only way people will hear the truth."

"It's not going to be easy. Want to do it for me?" She grinned when he shuddered. "Kidding, I'm kidding. I wouldn't throw you to the wolves that way."

"It's a good thing because our friendship might be over."

Amy glanced toward the shore where the other woman paced as she watched them. "Speaking of friendship, what about Dara? She seems a little possessive. I'm not sure Zoe would appreciate it."

He winked. "She's determined that I'm going to win. I think she wants a high-level appointment. And my wife actually hired her. They're friends."

"That's a relief." She looked back toward the waves. "We're missing the best ones. Race you!"

The beachgoers weren't out yet when Heather rode the bike to the pier. She'd gotten so used to getting up early for work that her eyes had popped open at five, and she'd decided to see if she could catch Edith out for her early morning surfing. Sure enough, Heather spied a figure in the waves and saw a canvas bag sitting on the dunes next to a pair of women's flip-flops.

Heather spread out a towel and settled on the sand to wait for Edith to return. There was no way she would get in that cold water herself. Grant had called last night and was not pleased at her lack of progress. She had to do better, which meant she had to get close to Edith. Simple.

The sun was warming her arms by the time Edith emerged from the water. A Jack Russell terrier trotted behind her. Edith's face was pink with cold and exertion. Her steps slowed when she saw Heather, but her smile beamed out.

She dropped her board a few feet from Heather. "You're out and about early, Heather. Did you go for a morning swim?"

Heather smiled and shook her head. "I wanted to sit and watch the sun come up. I can't seem to sleep in anymore since I've been working."

"It's a good habit to get into. The cold water keeps you healthy."

Heather looked at the gooseflesh on Edith's arms and grimaced. "I think I'd rather be sick."

"Typical young person." Edith pulled a towel from her bag and blotted the water from her hair.

Heather stared at the dog. "He goes surfing with you?"

"Oh yes, Sheldon loves it."

Heather watched her peel off her wetsuit to reveal a body in pretty good shape for an older lady. Maybe there was something to that cold water. The old gal looked younger than the fifty or so she had to be. "Where's Raine this morning?"

Edith stuffed her wetsuit in the bag and pulled out a bag of dog treats. "Sleeping. Curtis has babysitting duty until I get back."

"The waves are pretty nice out there. Bet you wished you didn't have to come in."

Edith tossed the towel back in her bag and gave the dog a treat. "I could have stayed out another half hour, but Curtis has to get on with his day."

From Edith's reserve, Heather knew she'd pressed a little too fast. "Good for him. I don't know many people here yet. Want to grab breakfast with me?"

Edith hesitated. "I really need to get back. But I know what it's like to be alone in a strange new place. Why don't you come with me, and I'll fix you my famous almond pancakes?"

Heather suppressed a shudder and managed to smile. "That sounds yummy. You sure you don't mind? I didn't mean for you to have to cook."

"I love to cook. And I make the best coffee on the island. Come along." She glanced toward the road. "You have a bike? You can either leave it here or wheel it along to the house."

"Is it safe here?"

Edith smiled. "Child, no one would dream of stealing your bike. This is Hope Island. It's perfectly safe."

"I'll just leave it then." Heather pointed to the cottage down the road. "That's your house?"

Edith picked up her bag. "It's Curtis's. He and Raine will be up and wanting breakfast by now. Come, Sheldon."

Heather and the dog fell into step beside her. "You have to cook for him? He's a grown man. Can't he fix his own meals?"

"He could, but I like to take care of him."

Heather's ploy to stir up some resentment was useless. The woman was determined to be taken advantage of. "I bet running after Raine wears you out." She had to increase her stride to keep up with Edith.

"Not really. It keeps me young."

Heather fell silent until they reached the sidewalk to the house. "It's a cute house." The cottage's shake shingles were a soft gray. A big porch with white posts wrapped the front. "It looks pretty new."

"Curtis had it built a few years ago." Edith opened the door and stepped inside.

The walls were soft yellow and were a nice contrast to the light-colored wood floors. Off the foyer was a pleasant living room with overstuffed blue plaid furniture. "It's pretty."

"When I moved in, it was a mess of used, mismatched furniture and broken-down end tables. I told Curtis I wasn't living like that, and he gave me a free hand to decorate it." Edith dropped her bag on the hall floor. "Curtis! I'm home."

Heather followed Edith through the living room and dining room to the kitchen. Curtis sat at the island with a bowl of cereal in front of him. Raine was in a high chair and had Cheerios in her hair. She babbled something to Edith when she saw her.

"I'll get your milk in a minute," Edith said, clearly understanding the little girl's request. "You should have waited, and I would have fixed you breakfast, Curtis. You need protein for breakfast, not carbs."

His grin was unrepentant. "Eggs and bacon would be great. This was just to hold me over." His gaze slid to Heather. "Hey, Heather. Where did you come from?"

"I was a vagrant on the beach, and Edith took pity on my lonely state. I'm starved." She strove for a light tone. "Hello, sweetheart," she cooed to Raine. "I was hoping to see you this morning."

The little girl stared at her with solemn eyes, then offered her a Cheerio.

"For me? Thank you." Heather took the moist Cheerio and tried not to grimace. She forced herself to put it in her mouth and swallow. "Anything I can do to help, Edith?"

"Just keep the baby occupied. Curtis, you need to get to work?" Edith got out a bowl and cracked eggs into it.

"Nope. I took the day off. I had quite an eventful day yesterday. Amy helped me rescue a pregnant woman on a shipwrecked boat, and then someone blew up my convertible."

Heather gasped. "That's terrible! Who did it?"

"We don't know yet. The authorities are looking into it. But it adds weight to Amy's theory."

What theory? Heather was dying to ask, but she knew her nosiness wouldn't go over well.

TWENTY

After surfing, Amy needed another cup of coffee and food. The earlier adrenaline rush from surfing had left her, and she wished she could go back to bed. Some faceless man chased her all night long in her dreams. Probably the result of the car bombing last night.

Her sluggishness called for drastic measures so she blended grass-fed butter into her coffee and sipped the rich concoction. The doorbell rang, and her energy level surged when she saw Curtis through the front door window.

"I didn't expect to see you." She raised her cup. "Coffee? It's Toomer's, infrared roasted. And where's my niece?"

"With Ede. I need your help." He followed her into the kitchen. "I took the day off since I knew I'd have to deal with police red tape today. Sure enough, I got a call at six this morning." He grimaced. "And a call from my boss on the heels of that. I knew I'd get in trouble for letting you in the chopper. The fact that we were nearly blown up softened his anger."

She handed him a cup of coffee. "What did the police say?"

"The bomb was a common type. No way to trace who might have done it."

She motioned for him to follow her back to the living room

where she curled on the sofa with her legs tucked under her. "Have they interviewed people who were there?"

He dropped onto the easy chair. "No one saw anything. There aren't any windows on that side of the hangar, and it was a slow day."

The memory of the convertible exploding had imprinted on her retinas, and she still shook with how close they'd come to death. She'd thought of dying often, but not in a car bomb. "Your poor car."

He shrugged. "I contacted the insurance company today. It's replaceable. You aren't."

She nearly shivered at the warmth in his eyes. "You were the one under the car. It could have been a lot worse."

"It sure could have been. I wouldn't want to lose you."

Her coffee was a welcome distraction from his intensity, and she relished the rich butter on her tongue. "God was looking out for us."

"Ready to search for Ben's wallet and log-in information?"

She liked sitting here in the sunshine with him, but she nodded and rose. "I almost looked last night when I got back, but I was too tired."

The morning light shone through the high window in the upstairs hall and touched the cheery yellow walls. On a day like today, the terror of yesterday seemed unbelievable. Ben's door was closed as always, but when Amy neared, she saw it was not firmly latched.

Curtis nearly ran into her when she stopped, and his big hands came down on her shoulders. "What's wrong?"

"Someone has been in his room."

"Are you sure?"

"I think so." She rubbed her head. "I suppose it's possible I didn't latch it the last time I was in there, but I didn't see it cracked open yesterday when I went past."

"Let me go first." He eased her out of the way, then pushed open the door. "It's been tossed. You'd better call Tom."

She peeked past him and gasped. Drawers hung open, and the closet door gaped. Clothes had been ripped from the hangers, and T-shirts and underwear spilled from the dresser drawers. After following Curtis into the room, she stood in the middle of the floor and didn't know where to look first.

"Call Tom," he said again.

"In a minute. My phone is in the living room." Clearly, the intruder was gone by now.

"Was your house locked?"

She shook her head. "I never lock it."

"I think you'd better start. And maybe consider getting a security system."

"The very thought is disconcerting."

"I'd normally agree with you, but Gina and Ben didn't find it very safe. And someone tried to kill us."

She shuddered at the reminder. "What could the intruder want?"

"Maybe the same things we're looking for—Ben's wallet and log-in information."

"If they were here, the intruder may have found them." A faint scent of cologne hung in the room. She sniffed. "Do you smell that?"

In two steps he was beside her. He sniffed the air, then shook his head. "Is it familiar? I don't smell anything."

"I've smelled it before, I think, but I can't quite place it." She sniffed again. "It's gone now. Maybe it was my imagination."

Curtis glanced around. "Did Ben have any hiding places in here?"

Hiding places. "You know, I found a leather address book of Ben's hidden in our special tree in the backyard. I couldn't make out anything about it though. It seemed to be in code. There are only a few pages in it."

"Could I see it?"

"I'll get it." She left him in the bedroom and rushed down to the living room where she dug the book out of her purse. She retrieved her cell phone as well and called the sheriff's office to report the break-in. When she returned, Curtis was in the back of the closet.

She held out the book. "This is the notebook. I called Tom's office. He'll be here in about an hour. He said not to touch anything."

Curtis's hair was disheveled from the hanging clothing, and he looked handsomely boyish. When he flipped open the book, he frowned. "It does seem to be in a code. Did you guys ever play around with codes when you were kids? It might be something simple."

"Not that I recall. I could check with some of his friends and see if they remember anything like that."

He tapped the book into his palm. "Mind if I take this? I'm good with codes. I might be able to decipher it."

"Sure. It's not doing me any good." She glanced around the room. "I doubt his wallet is here."

"Any idea where else we might check?" Curtis walked over to peer out the window. "He drove to the beach that morning, but it's close enough to have walked. Do you suppose he could have lost it on a previous jaunt?"

"He always hiked back and forth to the beach. I was surprised his car was found." A thought struck her and she gasped. "What if he didn't drive the car there? That would explain why he didn't have his wallet with him. Someone else might have parked it where it was found."

"But why?"

"To make it look like he was leaving the island. What if he wasn't leaving at all?" It was a weak argument, but it was the only reason she could think of. But maybe she was missing something. "I'm game to take a look along the path to the beach if you are."

"Lead on."

A walk in the springtime meadow with Curtis sounded near heaven to her.

———

Curtis took Amy's hand to help her over a fallen log along the rough path through the woods. He could have released her, but he liked her small hand in his. When was the last time he'd even held a girl's hand? It had been awhile, and it had never been this enjoyable.

She stopped in a clearing and glanced around. "Ben and I usually cut through here and didn't follow the path."

High grasses and wildflowers waved in the breeze, and trees fringed the large meadow. A fallen tree lay in the center of the field, but the opening from the dead tree allowed the blue sky to peek through.

She pointed out the dead tree. "We often paused there to rest when we were kids."

"You have a lot of great memories."

Her mouth went soft. "We had the best summers here."

She would have been a beautiful little girl as she roamed this island. He wished he'd known her back then.

She pointed to her left. "You go that way, and I'll go to this side."

He reluctantly let go of her hand and walked through the grasses. Kicking at the tall vegetation, he tried to see anything that didn't belong in the meadow. Blue jays scolded him from their safe perches, and bugs hummed in his ears. It didn't look as though anyone had walked through here in a while. There was no matted vegetation.

"There are lots of herbs here," she called across the meadow. "I'm going to come back and collect some. I see blessed thistle and cat's claw."

He turned to reply, and his foot struck something. Kneeling, he pushed brush and grass out of his way. There it was. The brown wallet was water damaged. Should he touch it? "Over here!"

She rushed through the meadow to join him. "You found it?"

When she reached for it, he grasped her wrist. "Leave it alone. There might be evidence."

Her eyes widened. "You mean maybe someone attacked him here?"

"It's possible. I don't want to contaminate the evidence."

"Do you think Tom will take it seriously?"

Drawing her up, Curtis slipped his arm around her waist, and they moved a few feet away. "He seems to want to get to the bottom of it, especially after my car blew up."

She cast a longing glance back at the wallet. "I don't like this at all, Curtis. This shows he didn't take the car to the beach."

"You're right. It's our first real clue that all was not as it seemed." He pulled out his phone and called the sheriff. "Tom will be here in ten minutes. He said not to touch anything. Let's wait over there on the log."

Her grief was etched on her face. "I was sure there was something, but to know that someone hurt Ben and made it look like an accident is almost too much to take in." She bit her lip.

He slipped his arm around her again and pulled her close with his chin resting on her head. The lemony fragrance of her hair slipped up his nose. "We'll find who did this, honey. We will."

Her fists clutched his shirt and she burrowed closer. "We have so little to go on. No motive. No real suspects."

He glanced back to where the wallet was lying. "Tom might find some clue. We have to be patient. And pray."

"I have been. I want justice for Ben. And for Gina." She lifted her head and stared up at him. "Have you looked for her log-in information?"

He forced himself not to look at her lips, only inches away. "Not yet. I'm going to go over her laptop and see what I can find."

"Maybe we can check it after Tom leaves?"

"Good idea." Plus, it would allow him to spend more time with her. He guided her onto the fallen log but left his arm around her as they sat in the warm spring sunshine. "I hate seeing you upset. Let's think about something else while we're waiting."

She pressed her lips together. "I'm all right. It was just a shock." She smiled but it was forced. "What else do you want to do? Help me gather wildflowers? Some of them are very good in tinctures."

"Tinctures? What is that? Some kind of drink?"

She laughed. "Sort of, but I doubt you'd like the taste of most of them. They're herbal remedies. I like natural medicine. Give the body the right nutrition and it heals itself. It's amazing the way God designed us."

He liked seeing her eyes light up. "Such as?"

She pointed out a woody vine with white flowers. "Take the passion flower. It's great for anxiety and insomnia. It can even be helpful with seizures. Barberry is great for skin ailments, even scurvy. And bitter orange helps with nausea."

He leaned in closer. "What about a love potion?"

She laughed, then her expression went somber. "I don't think you need any assistance."

His throat tightened at her words and the expression in her eyes. "You think I'd have a chance with a really beautiful new resident who doesn't know me all that well? Maybe I could slip her a potion, and she'd look a little more favorably on me."

"It doesn't take long for someone to see your qualities. Anyone who has caught your eye is a very lucky woman."

Her eyes fluttered closed, and she leaned in close enough for him to smell the minty freshness of her breath. He pulled her closer and his lips just brushed hers. Then a man hollered for them in the distance.

"Tom's here," he whispered. "But we'll resume this conversation at a later date."

TWENTY-ONE

Edith expertly taped the disposable diaper into place, then released the squirming toddler. "So Tom will let you know if he finds any fingerprints?"

"Or anything else." Amy held out her arms, hoping Raine would run into them, but the little girl giggled and ran for her Uncle Curtis.

"Dude!" she squealed, throwing herself against him.

Smart baby. That's where Amy wanted to be too, and the realization was uncomfortable. Sheldon thought Amy wanted him, and the terrier launched himself into her lap and licked her chin. She took solace in being wanted and rubbed the dog's head. He wiggled all over with delight.

Curtis picked up his niece, then sat on the sofa with his feet on the coffee table. His lids drooped, and there were dark circles under his eyes. "We need to go through Gina's things. I checked her laptop, but there's nothing in her history about logging in to a bank account."

Edith wiped her hands with a towelette. "It's all in the spare room. Most of it's in her cedar chest, but there are some boxes in the closet too."

"You didn't go through it, did you?" Curtis asked. "I thought you said you just packed it away until you had the heart to look through it." Raine grabbed a fistful of his hair and tugged.

Edith nodded. "That's exactly right. I threw her things into boxes and got rid of the furniture. All except for her chest and bed." She lifted little Raine from his arms. "Time for your nap, young lady."

The child cried, reaching out her hands for Curtis. When he shook his head, she turned to Amy and clenched and unclenched her hands. "Mom."

Amy couldn't resist. Edith didn't stop her when she took the baby from her arms. As she nuzzled the little one's soft skin, she caught a tender expression flitting across Curtis's face. She averted her gaze and began to softly sing "Amazing Grace" to Raine. The child sagged against her, and her head drooped. Amy swayed where she stood, and it was only minutes until Raine's breathing deepened.

"You have the touch," Edith said approvingly.

If only Edith knew how she longed to hug this baby tight and never let go. Raine would be the recipient of all the love stored up inside Amy's heart. "Could you show me her bedroom?"

Edith studied her expression, then nodded. "This way."

Amy followed her down the hall to the first room on the right. It was painted Cinderella pink and was charmingly furnished with white furniture and a block rug in pinks and lavenders. Edith lowered the side of the crib, and Amy laid Raine onto the pale pink sheet. The rail squeaked a bit as she raised it, but the little girl didn't stir.

Edith turned on the baby monitor and carried it out of the room with her. "She'll sleep a couple of hours. You two will have plenty of time to look through the spare room. If you don't mind, I'll run to the grocery store while she's napping."

"Of course." Amy took the baby monitor as Curtis joined them. "Where is the room?"

"Here." He stepped across the hall and pushed open the door to reveal a large bedroom painted in pale cream. A sleek black bed dominated the room. There was a cedar chest at the foot of it. "She loved that chest. Ben gave it to her."

"Looks Amish."

"It is."

"Call me if you need me." Edith walked away without waiting for an answer. Moments later the door to the garage closed.

Amy glanced around the room. "Where should we start?"

Tension radiated from Curtis. "The chest, I guess. It's hard to think about all the hopes she had packed into that chest."

She touched his arm. "I know this won't be easy. Would you rather I do it alone?"

The muscle in his jaw flexed. "I can do it."

A wave of protectiveness washed over her, and she wished she could hold him and soothe his pain. Instead, she cleared her throat and went to kneel by the cedar chest. "This is beautiful." The wood was smooth under her fingertips as she caressed it. She released the latch and raised the lid. A rush of aromatic cedar wafted into the air. "Oh, it smells wonderful."

There was a white silky garment on top. "Is this a wedding dress?" She lifted it out and saw the intricate beadwork. "It's lovely. Was it Gina's?"

"I didn't know she had it." Curtis's voice was strangled. "Her hope was always that Ben would marry her."

A week ago she would have bristled at the condemnation in his voice. Instead, she ducked her head and bent to her task. With the gown in her hands, she rose and shook it out, then laid it on the bed before returning to her perusal of the trunk's contents. The rest of the contents were paraphernalia like Raine's baby book, candles, classic Jane Austen books, a silver serving tray, stainless tableware, a blue-and-white teapot with matching teacups, and a set of nice dishes.

Some of the things seemed to be items that a woman about to be married would be compiling, and the realization brought tears to Amy's eyes. Poor Gina. And her pain was Ben's fault. If only Amy knew *why* Ben hadn't married Gina. Surely there was a reason.

One by one, she lifted the items from the chest until it was empty. She sat back on her haunches. "There doesn't seem to be anything here with bank information. No notebook or anything like that." It took less time to repack the chest than it did to empty it. She rose and picked up the gown again.

Out of curiosity, she glanced at the label. "This is a Vera Wang."

Curtis looked confused. "What does that mean?"

"It would have cost her the earth. Probably at least twenty-five thousand dollars!"

His brows rose. "You're kidding. Where would she have gotten that kind of money?"

"Maybe this is where some of that money went. We should hang this up." She shook it out again, and something fell onto the floor.

Curtis swooped down to seize it. "It's a journal. Maybe it will have some information in it."

Amy wasn't sure she wanted to know everything. She didn't want to see Curtis's disappointment in finding out more about Gina's activities.

———

Raine was still sleeping, and the house was quiet as they sat on the sofa. Curtis held the journal in his hands and tried to get the courage to open it. He was no coward, but he dreaded finding out something about Gina he would be happier not knowing. What if she'd been selling drugs or stealing? A thousand possibilities raced through his head.

Amy touched his hand. "Want me to read it?"

He shook his head. "I want to do it." He flexed the pages back and turned to the first page. The pastor's name was on the first line, followed by the words *STUDY TIME*. Then Libby's name was listed with the words *DUE DATE APRIL 19*. "I think it's a prayer journal."

He flipped to the next page and saw she'd written out prayers. She prayed for his safety, for Raine to grow up to be a godly woman. His eyes burned at the evidence that his sister took her faith seriously. Whatever she'd been caught up in, he was ready to bet that it had been inadvertent. She'd changed so dramatically after she became pregnant with Raine.

Amy's shoulder brushed his as she leaned closer to read the journal. "She loved you very much. And Raine." Her voice was choked.

"Gina had a lot of love in her. It wasn't always channeled in the best way. I'm not saying she didn't do something wrong that got her killed, but I'm sure where she is now." He started to close the journal, then stopped. "I guess we'd better read all of this. There might be a clue in what she prayed for."

"These are dated. Maybe start at the back?" Amy suggested.

He slipped to the back cover and found the last pages blank, so he fanned through them to find the last entries. "This one is two days before her death."

Amy leaned close again. "Mind if I read it with you?"

He moved the journal so it was half on his lap and half on hers. "You might pick up some clue I miss."

Dear Lord, I'm so afraid that Ben and I are in too deep. I should never have let myself get into this situation. Ben's arguments made sense at first—oh, who am I trying to kid? You know all things. You know I went into it with my eyes open. You warned us that the love of money is the root of all kinds of evils. It's true. It's so true. And so is vanity. I have tried to be truthful and honest, but I let my desire for Raine's future security sway what I knew was right.

I've been such a hypocrite. Help me make this right somehow, God. Maybe the truth needs to come out. In fact, I'm sure it does. I'm going to tell the truth. Protect us all, God.

"Wow," Amy said, her voice soft. "What could she be talking about?"

"I have a terrible feeling that it might be drugs." Curtis told her about Josh seeing Gina on Ocean Street.

She scooted away from him. "Why didn't you tell me before?"

"There was no proof, and I really didn't believe it. But it's clear she did something she knew was wrong because of money. And where else would she have gotten that kind of money?"

Her hands balled into fists. "You think Ben got her involved, don't you?"

"I don't think she would get into something like that on her own," he countered. "I'm sure you don't think your precious brother would do anything wrong, but unlike you, I try not to look at her through rose-colored glasses. Everyone has good and bad in them. Even Ben."

"Ben was a good man!" she fired back. She jumped to her feet. "I'd better go. Tell Edith I'm sorry I couldn't stay." She rushed toward the door.

Curtis started to go after her, then heard Raine cry out for him on the monitor. What could he say to Amy anyway? Until she was ready to look at her brother clearly, they were at an impasse.

TWENTY-TWO

Amy spent the next two days finishing preparations for setting up her clinic. Dr. Hollensby called and agreed to supervise her, so she was fully legal. She'd already received several calls from pregnant women who were eager to have her help them deliver, but she'd put them off. After such a busy time, she quickly agreed to meet Libby for lunch at the Oyster Café.

Libby was already seated under a red-and-white umbrella on the brick patio when Amy arrived. Noah slept in his carrier with his thumb corked in his mouth.

"I love to see a baby sucking his thumb," Amy said after she hugged Libby and settled into her chair.

Libby grimaced. "I'm not going to be excited about the orthodontic bills, but it makes for a happy baby. He hasn't even been getting up in the night."

"No wonder you look so rested." Amy picked up the menu.

Libby playfully smacked it out of her hand. "Oh no you don't. I want to hear about the car bombing. Curtis told Alec about it at work. You should have called to tell me about it."

"I didn't want to worry you. We're fine. Neither of us even got a scratch."

"But someone tried to *kill* you, Amy!"

Amy's heart faltered, but she managed a confident smile. "We

160

don't know that for sure. Maybe Curtis was the target or it was a random act."

Libby lifted a brow. "We both know better than that. And I bet you've turned up more evidence that Ben was killed, haven't you? Which brought about the car bombing."

Amy told her about the money and the wallet they'd found. "I think Tom is beginning to believe there might have been foul play, but it's so hard waiting to see what he can uncover."

"What else?"

Libby was way too perceptive. Amy shrugged. "Well, Curtis and I had a little fight." She told her about the prayer journal and Curtis's suspicions. "But I know Ben would never sell drugs. Never. It has to be something else."

"Whatever it is, it sounds like it was illegal." Libby's words were gentle. "You need to quit assuming anything. Ben wasn't perfect, honey."

Amy tensed. "I know he wasn't! But he was a good man. I don't like hearing someone trash his name. Not even Curtis." Her eyes burned, and her hands shook as she raised her water glass to her mouth.

"Why are you so mad, Amy?"

Libby's gentle words made her slump back in her chair. "I don't know. I'm just so . . . so angry that he's dead. That I didn't get to say good-bye. That he didn't get to raise his daughter. It's not fair."

Libby reached over and squeezed Amy's hand. "It's okay to be mad. It's not fair. And the whole situation stinks. You can yell and cry all you want with me. I'll listen."

Amy swallowed the thickness in her throat. "I guess I'm still just grieving."

"It takes time, a lot of time."

She noticed Libby's gaze wander over her shoulder. "What's wrong?"

"Ned Springall just came in."

"The guy who was surfing with Ben?" Amy twisted to look for the man. She'd never met him.

A man of about forty stood waiting to be seated. His grizzled hair hung down his back in a ponytail, and the sleeveless shirt he wore revealed arms covered in tattoos. He was as tanned as a chestnut and very fit. When Libby beckoned him, he headed their way.

He approached their table with a smile. "Miss Libby, you look like a happy mama. What a fine young man. Congratulations."

"Thanks, Ned. Would you care to join us? My friend here would like to talk to you. This is Ben's sister, Amy Lang."

His eyes were very blue in his tanned face, and he flashed a white smile at Amy. "Pleased to meet you, Miss Amy. I thought a wicked lot of your brother." His Boston accent put a broad emphasis on the A in her name. "And I'd hoped to ask you to help me get a community herb garden going in the plot behind the church. Think I could talk you into helping?"

His manner immediately put Amy at ease. "I'd be glad to. When do you want me to look at it?"

"Would you have time after lunch?"

She nodded. "It shouldn't take long." She liked the twinkle in his eyes and his easy manner. "I wanted to speak with you about the day Ben died."

Heather came to wait on them before they got into the discussion. She looked tired today, but her smile was bright. "Hey, Amy! I didn't realize I'd see you here today. My boss says I can give you my discount since you're like family. What can I get you?"

Amy smiled at her enthusiasm. When Heather had first come here, Amy thought she wouldn't last at the challenging job, but she'd buckled down. "I'll have the lobster bisque."

Heather scribbled down the order. "It's super good today."

While she took the other orders, Amy took a moment to think about what she wanted to ask Ned. She didn't want to forget anything. She had so many questions about Ben's death.

Ned took a sip of his water. "So what do you want to ask?"

She leaned on the table. "You said Ben was leaving for the mainland after surfing. That he'd driven to the beach, right?"

"Right." Ned nodded.

Amy studied his expression, seemingly open and honest. But who really knew what went on behind someone's innocent face? She was beginning to think no one ever knew anyone else. "Did you see him drive to the beach?"

Ned's eyes grew puzzled. "No. I was already in the water when he arrived, and I didn't pay any attention until I couldn't find him. I first noticed his car after I called the Coast Guard for assistance, so that's when I realized he'd driven instead of walked."

Maybe he was telling the truth. Amy wanted to believe him. "Did you speak to Ben that morning? Did he tell you he was heading for the mainland?"

"He'd told me the day before that he was going back home after we surfed. We grabbed a couple of great waves, then conditions started getting gnarly. The last wave I rode threw me down wicked hard. He went back for one last wave, even though I told him it was looking too dangerous."

"Did he act upset about anything? Worried?"

Ned frowned. "He wasn't himself on that last visit."

"In what way?"

"He was quiet, rather somber. You know what a jokester he was, always kidding around. He liked to go out at night and meet up with friends. There was none of that. Instead, he refused invitations and hung out at the house."

This was in line with everything Amy had heard so far. "What about Gina? Did he see her much?"

Ned sipped his water. "Yeah, she was at the house most of the time, her and Raine. I stopped by one day. Things were tense."

"Did you overhear anything that might indicate what the disagreement was about?"

He fingered the ring in his left ear. "Gina was laying into Ben something fierce. Something about a bad idea, maybe? His idea, she said."

"His idea," Amy repeated. "What did that mean?"

Ned shook his head as Heather brought their food.

His idea. Ben always had schemes to make money or increase business. His help had been invaluable to their father. Could it have anything to do with his business? Only her dad would know.

———

Amy eyed the angle of the sun and nodded to Ned. The large space behind the church was perfect for an herb garden. "I think there's enough space. You say Gina left this to the town?"

His ponytail swung when he nodded. "How much work do you think it will be?"

"Get a fellow with a tractor in here to till it all up, and we can get the plants in, or even seeds, if you want to do it more cheaply. I can draw up a list of what to plant where and what kind of soil and light the herbs prefer."

"That would be wicked good of you."

She touched his tattooed arm. "I have another question about Ben if you don't mind me asking."

He put his hands on his hips. "Sure. Don't know how much help I can be, but I'll try."

"You and Ben surfed a lot, is that right?"

He nodded. "Nearly every morning when he was here. That man was a born fish."

"Did he ever mention why he didn't marry Gina?" It was a personal question, but maybe he'd been close enough to be Ben's confidante.

Ned's smile faded. "Not exactly, ma'am."

"What does that mean? He did or he didn't."

Ned shuffled in his flip-flops. "He sometimes called his fiancée from the beach. I think he was torn between her and Gina, though he never really said so. But he was always a little quiet when he hung up."

"Did he talk to Elizabeth a lot in the weeks before he died? Their wedding was supposed to be next week."

Ned nodded. "I'd hear him talking about wedding plans." He nodded toward the hill. "Here comes Libby."

Amy turned and waved at her friend, but her thoughts stayed on her brother. How could he have kept two women on the string this way?

TWENTY-THREE

Amy expected her parents by seven on Friday night. She'd put fresh sheets on the guest room bed and had set out fresh flowers. She gulped when car doors slammed at 6:40. Curtis had originally offered to be with her when she told them about Raine, but after their tiff, she wasn't about to invite him over. The last thing she needed was for him to say something disparaging about her brother. Plus, she wanted to avoid any confrontation about Raine's custody. If her parents immediately planned to see an attorney, Curtis would not be able to hold his tongue.

She met them at the door. "You made it. Welcome."

Her mother, dressed in a tan suit, offered a sweet-smelling cheek. "Amy, you look positively brown. You haven't been wearing your sunscreen."

"I don't believe in sunscreens, Mom." It was a familiar argument. "I never get burned, and I want the vitamin D."

Her mother's eyes narrowed, but she didn't answer as she walked past Amy and sniffed. "You've painted recently."

"I've readied a room to see patients." Amy knew that announcement would not go over well. Her mother thought she should finish her training to be a doctor. And preferably set up practice down the street from where she grew up.

She stepped out of the way for her dad to lug in the two suitcases. "Hello, Dad. Glad you could make it." He barely paused long enough for her to brush her lips against his cheek before barreling into the entry.

He headed for the stairs. "Our usual room?"

"Yes," she called after him.

Her mother didn't follow her husband but wandered toward the living room. "I'd like some iced tea if you have any made up." She paused to study the pictures of Ben that Amy had put out a few days ago.

Her mother picked up a photo of Ben leaping high to clear a hurdle in high school track. "He still holds the school record, you know."

"I know."

Her mother put it back on the table, then went to her favorite chair, a pale lemon armchair by the fireplace.

"I'll get you some tea." Amy escaped to the kitchen.

It felt like a boulder was lodged in her stomach. No matter how carefully she approached the subject, it was going to be hard. Should she tell them together or approach her father first? He might be the most reasonable. Her mother was bound to get emotional, but she might be more upset if she thought Amy was trying to exclude her.

When she returned to the living room, her father was on the sofa working on his iPad. He barely grunted when she asked him if he wanted iced tea, so she placed her mother's glass on a table by her chair, then settled on the sofa beside her dad. She could put it off a few hours, but she'd be sick by nightfall if she didn't get this out in the open.

The breeze lifted the curtains at the window and blew in the scents from the herb garden: rosemary, cilantro, and oregano. Rosemary for remembrance. This was the time to remember Ben too. What he wanted. His dreams, the future he never had. If he wasn't willing to marry Gina, what did that say?

Her mother wiped the condensation on her glass. "You look like you just bit into rhubarb. Is something wrong?"

Amy inhaled and prayed for courage. "Dad, would you put your iPad down a minute? I have something important I need to tell you."

Her father looked at her over the top of his glasses, then set his iPad on the cushion beside him. "You look very serious. Are you in financial trouble? Or is this more nonsense about Ben's death?"

She wasn't about to get into what she'd found out about Ben's death. "Did you know Ben had a girlfriend here?"

Her mother frowned. "That's ridiculous, Amy. He was going to marry Elizabeth. The poor girl is still a wreck. Did I tell you I ran into her at the club the other day? She looked positively dreadful. So pale and drawn. She started to cry at the sight of me. Her father wants her to start dating again, but she says she'll never forget Ben." She dabbed at her eyes.

How much of Ben's reluctance to marry Gina had to do with his engagement? If only Amy could ask him.

She inhaled and her stomach tightened. "Ben had a baby with the woman here, Mom. A little girl."

The words fell into the silence of the room like an explosion. Her mother leaped to her feet. "That is impossible. Ben would have told us!"

Amy reached into the pocket of her jeans and pulled out a picture of Raine. "This is Ben's daughter." She extended the picture to her mother, who at first refused to take it. "Look at her, Mom. Her name is Raine, and she is a year old."

Her mother's fingers tightened on the picture, and she stared into Raine's smiling face. "Sh-She's beautiful." Her voice shook.

"What's this nonsense?" Her father got up and snatched the picture out of his wife's hand. "She looks nothing like Ben."

"She looks like her mother," Amy said. "Gina Ireland."

Her father stared at the picture. "I don't know any Gina from here on the island. Are her parents the Irelands who own the marina in Virginia Beach?"

"No, they're from New York. Wealthy. I'm not sure what their business is though."

Her mother took the picture back. "If she came from a good family, then he clearly wasn't ashamed of her. Why would he keep something like this from us?"

"I haven't been able to figure that out yet."

Her father's lips flattened. "Are you sure the child is Ben's?"

"Ben's name is on the birth certificate. Though I have to tell you all of it—Gina didn't have a very good reputation."

Her mother frowned. "Did Ben ever have a paternity test done?"

"I don't know."

Her father was looking more skeptical. "Where is the child now?"

"Gina's brother, Curtis, has custody. He's pretty amazing, really, and the baby clearly loves him."

"Surely he has to work. I suppose he puts her in *day care*," her father said, curling his lip.

"Actually, no. Curtis's aunt moved to the island to help care for Raine. She's wonderful with her. There are no worries there. I'm telling you because I know you'll want to be part of her life. I'm sure Curtis will be willing to let you have her over a weekend on occasion as she gets to know us all better."

Her father lifted an eyebrow. "We will want to raise her our-selves, of course." He looked at his wife. "Isn't that right, Mary?"

"Oh, of course!" Amy's mother sat upright in her chair. Spots of color in her cheeks brightened her eyes. "Once we're sure she is Ben's child."

The boulder in Amy's gut grew. "I can't support you in that, Mom and Dad. Raine belongs with her uncle. She's happy and he adores her. The upheaval wouldn't be right."

Her father squared his shoulders. "Children are resilient. I'll

COLLEEN COBLE

call my attorney at once." He turned around and grabbed his phone from the sofa.

———

Curtis was dragging when he got home from work. The Coast Guard unit had gone out on two rescues, and one of them had resulted in a death, something that always left them feeling defeated. Raine's bright smile always recharged him though.

The aroma of enchiladas wafted through the house as he sat on the floor with Raine and her blocks. Edith had said dinner would be ready in half an hour. When the doorbell rang, he half hoped it was Amy. He wanted to apologize about losing his temper. He started to smile when he saw her, then his gut clenched when he saw two people behind her. The woman was obviously her mother. She had the same eyes and hair color as Amy.

He opened the door and pasted on a smile. "You're just in time for dinner."

The man's mouth was set in a firm line. "You must be Curtis Ireland. We're here to see our granddaughter."

Amy mouthed *I'm sorry* at Curtis as he stood blocking the doorway. She managed a watery smile. "Um, Curtis, these are my parents, Oliver and Mary Lang. As you can tell, I told them about Raine. They'd love to meet her if it's convenient. I tried to call you, but it went to voice mail, and they were too eager to wait."

Her soft voice broke his stiffness. None of this was her fault. "My phone was dead, and I had it charging. Raine is in the living room playing. Come in."

Amy entered first. "Smells like Edith's famous Mexican."

He stood aside for her parents to enter. "Chicken enchiladas. I'm sure there's plenty if you'd like to stay for dinner."

170

Mary Lang glanced around the entry. "This is quite lovely." Her voice held surprise.

"Thanks. This way is the living room." He led them down the hall to the door on the left. Raine had a block in each fist. She waved one at him, and her small white teeth gleamed.

"Oh, she's darling," Mary said in a rush of breath. She stepped quickly into the room and knelt beside Raine. "What do you have there?"

Raine held up a block and smiled. "Block." It sounded more like *bock*.

"Can I help?"

The little girl examined both of the blocks she held, then handed Mary the one in her left hand.

Curtis turned to Oliver. "Can we discuss this privately? I'll take Raine to my aunt in the kitchen." He lifted the little girl into his arms and carried her to where Edith was chopping salad. When he explained what was happening, she gave Raine a cracker and put her in the high chair.

When Curtis returned to the living room, the tension was palpable. Mary stood off to one side, dabbing at her eyes with a tissue. Oliver paced in front of the fireplace. Amy sat on the sofa with her hands clasped on one knee.

Curtis dropped onto a cushion beside her. "Have a seat."

Mary sat gingerly on the edge of the armchair and looked at her husband. "I'll stand." He thrust out his jaw.

Curtis wasn't going to be intimidated by the way the big man stood over him. He rose as well. "Very well. I assume you're here to ask questions about all this."

Mary's lips trembled. "First and foremost, why weren't we told about Raine's birth? I don't understand."

"That's something I can't answer. Gina was always generous with Raine. I'm sure she would have been happy to share the baby

171

with you. It had to have been Ben's idea to keep it quiet." The truth was harsh, but he'd done nothing to soften the blow either, and he felt bad when tears filled her eyes. "I'm sorry."

Oliver picked up a picture of Gina with Raine just days after she was born. "There has to be more to it than that."

"It's all I know, all I was told."

Oliver pointed his finger at Curtis. "Your sister has been dead for several months. Why didn't you tell us about Raine when she died?"

"Dad, please sit down. This can escalate into an adversarial meeting if we aren't careful. That's not in anyone's best interest."

"I don't want to sit down! I want to know why this man"—he punctuated the words with a jab of his forefinger at Curtis's chest—"didn't tell me about my own granddaughter. If she *is* our grandchild. Was a paternity test done?"

Curtis clenched his teeth and exhaled. Getting angry wasn't going to fix anything. "Ben acknowledged the child. He signed the birth certificate. There was no need for a paternity test. And Gina wanted me to raise Raine. I love her, and I didn't want there to be any question of where she would live. So know this right now—I'll never give her up. You're wrong if you think you can come in here and demand to take her. Gina made her wishes clear, and I have legal custody. Ben never paid a cent in support either. You have no rights here."

Oliver thrust his head forward. "I have grandparent rights! I demand the right to see her!"

Curtis didn't back away. "I'll be happy to let you have visitation."

"If she is my grandchild, I intend to sue for more than visitation, young man. I want her permanently. And I can get the best attorneys. You'd be wise to give up without a fight."

"You may have money, but so does my family. A judge isn't

going to look any more favorably on you than on me. I'm younger and she knows me. If you want what's best for her, you'll drop the thought of custody."

"I want her to love us," Amy put in. "Not to tense whenever we show up. Think before you cause irreparable harm, Dad."

"Mary, we're out of here." Oliver wheeled toward the door.

Mary rose and followed her husband. "We'll be in the car, Amy."

"Don't you want to see Raine?" Amy's face was white.

"There will be plenty of time for that when we are sure she is Ben's daughter." Mary went out the door. Moments later the front door latched.

"I'm sorry," Amy said. "I don't know what to do."

"I'll handle it. No one is taking Raine away from me." Curtis knew his tone was hostile, but right now he blamed Amy too. For all he knew, she'd encouraged her parents to try to get custody. But it would be over his dead body.

TWENTY-FOUR

The church bells rang out twelve times, and Amy paused digging plant holes to wipe her brow. She inhaled the good scent of freshly turned dirt and glanced around at the community herb garden. Ned had wasted no time after their talk yesterday, and the plowed plot was ready for planting. She'd purchased the herbs herself as her contribution to the project. Townspeople populated the rows like ants scurrying to their mounds.

Working almost let her forget the way her parents had treated Curtis last night. Almost.

Alec and Libby's sister, Vanessa, worked two rows over. Libby was their cheering section and sat with Noah under the shade of a live oak tree. Even Libby's half brother, Brent, dug diligently in the dirt on the other side of the field. The Coasties had their own little spot where they were planting star-of-Bethlehem, rockrose, impatiens, cherry plum, and clematis. It was the concoction known as "Rescue Remedy," and it tickled Amy to see them so excited about it. She intended to make good use of it with her patients.

"Lunch!" Libby put Noah in his seat on the blanket and knelt to open the wicker picnic basket.

Amy wiped her dirty hands in the grass, then pulled out a

disposable towelette to clean up a little better. She handed one each to Alec and Vanessa, and they both wiped their hands as they went to join Libby. Vanessa looked like a slightly younger version of Libby, but she usually wasn't one to get her hands dirty, from what Amy had been told.

"I appreciate you coming out to help," Amy told her.

"I kind of like it." A smudge of dirt marred one of Vanessa's pink cheeks. She wore stylish capris and a sleeveless top that showed toned arms. "What's it like being a midwife? Sounds scary. What if something goes wrong? Have you ever lost a baby or a mother?"

Amy walked with her toward the shade where Libby had spread the tablecloth. "No, but I'm very careful to monitor my patients and refer them to a doctor if there's anything out of the ordinary. I know things can go wrong, and I've been lucky so far. A birth can take a wrong turn in a hospital too though. But most of the time births run smoothly. It's a natural process, you know. It's a modern Western notion to lock up a woman while she gives birth with the rest of her family cut off from the experience."

Vanessa nodded. "I guess I can see that. You did a great job delivering Noah. He's so sweet. I think he smiled at me yesterday."

"He might think you're his mother. You and Libby look very much alike."

Vanessa brightened. "We do, don't we? I like hearing that."

They reached the shade, and Amy's stomach rumbled in response to the smell of grilled chicken. Libby had brought a real feast of chicken, potato salad, seven-layer salad, baked beans, and even pie. "I'm starving. That's not coconut cream pie, is it?"

Libby smiled and set a bowl on the blanket. "It sure is. Delilah made it."

"I'm starved too." Vanessa waved at her brother, then went off to join him and his girlfriend at a picnic table by the church.

Quite a few of the townspeople quit for lunch too, and several of them stopped to thank Amy for contributing her expertise. She gave out several recipes for herbal remedies, including a recommendation to eat garlic and take echinacea for a cold. She was beginning to feel like a part of the community already.

When the hair on her arms stood at attention, she knew without looking around that Curtis had arrived. Why did she react so strangely to his presence? The entire situation was outside her comfort zone, and she didn't know how to handle this attraction. Never before had she been unable to ignore a man. And they were likely to be at odds until things were settled with Raine.

Curtis was smiling though. "You did all this?" He wore sandals and khaki shorts that showed his tanned legs.

He acted like he hadn't been furious when she and her parents left last night. Two could play that game, so she smiled and tried not to show that she was uncomfortable. "Not just me. I had lots of help."

"Your parents still here?" His mouth twisted. "Listen, about last night. I'm sorry I lost my temper."

"Apology accepted. It was tense all around. And yes, they'll be here until tomorrow." She pointed them out as they approached with boxes of fish and chips in their hands from the Oyster Café. "Looks like they're bringing a peace offering."

"For you, not for me, I'm sure."

"Don't leave," she said when he began to move away. "We have to learn to get along for Raine's sake."

Curtis hesitated and thrust his hands in his pockets. "I'll stay for you."

Her dad paused when his gaze lit on Curtis, but he tipped up his chin and marched toward them. "We brought some fish."

"Thanks. It smells good." Amy took the box of food from him. "I don't think you've met Libby and Alec. And little Noah." She introduced the family.

Her dad shook hands with Alec. "You own the big Tidewater Inn place. I've thought about investing in it, if you're interested in a partner."

Alec glanced at Libby, who gave a slight shake of her head. "Uh, thanks, but we're doing okay. It's been in Libby's family a long time. She has plans for exactly how she wants it to be."

"Of course, of course. Let me know if you change your mind."

Curtis visibly tensed. How were they going to keep Raine from feeling torn between them as she grew up? Amy hadn't realized until this week just how abrasive her father was. It was eye opening.

———

The rich scent of good dirt floated in the air. Curtis kept an eye on Amy as he dug holes two rows over from where she worked. Her pink cheeks and bright eyes told how much she enjoyed gardening. Several people stopped and asked her about using herbs for various ailments, and she answered all of them with a smile. Mud marred her white shorts, but nothing marred her spirits.

Josh nudged him. "Keep your eyes to yourself, buck."

Curtis straightened with a grin. "That's the pot calling the kettle black. You can't seem to quit watching Sara."

Josh grinned. "No crime in eyeing a pretty woman."

"Exactly." He thrust his shovel into the soft dirt with his boot. When he lifted it, he saw something white. "What do we have here?" Kneeling, Curtis brushed the soil away to reveal a plastic bag filled with white powder. "Whoa, I think we'd better call Tom over here."

"Cocaine?"

Both men had stopped their fair share of drug runners when they patrolled in a Coast Guard boat. Curtis motioned to Tom, who hiked up his pants and walked over the rows to join them.

Curtis stepped back from the cocaine. "Not sure how this got here."

Tom's eyes narrowed. "Someone buried it out here. Seems a weird place to hide it." He knelt and undid the twist tie, then stuck his finger in the powder and tasted it. Grimacing, he closed the top again. "Cocaine."

This plot had belonged to Gina. Tom probably knew that, which was why he was staring at Curtis so intently.

Tom poked in the dirt with the toe of his boot. "Did Gina come here often?" His tone was casual, too casual.

"She brought Raine here to play sometimes. It was quiet." The area was secluded by the church and obscured by a perimeter of trees.

"Can I have your shovel?"

Curtis handed it to him. "I stopped when I found this bag."

Tom grunted in response and began to turn up shovelfuls of dirt. A few minutes later four more bags lay drying in the sun. By now, several of the townspeople circled the three of them. Curtis looked around and saw Amy standing near him. Her eyes were wide. He knew it looked bad. He had to bite his tongue to hold back a defense of his sister.

Raine in her arms, Edith stepped to his side. "What's this all about, Curtis? That's not what it looks like, is it?"

"Looks like it's cocaine. Tom checked."

What a day for this to happen with the entire town out in force. News of this would race through the island. Raine reached for him, and he took her. She was getting tired, and he swayed and hummed when she put her head on his shoulder. The distraction helped him stare down the curious glances. What did Amy think? He didn't have to wonder long because she came to his side.

The sun gleamed in her hair. "Need help with Raine? Looks like you have your hands full here."

"You can take her when she's asleep. She'll squawk if I move her now." He gestured to the bags of drugs. "Guess you know what that is."

Her expression was resigned. "Gives a little more credence to our suspicions about drugs, doesn't it?"

"Not necessarily. Anyone could have put them here."

Even he could hear the defensiveness in his voice. Did he know Gina really? Or did she have a good mask firmly in place?

Tom straightened and thrust the tip of the shovel into the ground. "Looks like that's all there is. I'd better give the DEA boys a call. This is worth a lot of money."

"How long do you think it's been here?"

"Several months. The bags have drawn moisture."

Long enough that Gina could have put them here. "Have you heard anything about a missing drug shipment?" Had there been any alerts that had come through for the Coast Guard? He didn't typically pay attention to those since his current duties were more for rescue than for drug interdiction.

"Nothing current that I can think of." Tom heaved a sigh. "We can check for prints, but I'd guess nothing will show up." His penetrating glance pierced Curtis. "You notice anything off with Gina? Or Ben?"

Amy's hands curled into fists. "Ben had nothing to do with this."

Curtis straightened. "Just because Gina owned this property doesn't mean anything. Anyone could have hidden them here."

His words sounded lame. Edith dabbed at her eyes. Even she appeared to be ready to pronounce Gina guilty. Raine was a dead-weight in his arm, so he shifted her to the other arm. "I guess we'd better stop planting until DEA does their thing. They're liable to trample our herbs."

Tom shook his head. "They'll bring in dogs so maybe they won't have to dig up the entire field."

Amy came closer to Curtis's side. "I'll take her if you need to handle this."

He passed the sleeping child to her. "I think this is out of my hands. Tom can take it from here. How about we get something to eat?"

"You need something high powered. Like fudge." Amy's smile was impish as though she wanted to lighten his spirits.

"Only if it has macadamia nuts."

"And chocolate chips."

Edith fell in beside them. "And dried cherries."

Amy paused to shift Raine. "And peanut butter! It has to have peanut butter."

The farther he walked away from the field, the better he felt. Gina couldn't have had anything to do with the drugs. He'd bet his life on it.

TWENTY-FIVE

Amy's tongue still smiled from the fudge she'd eaten as she allowed the attendant on the back of the boat to strap her into the parasail rig harness beside Curtis. "I can't believe I let you talk me into this."

The only excuse for her insanity was the pain she'd glimpsed in his face when he found those drugs. She would have agreed to almost anything to bring his smile back.

His grin widened, and the lock of sun-lightened hair that fell over his forehead made him look about fifteen. "I'll hang on to you. I won't let you fall. Promise."

Such a dependable guy. She smiled back. "If I die, I'll come back to haunt you."

The bar in front of her looked sturdy enough, and she wore a life vest. The harness went around her thighs as well, so the rig fully supported her. Once they were in position, the attendant backed away and the kite began to fill with air.

Amy nearly shrieked when the first bump came that began to lift them from the platform. "I've changed my mind!"

But it was too late. The breeze lifted the kite into the air, and in seconds, the waves and the boat receded in the distance. The salty wind rushed through her hair and into her face. Mindless with terror, she clung to the bar in front of her. It was quieter up here than she had imagined. The purr of the boat engine seemed far away.

Curtis's eyes were laughing, but he reached over and put his hand on top of hers. "Breathe. Lean back and relax. Imagine God has you in the palm of his hand."

His words brought an image to her mind that calmed her breathing. She tried to do as he suggested, but she still clasped the bar in a death grip. All she wanted to do was get down from this thing.

The wind lifted them high enough to see the old lighthouse ruins and Tidewater Inn. He pointed out a glimpse of Rosemary Cottage to her, just past the maritime forest. She was beginning to relax when she saw a black car speeding along the shore road. Gina's neighbor had mentioned a black Mercedes.

She pointed it out. "Is that a Mercedes?"

He squinted in the bright light for a moment, then nodded. "I think so."

"You don't think it could be the same one, do you?"

"It's not likely." The car stopped at the quay parking lot. "I could be wrong though. It's parked by her condo. We're too far away to make out the license number. You're thinking about what Leah said."

From this distance, it was impossible to make out any features on the man who got out of the car. And Amy was certain it was a man because of the dark suit. "I think it's the same guy." She looked at the harness holding them aloft. "There's no way to get down there and see who it is, is there?"

"No, honey, we're stuck here. I can wave to the boat and let them know we've had enough, but it's going to take nearly an hour to get the boat to the dock, get my vehicle, and make it back to town." He pointed. "And he's leaving already."

The word *honey* on his lips sounded so good. She sighed and sagged in the harness. "What if he's the one involved in the drugs? There might be another contact at the condo. We only talked to Leah. There might be another person who knows something. We were so excited to get that flash drive that we didn't investigate further."

"True enough. A little shortsighted, I guess." He shuffled in the harness, and the kite veered in the wind.

She clutched at his hand. "Don't do that!"

"I might do it more if it means you'll hold my hand." His eyes held a teasing light.

"I've got you in a death hold." She tried to get her grip to loosen, but touching him gave her a sense of security.

His expression went serious. "I don't mind. I'm glad you came to the island, Amy."

She couldn't look away. "I'm glad too."

Clouds gathered above them, and the first few drops of rain began to fall. A shout came from below, and one of the men on board the boat waved at them, then made a cutting motion across his neck.

"Looks like our ride is about over. Want to go again?"

She looked down at the whitecaps. He'd kept his promise and hadn't let her fall. "You think I'll get over my fear if we try it again?"

"I'm sure of it."

"I'll think about it."

She looked again at the road. There was no sign of the black car, but whoever he'd met might still be around at the condos. "Let's take a jaunt to the condos when we get down. We saw which building he went in."

Curtis nodded. "Gina's." His voice was grim.

"What if she'd seen something and she had to be silenced?"

Curtis's brows rose. "You're beginning to believe in Gina?"

His hopeful tone made her lungs squeeze. It wasn't that she believed in Gina, but she wanted to see that haunted expression leave his face. "Maybe."

———

Before going to the condos, Curtis detoured to the ferry, but it had already departed with the black Mercedes aboard. He reversed direction, then drove back to town and parked in front of Gina's building. Settling his do-rag on his head, he got out and opened the door for Amy, who was running a comb through her wind-blown curls.

She got out. "I've got salt on my legs, and my hair is a mess."

"You look beautiful." He shut the door behind her. The wind-tossed look suited her pixie face.

Smiling, she shook her head. "I think you need glasses."

They walked to the front of the building. No one was at the entrance, though he heard a television blaring from inside. A couple of kids had drawn chalk figures on the sidewalk, but there was no sign of them now, even though it was Saturday. "We could start with Leah. Maybe she saw something."

"Good idea." She stepped into the hall where the stairway was and went up to Leah's door.

He rapped his knuckles on the door, but the television noise wasn't coming from inside her place. The apartment felt empty.

"They're on vacation."

He turned at the man's voice behind him. The speaker leaned in the doorway across the hall. About eighteen or nineteen, he wore exercise shorts that showed pasty white legs. A sweatband held his long hair out of his face.

"Do you know when they'll be back?" Amy asked.

The young man shrugged. "Next week, I think."

Curtis took a step toward him. "I'm Gina Ireland's brother. We saw a man driving a black Mercedes come in here. Did you see him?"

The guy nodded. "Grant something. Don't know his last name. He had a key to Gina's place and went inside for a few minutes."

"The condo is empty. At least I thought it was. The landlord hasn't managed to rent it again yet."

The kid shrugged. "I thought it was a little weird myself. Far as I know, no one has been in there since your sister left."

Curtis glanced at the door. "Was the apartment left unlocked?"

"I didn't try it." A female voice called behind the guy, and he started to close the door. "Gotta go."

The door shut and Curtis looked at Amy. "Let's see if we can get in. I have Gina's key. Edith found it in her things, and we never dropped it off to the landlord. I think it's in my glove box. Wait here."

He jogged out to the Jeep and found the key in the bottom of the glove box. When he returned, he found Amy trying the door. "Any luck?"

She stepped back. "It's locked, but I just realized I probably shouldn't have touched the knob. We could call Tom to see about getting prints."

"The guy didn't do anything illegal. At least that we know of." He inserted the key in the lock, then heard a click when he turned it. "The lock hasn't been changed at least."

The knob turned easily in his hand, and the door opened without a squeak. The rush of stale air made him wrinkle his nose. "Look." The carpet held foot imprints. "Looks like the landlord vacuumed, then someone tracked in here on it several times."

The prints led across the living room and through the bedroom door, straight to the closet, then back again. Whoever had been in here had made the trip at least twice. The closet door stood open, but the shelves were empty. He flipped on the light and examined the empty space. "I think there was a box there."

Amy stared at the shelf he'd pointed out, an eight-by-eight square that didn't have dust on it. "So whatever it was had been here awhile. Should we call Tom and suggest he talk to the landlord?"

"Yeah, I think we'd better." He whipped out his cell phone and placed the call. Tom promised to come right over.

As he talked to the sheriff, Curtis watched Amy wander the room. Her tousled dark curls framed a face rosy from their afternoon of parasailing. Expressions flitted across her face, emotions he wanted to examine to see what made her tick. Was she thinking about her brother and his role in Gina's life? Did she regret she'd never been a friend to Gina?

Curtis had plenty of regrets himself. His work demanded leaving family gatherings at the drop of a hat, and he'd often been distracted when Gina wanted to talk to him. If he could go back now and do it over again, he would have been more intent on listening to her and being there for her.

Guilt couldn't change anything now though. All he could do was go forward and not make the same mistake with Raine or Edith. Or even Amy, if their relationship led to more than friendship. He wanted to travel this little path in life's road with her and see if it led to a joined future. It just might. He'd never been so intrigued by a woman.

She turned around and smiled at his stare. "What? Do I have dirt on my nose?"

"No, I was just thinking about kissing you again."

Color bloomed in her cheeks, but she didn't look away. "That might not be the best idea."

He approached her. "Why? Am I moving too fast? I'm beginning to care about you, Amy. Don't you want to see where it might lead?"

He cupped her face with his palm, and she held her ground.

"There's a lot you don't know about me. I don't think we would suit one another in the long run."

"Why not?"

Pain darkened her eyes, but she didn't tell him what was holding her back. Was it his job or the fact that he was raising Raine? She liked children, so he couldn't see how the baby might give her pause.

"Tell me." His words were soft.

She opened her mouth, but Tom hollered from the living room.

"We'll talk about this later," Curtis said.

TWENTY-SIX

Delicious aromas filled Amy's kitchen as she and Libby put final touches on the Saturday dinner. She planned to have them all eat on the deck since there was a large table that seated eight out there. Her tummy rumbled at the aroma of crab chowder, steamed lobster, and au gratin potatoes. She'd even made coconut cream pie for dessert.

She glanced at Libby, who looked happy and healthy in her denim shorts and red-and-white sleeveless top. It was hard to believe she'd given birth two weeks ago. "Thanks for the lobster. We're going to have a terrific feast thanks to you." She held out a leftover spoonful of coconut pie filling. "Tell me if it's okay."

Libby licked the spoon. "It's perfect. Zach pulled in a big haul, and we were happy to share." She tipped her head and listened. "There's no screaming going on in the living room."

"Yet." Amy stirred the lobster bisque. "If there's a way to make peace between my parents and Curtis, I'd sure like to know what it is."

Libby put the spoon into the dishwasher. "Time, honey. That's the only thing that will work. And as they come to love Raine more and more, they'll appreciate all Curtis is doing for her."

"I'm worried the custody fight will turn our relationship into an adversarial one. No matter who wins, the loser will hold a grudge."

Libby nodded. "Curtis would never recover from losing Raine. He dotes on that child."

"She's all he has left of Gina. Just as she's all we have left of Ben. The battle lines are drawn, and it's going to be a bloody fight."

Libby leaned on the counter and crossed her arms. "There's a personal stake in this for you. I've seen the way you and Curtis look at each other."

Heat ran up Amy's neck to her cheeks. "I won't bother trying to deny it. He kissed me the other day, and I ran away. I can't risk my heart. Not after . . ."

"After?"

Amy set the spoon on the rest. "I was engaged once. Two years ago. The engagement lasted all of three months, until I got sick."

"I didn't know that. What happened?"

She turned to check the lobsters. They were nearly done. Maybe it wasn't the right time to get into this. "How important do you think honesty is to a relationship?"

"It's everything. It would be like hiding part of yourself from yourself. Curtis doesn't know about your engagement?"

Amy shook her head. "It's not the engagement that's the problem. It's why my fiancé broke it off. I think any man is going to run away when he finds out."

"Finds out what?"

She turned to watch Libby's expression when she heard the news. "That I had cancer. And I can't have any children."

Libby gasped, and the color drained from her face. "Cancer? Are you all right?"

Amy nodded. "I've been cancer-free for two years now, but every time I need to get checked, it's scary. I—I need to get my blood checked again, but I've been putting it off, which is silly. I can't image putting someone I love through that constant worry."

After losing Ben, she knew what it was like to be on the other end of loss. The guilt, the what-ifs, the regrets. The thought of putting Curtis through the roller coaster she went through every three months made her shudder. It was better to go through life alone than to cause that kind of pain in someone she loved.

Libby seemed to read her mind. "Since Curtis just lost his sister, you think he'll be quick to run from a relationship where he might face a loss again. He's a bigger man than that, Amy."

"Well, he *should* run from something like that. I would."

Libby rolled her eyes. "Let me get this straight. If you found out Curtis had faced cancer and had won, you would walk away just in case it came back?"

The wisdom in Libby's words stopped her. "I don't know. Loss is hard, Libby. It's a valley I don't ever want to walk through again. There have been days I didn't think I could survive Ben's death."

Libby's eyes softened, and she reached over to squeeze Amy's hand. "None of us wants to face death, but it comes to everyone. Death is part of life. I think you should tell Curtis."

"I don't want to. Not yet."

Libby pulled down glasses from the cabinet. "So you're going to let fear rule you."

Amy winced. "No, I'm just not going to go into something so personal."

"You're holding back who you really are from Curtis. Hiding the real Amy behind those eyes. Half an hour ago I would have said you feared nothing, but you do. You're afraid of being judged, yet you're judging how everyone else will react."

Libby's words hit her hard, and she pressed her hand to her stomach. "I'm not afraid."

But as she gave the denial, she knew it was a lie. She wanted people to like her. She was quick to judge others and to assume what people would think, but she was afraid to be up front about who she really was. Maybe Libby was right, but she couldn't bear to see Curtis retreat when he heard the news.

The thought of telling Curtis the truth made her quail. Could she trust him with the truth? What if he left her too? Her feelings about him were already entangled, and ripping them out by the roots would be more painful than she was prepared to face.

———

Raine slept on her chest, and Amy didn't want to move. The Bournes had gone home an hour ago, and her parents had gone to bed, but though Curtis had offered to take Raine and leave, she'd shaken her head and held the little girl close.

What if she pursued custody herself? Raine might be the only child she could ever raise. And she was a tiny piece of Ben. The thought grew in her mind. It would mean the end of any budding relationship with Curtis, but was there a future anyway? Her medical history indicated otherwise.

He tossed a pillow at her. "Penny for your thoughts."

"They're not even worth that." She shifted Raine a bit. The baby's hair lay in damp curls on her forehead. "She's as hot as an August afternoon."

"Lay her on the sofa." He rose from his favorite armchair by the fireplace and came toward her. "Need some help?"

"I can do it." She eased the sleeping child onto the cushion, then fanned herself. "I think I need some iced tea."

"Me too."

When she rose, she pulled the other cushion from the couch and dropped it on the floor so if Raine happened to roll off, she'd fall onto the soft surface. A couple of throw pillows tucked against the child helped ensure her safety. Curtis and Amy went to the kitchen where she poured glasses of iced tea.

There was a rattle outside. "What on earth? It sounds like someone is in the trash." She threw open the door and stepped onto the deck. The banker pony was nosing in her metal trash can. His tail swished as if he liked whatever he was eating. "I didn't know horses ate garbage."

"Bet you've got the corncobs from dinner in there, don't you? They love corn." He tried to shoo the horse away, but the pony ignored him.

"Fabio, get out of there." She slapped the horse on the rump, and he backed his head out and snorted as if to ask her why she was being so mean.

Curtis lifted a brow. "Fabio?" He snickered. "What kind of name is that for a horse?"

Her face went hot. "Er, Fabio is a male actor who poses on romance novels. Don't you think my horse looks like a star?"

His grin widened. "Romance novels, huh? You read those things?"

"Every woman likes a little happily-ever-after."

She tugged on the pony's mane and managed to get him away from the trash can. Fabio snorted and jerked his head but went along with her bidding. She hadn't realized that Curtis had followed until his hands came down on her shoulders. From behind, he pulled her against his chest and rested his chin on her head. Cradled like this, she could enjoy his touch without him seeing her expression.

"I think even guys like to think happiness with one woman for life exists." His breath stirred her hair as he spoke.

One partner for life. Was it too good to be true? She opened her mouth to tell him about her situation, then closed it again. Wouldn't he think it presumptuous to tell him when he hadn't said a word about holding any special feelings for her? For all she knew, he might not have the same strong yearning squeezing his heart that she had pressing on hers. This romance stuff was hard.

Fabio hadn't wandered far. He stood a few feet away, tossing his head as if he wanted her to notice him. "Do you think he'd let me ride him? By now, he knows me pretty well."

"The bankers are pretty docile, but he might throw you."

She moved out of the shelter of his embrace to lay her palm against the horse's rough coat. Fabio's skin quivered under her fingertips. "Easy, boy." She ran a caressing hand along his back. "Give me a boost, Curtis."

"I'm not so sure about this." But he came to her side and laced his fingers together for her to step into.

She put her bare foot in his hands, and he helped lift her onto Fabio's back. The horse jumped when her weight settled on his back. He stamped his feet and neighed, a nervous, high-pitched sound. She patted his neck. "Easy."

Her fingers tangled into his mane, and she touched her heels to his flank. He reacted immediately and bolted for the trees. "Whoa, whoa!" She tightened her grip on his mane and held on as best she could, though her backside was sliding to one side.

The trees loomed nearer, and she leaned down with her cheek to the horse's sweaty neck. His eyes rolled back in his head. It would be better to bail off now before he entered the trees. At least there would be grass to stop her fall. She was sliding more to the left, so she kicked free and released her grip on his mane.

In the next moment, she hit the ground. She felt the jar in every bone of her body. Pain traveled up her arm and into her neck, and the fall knocked the breath from her lungs. She lay on the ground and struggled to draw in a breath.

"Amy!" Curtis was by her side. He touched her head and ran his fingers down her cheek. "Are you hurt? Can you talk?"

She wanted to tell him she'd be fine if she could just get her lungs to work, but she didn't have enough breath to speak. Then a rush of oxygen expanded her chest, and she drank in the sweet taste of the night air. She nodded, and he slid his hand under her and helped her into a seated position.

He cradled her close. "You scared the fire out of me. I couldn't lose you too." He pressed his lips against her forehead in a fervent kiss.

Her fists clutched his shirt, and she clung to him and willed him to kiss her. His lips came down on hers, and as she tasted the passion in his kiss, she allowed herself to believe that maybe, just maybe, they had something enduring between them.

TWENTY-SEVEN

A my palpated Mindy Stewart's belly, then listened to the baby's heartbeat. She looped her stethoscope around her neck and smiled. "Everything looks good, Mindy. The baby is growing, and your weight is excellent. Your little one should be making her appearance in about four weeks."

Mindy swung her legs off the table and hopped down. "I'm so glad you're here, Amy. Can you give me a list of the things I need to have ready for a home delivery?"

Amy handed her a list of the items to purchase. "If you'd like to order a kit online, some companies I work with will send everything together. They have a fair price on it too."

She walked Mindy to the door and waved her off. She loved this part of her chosen career—the excitement of preparing for new life, the visualizing of the new family unit. Women on the island had heard she was staying. Her week already had a few appointments, and she made a mental note to call her supervising physician and give him a list of the new patients. Though he would not see them, he needed to affirm the fact that she wasn't taking on too much.

And she'd finally made an appointment to get her blood drawn again. Now she would be on tenterhooks every time the phone rang.

Her parents had left this morning, thank goodness. Now she could get back to figuring out what had happened to Ben. There were no more patients today, and she intended to track down Curtis. Saturday night's interlude still made her breath catch in her throat. She was going to have to tell him, though she dreaded it. If he wasn't busy today, she'd spill the truth. Her parents had attended church with her yesterday, and Curtis hadn't been there. Amy had heard he was working, but she had to wonder if the kiss they'd shared had kept him up half the night like it had her.

She changed from her skirt to a pair of shorts, then grabbed her keys and headed for the door. A Harley rumbled to a stop in her drive, and Curtis dismounted. A scowl darkened his expression, and he clutched a piece of paper in his hand. With a sinking feeling, she suspected she knew what was on it. The warm feeling she'd started the day with evaporated.

She waited for him on the porch. "Hi, I was just coming to see you."

He waved the paper in the air as he bounded up the steps. "Your parents didn't waste any time. This is an order to have a paternity test done on Raine."

"You can't blame them for wanting to be sure." She sat on a white rocker and pointed to the other one. "Have a seat."

He paced the floor in front of her. "I called my attorney on his vacation, and he said it's standard procedure to establish paternity before suing for custody. So that's clearly their plan."

"I'm sorry, Curtis. Truly. It's what I feared would happen, but I tried to talk them out of it." She softened her tone in hopes that it would help him calm down.

He dropped into the other rocker. "It's about Gina's past, isn't it?" His gaze cut away, then came back to her. "I know there was a revolving door of men in her life. One-night stands, relationships that lasted two weeks, and everything in between. But that all changed when she became a Christian. It really did, Amy. Then she had Raine and she was so happy. She wasn't seeing anyone but Ben and hadn't since she got pregnant." He held up the papers. "But this makes me wonder if your parents heard of her past."

Amy didn't want to tell him, but she had to be honest. "I told them about Gina's past, Curtis. I thought it would be better coming from me than for their attorney to dig it up. It's not like it was a secret."

He stared at her. "*You* told them?"

"This is a small island. They would have heard it sooner or later."

"And you judged her. You haven't believed a word I've told you about how she changed."

She ducked her head. She had been judge and jury to Gina. But didn't she have the right to question everything? The entire tapestry of Raine's heritage was woven with deceit. "I'm sorry, but can you blame me? You never even told us of her existence. We've all been shut out of the relationship. I wondered if this was why Ben didn't marry her," she said. "Ben had political aspirations. He'd been considering a run for the North Carolina House of Representatives. Reporters would have been quick to dig up any dirt on Gina."

His mouth opened, then he clamped it shut and looked away.

She didn't care for his expression—as if he'd bitten into something rotten. "What?"

He shrugged. "I didn't much like Ben, Amy. I'm sorry if that hurts you, but a real man would have stepped up to his responsibilities. Regardless of her past, the fact was that he brought Raine into the world. He needed to be there for her. To love her and care for her needs."

Her chest tightened. "Maybe he wasn't sure Raine was his."

He stared at her. "I had no idea you'd judged Gina so harshly. Haven't you ever made a mistake? Or do you keep it all covered up?"

"Like you're a paragon of truth!" she shot back, panicked that he would see the truth in her face. "Raine is a year old, and you didn't bother to tell us." When he flinched, she knew her barb had struck home. His words had hurt her too. There was much about her past that she hadn't told him. Her own cover-ups were much worse than Gina's. Why hadn't she been honest the minute she stepped foot on this island? After this argument, she doubted she ever would.

She rose and walked toward the front door. "I think we need some refreshments."

He leaped up and caught her arm, then turned her to face him. "Don't walk out on this discussion."

She tugged her arm from his grip. "You didn't really know my brother!" The way her voice rose and then wobbled horrified her.

"Maybe not. But are you sure you did?"

"Are you sure you knew Gina? What about the drugs in the field and the man in the dark suit?" His eyes flickered, and she wished she could take back the words.

He swallowed and nodded. "She might have made mistakes, but she wasn't afraid to own up to them. And she was never a hypocrite, saying one thing and thinking another."

Amy rushed for the screen door and gave it a satisfying slam behind her. She was no hypocrite. It wasn't a sin to hold her tongue.

———

All evening Curtis had regretted calling Amy a hypocrite. He'd been angry when he got that court order, and he lost his cool. Everyone kept their feelings secret, just a little. How many times had he heard his mother say she was fine when someone asked her how she was at church? And he knew perfectly well she was suffering with her arthritis. Or how about the family who was about to lose their house but didn't tell a soul? And he had judged Gina when she was at her wildest himself. It was only later that he began to understand why she acted out.

After tossing and turning all night, he strapped Raine in her car seat and drove to Amy's house. She'd mentioned that she would do office appointments on Mondays and Fridays and do home visits as needed on the other days. Her car was in the drive, so he laid on the horn until she came to the door.

"Sorry, I didn't want to get Raine out of the car seat," he called through the open window. "Want to come with me today? I have to get her DNA testing done at the court, and I thought we'd check on the investigation into the car bombing. Unless you're working."

She didn't smile. "I don't have any home visits today, but why aren't you at work?"

"I took the day off."

She looked cute today with her dark curls caught back in a red headband that had a flower on it. She was barefoot and wore denim shorts that showed off her fabulous tanned legs. He could look at her all day and never grow tired of it.

"Want to come, then?" When she hesitated, he added, "I'm sorry about last night. I was out of line."

Her nod was grudging. "Let me grab my sandals."

When she disappeared back inside the cottage, he let out the breath he was holding. Inhaling, he prayed that he could let go of the anger he'd been carrying around. It wouldn't do any of them any good. They were supposed to be working together. And if he was honest with himself, he wanted more than friendship to develop between them.

That kiss Saturday night had changed something between them. He handed Raine some cheese crackers and waited.

When Amy came back out, she had changed her top to a blue ruffled one, and she wore some kind of woven shoes on her feet.

When she buckled the seat belt, he caught a whiff of a flowery scent that wasn't artificial.

"I smell flowers. Been working in the garden?"

She nodded. "I planted a lot of herbs today, medicinal and kitchen. That dratted Fabio keeps tearing up my patch, so I hired someone to fence it in. It's safe from the pony now. He seems to like me, even though he about had a heart attack when I got on his back."

He slanted a grin her way. "Who wouldn't like you? And can I help with the gardening?"

"I can do it. I like gardening." Her tone was still stiff. She turned around and smiled at Raine. "Hello, sweetheart."

Raine held up a book. "Read."

"In a little while."

"Now." The baby threw the book to the floor.

Amy glanced at him without smiling. "She's quite the general." She released her belt and leaned over to grab the book. Raine grabbed it and began to flip through the pages. Amy snapped herself back into the seat belt, then kicked off her shoes.

He rolled his eyes and nodded. "I have to start curbing that, but it's so darn cute." He started the Jeep and put it in drive. "I said I was sorry, Amy. I think you're still mad at me."

She stared straight ahead. "Maybe I am. I don't know that it's wise for us to be friends, Curtis. This is going to end badly, no matter what happens."

What did she mean? Or was it his imagination that she put special emphasis on the word *wise*? And how could she know it would end badly? There were worse things to overcome than prickly parents.

He said nothing at first as he concentrated on steering the Jeep around some tourists heading to the water with boogie boards and beach bags. "It's not going to be easy, but when I got home last night, I realized that I'm not willing to give up our friendship just because we might have a spat or two. If we keep things out in the open between us, we can navigate through this."

He glanced at her when she didn't answer. What was she thinking? His words should have reassured her, not caused her face to go pale. She looked out the window at first too, and not at him.

The leather seat squeaked when she finally turned a bit to face him. "And what if my parents get custody? I don't think that's a hurdle we can get past."

He pressed his lips together. "They won't get custody."

Sadness and resignation hovered in the depths of her eyes and in the twist of her mouth. "And how will I deal with being caught between you and them? Because I know my father, Curtis. If he loses, he won't forget it. And he'll consider you an enemy as long as he lives."

He knew what she was saying. The things that drew them together were tenuous, and the feelings were beginning to be deeper than mere friendship. So what if their relationship progressed to something more—like marriage? How could it survive open hostility from her parents?

He parked in front of the courthouse. "Let's worry about that if it comes."

None of the businesses were open yet, but the town offices opened at eight. The ice-cream store across the street wouldn't hang their sign out until eleven. The no-parking zone in front of the town office had been freshly painted a gleaming yellow, and he pulled into the small parking lot instead. The nurse's office was in the basement of the big stone building with a green door. She dispensed immunizations, and Tom had told Curtis that she could collect a court-approved saliva sample.

He got out and unbuckled Raine. "Why don't you go talk to Tom while I have the nurse collect the sample?"

Amy hopped out and looked doubtfully at Raine. "Will it hurt her?"

"It's just a cotton swab. I'll meet you there in a few minutes."

Curtis was glad to escape into the cool confines of the basement. Amy's warning still reverberated in his heart. Maybe they needed to go their separate ways. Someone was going to get hurt.

TWENTY-EIGHT

Tom leaned back in the chair with his feet on his desk. He had a cup of coffee in his hand when Amy stepped into the sheriff's office. There was one bulb out in the overhead fixture. The dimness of the lighting made her think of an old-time movie where the heroine was in a private detective's dingy office building. The only part of this scene that didn't match was the female deputy filing paperwork in a shiny gray cabinet.

Amy had forgotten Mindy worked here. "Mindy, your ankles look a little swollen. Can you do some of that work at your desk with your feet up?"

Mindy turned with a smile. "I'm nearly done here, and then I'll rest. I haven't been working too hard."

Tom's feet hit the floor. "Amy. I was going to call you today." He perched his cup precariously on a stack of papers and reached for a manila folder on his right. "Got an interesting report back from the shark expert. Coffee?"

The coffee smelled stale from here, and the concoction in the pot behind him looked as thick as tar. "No coffee for me, thanks." She took the folder he extended. "Interesting in what way?" Without waiting for his answer, she flipped open the folder and glanced at the paper. "'Not consistent with any known species of shark.' What does that mean?"

His expression perplexed, he leaned back. "It means the bite marks on Ben's board weren't made by a shark."

"What made them, then?" She eyed the picture that came with the report. "They are clearly teeth marks."

Tom raised his brows. "If you read the second page, you'll see my expert thinks they were man-made to mimic a shark."

"Mimic a shark? That's just plain weird. Unless the murderer was trying to make sure no one went looking for Ben's body and found a bullet hole in it."

"You might be right."

A lump formed in her throat. It was one thing to suspect someone murdered Ben and quite another to be faced with this reality. Who could hate him enough to want him dead?

"So this adds weight to the murder hypothesis," Tom said, his tone heavy. He poured more of the black mud coffee into his cup, then took a swig and exhaled. "That's good stuff."

She swallowed past the constriction in her throat. "What about his wallet? Did it tell you anything?"

"No fingerprints except for Ben's." Tom's gaze lingered on her face. "I gotta tell you, Amy, we saw signs of a struggle in the clearing where you found the wallet. I think he might have been killed there, then dumped in the Atlantic. And another thing—his cell phone records are missing. All those things seem to point to foul play of some kind."

The strength went out of her legs, and she grabbed the back of the chair, then sank onto the seat. "But what about Ned? He saw Ben surfing. Is he a suspect?"

"Let's say he's a person of interest. Right now he claims he didn't see Ben for several hours and finally called the Coasties. It's possible Ben got out and Ned didn't see him. Ben could have headed back to the cottage for something, been accosted there, and then disposed of when Ned wasn't watching. But I could be wrong about Ned."

She shook her head. The door opened behind her, but the noise barely penetrated Amy's daze. "What motive would Ned have for killing Ben though? I like him. He doesn't seem like the murderous sort. I don't suspect him, not really."

Curtis spoke behind her. "What's going on? Amy, are you okay?" His hand touched her shoulder and settled there.

She covered his hand with hers and turned to face him. Raine smiled and reached for her, and she cuddled the baby close, relishing the bit of Ben she had left in that moment. "We have more evidence that Ben was murdered." She handed him the report and explained what it meant.

He exhaled and went white, then looked at Tom. "What about Gina? Any progress on finding the person who struck her? Because if Ben was murdered . . ."

"Then there is likely more to Gina's death too."

Tom shook his head. "I pursued every lead when she died, but that ski boat never surfaced. You said it had blue lettering, but all you could make out was an *S* and a *Y*. There wasn't much to go on."

"It was too far away to see well." His gaze was intent. "And what about the condo? Anything turn up when you had forensics go over it?"

"One interesting fact. There was a trace of cocaine on the bedroom shelf."

Amy gasped, and Curtis took a step forward. "The same stuff as we found?"

Tom shrugged. "We don't know that yet. It's still in the lab."

If Gina was selling drugs, did that mean Ben was involved? Amy saw where this was heading, and she didn't want to believe it any more than Curtis wanted to believe it of his sister.

She turned to stare into his face. Raine was asleep on her shoulder. "Could you see who was driving, whether it was a male or female?"

He sat down and put his hands on his thighs. "No, nothing. I was too focused on trying to save Gina and didn't grab my binoculars." His voice was flat and controlled, but his fingers tightened convulsively on his pant leg. "I was too late."

"It's just horrible," Amy whispered. "Why would someone want them both dead? There has to be a connection we're missing."

Curtis looked at the report in his hands again. "Any lead on the money I told you about in both their accounts?"

The sheriff shook his head. "Not yet. We haven't even figured out what bank the money is in. Once we do, I can get a court order to track where it came from."

As they said their good-byes to Tom, Mindy finished her filing and moved toward her desk. When she turned around, Amy noticed her face was swollen and red now too. The long pants she wore strained at the seams, and they weren't long enough to hide the way her ankles dripped over her shoes. She passed Raine to Curtis and moved to intercept Mindy.

"Are you feeling all right?" She took Mindy's hand, then pushed her thumb against the woman's swollen wrist. When she released her thumb, there was a remaining indentation in Mindy's skin.

Mindy put her hand to her forehead. "I—I don't feel very well. My vision is a little blurry, and I think I might have the flu."

Amy guided her to a chair. "Feel like you're going to vomit?"

The deputy nodded. "And my head is pounding." Her skin was white with a greenish tint.

"I think you have preeclampsia." Amy glanced at the sheriff. "She needs to go home and get straight into bed. I'll get my ultrasound and pressure cuff to check her out. She might need to go to the hospital."

Looking concerned, Tom got up and came around the end of his desk. "Can she drive? I can run her home."

"I'd rather she didn't. We'll take her home." She looked to Curtis for agreement and he nodded. "When did you have your last checkup with the doctor?"

Mindy licked her lips. "Two weeks ago. I was fine on Monday when I saw you. Is this serious?" Her brown eyes were scared. "Is my baby all right?"

"I need to get your blood pressure, and we'll assess what needs to be done. For now, you need to get into bed on your left side so the baby is off your organs. No salt either. And you're going to need to eat more protein and get more water in you."

"But the baby?"

Amy patted her shoulder. "The baby is fine. Now let's get you home."

At least she knew what to do for Mindy. Amy had no idea how to bring justice to her brother.

—

Curtis's call to Edith went directly to voice mail. She was probably surfing. He'd told her she had the morning to do what she wanted, but he hadn't expected an emergency to pop up. Amy was too tense for this preeclampsia thing to be minor. He had no choice but to bring Raine along with them to Mindy's house. At least the little one was sleeping and wouldn't pick up on the seriousness of the situation.

They exited into bright sunlight and the smell of exhaust from a passing truck. The *putt-putt* of a fishing rig going out to sea came over the noise of a couple of bicycles going past, and several fishermen called out their catches at the pier.

Mindy winced and stopped at the curb. "The light hurts my

head." She doubled over by the storm sewer grate. "I'm going to throw up!"

Amy shot an alarmed glance at Curtis. She went to Mindy's side and soothed her as the woman vomited into the street. "Better?"

Mindy nodded and wiped her mouth with the back of her hand. "I need to lie down." Her voice was a whisper.

"Yes, you do." She maneuvered Mindy into the backseat of Curtis's Jeep, then stepped out to his side. "I think she might need to be taken to the hospital. This seems to have escalated into eclampsia. I'll stabilize her while you get the Coasties chopper readied."

"You can't help her?"

Amy shook her head. "If she has full-blown eclampsia, she'll need to deliver right away. And it can be dangerous for her and the baby, so she needs a doctor. It will likely take a C-section."

"How can you tell if it's the full-blown kind?"

"There are certain signs—" Amy's eyes widened as she looked at the vehicle again. "Oh no!"

Was Mindy thrashing around or asking for help? Her arms were jerking in the air.

Amy jerked open the back door. "She's convulsing! Call for a chopper. We've got to get her to a hospital!"

He yanked out his cell phone and called headquarters. The Coast Guard helicopter could lift her to the hospital in Nags Head. Once they were readying the chopper, he tried Edith again but still didn't reach her. What was he going to do with Raine? She awakened and smiled at him. He had to find someone to take her, or he'd have to ask the Coast Guard to find a substitute for him.

He saw a familiar figure across the street, and relief coursed through him. "Heather!" Waving her over, he went to meet her at the edge of the walk.

She wore a cover-up over her bathing suit and flip-flops. A red, white, and yellow beach bag was slung over one shoulder. "Hi, Curtis. Is everything okay? You look upset. I decided to make it a beach day today. It's way too nice to be inside."

He didn't try to hide his urgency. "Are you busy? I'm in a bit of a bind. We need to fly a patient to the hospital, and I can't get hold of Edith."

Her eyes brightened, and she dropped her beach bag onto the sidewalk. "So you need me to take Raine for you? I'd be glad to." She reached for his niece, and he handed her over.

"Would you mind? Edith should be back home in an hour. Here." He pulled forty dollars from his wallet. "This should cover it."

She pushed away the bills. "Whoa, I won't take money for helping out a friend. Does she have a diaper bag?" Shifting Raine to one shoulder, she dropped a kiss on her hair.

He ran to the Jeep and extracted the diaper bag, then carried it back to where Heather stood with Raine. "I can't tell you how much I appreciate this. You're a real lifesaver."

She kissed Raine again. "I'm glad to help. Really. I've been wanting to watch her for ages."

He took several steps back toward his vehicle. "You can wait at my house for Edith. Raine's room is upstairs. You can't miss the baby bed." He grinned, relieved he'd found a solution to his problem. "The house is unlocked. Help yourself to anything in the kitchen. I think Edith was making guacamole. The chips are in the corner cupboard."

Heather smiled. "Don't worry. I have it all under control. Go save whoever you have to."

He watched her carry Raine down the street in the direction of his house. A vague disquiet disturbed him, and he pushed it away. There wasn't anything wrong with asking for help.

He retraced his steps to the Jeep and slid behind the wheel.

"The chopper is waiting. Let's get her loaded. How is she?" Amy had gotten Mindy on the seat with her feet elevated by the car seat.

"A little more stable. She's not convulsing at the moment." She frowned. "Where's Raine?"

"I couldn't reach Edith on the cell. Then I saw Heather and asked her to take her to my house to wait for Edith. It shouldn't be longer than an hour or so."

She bit her lips. "Oh, Curtis, I wish you hadn't done that. She's not very forthcoming about her past, and I'm sure you never checked her references, did you?"

His unease deepened, and he shook his head. "I never intended to hire her so I didn't bother. I'm sure it's fine. It's only an hour." He slammed his door, then jammed the key into the ignition and started the car.

They were both being unduly nervous about a perfectly innocent request for neighborly help. But the more he argued with himself, the more he wanted to wheel the vehicle around and go retrieve Raine. He had no choice though. Mindy and her baby could die if they didn't get help.

By the time he reached the Coast Guard headquarters, the rest of the team had assembled at the pad. Sara and Josh helped get Mindy aboard. Sara administered magnesium sulfate to make sure Mindy didn't have another seizure on the way.

He started to help Amy aboard, but she stepped back and shook her head. "She'll be safely in the ER in minutes, but I want to go check on Raine. You have Sara. She's well trained in things like this."

"You think there's really something to worry about?" He glanced at the helicopter. "They can go without me. We aren't doing a water rescue."

Her smile looked forced. "I can't even put my finger on why I'm worried, but I am. I'll feel better when I get to your house and see the baby is safe."

Sara beckoned from the helicopter door. "Curtis, come on!"

"Go. It will be fine. I'm sure I'm just being cautious for no good reason."

He gripped her shoulders and brushed a kiss across her lips. "You're a good woman, Amy Lang. Text me when you get to the house, okay?"

She nodded. "And let me know when Mindy is safely delivered to the hospital. I'll be at your house when you get back."

Reluctantly, he released her and headed for his chopper. The ten-minute ride was going to be an eternity. There wasn't anything he could do but pray, and really, wasn't that the best thing anyway? He was worrying for no reason.

TWENTY-NINE

Heather smiled as she stood on the remote beach watching for a boat. The sea breeze ruffled her hair, and Raine's baby girl scent filled her head with success. It had all been so easy. She'd been making plans to enter the house when no one was looking and snatch the baby away, and here fate had just handed her the answer. She wasn't about to refuse a sweet gift like this. She hugged Raine to her. Cute little mite was about to bring her everything she'd ever wanted.

Grant had been elated when she'd called with the news. Her reward had been in hearing him praise her. She shielded her eyes from the glaring sun and looked out to sea. Where was the boat? They had to hurry. No telling how long Curtis would be gone. And he might call Edith to check on Raine. When he found out neither of them was at the house, he'd call the sheriff. No way did Heather want to have her fingerprints taken.

Raine stirred against Heather's shoulder. One small hand curled around a lock of Heather's hair. Heather smiled and touched the tiny fingers. Such a sweetheart. She wished she didn't have to make Curtis and Amy so unhappy. They were going to be really upset when they got to the house and realized Raine was missing.

Her smile faded. They'd know who had taken her too, unless

Grant had a good cover idea. She could only hope he had their tracks covered in some way. Otherwise, her picture would be plastered all over the news. She chewed her lip and considered her options. There weren't many, but she was too elated over her success to think it through. But Grant would know.

The sound of a motor carried over the water. Heather shaded her eyes again and squinted through the glare of the sun on the sea. The white-and-blue boat drew nearer, and she recognized one of Grant's employees at the helm. She thought his name was Vince, but people just called him Bossman. She'd thought Grant would come get her himself. But he was a busy man. An *important* man, so she needed to realize he couldn't always do what he wanted. And once she was taken to him, they could go away on that vacation he'd promised.

She imagined a white-sand beach and turquoise water. A grass-thatched hut where they had a couples massage while they drank piña coladas. Grant would be blown away when he saw her in the new bikini she planned to buy. He'd think she was hot, hot, hot. Life was about to get very fun.

She waved, and the boat veered toward her. She gave Bossman a big smile. "I got her."

He merely grunted and tossed the anchor overboard, then motioned for her to board. No words of praise from him. But she didn't care. Not when Grant was waiting.

She shuffled the baby higher in her arms. "Hold my neck, honey. We're going into the water."

Raine clutched at her and pointed, jabbering something. Wading into the water, Heather made her way toward the craft, a big Sea Ray, as it floated about ten feet offshore. The name on the side read *Sea Nymph*. By the time she reached the boat, she was soaked to her bra line. Raine squealed and reached for the water as if she wanted down.

"Not now, honey." She handed the baby to the man, then climbed the ladder and practically fell onto the deck. "Where's Grant?" Until she boarded, she'd hoped he was belowdeck, but it was clear this boat had no cabin.

She reached out her hands to retrieve Raine, but Bossman shook his head and pointed to a seat. She longed to have the little girl back in her arms. Something about the man had always given her cold chills, and she didn't trust her little cargo with him. "She knows me."

"She'll get to know me." Bossman shifted the little girl to his other arm. "Grant's a busy man. He had me handle this for him."

Handle this. What did that mean? She eyed him, not sure if he was telling her the truth. "He didn't tell me that. He said he was going to come himself."

Bossman shrugged. "What you see is what you get."

Was he laughing at her? She studied the glee in his eyes and tried to decipher what it meant. Maybe he was as glad as she was that their plan had fallen into place. "We need to come up with a cover story. Curtis will know that I took Raine. There needs to be some way to throw off suspicion. Maybe I can call Curtis and say we've both been kidnapped."

Bossman absorbed her fears in silence. Setting Raine on the deck, he reached toward the compartment in the dash and pulled out a revolver. "We've got that covered too." He turned the gun barrel toward her. "I think when they find your body, they'll assume the kid is dead too."

She didn't argue, didn't try to plead with him. Everyone knew this guy was as dangerous as they came. He'd shoot her without blinking an eye. Without thought, she flung her leg over the metal railing that enclosed the deck, then leaped over the edge and into the sea. The cold water closed over her head as she heard a shot.

Something struck her arm, and blood darkened the water.

The salt stung her eyes, but she kept them open anyway so she could see what he was doing.

Bossman looked ghostly through the blur of the water. He leaned over the edge of the boat looking for her.

Panic closed her throat. She kicked as hard as she could and swam under the boat to the other side. Her lungs burned for air, and she had to go up to draw more oxygen in. When she emerged near the back of the boat on the leeward side, she saw him still staring into the water on the other side of the boat. Another boat motored their way, and Bossman muttered a curse. Drawing in silent, shallow breaths, she huddled as close to the side as possible.

Keeping only her nose and eyes above the water line, she watched him fumble with the key. The engine came to life. She dove down as fast as she could. As long as he didn't see her, he would surely see the blood in the water and think he'd killed her. It was her only hope. Lucky for her the other boat made him hurry to escape. If he'd stayed, he would make sure he saw her body.

Her hands touched sand, and she lingered on the bottom as long as she could. Her lungs burned, and she knew she wasn't going to be able to stay under any longer. Swooping around, she kicked against the bottom and zipped toward the top. When her head broke water, she inhaled a great gulp of air.

A wave struck her in the face, and she choked on salty water. Struggling to keep her head above the surf, she struck out toward the shore. If Bossman looked back toward the shore, he'd see her, but she had no choice. She'd drown if she didn't get to land.

Her knees scraped bottom, and she heaved herself out of the water and drew in a breath clear of moisture. She staggered to the beach and collapsed onto her knees, then vomited up seawater. Only then did she turn her head to look out over the seascape. The boat was a tiny speck in the distance. She doubted she'd been seen.

But what about Raine? Hugging herself, she was surprised to

find tears leaking from her eyes. Though she didn't really know the little girl, she loved children. That much hadn't been a lie. She had to contact Grant and warn him that Bossman had gone rogue. He wouldn't be happy.

But as she started down the beach to try to find help, her legs gave way and darkness took her under.

———

Amy turned up the music as she drove to Curtis's house. Mindy would be all right, and for the first time in a long while, Amy saw her way to a future without Ben. And that future included sweet little Raine. Amy wanted to hold the toddler and think about how lucky she was.

Edith stood sweeping the porch when Amy pulled into the drive. She'd hung out colorful new flags of red and white that blew straight out from the posts in the breeze. Dressed in capris and a sleeveless white top, Edith looked happy and content after her morning in the water. Her hair was still damp.

Even though it was likely Raine was sleeping, Amy frowned when she didn't see the child. She got out of the car and shut the door. "Good morning." She walked past new flowers pushing up in the beds along the sidewalk.

Leaning on her broom, Edith paused and smiled. "I thought maybe you went with the helicopter. I got Curtis's message about having to do a run." She sobered. "I hope the patient is going to be okay."

"Sara was there, so I wasn't needed. I'm sure the patient will be fine." She looked past Edith through the open door. "So everything was okay with Raine and Heather?"

Edith's brows rose. "I assume so, though I'll admit I thought they would be here by the time I arrived."

Amy's gut tightened. "You haven't seen them? I don't like that. I'd better call and tell her to bring Raine home right now." She went back to her car and got her purse. She pulled out her cell phone and placed a call to Heather. It rang six times, then went to voice mail. "Heather, where are you? Call me."

"She didn't answer?"

Edith was biting her lip and frowning so Amy forced herself to smile. "They probably stopped off for ice cream or went to the playground. Heather was excited to have her, so I'm sure she wanted to make sure Raine had a good time."

"I suppose you're right." Edith glanced at her watch. "Heather has had her, what, about an hour? It's 11:10."

"We got to the sheriff's about nine. We talked with him awhile, then realized, ah, the woman we helped was in eclampsia." Just in time she caught herself from mentioning Mindy by name. Getting her to the car and dealing with the convulsions had taken awhile. "I'd guess Heather took Raine a little before ten, so maybe she's had her an hour and a half."

Edith's frown came again. "Plenty of time to get here, then." She shaded her eyes with her hand and looked toward town. "She's still not coming."

"Let me try to call her one more time." Amy pulled up the phone number again, but there was still no answer. She dropped her phone back in her purse. "I'm going to go look for her."

Edith leaned the broom against the wall of the porch. "I'll come with you."

"You should probably stay here in case she arrives."

Edith bit her lip. "It feels wrong to stay here and do nothing. I don't like this, Amy. Something feels wrong."

Amy felt it too, but she chalked it up to nervousness about the upsetting morning. "I'm sure there's an innocent explanation for what's happened."

Edith shook her head. "I can see the worry in your face. You warned Curtis to check her references. You don't trust her."

"She's just young and flighty. I bet they're at the playground." She got back in her car and ran the window down. "I'll call you when I find them. Let me know if you hear from them."

First, she checked Rosemary Cottage, just in case, but it was empty with no sign that Heather and Raine had been there. She drove slowly down Oyster Road, watching for any sign of a woman and child. At the playground, she got out and walked through the swings and slides, but Heather and Raine were nowhere around. She peeked in at the ice-cream shop and asked if the server had seen them there. When the answer was no, she went to the toy store, then to the candy shop. The answer was the same everywhere. Next she called the ambulance service that took injured people to the ferry. Maybe one of them had been hurt. Raine could have run in front of a car or fallen.

But when she asked if there had been an injured woman or child brought in, the dispatcher told her no. She called Edith to report in, but the other woman hadn't heard anything either. Though she hated to do it, she had to call Curtis. Her chest squeezed, even though she kept telling herself there was an innocent explanation.

He answered on the first ring. "Hey, I was about to call you. I just landed back at the Coast Guard airfield. You want to come pick me up?"

"I'll be right there." She drove slowly through town and out to the field, hoping she wouldn't have to tell him that Heather and Raine were missing. But there was still no sign of them, and Heather hadn't returned her call.

He came toward her before she pulled into a parking place. She stopped and he hopped in. His smile vanished when he looked at her face. "What's wrong?"

"We can't find Heather and Raine. They never showed up at your house, and Heather isn't answering her cell phone."

"Where have you looked?"

"Everywhere. The playground, the ice-cream shop, the candy shop, the toy store. My house too, just in case they went there."

"Well, let's not panic. I'm sure there's a perfectly good explanation. Did you try the café?"

She slapped her head. "No, I didn't even think of that. Maybe Heather took her there to have an early lunch." Of course that's where they were. It made perfect sense. "Keep an eye out on the way. How is Mindy, by the way?"

He stared out the window as the car moved slowly through town. "They rushed her in for a C-section, but they thought she'd be okay."

Two minutes later she parked in front of the café, and they both ran to the entrance. When the server told them she hadn't seen Heather today, they checked with Imogene back in her office. She told them Heather had called in at nine thirty to say she wouldn't be working today.

"That was before you asked her to watch Raine, I think," Amy said when they were back outside. "She must have decided to take the day off."

"She was dressed for the beach." His mouth tight, Curtis glanced down the road. "I think we'd better talk to Tom."

"You mean, report Raine as missing?" Her voice trembled, and she swallowed hard. She warned herself not to fall apart. There had to be a logical reason for this.

"She was told to go directly to my house and she didn't. So, yeah, I'm going to report her missing."

He took her arm, and they dashed across the street between a family of four on bicycles. Tom's SUV was still in front of the sheriff's office, but they nearly collided with him on his way out the door.

"Sorry, I have to run. I don't have anything new to report." He went past them to his vehicle.

"Hold on," Curtis said. "Raine is missing."

Tom paused with his hand on the door of his SUV. "Missing?"

"I asked Heather Granger to take her to my house and wait for Edith to get back from surfing. They never arrived, and she's not answering her cell phone." Curtis spoke in a clipped voice.

"I'm on my way to Rocky Corner. A fisherman found Heather unconscious on the beach. When he revived her, she was babbling about some man who took the baby. Given what you just told me, I think we have to assume the baby she's talking about is Raine."

The words hit Amy hard, and she nearly sagged to her knees. Raine had to be all right. She had to be.

THIRTY

Its lights still flashing, the ambulance rested along the side of the dirt road parallel to the beach. Two paramedics tended to someone on a stretcher. Curtis leaped out before Amy's car had rolled to a stop. Amy hurried behind him as he approached the young woman on the stretcher behind the ambulance.

A paramedic tried to stop him, but he brushed past him. "It's my niece who's missing."

Heather's eyes fluttered in her white face. Her hair and clothes were drenched, so she'd been in the ocean. He couldn't make out the words she muttered until he leaned closer.

"Tried to shoot me," she whispered.

He took her hand. It was ice cold. "Heather, where is Raine?"

Her head lolled from side to side, and her eyes were wild. "Took her. He took her."

Curtis gripped her hand. "Who took her?" By some miracle he kept his voice strong and confident. He'd find her, and the man who had taken her would wish he'd never been born.

Heather's eyes opened but were unfocused. "Boss. Boss took her. He tried to shoot me." She tried to sit up and shook her head. "I was bleeding." She stared at her arm. "See? He shot me." She squeezed his hand. "Don't let him get me!"

221

The bullet had dug a furrow in her arm, but it had stopped bleeding by now. "You're going to be okay." He glanced at the paramedic. "Can you give her something to bring her around? My year-old niece was in her care. I have to find her."

The paramedic, a tall man in his thirties, shook his head. "Sorry, dude. We stabilize the patient and get them to a doctor in Nags Head. That will be the doctor's call."

Amy approached Heather's other side. She smoothed her hair back. Her touch calmed Heather's agitation. Her lids fluttered again, and she opened her eyes. They were clearer, more aware.

"Amy, don't let him kill me."

Amy rested her hand on Heather's forehead. "You're safe now. The paramedics are here. You're going to be all right. No one is shooting at you now."

Heather's eyes filled with moisture, and tears leaked from them. She released Curtis's hand, then gripped Amy's arm and tried to sit up. "He took her! Bossman took Raine! It's not my fault, I swear!" Her cries grew more frantic.

"Easy." The paramedic tried to push her back against the pillow.

She fought him and sat up, then swung her legs to the side of the stretcher. "We have to find Raine. She wasn't supposed to be hurt!"

Amy exchanged an alarmed glance with Curtis. "What do you mean she wasn't *supposed* to be hurt? Did you take her somewhere?"

Heather began to cry in earnest now, and her face contorted. "He promised she wouldn't be hurt. She was just supposed to get a paternity test."

"What?" Curtis wanted to grab her and shake her. "Who wanted her to have a paternity test?" He glared at Amy. Had her parents arranged for this?

She gave a slight shake of her head. "Think, Curtis. They went through the law. They wouldn't do anything to jeopardize their chances of gaining custody. Thuggery isn't my father's style."

"Then who? And why?" He wanted to shake it out of Heather, make her tell him where his Raine was.

Tom finished talking to the men who had found Heather. He joined them, and Curtis filled him in on what Heather had told them.

Tom stared past Curtis to where Heather was getting more upset. "I think you'd better let me question her." He shuffled to the stretcher. "Who wanted the paternity test, Heather? What reason were you given?"

Heather hiccupped and rubbed her wet face with the back of her hand. "M-My boyfriend. He said he could make a lot of money on Raine's parentage, but that he just had to prove it."

Amy looked as stunned as Curtis felt. "But Raine's father is dead. I should know since he was my brother. This makes no sense." She stared at Heather. "Did your boyfriend intend to try to get money out of my parents?"

"I don't know anything," Heather wailed.

The way she cried reminded Curtis that she was just a kid herself. Though technically an adult, she was still in her teens. "What were you told to do?"

Tom shot him a glare. "Questioning the witness is my job, Curtis."

"It's my niece who's missing," he fired back. "*Who*, Heather?"

"I was supposed to meet Grant at the beach. He was picking us up on his boat. He'd take her to get the test."

"Then what?" Tom asked.

"I—I assumed we'd give her back." But her gaze wandered away from his.

Curtis's stomach roiled, and it was all he could do not to throw up. "You're lying. She wasn't going to be given back, was she?" Where was Raine? This girl knew more than she was telling.

"I don't know," she said in a low voice. "Grant never really said. But he's a good man. He wouldn't do anything to hurt her."

"He had his goon try to shoot you," Amy said quietly.

Heather straightened and shook her head. "Oh no, I'm sure he didn't tell Bossman to do what he did."

Curtis dug his phone out of his pocket and handed it to her. "Can you call this Grant and ask what he's done with Raine?"

"I—I don't know the number. It's programmed into my phone, and I never have to dial it." She patted her pockets.

"Do you have your phone?" Amy asked.

"I guess I lost it in the water."

Tom took out his notebook. "What's Grant's last name? We'll track him that way."

Heather looked down at the ground. "He told me it was Smith, but I don't think that's his real name."

Curtis paced the dirt road. "Oh, come on! That's pretty hard to believe you would swallow the lie and not ask him about it."

"It's true. We met at a party. He said, 'Hi, I'm Grant. You're the most beautiful girl I've ever seen.' No one had ever told me anything like that. I only get to see him once a month or so. Last names just didn't seem to be important."

Amy put her hand on Heather's arm. "Is he married?"

"Of course not!" Heather ducked her head. "I mean, I don't think so. He never said he was, and he doesn't wear a wedding band."

"You poor, naive child." Amy's voice was sympathetic. "He's manipulated you."

Heather flushed. "He hasn't! He loves me. When this was finished, we were going on a long vacation." She blinked rapidly. "That's over, isn't it? He's going to be in a lot of trouble. But it's not his fault, really! Bossman took her."

Curtis had had enough of pussyfooting around this girl, and

he grabbed her arm roughly. "No, *you* took her. You're the one who's going to be in a world of hurt. Kidnapping for one. You have to know where she is." He wanted to shake the truth out of her.

"You gave her to me!" She struggled to get out of his grip.

"But you were supposed to take her to my house, not to meet some guy on a boat. You kidnapped her, Heather." He glared at Tom. "Arrest her, Tom."

Tom's big head nodded. "I'm afraid he's right, Miss Granger. You're under arrest for the kidnapping of Raine Ireland."

———

The salt-laden air lifted the curls off Amy's hot neck. The distant roar of a Sea-Doo floated over the surf. She kicked a broken shell out of the way with her flip-flop, then glanced at Libby, who walked beside her. "I don't know what we're doing out here. We're not likely to find anything."

Her Raine was out there somewhere. And she did think of the child as hers. She already loved the little mite with the dimpled smile. They had to find her. *Please, God, hold her in your arms. Protect her and let her feel no fear.* Raine never seemed to know a stranger, so Amy's biggest hope was that she wouldn't be frightened.

Libby shifted her sleeping son to the other shoulder. "I know, but I wanted to do something. Maybe Curtis and Alec will find the boat. The Coast Guard is on it. They'd all be mobilized. An AMBER Alert has gone out too. They'll find her."

Amy shaded her eyes with her hand and looked out over the waves. "I bet the kidnapper is long gone. It wouldn't take long to get to Kill Devil Hills or even the mainland. He had plenty of time to get to safe harbor."

"You can't give up hope."

She'd seen too many horrific stories on the news, had witnessed too much pain in the world. Though she knew God was in control, what made any of them think that they were somehow special and nothing bad would happen to them? She couldn't speak past the constriction in her throat. What if they never found Raine, never knew what had happened to her? She couldn't go through that again. Never being able to bury Ben was bad enough—they had to find Raine.

The sea deposited foam and kelp on the shore before rolling back for more. They walked close to the water's edge and nearer to the rocks that jutted into the ocean. There were no clouds in the sky, but the air was heavy with humidity and thick with the scent of kelp.

"Hey, what's this?" Libby stooped and grabbed an object in the sand. "It's a cell phone. Does it look familiar?"

Amy took it from Libby. "Heather's phone was similar. I don't know if it's hers or not. It doesn't feel wet. Could she have dropped it before she got on the boat?"

"See if it comes on."

Amy pressed the top button of the iPhone, and the screen came on. "It's working!" The background was of Heather and another young woman Amy didn't know. "And it's Heather's." Her phone was a similar model, so she called up the contacts list and dragged her finger along the screen to see if there was a Grant listed. "Here he is." Her pulse hammering in her throat, she touched the phone number. She would *beg* the man to return Raine. But the phone blinked off. "Oh no, there's no signal here."

Libby turned back toward the road. "Let's get this to the sheriff. He's probably going to have a fit that we touched it. I didn't think about it being evidence when I grabbed it."

"I would have done the same." She held up the iPhone. "And I'm calling this number as soon as we get a signal."

The women hurried to Amy's car. She'd just buckled her seat

belt when her phone rang. Her gut tightened when she saw it was Curtis, and she quickly answered it. "Any sign of the boat?"

"The cutter out searching stopped a few fishing boats, but they didn't find her." Pain laced his voice. "We've flown all over the sound and along the shore and haven't seen anything. We've called in the FBI, and Raine's picture will be all over the news tonight. The entire state's been mobilized. Maybe the AMBER Alert will get some calls."

He didn't have to tell her that all the effort in the world might not be enough. "Libby found Heather's cell phone." Maybe that news would encourage him.

"You're kidding! I bet the FBI can retrieve some data even though it's been in the sea."

"It's not wet. I think she dropped it on the beach. I tried to call that Grant, but there are no cell bars out here."

"Don't call yourself. You might scare him off. Meet me at the jail. We'll get Heather to make the call while law enforcement is listening in. She'll be able to get more information out of him. And if she can keep him on the call, they can triangulate his location. Hurry!"

"We'll be there in fifteen minutes." She ended the call and started the car. As she drove to town, she told Libby what Curtis had said.

"The phone might be our lucky break." Libby looked in the backseat. "Noah's wide-awake and sucking his thumb." She smiled at her infant son.

Amy's chest constricted at the thought that she might never see Raine's sweet smile again. "Do you want me to drop you off at Tidewater Inn? Alec will be home soon."

"Are you kidding? I want to be right there when we find her." She shuddered. "I can't even imagine something as terrible as this. And besides, I'm sure Alec won't be in until it's too late to look for the boat. He'll be turning over every rock. I'm sure he's hurting for Curtis."

Amy shot her a glance. "I—I could use the support. I feel a little out of place. I love Raine already, but that whole custody thing is going on, and I'm not sure how Curtis feels about me now that my parents are involved." She should have known better than to let her emotions get so involved.

Libby reached over and patted her hand. "Have you called your parents?"

"No, but I'll have to. If they see it first on the news, they'll be livid." The clock on the dash glowed the time of 3:10. "It might already be on the news."

"Will they blame Curtis for handing her over to Heather?"

"Probably." Amy's jaw tightened. "Honestly, I even blame him a little."

"Oh, Amy, you don't! He had no way of knowing she had something like this planned. And it was an emergency."

Amy sighed and tried to push away the anger that had been growing toward Curtis all afternoon. And she was angry at herself as well. She was as much to blame as Curtis.

THIRTY-ONE

Clouds billowed above him, and thunder rumbled in the distance, nearly obscured by a boat horn in the harbor. The weather seemed to punctuate the terror clawing at Curtis's gut. It was all he could do to hold himself together. The panic grew with every minute that passed. He had to find Raine.

Edith hadn't stopped crying since he'd picked her up. Her face was red and blotchy, and he held on to her arm to keep her from collapsing to the pavement. He murmured some kind of comfort he didn't believe himself as he watched for Amy's car. When her small compact pulled into a parking space in front of the jail, he settled Edith on a stone wall and went to meet Amy and Libby.

Libby got out of the passenger side, then opened the back door and reached inside to get little Noah. Curtis's heart squeezed at the sight of the baby. Just a year ago Raine had been that size, and now she was . . . gone.

Amy's eyes were huge in her white face, and her expression pleaded with him to tell her good news.

Swallowing down his pain, he met her on the sidewalk. "I told Tom you found the phone. He's squawking about contaminating the evidence, just so you know."

"I knew he would be. So still no news?"

He shook his head and took the phone she handed him. "There are four bars now, so we're good. Tom is going to move Heather to an interrogation room. He's got some kind of equipment where he can listen in on her call without her knowing about it. So we can hear more than what she's saying. We'll be able to hear the scumbag too."

Amy nodded but her eyes looked distant, as though she was thinking of something else. "I have to call my parents before I go in. I just heard something about it on the radio, so it's going to be all over the country."

"It will take a few minutes to set things up anyway. Go ahead." He needed to call his parents as well, but not until he managed to regain a steady tone. His mother would fall apart, and he needed to be strong enough to help her.

To give Amy privacy for the call, he started to walk away, but she grabbed his hand as she placed the call. "Stay. I could use the support."

She settled on the wall that ran the perimeter of the yard. Libby gave her an encouraging pat as she settled beside her.

"Hello, Dad? Listen, there's trouble here." She told the whole story, ending with finding Heather on the beach. "And Raine's still missing, kidnapped from Heather by this unknown man."

Her father's voice boomed out of the phone, loud enough for Curtis and any passerby to hear. "What do you mean kidnapped? I knew that Coast Guard fellow couldn't care for her properly. We'll be there first thing in the morning. I have a meeting tonight I can't get out of."

Amy was white when she dropped her phone back in her purse. "Sorry that you're going to have to contend with them. My dad will use this as ammunition to bolster his fight for custody."

"Right now we need to get her back. Then I'll worry about your dad." She nodded, but he didn't like the way she didn't meet his eyes. "You think it's my fault, don't you?"

She rose and slung her purse strap over her shoulder. "It was my fault too, Curtis. We were running on pure adrenaline and didn't stop to use our heads. Neither of us knew Heather well enough to entrust her with Raine. We should have called Libby or even a neighbor we knew." Her voice broke. "This is going to be hard to live with for both of us if—"

The doubt in her eyes nearly buckled his knees. "We *will* find her!" Hope was all he had to cling to. No one was going to take that away from him. He would search for Raine until his dying breath.

She nodded. "Of course. Did you call your parents?"

He paused. "No, and I need to. I don't want them to hear about it on the news." With his shoulder brushing hers, he placed the call and got his mother. Dad would likely be in meetings. "Mom?"

"Curtis, I was about to call you." His mother's voice quavered. "I was watching the news. That isn't our Raine who's been kidnapped, is it? Please tell me it isn't."

"I'm afraid so, Mom." He plunged into what had happened, sparing no details and taking the full blame. His mother cried softly on the other end and promised she and his father would get there as soon as they could. Sighing, he put his phone away. "They'll be here in a few hours too. Dad will come in on his private plane."

Amy gripped his hand. "I heard what you said. It wasn't your fault, Curtis."

"A few minutes ago you weren't so sure." He started to pull his hand away, but she held on and shook her head. "It *is* my fault. I handed her right over to Heather without a care in the world. I should have known better. I wasn't thinking."

She held his gaze. "Neither of us was. An emergency can do that to a person. Blaming ourselves isn't going to get her back. And we *will* get her back, Curtis."

The way her voice held conviction gave him hope. He took her arm. "Let's get inside and make Heather call that monster."

The air-conditioning in Heather's holding room gave a thump and a wheeze before it let go of slightly cooler air that did little to alleviate the stuffy space. She sat on a metal chair covered with the thinnest cushion she'd ever seen. The table was metal as well, and four other chairs were grouped around it. Sniffling, she willed herself not to cry, but her eyes kept burning and flooding with tears. She'd been so *stupid*. There should have been some way to prevent Bossman from taking the little girl.

Down the hall, a door slammed. Footsteps came toward her door, and she rose with her hands clutched together. There had been no one to call to get her out of jail, and she had little hope that whoever approached would help. If she could just call Grant, he would know what to do to get her out of this.

The metal door of her room swung open, and the first person she saw was Amy. Curtis and Sheriff Bourne, Alec's cousin, were behind her. Heather wanted to rush forward and throw herself into Amy's arms. Amy had a gentle, competent way about her, and Heather was sure she could help her. But *would* she? She had no real cause to help when it was Heather's fault that Raine was in the possession of that awful man.

Amy gently took Heather's shoulders and disentangled herself from the young woman. "Heather, how are you?" Her tone held interest without condemnation. Her face was pale and full of pain.

Heather searched the other woman's face for signs of sincerity. Did Amy *really* care that she'd been thrown in jail? Her green eyes were warm with compassion.

"It's hot in here. And I'm scared." Heather's voice broke. She stepped back and rubbed her burning eyes. When Amy took her arm and settled her back in the chair, Heather leaned into her. Right now anyone's touch was welcome. She felt so alone.

Amy pulled out a metal chair and sat beside her. "Could we get her a glass of water?"

"Or a Mountain Dew?" Heather put in.

Sheriff Bourne's lips tightened, but he inclined his head and went to the door. Sticking his head out, he told someone in the hall to bring her a drink.

"Amy, what's going to happen to me? I've seen movies about women who went to jail. Something like that couldn't happen to me, could it? If I told them I'm only seventeen, would that change things? Maybe juvie would intervene. If I have to go to jail, being with girls my own age would be better than prison."

Amy chewed on her lip. "Honey, that's up to the sheriff. I don't know anything about the legal stuff."

When the sheriff turned back to the table, he pulled out a chair and dropped into it. "Curtis, have a seat." He reached into his pocket and pulled out a phone. "This yours?"

She reached for it eagerly. "I think so!" Her fingers closed around it, and she recognized the slice in the plastic cover on the back. "It's mine. Where did you find it?"

Amy kept hold of her hand. "On the beach. I think you dropped it before you got in the water. It still works, and I don't think it's ever been wet. We want to help you, Heather, but to do that, you have to help us."

Heather didn't like the sound of that. "Are you talking a trade? I turn Grant over to you and you'll let me go? I can't do that. I love him. And besides, I don't think he had anything to do with what Bossman did. I think he'd help us get her back though. Once I tell him what's happened, he'll figure it out."

The sheriff gave an exasperated *humph*. "Girl, that man was using you, and you're too dumb to see it. He's letting you rot in jail while he does whatever he set out to do. I'm expecting a ransom demand."

Curtis's head shot up. "Ransom?"

"Your folks have money. It makes sense. And Heather said something about using the kid to make a lot of money."

Heather shook her head. "I don't believe Grant would ask for a ransom. I know he wouldn't hurt her. Let me call him and tell him what Bossman has done. I'm sure he doesn't know. He'll help us track down Bossman and get Raine back." Sobs surged in her throat. "I never wanted to hurt the little girl. I like kids. Truly."

The sheriff's frown darkened. "Yeah, well, prove it. Call your fella, and let's see what he says." He motioned to the rest of them to follow him. "We'll give you some privacy so you can talk."

They exited the room and Heather exhaled. It would have been awkward to have them listening. Her hands trembled as she called up Grant's number. What if he wasn't there? Or what if what the sheriff said was true and Grant had been using her?

The phone was answered almost immediately. "Heather, you're supposed to wait for my call."

She exhaled. "Oh, Grant, thank goodness you're there."

"Of course I'm here. Where else would I be? And why are you calling?"

"It's Bossman. He picked us up. He tried to *kill* me, Grant. He got out a gun and shot me." Her fingers crept to the furrow in her arm. "Be careful with him. I escaped, but he took Raine."

"And brought her to me. I didn't tell him to hurt you though. Are you exaggerating?"

Heather licked her dry lips. "Of course I'm not exaggerating! Hang on." She quickly snapped a picture of her injured arm and texted it to him. "I just sent you a picture of what he did. He tried to kill me."

There was a pause. "It looks like a bullet, all right. And Bossman did this?"

"Yes." A sob escaped her throat. "Is Raine all right?"

"She's fine."

"You have to bring her back. You have to, Grant! They know I took her, and they'll send me to prison. Bring her back and everything will be okay. We'll go on our vacation and forget about this nightmare."

He gave a heavy sigh. "Listen, I'm seeing someone else now. It's time we both moved on."

"But you said you loved me, and that you'd already bought tickets to the beach."

"Grow up, Heather. You did what I asked, and we're both moving on." His voice was hard. "Now leave me alone. And don't go to the police. You'd just get yourself in trouble since you're the one who took her. And even worse, I'll sic Bossman on you, so keep your mouth shut if you want to live."

The phone clicked in her ear, and she let it slip from nerveless fingers. She felt frozen inside and out. He couldn't have meant what he said. He couldn't.

The door opened, and Amy stepped back inside with Curtis and the sheriff. Amy slid back into her chair. "Are you all right? You're pale. Did he say where Raine is?"

"He has her, but he's not bringing her back." She put her hand to her mouth. "He *used* me."

Amy reached over to take Heather's hand. "Help us find Raine, Heather. What can you tell us about Grant? Anything you can think of will help us track him down."

Heather tried to think past the pain squeezing her chest. Was this what death felt like? "H-He's in his early thirties, I think. Blond hair and the bluest eyes you've ever seen. He always wears polos and khakis with deck shoes. He said he lived in Atlantic City, but I bet that's not true either." Bitterness laced her words, and she suddenly wished she had a gun. She'd track him down and shoot him in his black heart.

"Not much to go on," Sheriff Bourne said.

Heather reached for her phone. "Wait, I have a picture. He'd kill me if he knew I took it, but I just wanted to have something to look at when we were far apart." She called up the photos and whipped through them to find the one she wanted. "Here." She passed it to the sheriff, who looked at it and nodded.

"I'll see if we can find a match."

"Can I see it?" Amy and Curtis asked at the same time.

Sheriff Bourne shrugged, then handed the phone to Curtis, who stared at it and shook his head. Curtis offered it to Amy.

She took one look and gasped. "I know this man. He was a friend of my brother's. His real name is Grant Davidson. He lives in Washington DC."

The sheriff was scribbling things in his notebook. "We'll find him."

THIRTY-TWO

The house had been close and hot all night. When dawn came, Amy was still wide-awake, so she got out of bed and grabbed her gear. She had to lose herself in the cold sea, to talk to God in the ocean. The sea was cold and gray this morning, much like she felt inside. Plunging into the chilly water, she cried and raged at this turn of events as she clung to her board and let the sea carry her to and fro.

Why, God, why? You have to be with her. Keep her safe. Help us find her today. We can't go on without her.

Finally spent, she let the foam carry her to the sand where she lay exhausted and broken. The sun had come up half an hour ago, but pink and orange still tinted the eastern sky. Clouds piled high to the south as a predicted storm headed this way.

She pulled off her hoodie and inhaled the scent of sea and salt, then cut through the maritime forest to her house. Her feet kicked up the scent of pine. Her skin was cold as she approached her house. The first few drops of rain hit her face as she stepped onto the back porch. The first thing she grabbed as she came in the door was her cell phone in case Curtis had called with news, but there were no messages.

"Is that you, Amy?" her mother's voice called from the living room.

Amy stopped and took a deep breath. They'd gotten up early if they were here already, though it was a relatively short flight in her father's private plane. "It's me, Mom. Just got in from surfing." She was not ready to deal with them.

Footsteps sounded on the wooden floors, and her mother appeared in the doorway to the kitchen with Amy's father behind her. Her mother's hair was perfectly coiffed, and she wore slim white capris and a red-and-white top. Her father had his hands in the pockets of his khakis. They didn't even look all that worried. Amy bet they'd slept perfectly fine all night. They'd awakened with the alarm and come up as if it were a vacation.

"Look at you," her mother scolded. "Your face is red from the cold water, and you've lost weight. And you should be here monitoring the phone in case the kidnapper calls. Your father brought a suitcase full of cash in case there's a ransom demand." Her tone indicated she expected high praise for their planning.

Amy grabbed the towel she'd left on the back of a chair and dried her hair with it. "If the kidnapper calls, he'll phone Curtis or his parents, not me."

Her father bristled. "I have more money than the Irelands."

"It's not that well known who Raine's father is. After all, even *we* didn't know." Tossing the towel back onto the chair, Amy went to pour coffee. "Want a cup? It's Toomer's. And how about breakfast?"

Her mother went to the cupboard and pulled out two more mugs. "How could you even be out surfing at a time like this?"

Amy poured cream in her coffee before answering. "I didn't sleep all night. I prayed while I was in the water, and I think I can deal with the day now."

To her surprise, her mother's face softened. Mary Lang was not known for her compassion, not even for her children, but something this horrific made a dent even in her brisk manner.

She put her hand on Amy's shoulder. "We're here to help now."

She handed a cup of coffee to her husband. "Your phone rang and I answered it. The nurse assumed I was you and told me your CA-125 was 10."

Amy closed her eyes and exhaled. *Thank you, God.* But her usual elation was missing. There was no joy in anything with Raine missing. What difference did it make if Amy lived another fifty years or not when that darling baby was missing? Worrying about something like her cancer returning was no way to live when there were more important things in the world. She wasn't going to do it anymore.

"That's good," Amy said.

"I've contacted a private investigator as well," Oliver said. "He'll be here later this morning."

Amy wasn't sure why the announcement made her tense, but she feared that the more people who got involved, the farther the kidnapper might run. "I have something to show you."

She pulled out a chair at the table and reached for her notebook. She'd spent all evening jotting down everything she could remember about Grant Davidson. It wasn't much, but her father might know more.

She pushed the paper in front of him. "Recognize the name Grant Davidson?"

Her father's brow furrowed. "Sure. What's he got to do with this?"

"He's the one who took Raine."

Her mother gasped. "That's a very serious accusation to make against someone like Grant. I suppose Curtis put the notion in your head."

Amy frowned. "Curtis had nothing to do with it. The girl who took Raine, Heather Granger, identified him. She called him from jail, and he told her that he had all he wanted from her. Where can we find him?"

Her father pulled out his phone and touched the Contacts icon. "Preston Kendrick will know. I'll call him."

"Preston? Why would he know? The last I heard, Grant was a financial consultant with a big firm in DC."

"Preston brought him on to be the state finance chairman. I hear he's done a great job so far."

Amy reached for her cell phone. "I have to tell Sheriff Bourne. You call Preston and get the contact information."

Her father's hand closed over hers. "You can't implicate Preston's staff this way. It could affect the campaign."

She jerked her hand away. "Then it affects the campaign! I will do anything and everything to get Raine back. The campaign is the least of our worries right now."

"You don't even know if she's Ben's daughter yet."

Amy gaped at her mother. "Do you hear what you just said? I don't care if Raine is or isn't Ben's child. She's a year old, and she's been stolen from her family, no matter what family she belongs to. We have to find her—right away!"

"Of course, of course," her mother soothed. "But your father is right. Don't do something we'll all regret."

"I won't regret it." Amy rose and slipped out the back door onto the porch, where she sank into a wicker chair. She couldn't believe her parents. They were *not* helping her stress level. She placed the call to the sheriff's cell phone. Tom promised to contact the senator's staff and see where Grant could be found.

She heard the doorbell through the open screen door and hopped up, hoping it was Curtis. When she stepped into the kitchen, she heard Curtis's deep voice in the living room. Her father was offering his sympathy when she joined them. A little different from what he and her mother had just been saying.

"I have news," she said when he directed a smile her way. "My father said that Grant works for Preston Kendrick."

Curtis's eyes widened. "You're kidding. What a lucky break! He'll be easy to find, probably right at campaign headquarters. You called Tom?"

She nodded. "He's on it." She glanced at her father. "Did you get hold of Preston?"

He shook his head. "But I spoke with Zoe. She was going to find Preston and get Grant's address and phone number for me. She was horrified."

Curtis dropped into the chair by the fireplace. The skin under his eyes was dark, and she was sure he hadn't slept last night either. "Want some coffee?"

"Sure." His eyes glistened. "I prayed all night that she wasn't afraid and that whoever had her was taking good care of her." He took off his do-rag and ran his hand over his still-damp hair. "Maybe this nightmare will be over today and she'll be safely home."

Amy handed him her cup of coffee since she hadn't drunk out of it yet, then went to pour herself more. As the black liquid spilled into her cup, she prayed for Curtis and Edith. This was harder on them than on her. When she returned to the living room, she tensed at her father's voice. They settled down to wait for the phone to ring.

She was so tired. Closing her eyes, she drifted to sleep. When she awakened, she glanced at the clock on the mantel. "Have I really been asleep for two hours?"

Curtis opened his eyes at her voice. "You needed some rest. I took a snooze myself."

Dad stretched. "Did you take Raine in for the DNA test?"

She fixed a quelling stare on her father. "Dad, that's not appropriate to ask now. It doesn't matter."

Curtis nodded. "I did. Should have the results back in a few days."

Amy's phone rang, and she glanced at the screen before she answered it. "Any news, Tom?"

"The worst kind."

Her stomach clenched, and her knees went weak. She gripped the phone with tight fingers. *Please, God, not that.* "W-What is it?"

Curtis stepped to her side and put his hand on her shoulder. "What's wrong?"

She put her fingers to her lips. "Tom?"

He inhaled. "Davidson's body was found in the Atlantic with a bullet in his head."

"A-And Raine?"

"No sign of her. The FBI is going to question Senator Kendrick, but it looks like we're at a dead end."

She ended the call. "Grant is dead. Murdered."

———

They'd all gathered at Curtis's for dinner, but the tension between both sets of Raine's grandparents was so thick in the living room that Curtis wished he hadn't invited them over. He'd thought they could all support one another, but his father and Amy's dad had been sniping at each other for the past hour. Well, Amy's dad mostly, but Curtis could see his father beginning to react to the jabs.

Edith's eyes were red and swollen from crying. "I'd better check on dinner." She jumped to her feet and rushed out of the room.

Curtis had tried to take as much stress off of her as possible, but nothing would relieve it until Raine was back. "I'll be right back." He followed her to the kitchen. "Anything I can do to help?"

Edith shook her head. "Dinner will be ready in about fifteen minutes. You'd better stay in the living room and make sure open warfare doesn't break out between your parents and Amy's family."

"I'm sorry you have to listen to this."

She pressed trembling lips together. "Family should hang together in bad times like this. Amy's parents seem determined to be in charge. They don't even know Raine. Or love her." Her voice broke.

He hugged her, and her trembling body began to calm. "We'll get through this, Ede. We will. And we'll find Raine."

"I want her back. Tonight." Her voice was a whisper. "I can't bear seeing her empty crib."

"Me neither." He released her and headed for the living room. The tension could explode between them any minute, though he wasn't sure what he could do to avert it if things began to heat up. He took the hard-backed chair by the desk and pulled it into the circle of people grouped near the fireplace.

Amy was pale. "Is Edith okay? I can go help her."

He shook his head. "She's got it under control. Should be ready in fifteen minutes or so." He left her question unanswered. None of them would be okay until Raine was safely home.

Mary Lang crossed her legs. "Your mother was just telling us about Gina's work with disadvantaged children in the church. Very admirable."

She wore a short blue dress that most women her age wouldn't have attempted, but she managed to carry it off. He suspected she spent a lot of money maintaining her youthful appearance. His mother, Cindy, was slightly overweight, but with a soft, gentle expression that was much more appealing than Mary's face, chiseled with plastic surgery.

Curtis nodded. "Gina had a lot of compassion for other people."

"Probably because she hit the bottom herself," Oliver said.

Curtis saw his father bristle, and he quickly changed the subject. "You flew your plane in yourself or do you have a pilot?"

Oliver sat back in the sofa. "I fly myself. Learned in 'Nam." He launched into the merits of his plane, and the two dads discussed various planes.

It was a safe subject for now, but watching Oliver, Curtis

wanted to ask him if he was worried at all about Raine. Why was he here? There had been no real discussion of how they were going to find her. The room went silent as Oliver finally stopped talking. Curtis glanced at Amy and saw she was on the verge of tears.

She held his gaze a moment, then wiped her eyes. "It's so hard not knowing if she's all right. You'd think the FBI would have heard something. I mean, they know who took her."

"Who allegedly took her," her father corrected. "If you can believe the word of that girl."

"We listened in when she called him," Curtis said. "But he was killed before they could interrogate him. That made everything harder."

Oliver shrugged. "Fine, but I'm not convinced Grant was even involved. I was impressed with him when I met him."

"Why?" Amy fired back. "Because he was good with money? That doesn't mean a thing."

Her mother stared at her. "You've never really appreciated all the things we've given you, have you, Amy? Money sent you to the finest schools and gave you all the opportunities you have now."

"Her hard work got her further than money and advantages," Curtis said.

Oliver rose and pointed his finger at Curtis. "You've known her, what, all of two weeks, going on three? I think we know our daughter better than you do."

"I've known her a long time, more than a year." Curtis barely held on to his temper.

Curtis's father stood. "I think we'd do well to remember why we're here." His gravelly voice held an edge. "My granddaughter is out there somewhere, and she's all that matters right now. Bickering about inconsequential things is stupid. Your granddaughter needs you to help find her."

"*Your* granddaughter, Edward. Whether she's ours or not

remains to be seen. There must have been some reason my son didn't marry her."

Amy leaped to her feet. "Dad, that's enough! If you can't be civil, you can go home. I thought you wanted to come here to help and be supportive. Your attitude is not helping."

Confusion mingled with Oliver's bullish expression. "Well, we don't know yet. Not until the paternity test comes back."

Mom pulled Amy back onto the sofa and patted her leg as she stared up at Oliver. "You think our daughter would actually lie about something like this?"

"Well . . ."

Mom held up her hand. "Your son claimed Raine as his daughter. Are you calling him a liar as well? I feel sorry for you, Mr. Lang. So little trust in your life."

Oliver's face reddened. "Mary, I think it's time we left." He didn't wait for his wife but stomped toward the door.

Amy followed her mother. "I'll run them home and then come back."

Curtis went after her and stopped her at the door. "Don't let them talk you out of coming back."

"I wish they hadn't even come," she said, her voice choked. "Raine is all that matters, and they're just making things worse. I'm sorry for the stress they've brought you and your parents."

He put his hand on her arm. "It's not your fault."

She gave a slight smile and shook her head. "It's days like this that I wish I were adopted."

THIRTY-THREE

Curtis's eyes burned from two nights of no sleep. He'd prayed, put up posters, done interviews with multiple news stations, and had made a nuisance of himself with his FBI contact. There was still no sign of his Raine. He found himself playing endless games of FreeCell on his computer.

Saturday morning he mowed the yard with his cell phone in his pocket, but it hadn't rung. The scent of fresh-cut grass hung in the air as he put his mower away and headed for the house. Amy's car pulled into the drive, and he changed course to meet her.

There was a plate of cookies in her hand when she got out of the car. "I know it's silly, but I felt compelled to bake cookies this morning. I'll eat every one if I leave them in the house, so I thought I'd share the pounds with you." She looked him over. "You've lost weight."

"I smell peanut butter."

"Any real man loves peanut butter. These are healthy too with real butter and almond flour."

He put his hand on her shoulder. "I appreciate the effort you're making to cheer me up."

"No word?"

He shook his head. "It's killing me." He selected a cookie, then bit into it. The peanutty taste was good on his tongue, but his stomach still felt like lead.

"I can only imagine how you and Edith feel. I love Raine already but not like you two."

The mailman's arrival distracted his attention. The DNA test was only supposed to take a couple of days. Not that it mattered right now. Oliver's custody case was a gnat compared to the overwhelming worry about Raine. He went to meet the mail carrier, who passed over a thick batch of envelopes. Nothing, nothing, then he paused. The official-looking envelope made his chest tighten.

He showed it to Amy. "The DNA test came back."

"I thought so. You went a little pale." She swallowed and stared at it. "I'm afraid of what my parents will do, Curtis. They may try to take control of the investigation into her disappearance away from you. Not having those results is the only thing that has kept them corralled. The private investigator they hired has been poking around, but I think he's pretty useless. Maybe my father just had to do something. Maybe you shouldn't read it. If they don't know the truth, they won't interfere."

He offered her a tight smile. "I'm prepared for him to try to take charge. I won't allow it. Raine is *mine*." The flap resisted his finger, then he ripped it open and scanned the page.

Negative. Not a DNA match.

This couldn't be right, and he read it again. *Negative.* He whistled through his teeth. "Holy cow."

"What is it?" She took the letter he held out and read it. The color leached from her cheeks. "It can't be!" Her eyes were stunned when she looked up at him. "Ben isn't Raine's father? Then who is?"

"He claimed to be her father." Curtis took off his Harley do-rag and wiped his forehead, then adjusted it back in place. Anything to avoid facing the implications of this result. "They both lied. But why?"

"If we knew that, we might know why Raine was taken." She bit her lip. "My parents won't know how to behave about this news."

"At least they'll drop the custody battle." He winced. "I'm sorry. This means she's not your niece."

Her eyes widened. "Not my niece." Her voice trembled. "I—I have to admit this is a blow. I thought she was a small piece of Ben left in the world."

He took her elbow and guided her to the house. "Edith isn't going to believe this. I'm not sure I can."

Edith opened the screen door for them. "I won't believe what?" Her pallor had grown worse with every hour Raine was still missing.

"The DNA results show that Ben is not Raine's dad." He let the door shut behind them and headed to the kitchen to start coffee. The women followed him. "Yet Gina and Ben both claimed he was the father."

Amy stepped past him and put coffee in the grinder. "Maybe Ben suspected he wasn't the father and that's why he didn't give her any support."

She needed a dose of reality about that brother of hers. "We can talk about it over coffee and cookies."

Her chin was tipped up aggressively, and her green eyes sparked fire. "How could Gina lie about something like that? Did she not even know who the father was and picked Ben as a likely sucker? This is despicable!"

Curtis clamped his lips shut and put water in the coffeepot. She was judging Gina just like everyone else. Gina had changed. Why she'd lied was still in question, but he'd bet everything he owned that Gina knew exactly who Raine's father was.

———

The gray deck looked new with a pergola overhead for shade. Baskets of geraniums hung from the beams. Birds chirped overhead as Amy settled into a chair at the outdoor table. The beauty of the day did little to calm her agitation.

Raine wasn't her niece.

The information kept slapping her in the face. Everything she thought she knew was suddenly in question. Even her decision to settle here. Being close to Raine had been part of the draw.

The thought of eating a cookie turned Amy's stomach, but she set the plate of treats on the patio table. Curtis's eyes seemed to look through her as he sat in a chair beside her and sipped his coffee. He hadn't condemned his sister's actions, but he should have. And if he thought what Gina had done was okay, then whatever relationship developing between the two of them wasn't going anywhere. First drugs and now a blatant lie about her brother. Who was Gina really?

"You look shell-shocked." Curtis set his cell phone on the table and glanced at his aunt. "You okay, Ede?"

Edith's lips trembled. "I feel like I didn't know Gina at all. Everything is such a jumble."

How could he act so unaffected by this news? Amy stared at his tanned face under the Harley do-rag. "Don't you feel the same? I've been told Raine is my niece, only to discover it was all a lie." She blinked rapidly at the burn in her eyes. "I feel a sense of loss, okay? How would you feel if you found out she wasn't related to you at all?"

He held her gaze. "I'd still love her."

The rebuke in his words brought her up short. Did this change how she felt about the tiny girl? No, it didn't. She'd already given her heart. Every moment that went by with her missing was agony. "And I do love her." She exhaled and slumped in the chair. "But it's still hard to swallow. This surely means something, but what?"

"I think it's all connected to her kidnapping."

"Why do you say that?"

He stared at the hummingbird feeder where two tiny birds

fluttered. "Intuition. Two deaths and now Raine gone. And we suddenly find out even Raine is not who we thought."

Edith stirred cream into her coffee. "Have you heard from the FBI about their questioning of the senator?"

Curtis nodded and glanced at Amy. "I didn't get a chance to tell you, but they called this morning. Senator Kendrick didn't know anyone called Bossman, and he says he didn't know Grant that well. I guess he was recommended by his campaign manager."

"Then we need to talk to the campaign manager."

"They plan to. The boat hasn't been found either, even though Heather told us the name and make."

Amy watched one of the hummingbirds dive-bomb the other one, trying to drive it away from the feeder. Territorial behavior even in the bird kingdom. Did Raine's kidnapping have something to do with her father's rights? Could she be safe and sound with her real father—someone who didn't want to admit he was related to her?

She pulled out her phone. "I'd like to talk to the senator myself. He might be a little more forthcoming with me."

"You think he'd be honest on the phone?"

She shrugged. "Maybe you're right. I think he's doing a campaign drive in Kill Devil Hills tomorrow. I could show up and talk to him face-to-face."

"Want me to take you?"

She hesitated, then nodded. "I'd appreciate the company."

She studied his expression and the sadness in his eyes. What did he think about his sister now?

"What are you thinking?" he asked softly. "I see the judgment in your eyes. You blame Gina, don't you?"

"Shouldn't I? She lied to you, to Ben, to Edith, everyone."

Curtis's gray eyes flashed. "My sister cared about everyone. You can't judge her based on this one incident."

"You appear to be deliberately ignoring the evidence. I thought better of you than that. Look at what's right in front of us, Curtis! The truth is here."

"Truth—whose truth? And who are you to judge her?" he countered, his voice raised.

Her anger spiked at his dismissive tone. "She lied to my brother! I think that's reason enough for me to question her virtue."

His eyes flashed. "I'm not going to sit here and let you trash my sister, Amy." He snatched his cell phone and coffee, then got up and went inside.

"Oh dear," Edith said. "That was rather unpleasant. And you are making judgments, honey. Judgments that aren't yours to make. None of us knows what is in another person's heart or the circumstances that rose in a person's life. I'm not saying what Gina did was right, but God is her judge, not you or me." She took a sip of her coffee. "And what of your brother's involvement? I don't believe he was lily white in this situation."

Amy bristled at Edith's tone. "What do you mean? He was hoodwinked like everyone else."

"Was he? I don't think so. I suspect there is something much deeper going on than we know. And Ben didn't have a stellar reputation either."

Amy jumped to her feet. "I won't listen to anyone talking bad about my brother. Not even you, Edith."

She marched around the edge of the house to her car. Her pulse thumped against her temple. Neither Curtis nor Edith knew her brother all that well. Not like she did. But as she drove toward home, she wondered what reputation Edith was talking about. Ben had been well liked. At least she'd always thought so.

THIRTY-FOUR

His chest still burning from his argument with Amy, Curtis stood in Raine's room. Two walls were pink and two were lavender. Her favorite three stuffed bears sat in the tan rocker in the corner. He stepped to her empty crib and picked up her blanket. If she'd had this, it might have been of some comfort to her. Holding it to his nose, he inhaled the aroma of baby lotion and little girl. Was she warm and fed? Crying for him and Edith?

His eyes stung, and tears choked his throat. How could he bear it if he never got her back? He stood and prayed for a long time by her crib, then wiped his eyes and closed the door behind him before stepping into Gina's room.

Boxes littered the room, and everything in the dresser drawers hung out. The fuzzy pink rug had been kicked up to reveal the wood floors underneath. Edith knelt in the closet on her hands and knees. Her expression was almost wild when she looked back at him.

He hauled her to her feet when she held out her hand. "What are you doing?"

Her short hair stuck up on end. She wiped dust on her capris. "Looking for something, anything, that will put an end to this nightmare." Her face crumpled. "I want my Raine." Tears rolled down her cheeks.

His own tears welling again, he pulled her against his chest. "We'll find her, Ede, I swear we will." They'd both been rocked to their cores.

"She's never been away from us. I'm so afraid, Curtis." Her words were muffled against his shirt. "I can't stand this."

He patted her back awkwardly. Edith was one of the strongest people he knew. She'd managed to hold it together, but the waiting was destroying all of them. Their Raine had been gone four days, an eternity.

She finally pulled away and wiped her eyes. "There has to be something we're missing. Want to help me look?"

He nodded. "I came in here for the same reason. I'd like to find out where she got the money for that expensive wedding dress. Or I guess someone could have bought it for her. There's no record of such a purchase in her regular bank account."

"Amy said it was expensive."

"Like twenty-five-thousand-dollars expensive."

He moved to the bed and stripped off the bedding to reveal the mattress beneath it. He removed the pillowcases and felt inside the down pillows but felt nothing out of the ordinary.

"Check under the bed," Edith said.

She went around to the other side of the bed and stooped. He dropped to his hands and knees and examined every inch under the queen bed. Nothing. Not even dust bunnies. He heaved the mattress onto its end on the floor to expose the box springs. Was that an envelope?

Edith gasped and swooped in to grab it. The envelope shook in her hand as she struggled to open the flap, so she handed it to him. "I can't do it."

The paste on the flap was gummy, but it wasn't stuck tightly.

It appeared the envelope had been opened and reopened numerous times. He lifted the flap and pulled out a sheaf of papers. "It looks like a bank statement and old receipts." Perching on the side of the box springs, he began to go through them. "Look at this, Ede. Two large deposits made three months apart, each a hundred and fifty thousand dollars."

Edith's eyes were wide. "Is it possible this is support from Raine's father?"

He should have thought of that himself when he discovered Raine wasn't Ben's child. "I bet you're right." He glanced at the clock, then remembered it was Saturday. "We'll have to wait until Monday to get any answers on where the deposit came from. According to the statement, they were electronic deposits, but the bank can trace where they came from. And now we have the bank information and account number."

"Could Tom find out something sooner?"

"I don't know. Maybe." He pulled his cell phone from his pocket and called the sheriff, but the call went to voice mail. He told Tom what he'd found and ended the call. "I'm sure he'll check it out. The bank name and account number will tell us a lot."

"What about Ben's address book? The one that was in code."

"I haven't had a chance to work on it. I'll see what I can figure out on it tonight."

"Is there a purchase of the dress?" she asked, looking over his shoulder.

Line by line, he went through the transactions. "Nope, it's not here."

Edith frowned, then her expression cleared. "Let me go through the receipts." She spread them out on the bed and began to go through them. "Here it is!" She stared at it, then glanced up at him. "It was bought just before Raine was born."

He took the receipt. "Yet they never married. And where

would she have gotten that kind of money? It came from a bridal shop in Virginia Beach. I'm going to go talk to them about it. I can be there by midafternoon. You should stay here in case there's a ransom call."

She nodded. "Of course. The FBI has the line tapped too, right?"

"Yeah, but I don't think we're dealing with a ransom. We would have heard by now."

"I think so too." She exited but left the door open behind her.

He went to his room and carried Ben's coded book back to Gina's room. Might as well start with something simple. Once he began to look at it, he recognized the simple code he'd used in school as a boy. The beginning letters had been reversed so *a* equals *z*, *b* equals *y*, and so on. Simple enough. He found a pen and deciphered the few entries, but an hour later there wasn't much sense to be made of it all.

The book was what it seemed—an address book. The few notations were Amy's address, Ben's address, and another one on Hope Island he suspected might be a fish house since it was out near the four-by-four beaches. A dead end.

Curtis looked around the room. Amy's accusations still rang in his ears. How well did he really know his sister? He would have guessed he knew her very well, from her wilder younger years to the new Gina who had emerged a couple of months before Raine was born. That Gina had been gentle and wise. Full of faith and hope. An inspiration to him and others. But had she deceived him? Was there something much darker under the surface that he'd missed?

Her pink leather Bible was on the nightstand. Flipping through the well-worn book, he noticed she'd marked many passages. This hadn't been a table ornament, but a living, breathing comfort to her. How did he reconcile this with the lies?

———

Amy stormed into the house and tossed her purse on the sofa. Her parents were in the living room and would have to be told. She found her mother curled up on the sofa reading a magazine, and her father smoked his vile pipe while he looked at his investments on his laptop.

Neither of them saw her until she cleared her throat. "I need to talk to you."

Her mother was dressed in a silky pink top and white capris that screamed expensive. She tossed aside the *Cosmopolitan* she'd been reading and stared at her. "What's happened? You look terrible. You should try some of my face cream."

"Dad, shut the computer." She waved smoke out of her face. "And I don't want you smoking in here. Some of my patients are allergic to smoke. Come outside with me." When he didn't move fast enough, she shut the lid for him, then took the computer with her.

"Hey!" He sprang to his feet.

Her mother got up and followed her. "What's this all about, Amy?"

She walked out the back door to the seating area on the back deck and dropped into a chair. She was unutterably weary. There was no way this was going to go well. "Have a seat. I have something important to tell you."

Her mother's face crumpled. "Is she dead?"

Amy shook her head. "They haven't found Raine yet. But Curtis got news today. I'm sure your attorney will be calling as well since a copy was mailed to him. The DNA test came back. Ben is not Raine's father."

Her mother's eyes went as wide as sand dollars, and her mouth sagged. A filmy moisture filled her eyes. "Not Ben's? Then Raine isn't our granddaughter?"

"No. Gina lied about it." It was all Amy could do to choke out the words. Little Raine wasn't hers. Every now and then, she'd thought she'd caught glimpses of Ben in the child's expression or the shape of her eyes. Amy had deluded herself as much as Gina had deluded them.

Her father took a puff of his pipe, then exhaled a stream of smoke. "But you said Ben claimed to be the father. Why would he do that?"

"I'm assuming it was because she convinced him of the lie. Maybe she saw him as a good father for Raine. Maybe the real father was married." Pain throbbed behind her eyes, and she pressed her hand to her forehead. "I don't know, it's all such a jumble."

"So we don't have a granddaughter at all. Ben is truly gone." Mother's mascara was running now, and little hiccups escaped her.

At least her mother seemed to have some real sentiment for Raine. "I'm upset too. I thought we had a little piece of Ben left to love. But that doesn't change the fact that Raine is still missing. I love her and want us to do all we can to get her safely home."

"I think that's up to the FBI now," her father said. "It's not our business."

"Gina was Ben's girl, Dad. I think we still have a responsibility to do what we can. Maybe offer a reward."

"That's ridiculous, Amy." He tamped out his pipe. "Elizabeth was his girl. Not some woman he was too ashamed to introduce to his family."

"Ben had funds he left. We could use that to search. And what about that money? Why was it in a secret account? Have you looked at it?"

"All his possessions passed to me. Of course I looked at it."

She shouldn't have to beg her own father. Why couldn't he see that this might be important? "I'd like to see the statements. Do you still have them?"

He shifted in his chair and frowned. "Not with me, of course."

257

"What about online access?"

"Why are you pushing about this? There's nothing in some old bank statements that will lead you to Raine's kidnapper."

Amy slumped into her chair. "I don't know where else to look. Something they were involved with got them both killed and Raine kidnapped. We have to start somewhere. Dad, this is important. Please, just humor me. What could it hurt? A little girl's life is at stake." Her voice broke.

Her father studied her face, then shrugged. "I can give you the log-in information, and you can take a look, I suppose." He held out his hands for his computer, and she handed it over. "I think I've got it saved on here." His face intent, he navigated through a few sites, then nodded. "Ah, here we are."

With a rising sense of excitement, she took the laptop and saw the bank was in Western Europe. "A Swiss bank?"

"Ben was always very careful. I have two accounts there myself."

Something about it seemed fishy to her. Underhanded. "But why? Isn't that kind of account used for hiding money from the government?" Could it be illegal money he'd stashed away there?

His eyes narrowed, and he flushed. "They pay good interest and are extremely secure. It's smart business to sock some away there in case our economy ever falters again."

The economy was so worldwide now that she didn't see it would make any difference, but she didn't argue with him. Hunching over the screen, she called up the statements one by one. "The deposits are all electronic. Two large deposits three months apart and exactly the same amount, one hundred and fifty thousand dollars. That's it. No drafts out, no purchases. It appears you left the money there?"

"It was a good, safe place."

"Is there a way to find out who made these deposits?"

He shook his head. "The Swiss guard anonymity with great diligence. That's the beauty of doing business with them. So see, just as I said. This didn't help you at all."

"I guess not. Thanks, Dad. I'll leave you to your pipe." She went back inside and down the hall to Ben's room. Tears felt very close and had ever since she'd heard the news. What was true and what was false? She didn't even know anymore.

What if Ben had been involved in something unsavory? The idea hurt her chest. She had defended his memory over and over again, but what if she had been willfully blind? Ben had been a good man, but even good men sometimes found themselves going in the wrong direction. Maybe he'd gotten in over his head.

Her cell phone rang, and Curtis's face flashed across her screen. Maybe Raine had been found. "Curtis, is there news?"

"Not the kind you're hoping for. But Edith and I tossed Gina's room. We found the bank information we'd been looking for. And I know where she bought the wedding dress. I'm heading there now. Want to go with me?"

Part of her wanted nothing less than to go with him, but she heard the note of desperation in his voice. "I'll be ready when you get here."

THIRTY-FIVE

The sun blazed down, and a few tourists strolled the streets of Hope Beach as Curtis drove his Jeep to Amy's cottage. He breathed a sigh of relief when she came out as soon as he parked in the drive. He'd been dreading hearing her parents rail on Gina the way Amy had done.

He smiled at her when she slid into the passenger seat. "Glad you could come."

"Thanks for asking me." Her voice was a little stiff. "So how did you figure out where that beautiful wedding gown was purchased?"

He told her about finding the bank account information. Her face changed when he mentioned the large deposits. "What is it?"

"The exact two deposits were put in Ben's overseas account. I talked my dad into letting me look at it. What were the dates of Gina's deposits?"

"Last September fifteenth and then October fifteenth."

"Those are the same as Ben's." Her eyes were wide. "What could it mean?"

"Obviously someone paid them both for something. We have to figure out what it was."

She looked out the window. "It's sort of sad to know she bought that dress and never got to wear it. Makes me think less of Ben."

Finally.

Her eyes swam with tears when she turned to look at him. "I don't like to think that he might have had feet of clay. I idolized him. All my life he's been my hero."

Just in time he bit back a caustic comment. She didn't need to hear his opinion. Let her form her own as the truth began to come out. "How well do any of us know other people? Most keep their masks firmly in place."

"I know I do," she said so softly he nearly missed it.

He reached the ferry boarding and got the vehicle in line behind an old blue pickup and a tan minivan. The stench of the fuel washed in his open window, but he left it down so he could hear when he was told to pull the vehicle aboard. A few minutes later they were on the deck of the ferry.

They got out and went to sit on a bench at the bow of the boat. Seagulls squawked and swooped overhead, and waves lapped against the ferry as it headed to Hatteras Island. The sea breeze blew strongly here.

She brushed her blowing hair from her eyes. "Preston's rally in Kill Devil is at six. He's probably there now. Would there be time to talk to him on the way to Richmond?"

"The shop closes at nine so we should be fine. Where can we find him?"

"He has a house on the water in Kill Devil. I have the address." She pulled out her phone. "He threw a party for Ben's birthday one year. Here it is, on Virginia Dare Trail." She read him the address.

"We'll be going right through there anyway." He glanced at his watch. "It's two. We should be there by three. Shouldn't take longer than half an hour unless he has something really stupendous to tell us that derails our stop at the bridal shop. It's less than two hours to Virginia Beach. We should be there by six. We can talk to the owners at the shop, then get dinner. Sound okay?"

"Yes." She looked down at her hands. "I want to apologize for how I acted this morning. I was out of line."

Yes, you were. He bit back the words. "But you haven't changed your mind, I bet."

"I don't know what to think right now. That money in Ben's account too . . ." She shook her head. "And it's in a Swiss account. It felt secretive. So nothing makes sense to me."

He didn't much like what he was learning about his sister either. "Let's try to put aside our reservations about both of them. The most important thing right now is to find Raine. We're only following the trail of the money in hopes it will lead us to her. She's all either of us cares about."

"Right," she said.

"Oh, and I deciphered that book of Ben's. I'm not sure why he had it hidden. Not much in it." He told her about the addresses he'd found. Hatteras Landing with its docks and building was just ahead. "We'd better get back to our vehicle."

———

Curtis rolled his window down and let the sea breeze blow through the Jeep. For a moment he let himself dream that his phone would ring with the good news that Raine had been found. Where was she? The thought that she might not still be alive squeezed his heart.

The businesses of Kill Devil Hills sprinkled both sides of the Croatan Highway. Amy stared at the GPS app on her phone. "I think we turn on E. Wright Avenue."

Curtis braked. "Right here."

He steered the car toward the Atlantic and turned onto Virginia Dare Trail. The houses were typical beach houses on stilts, two stories high, in bright colors with decks and beach furniture. Several people carried blankets and chairs toward the access path to the water. The sound of the waves carried through his open window, and the smell of the sea was strong. Banks of sand dunes blocked the view of the sea in most places. Reading the numbers on the houses, he looked for the address they sought.

Amy pointed to a blue house with wraparound decks. "There it is. I recognize it from here."

The place had four cars parked around it. "Looks like he has company. I'll have to park down the road."

Though the Croatan was called a highway, it was more a wide country road with sand blowing across it. He found a place to pull off and got out. "You think he'll talk to us?"

"Why wouldn't he? He's a family friend."

"Who is afraid of getting pulled into a murder investigation. His finance manager is dead. This could derail his campaign."

"I'm sure he wants to get to the bottom of it too." She shaded her eyes with her hand and squinted into the sun. "I think that's him on the deck. Looks like his wife is with him. And his girls." She smiled. "I haven't seen the girls in ages." Her stride quickened.

Blowing sand bit into his skin, bare below his shorts. When they reached the driveway, two suited men stepped between them and the steps to the deck. They looked grave and imposing. "This is private property," the older one with glasses said, blocking them. "You're trespassing."

Amy tipped her chin up in a friendly smile. "I'm Amy Lang, a friend of the Kendricks. If you'll let Preston and Zoe know we're here, I'm sure they'll be glad to see us."

"Wait here." He left them and stepped into the yard with his phone to his ear. Moments later he motioned to them. "You can go up."

Sandbags were stacked under the deck to help with beach erosion, and wooden picket fences marched as far as he could see to help prevent sand drifting. The dunes were huge here, but he caught a glimpse of blue water as they approached the stairs.

As they reached the bottom of the steps, an attractive brunette dressed in shorts ran down the stairs toward them. "Amy, I can't believe it! I was just telling Preston that I should call you and see if you had time to meet." She and Amy hugged, and she glanced at Curtis. "Who's your handsome escort?"

"This is Curtis Ireland. His niece is the little girl who was kidnapped. Curtis, this is Zoe Kendrick."

Zoe's pert smile vanished as she took his hand. "I was appalled to hear about this, Mr. Ireland. I'd hoped once the FBI talked to Grant, it would all be cleared up. His death was a blow both to us on the campaign trail and to you who needed to discover what he'd done with Raine. I assume the FBI is looking for his bodyguard?"

He returned the pressure of her fingers. "Call me Curtis. And yes, they're looking, but so far they haven't been able to locate him. We're praying the FBI can find her quickly."

"Of course." She turned and gestured to the deck. "Come on up. Preston is excited you've stopped by too. And the girls, of course. You're one of their favorite people, Amy."

When they stepped onto the deck, two little girls of about seven and nine rushed to Amy. Curtis watched with his heart thumping in his chest. Would his Raine ever have a gap-toothed smile like the youngest? Would she ever get a chance to wear those cute pink shoes with sparkles? It was all he could do to smile and shake Preston's hand.

Zoe put her hand on her oldest's head. "Girls, would you help me with some snacks?" The girls grumbled but followed her through the back door.

Preston motioned to the chairs, expensive blue-and-white-striped ones that wouldn't bring shame to a Sandals resort. "This is a surprise. Did you try to call?" The rebuke was subtle but present.

Amy shook her head. "We were heading to Richmond when I remembered your rally tonight. I took a chance you might be here. I hope you don't mind."

Preston studied Curtis's face. "Not at all. I'm cooperating fully. I'd be glad if anything I knew helped you locate your little girl. I imagine you're here to see if there's anything else I might remember about Grant."

"Anything might be helpful. I'm desperate to find Raine." His voice broke and Curtis cleared his throat. "Did Grant have any vacation homes or places he liked to go where his bodyguard might head?"

"As I told the FBI, I didn't know him all that well. But my campaign manager is here. I'll let you talk to him." He pulled out his phone and placed a call.

A few minutes later a man of about forty with wings of gray at the temples came up the steps. Dressed in an impeccable navy suit, he looked wary as he approached. "Something wrong?"

"They'd like to ask you some questions about Grant."

"I already talked to the FBI." He looked puzzled but not impatient.

Preston waved his hand at Curtis and Amy. "This is Curtis Ireland, Raine's uncle. Curtis, Amy, this is my campaign manager, Andrew Morgan."

Curtis shook his hand, and the man returned the pressure. He didn't seem ill at ease when he heard who they were and what they wanted. "Thanks for any help you can give me. We're trying to figure out where Grant's bodyguard might have taken Raine. Do you know of any vacation spots Grant liked? Or maybe a family member who would be close enough to shelter him?"

The concern in Andrew's eyes seemed genuine. "I told the FBI that he had a house in Maine. In Kennebunkport. And his sister lives in Myrtle Beach. I gave them the names and addresses

I know. Well, the sister's name. And I had the address in Maine because he let me use it for a long weekend."

"I'll follow up with the FBI," Curtis said.

Amy leaned forward in her chair with her hands clasped in her lap. "There has to be *something* you're forgetting, something that seems inconsequential. Did he have any plans in the few days leading up to his death? Did you see him talking with anyone who struck you as unusual? Any phone calls that seemed odd?"

Andrew started to shake his head, then he paused and frowned. "I just thought of something. His voice mail was acting up, and the old account wasn't working. Our IT department set him up with a new one temporarily. I wonder if they ever got that main one up and going." He pulled out his cell phone and placed a call.

"Anything?" Amy asked when he hung up.

"They have it going, but there weren't any messages on it." He looked disappointed. "I'd hoped we might have something. I really want to help find that little girl."

Curtis heard the ring of sincerity in his voice. "Thanks. Was Grant married?"

"Yeah." Andrew paused. "And he had a teenage girlfriend on the side. I met her once. She's the one who got pulled into this whole mess, poor kid."

Amy leaned forward. "You met Heather? Where was this? And when?"

"About a month ago. We had just finished up a campaign meeting, and she showed up at the apartment he rented in DC. His wife and family have a house in the burbs, and it's convenient to have something closer for business. He was livid. Yelled at her and she cried. I felt sorry for her. I told him it wasn't cool, but he told me to mind my own business."

Amy's eyes widened. "Heather was in DC? Do you know where she lived? And did she ever have any contact with his bodyguard?"

Curtis eyed her. Excitement was coming off her in palpable waves. Where was she headed with this line of questions?

"Yeah, she had a house that he rented for her in Virginia Beach. It was in Preston's name, but Grant paid for it."

Preston grunted. "That's not okay, Andrew. Why am I just hearing about it?"

"I took care of it when I heard about it. He said he'd change the name on the lease, so I thought that was the end of the story."

"Did he?" Preston growled.

Andrew didn't cower before Preston. "I don't know. I'm ashamed to say I didn't follow up once your campaign got into full swing."

Curtis rose. "You think Bossman might have taken Raine there?"

Amy's cheeks were pink. "I don't know, but it's worth checking. Did you tell the FBI about this?"

Andrew shook his head. "I didn't think about it until now."

Curtis whipped out his phone. "I'll have the FBI check it out."

THIRTY-SIX

The brick building housing the bridal shop sat on a corner facing a row of high-end shops. Dresses dripping with sequins and glitter hung on mannequins in the window. Just looking at them made Amy feel a little sick, but she squared her shoulders and followed Curtis. The smell of new clothes hit her when she stepped inside. She well remembered the day she'd picked out her wedding dress. Full of anticipation, she wandered the aisles of dazzling dresses until she found the perfect one. She had no idea that a few months later her lovely wedding would be canceled.

A young woman in a tailored garnet suit stepped forward. "May I help you?" She appeared to be around forty and wore her dark hair in a French knot in a Katharine Hepburnish look.

Curtis nodded. "We'd like to see the manager."

The woman's smile widened as if smiling could ward off whatever problem was about to descend on her head. "That would be me. How can I help you?"

"I need some information about a gown my sister purchased." Curtis dug a paper out of his pocket. "She bought it a year ago."

Amy glanced around as he rattled off the details of the gown and the date it was purchased. What was Ian doing now? Had he found another woman, a whole one who could bear the large family he wanted? She didn't doubt he had. Women flocked to him like egrets to newly mown grass.

She tore her gaze away from the rows and rows of wedding dresses and bridesmaid gowns.

"I remember your sister," the manager said. "And the dress, of course. We don't sell one of those every day. I'm sorry for your loss. She was a sweet young woman."

"Thank you. So the gown was unusual?"

The woman nodded. "Her fiancé had ordered it, and she came in to see it and try it on. We don't typically stock something that expensive."

"Who came with her?"

Curiosity flashed through the woman's eyes, but it was quickly masked. "I have a card on her wedding. Just a moment." She stepped to the computer at the counter and called up a program. "She was engaged to a Preston Smith, but the best man, Ben Lang, helped her pick up the dress. There were several possible brides-maid dresses chosen as well, but there's no mention of names or sizes for those."

Amy barely managed to hold back a gasp. Ben was the *best man*? But everyone thought she wanted to marry Ben. *Preston Smith*. Amy rolled the name around in her mind. The only Preston she knew was Preston Kendrick, but he was married with a wife and children. Smith, just like Grant's fake last name. Surely her stirring suspicions couldn't be right.

Curtis's face seemed etched in stone as he thanked the woman and led Amy back into the sunshine. She didn't say anything until they were back in his Jeep. "I don't understand this. I thought she wanted to marry *Ben*. So not only is he not Raine's father, he's not the man she loved either. So why did he pretend to be?"

"I thought she was crazy about Ben. They spent so much time

together." He started the vehicle and turned the air-conditioning to high. "I think I mentioned she was involved in some political campaigns on occasion. Preston Kendrick's was one of them."

"So you're thinking like I am—Smith is a fake name, and she was in love with Senator Kendrick."

A muscle in his jaw twitched. "I think it's pretty obvious."

The fan cooled her hot cheeks, but her thoughts continued to churn. "I think we need to talk to Preston. Maybe there's some other explanation."

"I sure don't know what it would be. And how do we get him alone? I don't want to accuse him in front of his nice wife or children."

Something about the situation still didn't sit well with her. "I've always admired how much he loved Zoe. I can't quite believe this. What if Gina was seeing Grant instead, and he used Preston's name?"

"That's quite a stretch. She would have known who Preston Kendrick was. She wasn't a gullible girl like Heather. But then, Preston's campaign manager mentioned how Grant had used Preston's name once before. Maybe she knew who he was, but he used Preston's name to buy the dress." He frowned and glanced at her. "We should probably call the FBI."

She shook her head. "Oh no, not yet. Not until we know more. I'd hate to implicate him if there's a reasonable explanation." Amy pulled up a browser on her iPhone and navigated to Preston's campaign schedule. "Tonight's rally is over at eleven. I doubt Zoe will be there until the end. She usually stays for the speech, then takes the girls home to put them to bed."

"So basically waylay him when the rally is over?"

Confrontation wasn't something she relished, but she nodded. "We know Ben wasn't Raine's dad. What if Preston is?"

"And what if he arranged to have her kidnapped?" Instead of anger, hope radiated in Curtis's voice. "I intend to make him tell me where she is."

"But why would he kidnap her? The FBI is involved."

"Maybe he wanted custody."

Amy didn't see the sense of that. "Would he risk that when he could contact you and tell you he was Raine's father?"

The hope in his face faded. "Well, he'd have to get into a custody battle that could be deadly for his campaign."

Amy frowned. "But being arrested for kidnapping would be even deadlier for reelection. He'd be better off waiting until it was all over and then seek custody. Once he was elected, it wouldn't matter much."

"I guess so. For just a minute . . ."

She reached over and squeezed his hand. "I know. But we're going to find her. Preston might know where she is." She couldn't imagine what he might have to do with this, but she planned to ask him. It was all very strange.

"Let's get some dinner," Curtis said, pulling into the busy traffic. "It's rush hour, and we'll make better time if we stop for food now."

"Okay. I'm hungry anyway." She pointed out a raw bar and grill on her side of the road.

She would need all the strength she could get for the long night ahead.

———

Curtis listened to Preston's stump speech in the park by the water. The senator knew just how to inspire the crowd with specific promises on how to fix corruption in government and lower taxes, both issues he'd actually followed through with in his previous term. Until today, Curtis had always liked the senator. Now it was all he could do to keep from curling his lip.

Preston and Gina. Even knowing it was likely true, he saw no evidence of a relationship. Gina stayed on Hope Island most of the time, only going to the mainland four times a year for shopping. Could a clandestine affair have been going on so infrequently?

Voters crowded around Preston after the speech. Curtis stood off to one side with Amy and waited for the throng to thin out. The stars were bright tonight, and the warm, humid air dampened his forehead. Someone had shot off fireworks, and a wisp of gunpowder floated in the air with its acrid smell.

She leaned close to whisper, "I just saw Zoe leave with the girls."

Her breath on his neck felt good. They were in the shadows, and he wanted to slip his arm around her waist. Her closeness would give him courage. But the roadblocks between them felt insurmountable tonight. Each of them defending their dead sibling, her parents. He shifted away as a wave of guilt swept over him. It felt wrong to even feel this attraction when his little Raine was out there somewhere. Was she even alive? He gulped as fear gripped him again.

She had to be all right.

The minutes ticked by as people trickled off to their cars. Finally, only the senator and his aides stood talking. A technician switched off the bright lights and left them even more in the dark.

Curtis took her hand, his fingers curling around hers. "Let's go see him."

Her cold fingers clutched his as though she was nervous. "You know he's going to deny it. I don't know how we'll get him to tell us the truth."

Before Curtis answered, Preston saw them and smiled. "I thought you two were in the crowd. How did I do?"

"Everything rang true. Listen, can we talk to you a minute?" Amy glanced at his aides. "In private?"

The senator's smile faded. "Sure." He turned to the others. "I'll meet you at the van in a few minutes." He joined Curtis and Amy. "What's up?"

There was no easy way to segue into the discussion. No matter what Curtis said, it was going to sound accusatory. "How well did you know my sister, Gina?"

Preston's brow lifted. "She worked on my campaign a few years ago, but I'm sure you know that already."

Curtis dropped Amy's hand and stepped closer. Was Gina's murderer standing in front of him? "How about in a personal way?"

Spots of color came into Preston's cheeks. "I don't know what you're implying."

"I'm not implying—I'm asking if you're Raine's father." Curtis curled his fingers into his palms and struggled not to grab the guy by the collar and demand to know where his niece was. Preston's reaction was proof enough.

"Of course not. What a crazy accusation!" Preston glanced at Amy. "You don't believe this lie, do you? Where's all this coming from?"

She edged a little closer to Curtis. "Someone ordered a fancy wedding dress for Gina. Someone named Preston Smith."

"And is my last name Smith?" Preston's voice rose. "No, it is not. You, of all people, shouldn't be accusing me. You know me too well for that, Amy."

"Ben wasn't Raine's father," Amy said. "You're the only Preston we know."

He clenched his fists. "And that automatically makes me a suspect? I thought we were innocent until proven guilty in this country. You're both about to hang me without even letting me defend myself."

Could he be right? It's not like there were no other Prestons in the country. Curtis took a step forward. "Would you be willing to take a paternity test?"

"I will not! I love my wife." He stared at Amy. "You know how close we are. And all it would take is a whiff of this to hit the press and my campaign would be over. This conversation is over, and I never want it to be brought up again. Don't you find it odd that you're accusing an honest family man when Gina's life tended toward the wild side? I'm not the one who should be on the defensive. In fact, I refuse to be."

As he started away, Amy put her hand on his forearm. "Preston, I'm sorry if we offended you. Surely you see that we have to leave no stone unturned. There's a little girl missing."

Preston's eyes widened. "You mean you actually thought I kidnapped that baby? Amy Lang, if your father knew you'd accused me of something so heinous, he'd have something to say about it."

"I realize that," she said softly. "Raine has been missing for four days. We're all going a little crazy."

"You believe me, don't you?" Preston's eyes were anguished. "I would never harm a child. Never."

Even Curtis was beginning to doubt his assumption, so he was not surprised when Amy nodded her head.

"I believe you, Preston, and I'm sorry. Truly. We just had to ask."

"No, you didn't. You should have known better. I'm disappointed in you, Amy. I don't think I can ever feel the same as I did about you. It's going to be hard to look at you and not remember your accusations."

"Blame me, not her," Curtis said. "And how about you knock it off with the guilt trip? If one of your daughters were missing, you'd do the same thing. You wouldn't worry about offending someone. You'd run roughshod over anyone in a quest to find her."

Preston stared at him, then finally nodded. "True enough. All right then, I accept your apology. But no more of this. And if I hear that my wife got wind of your suspicions . . ."

"We deliberately waited to talk to you in private," Amy said.

"I should be happy for small favors," Preston muttered as he walked away.

Amy exhaled. "That didn't go well. And I guess I can't blame him. We jumped to conclusions pretty fast."

"I think our assumptions were logical."

She glanced at him. "You believed him, didn't you?"

He wished he could say no, but he nodded. "Yeah, I believed him. I've always thought he was a good guy, and we don't have any real evidence proving otherwise."

As they walked back to the car, he prayed for Raine, that she was all right and that God would lead them to the right clues to find her.

THIRTY-SEVEN

Heather blinked at the bright sun as she stood on the sidewalk outside the jail. She'd seen little of the sun through the small window in her cell. She was free, if you could call it that when she had no idea where to go or what to do now. Grant had cut her off, and there was no way her parents would help her.

Someone called her name, and she turned to see Amy beckoning from her small red car. She looked serious, though her lips tipped in a smile that didn't reach her eyes.

"Hi." Heather bent over to speak through the open window. "You heard I got out, huh? Did you bring my things?"

"No, I came to take you home."

"T-Take me home?"

"Yep. Get in."

Heather didn't waste time with questions, not with people staring curiously at her. Once she was in the passenger seat with her belt fastened, she ducked her head. "Thank you."

"You're welcome. I thought you probably didn't have anywhere else to go."

Heather kept her head down, allowing the swing of her hair to hide her face from Amy. "I don't," she mumbled. "Did you post my bail?"

"I did."

Heather caught her breath and finally looked up. "Why? I would have thought you hated me now."

Amy's eyes were kind when she glanced her way, then back at the road. "Tom told me how old you really are. Seventeen."

"So?"

"You were taken in by a con man. Tom called your mother, you know."

Heather's fingers tightened around the armrest. "Why would he do that? He had no right!"

"I suppose you already know what your mother told him."

Heather swallowed, knowing full well the depth of her mother's hatred. "She said she doesn't have a daughter. She tossed me out long ago."

"How long have you been on your own?"

"Two years."

Amy pulled into the drive and turned off the car before she faced her. "Care to tell me what happened?"

The muscles in Heather's throat gave a convulsive twitch. It wasn't something she'd told anyone. She looked down at her hands. "My mom's boyfriend made a pass at me. Okay, more than a pass. H-He—"

Amy put her hand on her arm. "I get the picture. Your mom found out and blamed you?"

Heather touched her suddenly wet face. "How'd you guess?"

"I've heard it before." Amy sighed. "In my line of work, I see more than you can imagine." She pushed open the passenger door. "Come on inside. I'll fix you some lunch."

In her cell at night, Heather had pictured Rosemary Cottage. The roses rambling up the porch, the herbs swaying in the breeze, the crisp paint. She still wasn't sure how it had happened that the cottage had become home when she'd never felt at home anywhere.

Once there, she followed Amy up steps she never thought she'd see again. "Why are you doing this? It's my fault Raine is missing."

Amy opened the screen door and motioned her inside. "I don't know, really. I guess I felt sorry for you when I saw you at the jail. And I'm hoping you will want to help find Raine."

"I do, oh I do!" She followed Amy to the kitchen and watched as she got into the refrigerator and pulled out hummus and cheese. "A-And I want to see Grant pay for what he did to me."

Amy gave a small gasp and turned. "No one told you?"

"Told me what?"

Amy's mouth was soft, and her eyes held sympathy. "Someone murdered Grant, honey. His body was found in the bay the night Raine went missing."

The strength ran out of Heather's legs, and she grabbed the counter. "He's dead?"

"Yes. Are you okay?"

Heather's eyes filled. She thought his actions had ripped every root of love from her heart, but she was suddenly sobbing. Amy quickly embraced her, and she buried her face in the soft cotton of Amy's shirt.

Amy led her to the table and pulled out a chair. "I shouldn't have told you so abruptly. I'm sorry. I guess you still have feelings for him. Let me get you some iced tea." She moved to the counter. "We have no idea how to find Raine. Or this Bossman fellow."

While Amy rummaged in the refrigerator, Heather tried to collect herself. Grant was scum, a con artist, and who knew what else, but he'd been all she had, and she'd been holding out hope that he would call her and ask her to join him. That he wasn't as bad as it first appeared when she called from jail.

Now she was truly alone.

She clutched the cold glass of iced tea and took a gulp. "Do you think I still have a job?"

"I don't know, Heather." Amy hesitated, then shook her head. "I'm sure Imogene has heard what you did."

"And likely will terminate me." Heather put the glass on the table and buried her face in her hands. "I've so screwed up my life. There's no way of fixing it."

"There's always a way of redemption."

Heather lifted her head. "You're talking about God, I suppose. Let's get real, okay? I'm a lost cause, even for him."

"No one is ever a lost cause." Amy paused. "Have you ever thought about going back to school? You never finished, did you?"

Heather shook her head. "It's impossible. I have to work to support myself." Rising, she went to look out the window. "There has to be a way to find Bossman."

"What do you know about him?"

What did she know? The man had been an enigma. Always hovering near Grant with that ominous bulge in his pocket she'd assumed was a Glock. He looked the sort to carry a heavy-duty gun like that. And why did Grant need protection?

She turned abruptly. "He was a bodyguard. From things they said, I thought he'd been with Grant a long time, years. He had a Boston accent. I heard Grant call him Vince once, so that might be his first name."

"You have no idea why you were supposed to take Raine?"

Heather went back to the table and sat down. "I told you—it was about paternity and money."

Amy's face was full of pain. "That makes a lot more sense now that we know Ben isn't Raine's father."

———

Amy's eyes were gritty as she sat on the sofa with her legs curled under her. She couldn't remember when she'd last had a good night's sleep. With the baby still missing, she tossed and turned, praying most of the night. And five days later they were no closer to finding Raine.

Ever since she'd gotten back from the jail three hours ago, Heather had barely moved from her bedroom. It was as if she feared saying the wrong thing and ending up back at the jail. Heather's cell phone rang, and Amy picked it up to take it to her. And froze.

Ben's picture flashed on the screen.

Amy stared at it. It was like hearing from a ghost. She had to know. She flicked it on and muffled her voice. "Hi."

"Heather, that you? You sound like you have a cold."

It was her brother's voice in her ear. No other voice had that deep rumble, that resonance that made you want to do whatever he wanted. Amy's throat closed, and she couldn't speak as tears flooded her eyes. Was this some kind of prank? A recording that some cruel person had used to hurt her? She looked again. Wait, this was Heather's phone, not hers. Why would someone play a prank on Heather?

"Heather?" Ben asked. "You there?"

It was no recording. "Ben," she managed to say. "It's Amy."

There was a long pause. "I don't know any Ben. I'm looking for Heather." The phone clicked in her ear.

Shaking and crying, Amy ran up the stairs and flung open Heather's door. The girl was sprawled across the bed with a *Seventeen* magazine in her hand.

She bolted upright. "What's wrong?"

"You got a call," Amy choked out. "It was Ben."

"You answered my phone?"

Amy held up the phone. "I saw my brother's picture on this phone. Of course I answered it!"

"What are you getting all upset about? So what if he called me?"

"He's dead!" Amy threw the phone onto the bed. "At least I thought he was until today."

Heather got up. "Oh. Yeah, that."

"What is going on? I have to know right now. And where is my brother? I want to see him. Immediately." She began to shake so hard she could barely stand, so she grabbed the edge of Heather's desk and held on. "You have to tell me."

The girl bit her lip and sat on the edge of the bed. "It's not my business. You'll have to ask him."

Amy knew she should be elated to discover her brother was alive. But she had a sick feeling in the pit of her stomach that she wouldn't like the reason behind all the deception. "I'll be happy to do that. Where is he?"

"He's going to kill me," Heather groaned.

"If you don't want to go back to jail, you'll tell me right now where he is."

"He's at a house on White Swan Beach."

"One of the four-by-four beaches?" There were fabulous houses along that northern stretch of Hope Island, but the only access was with a four-wheel drive.

Heather nodded. "It's a big blue house."

Amy grabbed her arm. "You're going to show me."

Heather tugged her arm out of Amy's grasp. "We can't get there in your little car."

"Curtis will drive us." Amy rushed out of the room and back downstairs to get her cell phone. Her heart pounded as the call rang through. Ben was alive. What did it all mean?

"Amy. Is there news?"

Sobs erupted from her throat. "I-It's Ben."

"Ben? What do you mean?"

"He's *alive*, Curtis." She told him about the call. "Can you come? The only access is with a four-wheel drive."

"I'll be right there. Oh and, Amy . . . ?"

She'd started to hang up. "Yes?"

"I'm glad he's alive, honey."

Her throat closed. "Thanks, but I—I don't know what to think. He's *lied*, to all of us. How can he even explain that? See you in a few minutes." She ended the call and dropped her phone into her purse.

Was that the back door? Her legs barely carried her to the kitchen, but the room was empty. A flash of movement caught her eye through the window. It was Heather, running for all she was worth into the trees.

Amy leaped for the door and jerked it open, but by the time she reached the deck, the girl was gone. "Heather!"

She raced in the direction she'd seen the girl, but though she called and searched for fifteen minutes, she couldn't find her. There was a distant voice. Curtis had arrived and was calling for her. He sounded almost frantic. Retracing her steps, she rushed back to the cottage. He was standing on the back deck.

Relief lit his features when he saw her. He leaped from the deck and caught her in his arms. "I was so worried when I couldn't find you." He pulled her close and rested his chin on her head.

His heart thudded under her cheek, and she felt cradled and protected. His lips grazed her forehead, and she closed her eyes, savoring the moment of safety and contentment. Then reality intervened. Ben was out there, alive somewhere.

She pulled away a few inches. "Heather ran off, Curtis. Without her, we have no idea which house. All she said was it was blue."

His breath whispered across her cheek. "We can stop at every blue house we see. We'll find him. I can have the sheriff look for her too. She can't get off the island without being seen." Keeping one arm around her, he pulled out his phone. "I have to let go a minute, honey. I think you're in shock. You're still trembling." He led her to the deck and got her seated on a step, then placed the call.

Amy felt as though she were about to shake into a million pieces. How could Ben do this to her—to their parents? He'd let them believe he'd drowned and was eaten by a shark. Who was he, really? Not the brother she thought she knew.

THIRTY-EIGHT

Curtis had taken the top off his Jeep for better visibility. The big tires ate up the distance along the sand, smoothed by the outgoing tide earlier. The ocean breeze blew Amy's curls into a tangled riot around her face. A few puffy clouds floated in the brilliant sky overhead. It was a perfect late afternoon—or would have been if they'd been out here for any other reason.

So far, the few houses where they'd stopped had been either empty or occupied by someone who looked at them oddly for inquiring. The dunes had seemed endless when they started, but now there wasn't much left of this stretch of beach before they would need to give up and turn around. There was no cell phone service out here either, so they would have to go back to a place where they had service to see if the sheriff had found Heather.

The dunes rolled into maritime forest to their left, but he stayed at the waterline where the moisture had packed the sand into a smooth stretch of makeshift road. The recent storm had deposited more than the usual amount of kelp and seaweed.

He glanced at Amy, who wore a pensive expression. "I can see the wheels turning. You've thought of something?"

Her eyes were wide, and she bit her lip. "It may mean nothing, but Preston has a vacation house out here. He rarely uses it, but my parents visited once. It's blue. I don't know—it may be a wild card."

"I thought you'd absolved him of all guilt in this."

She peered ahead, then looked back at him. "It's a little too coincidental, don't you think? That he would have a house out here where Ben is?"

"Maybe. Where is his place?"

"Clear at the end."

Something niggled at the edges of his memory. "Wait a minute. That address book of your brother's. There was an address listed out this way. I thought it was a fish house. Could it be Preston's house?" He drove back the way he'd come until he had two bars, then pulled to the side of the road and called Edith and asked her to look at the note on his desk. He jotted down the address she gave him. "Let's check this address."

She nodded, but tears stood in her eyes. "Why would Ben pretend to be dead? I don't understand any of this."

He glanced at her. The anguish in her voice told him a lot. If he'd suddenly found out Gina were alive and had let Edith and him grieve all this time, he would have been devastated too. It was the height of selfishness. Though he'd disliked Ben, Curtis would never have pegged him as deliberately cruel to his family. Unless that money had been stolen or something. Maybe someone was after him.

He drove along the beach and watched the signposts that designated the addresses.

"That's it!" She pointed to a large blue beach house set off at the edge of the maritime forest. "I recognize the widow's walk on top."

"And that's the address in your brother's book." He slowed the Jeep and turned toward the house. From here, it didn't appear to be occupied. The hurricane shutters were shut, and the house had a closed feeling. The driveway was empty, but he drove on past and parked along the beach down the road. "I don't want to warn him that we're here."

Amy got out as soon as he parked. "I'm going to go around back. Lots of people out here hide keys."

"You don't want to knock?" He followed her down the road and around the side yard.

"No. He might not answer." Her voice was tight.

They reached the back, and she began to check the yard. Nothing under the mat or on the windowsill. No key around the garage. She headed for a small wishing well. All the bricks were right with nothing hidden.

"I don't think it's here," he said.

"Just a minute." Lifting the flowers in the bucket of the wishing well, she exhaled. "It's here." She extracted a key, then headed to the back door.

The big deck on the back appeared to have been coated recently with solid gray stain. The red-and-white-striped deck furniture looked clean and new, and there was no debris in the chairs, so someone had been here in the not-too-distant past, at least long enough to clean. He said nothing about it, though, as she stepped past the table and peered in the window of the red back door.

"See anything?" He looked over the top of her head. "Looks like someone has been here. Dishes and glasses are on the counter." They looked fresh too. The half-eaten peanut butter sandwich wasn't moldy.

"Peanut butter and jelly is Ben's favorite." She inserted the key in the door. When it clicked, she twisted the knob and opened the door. The aroma of some kind of soup rushed to greet them.

Her face went even whiter. "Smells like tomato soup. Ben eats it nearly every day."

He followed her into the kitchen. Touching the pan on the

stove, he nodded. "Still warm." The distant sound of a television's canned laughter came through the doorway.

She tipped her head and listened. "*MASH*. Ben loves it." Color washed up her cheeks, then faded, leaving her deathly pale again.

He put his hand on her shoulder. "Are you okay? Want me to go first?"

She tensed. "No, I want to see his face and catch his first expression."

"Are you sure you're ready for this, honey? It's going to be hard. We both are pretty sure who we're going to find in there."

She covered his hand with hers. "I realize now I don't know my own brother. If Ben could deceive me so completely, what does that say about me and my discernment?"

He wasn't sure how to answer her. Little by little, he'd gotten past her defenses, but he could feel her closing up, pushing him away. And who could blame her? What Ben had done was indefensible. It would shake anyone's foundational beliefs about human nature.

He pulled her into an embrace, but she came stiffly with her arms hanging to her sides. Her shoulders were rigid. "Let's take this one minute at a time, okay? Don't borrow trouble. Remember the money in the bank. Maybe he was hiding out for his own safety and didn't want to pull his family into danger."

A bit of the tension eased from her body at his words, even though he didn't necessarily believe them himself. He hoped it was possible Ben had done this unselfishly, but from what Curtis knew of the man, he doubted it.

Her head on his chest moved, and she nodded. "I hope you're right. Otherwise, this will kill my parents. And me." She pulled away and wiped at her wet cheeks. "I'm ready."

She squared her shoulders and marched toward the sound of the television.

Amy had heard this episode of *MASH* a dozen times or more. It was Ben's favorite, where Hawkeye invents a Captain Tuttle to be able to get supplies to a nun. How appropriate that Ben's favorite would be about inventing a person who never existed. She doubted her brother had done this for any kind of altruistic motive like Hawkeye.

She moved to the doorway of the living room. A man sat on the sofa facing away. She immediately recognized the shape of his skull, the curve of his jaw.

Her brother was alive and well, at least until she had a chance to kill him personally.

Her first impulse was to rush in and hug him to death, even though what he'd done was incredibly selfish and hurtful.

Tears welled in her eyes, and she recognized them as tears of joy, but she knew tears of disillusionment and pain would follow on their heels. Alive. Ben was alive. She couldn't quite wrap her mind around the truth as she stood and stared. He must have felt or heard something because he tensed. Ben slowly turned his head, and his green-gold eyes, so like hers, widened when he saw her.

He rose, squared his shoulders, then held out one hand. "Amy."

"Ben," she choked out. "I *knew* it was you on the phone."

His gaze flickered to the man behind her, and his lip curled. "Curtis. Is this your doing?"

Amy clenched her fists and took a step toward him. "Is *what* his doing? The fact that you lied to me and to our parents? The fact that you told everyone Raine is your daughter?" She glanced around. "Is Raine here?"

A muscle in his jaw twitched. "No, I don't know where she is. I'd hoped to keep her safe."

"Safe from who?" Curtis put in. "I have to say this is pretty low, Ben, even for a scumbag like you, but we'd hoped you had her."

She'd known Curtis didn't care for Ben, but she hadn't realized until now how deep that dislike went. What had he seen that she'd missed? The deceit in the man, the selfishness?

She swallowed the boulder in her throat. "Why?"

Ben shrugged. "Better sit down. This is going to take awhile."

A woman spoke from the steps. "I don't think so."

Zoe Kendrick stepped into view with a big pistol in her hand. It was pointed at Amy.

"Zoe?" Amy couldn't take her eyes off the woman's cold eyes. This woman was nothing like the smiling, vivacious wife of a senator she'd always known. "What are you doing?" A familiar fragrance wafted toward her. It had been Zoe's musky cologne in the house after the break-in.

"Your brother won't have the guts to do what needs to be done now, so I'll take care of it myself. Luckily, we have no neighbors out here." Zoe gestured with the gun. "Out the back. I don't want blood on my floors."

Ben clenched his fists. "This isn't necessary, Zoe."

"Good grief, Ben. Do you think either of these two are just going to go back to Hope Beach and forget they saw you? You should have thought of the consequences before you tried to blackmail Preston."

Blackmail? Amy stood rooted to the floor, unable to move a muscle. She had to understand this. If Ben had blackmailed Preston, would it have been about Gina? Maybe Raine was Preston's child. Could he have had Raine kidnapped to protect her from Zoe?

Curtis took a step. "Where is Raine?"

Zoe's finger tightened on the trigger. "If you move again, the bullet will go straight into Amy's heart. I'm a very good shot."

Curtis held up his hands. "Fine, I'm not moving. But where is Raine?"

Zoe's eyes glittered. "Ben was going to help me eradicate the evidence. I suspect that somehow Preston figured out what was going on and had her moved to safety. But he has no idea I have Bossman in my pocket too. I was about to go take care of that problem when you arrived."

"You always said you wanted to be First Lady someday," Amy said. "Preston's affair with Gina and his out-of-wedlock child would derail all his political ambitions."

Zoe smiled. "I never would have known about her if Ben hadn't gotten greedy, so I have him to thank for that. It requires a ruthless hand to cover these kinds of problems."

Amy could see the entire convoluted pattern. "Did Preston really love Gina? He bought her an expensive wedding dress. I bet he was going to leave you. Did he send me the e-mail suggesting Ben's 'death' wasn't all it appeared?" The expression on Zoe's face confirmed her suspicions.

Ben stood clenching and unclenching his fists as he stared at Zoe with an uneasy expression. "Is that how you ended up on the island? You got an e-mail about me? I wondered why you suddenly started poking into things."

Amy stared at the face she'd always loved so much. "But how did you get involved, Ben? I don't understand."

Comprehension flashed over Curtis's face. "I bet I know. Amy, you mentioned that he's good friends with Preston. I bet he asked Ben to pretend to be Raine's father to throw off suspicion when she became pregnant after working on his campaign."

Amy stared at him. "Ben?"

Her brother didn't meet her gaze. "Things got kind of out of hand. That's why I faked my death. I had a friend pick me up while I was out surfing. I tossed my wetsuit overboard and made teeth marks in my surfboard."

"I think you see we have no choice but to eliminate them.

They've figured it out." Zoe gestured with the gun. "Move. Out the door. The floor is tile, so I can shoot you here if you leave me no choice. Easy cleanup."

Amy didn't know this hard-eyed woman, but she knew determination when she saw it. And outside, they might have a chance to escape. When Zoe cocked the gun, Amy headed for the back door. "Take it easy, we're going."

"Slow down!" Zoe snapped. "My gun is on lover boy's back, so if you try to run off, he goes first."

Amy slowed and took Curtis's hand. They might be able to communicate by touch. They reached the deck and she paused, gauging what they might use as a distraction or a weapon. Would Ben allow this woman to shoot them? Amy couldn't fathom the brother she knew standing aside and doing nothing to help them. She glanced back at Ben, but he didn't meet her gaze as he brought up the rear of their little death march.

The trees were thick where they walked along the back of the property. She could pretend to trip when they entered the forest. That might provide enough distraction for Curtis to grab the gun. But how to tell Curtis what she planned?

She glanced at the path. The mulched walk turned before it ended. Branches littered the ground. A likely culprit to cause her "accident" was ten feet ahead. Squeezing Curtis's hand, she tried to signal to the branch with her eyes and stumbled a bit. He gave a slight shake of his head, and she could only pray he understood what she planned. His fingers left hers as he reached to his head and adjusted his do-rag.

They reached the branch, and Amy tensed. Her foot touched it, and she pretended to falter, then rolled across the limb. A shot rang out, but she was facedown breathing in the scent of pine needles. Rolling quickly out of the way, she sprang to her feet and turned to face Zoe.

THIRTY-NINE

Birds chirped overhead, and his feet kicked up pine needles as Curtis launched himself at Zoe. A shot rang out, and something ripped into his arm. He knocked the gun out of her hand as they both went down in a tangle of arms and legs.

Zoe clawed at his face. "Get off me!"

He grabbed her wrists and hauled her to her feet as blood trickled down his arm. The wound didn't hurt that much, at least not yet. She fought like a wolverine, and though he was bigger and stronger, he struggled to keep her pinned.

"Amy, grab the gun," he said, panting.

When he turned to look, the gun was in Ben's hand, not Amy's. And it was pointed at him.

"Let her go." Ben's finger caressed the trigger as if he wanted to pull it.

Curtis glanced at Amy. She stared at her brother with wide eyes. Her shoulders sagged as the fight drained out of her.

When she took a step toward Ben, he shook his head and motioned with the gun for her to go over by Curtis. "I'm not going to tell you again to turn Zoe loose."

Amy reached Curtis's side as he reluctantly released the struggling woman. "Your arm." She touched his hand.

Curtis kept his eye on the gun. "It's just a scratch." Would Ben really shoot his own sister?

Zoe glared at Ben and swiped her hair out of her eyes. When she moved to Ben's side, she reached for the gun, but he jerked it away. She frowned, then dropped her hands back to her sides without a word.

Ben gestured to Zoe. "You can join them." She gasped and reached for him, but he turned the gun on her. "Do what I said, or I'll shoot you where you stand."

"Ben, we're in this together." Her voice quavered, but she shuffled to where Curtis stood.

Ben's lips flattened. "I think it's time we broke up the partnership. I can't trust you. With you out of the way, I can take my money and disappear into Central America, just like I planned."

"But everything is nearly over now, once we clear up this little detail."

"Look, when Grant's cover was blown, I took care of him for you, but you keep upping your demands. If it hadn't been that you needed another henchman with Grant gone, I'm sure you would have killed me too. I'm sick of it. I want out." He motioned with the pistol. "Get going."

Took care of Grant. Ben must have killed Grant or arranged to have him killed before the authorities could question him. If Curtis didn't do something, the cold-eyed man might really kill his own sister. Zoe bit her lip and started off down the path. Curtis glanced at Amy, then took her hand and followed. How did he plan to dispose of them?

Amy squeezed his hand, then pulled loose and turned to face her brother. "Ben, you're not going to shoot me. You and I both know it. I'm tired and Curtis is hurt. I'm going back."

The gun shook in Ben's hand. "I don't want to hurt you, Ames, but I'm in too deep. I don't intend to go to jail. Surely you wouldn't want that either. Can you promise me you'll let me leave the country and never tell Mom and Dad what happened here? I know you'll keep your word."

Curtis cast a surreptitious glance around. Ben stood on uneven ground. If Curtis tackled him, it should be easy to take him over.

Her eyes soft, Amy held her hand out toward her brother. "Give yourself up. Tell the police what really happened here."

Ben shook his head. "I killed a man. I never thought I'd sink so far, but things just got out of hand. I have enough money to get out of the country now and live well. I intend to take this second chance."

Amy glanced at Zoe, who was looking more and more panicked. "She had Bossman kill Gina, didn't she? And then forced you into killing Grant. Once his identity was revealed, she knew it would only be a matter of time before the police found out what she'd done."

Ben shook his head. "Zoe tried to have me killed too, but I realized what was going on and faked my own death so I could get the heat off until I figured out what to do. I knew she'd gone too far when she had Bossman plant that bomb in Curtis's car. You could have been killed! I never wanted to see you hurt."

"You started it!" Zoe said. "Demanding more and more money. I had no choice."

Bile rose in Curtis's throat. This woman had had his sister killed. "Why did she have to die? She loved Preston, I know she did. The money in her account. I can't believe she would blackmail Preston."

Ben had the grace to look ashamed. "I told her the money was support from Preston. I didn't want to leave her with nothing."

Amy gasped. "You loved her?"

He nodded. "I would have taken her with me if she would have gone, but she loved Preston in spite of his weakness. When she started going to church, she broke it off though. And she was livid when she found out the support money had been blackmail money."

"Which is probably when you had the big fight Leah overheard." Curtis felt more and more sick. His sweet sister had been so naive, but hadn't they all? "So you went into hiding until Zoe found you and agreed to pay up if you'd finish one little detail and eliminate Grant so he couldn't spill the beans about who hired him."

"That's it in a nutshell," Ben said. "I leave tomorrow, and this will all be over."

"What about Heather?"

Ben shrugged. "I thought she might know where Raine was. I wanted to get her to safety."

Tears rolled down Amy's cheeks. "You could have asked Dad for money. There was no need to resort to blackmailing Preston."

Ben kept the gun trained on Zoe. "I owed some bad people a whole lot of money. Dad would never give it to me, and I know enough about these dudes to be certain that I'd be in a box if I didn't either pay up or get out of the country. I decided it was better to skip out, just disappear."

"And we'd never know you were alive and living somewhere else." Amy's voice was choked. "You're not the man I thought you were. You hid your true nature very well."

He shrugged. "Sometimes you have to do what you have to do. One thing leads to another, and then you're too far in to back out without losing everything. So how about it, sis? I don't want to hurt you. Do I have your word?"

She wiped her eyes with the back of her hand. "What about Curtis and Zoe?"

"I can't trust them like I can you. I don't have any choice here."

Amy's cold fingers crept back into Curtis's hand. "Then no. I love Curtis. I can't stand by and watch him die."

Curtis's heart kicked in his chest at her admission, but there was no time to examine what she'd said until he took down Ben.

Something rustled in the vegetation, then Fabio stepped into their path. The horse neighed. Amy's eyes widened, and she gave that peculiar whistle. The horse trotted toward her, though he rolled his eyes at Ben. She dug out a handful of dried herbs from her pocket and fed it to him.

Ben's attention was on the pony. "Did you call that horse?"

While Ben was distracted, Curtis leaped without waiting for another opportunity. His body barreled into Ben's, and they both toppled into the marsh. The water was only a foot or so deep, but it smelled of swamp and mud. Curtis came up spitting the nasty stuff, but at least he had Ben by the throat. He staggered to his feet and dragged Ben up with him. The gun was gone, lost in the marsh. He had to manhandle Ben to shore.

When they stepped onto dry ground, he found Amy had Zoe pinned to the ground on her stomach. He took off his belt and tied them both as well as he could.

"Now to turn them over to the police," he said.

Amy nodded, but her eyes were filled with tears. There was little joy in this turn of events.

———

Heather bent over with her hands on her knees as she struggled to draw in a breath. With the sun falling, it was dark in the woods, but she held on to what bit of courage she had left. Watching Amy, she'd come to realize how selfish and cruel she'd been. Helping to take that little girl. What had she been thinking? Now that it was over, she hated herself. Hated how gullible she'd been, how easily deceived.

The only way to redeem herself was to find that baby and get her back. As she'd run away from Amy, Heather remembered something Bossman had said. *The hole in the wall.* He was supposed to meet Grant there. They might still be there. It had been easy to catch a ride in the back of a truck. She'd waited until the driver wasn't looking, then hid under the tarp. Grant had often referred to his tiny house at the tip of Hope Island as his hole in the wall. If Bossman knew about it, he might have taken the baby there.

Her feet hurt, and her lungs burned from running. She had to have hiked a good five miles by now. She stood and took another deep breath, then got going again. The place was just ahead with a lone light shining out the back window. If he was there with the baby, what was she going to do? How could she get Raine away from him? He was much too big for her to take on by herself, and she'd left her cell phone behind when she'd run away from Amy.

Her feet touched the damp grass of the yard. She took off her sandals so they'd make no noise and tiptoed to the back door, then peered in its window. The place was just a two-room shack, but Raine sat in a crib shoved into the corner. She was sucking her thumb. Heather almost cried when she saw the little one alive and in relatively good condition. She wasn't crying or anything, so maybe he'd been good to her. There was even a little doll on her lap.

His head against the back of the broken-down sofa, Bossman slept with his mouth open. A woman in the other piece of furniture, a wooden rocker, sat knitting. She was older and had Bossman's chin and nose. His mother? It was hard for Heather to wrap her head around the fact that a man like Bossman could even have a mother. She noticed a beer on the little stand by the sofa and prayed he might be too drunk to see her sneak in and grab Raine. But she still had to contend with the older woman.

What if she distracted her? Maybe broke something in the front yard that she'd go to investigate. Then when the mom went out the front door, Heather could zoom in the back and grab Raine. It was worth a try.

Heather rummaged in the trash and grabbed the necks of four beer bottles. Rounding the house, she hefted two bottles in each hand and tossed them to the center of the road. As they shattered, she darted around the back and raced to the door.

Through the window, she saw the woman get up and hurry to the door. Bossman was still in a drunken stupor. Heather eased open the door and dashed through the kitchen to the crib. In seconds, she had Raine in her arms and was hightailing it out the back door. The little girl's hands clutched Heather's neck, but she didn't cry.

Heather raced out the door and pulled it shut behind her. She glanced over her shoulder and saw the older woman entering the front door.

Without waiting to see if she'd notice the child gone, Heather ran with every bit of strength she could muster for the shadows. There was help just down the road, a neighbor. Once she found other people, she would ask them to call the Hope Island sheriff's department or the FBI.

"Dude?" Raine asked. Her fists were tangled in Heather's hair.

"We're going to find him," Heather promised. Her heart squeezed when Raine smiled and put her head on her shoulder.

She glanced behind her and saw a wash of light from the open back door. Either Bossman or his mother was looking around outside. Putting on more speed, she raced for the dim light of a house in the distance.

A man's voice bellowed behind her, and she dared another glance behind. Bossman was running this way, but she wasn't sure if he'd seen her or if he was just looking. When she jogged to the right, he did too, and her stomach plunged.

He'd spotted her with Raine.

She wasn't going to make it to the safety of the other house. And did she dare bring down his wrath on some unsuspecting occupants? Her gaze frantically scanned the landscape. There was a rowboat along the shore to her right. Changing directions, she leaped to the pier where it was docked and untied it.

She stepped into it with Raine, then put the baby down and grabbed the oars. Raine started to wail. "I'll hold you in a minute, baby." With a few strokes, she was away from the dock and heading away from land.

Shouting and swearing, Bossman stood swaying on the dock. He raised his fist. "Come back here and I won't shoot!"

Heather rowed harder, her back protesting at the unfamiliar exertion. Bossman shouted again, then dove into the water. His big head popped out of the waves, and his muscular arms pulled him quickly toward the boat.

What was she going to do? A few more strokes and he'd reach them. He was liable to tip them all into the water, and Heather didn't have a life vest on Raine, who was wailing even louder where she sat on the bottom of the boat.

Her gaze lit on a metal fishing box, and she picked it up. It was heavy enough to do some damage. Standing up with it in her hands, she waited for him to get nearer. When his meaty hand grasped the side of the rowboat, she brought the box down on his head with all her might.

He didn't make a sound, but his hand fell off the boat, and he disappeared under the water. Heather grabbed the oars again and rowed for the next house down.

FORTY

An FBI SUV and Sheriff Bourne's truck, both with lights flashing, were parked in front of the Kendrick summer-house. Ben and Zoe had been taken into custody, and a news helicopter circled the property looking for a place to land as Amy walked away with Curtis. The sand would be crawling with media in another hour. This was big news and would be retold on crime shows for years to come.

Sunset hovered on the horizon with calming golds and lavenders that eased the tension from her shoulders as she walked the dunes with Curtis holding her hand. The FBI agents had practically thrown him out of the house so they could interrogate Zoe to find out where Raine had been taken.

He stopped and looked back at the house. "They have to get it out of her."

She squeezed his fingers. "They will. Let's give them a few more minutes. If she doesn't crack, I'll get them to let me talk to Ben about it. He's pretty broken now."

The dunes were thick here. She stood in the soft sand and watched the sky darken over the ocean. "I should call my parents and warn them."

"There's no cell service out here. Once we're allowed back inside, we can use the landline."

She nodded. "I'm not looking forward to it. There's such a mixture of feelings—joy that Ben's alive and total despair over what he's done. I don't think they'll take it well."

He squeezed her hand. "Who would?"

His dear face, so open and honest, made her heart hurt. He'd never been anything but the man he showed on the outside. The events of the past few months had shown her how much she'd deceived herself and others. She hid too much of who she was, but no more. From now on, she was not going to be the hypocrite her brother was. She intended to let other people in, to show her faults and trials. No one was perfect. Trying to make believe only led to heartache.

His smile broadened, and she glanced at Curtis from the corner of her eye. Would he say anything about what she'd said to Ben? About loving him? She kept trying the feeling on for size, and it fit amazingly well. Love. She'd never thought to find herself in this situation again. She thought Curtis felt something for her, but watching his face, she wasn't sure it went nearly as deep as her own feelings.

"Penny for your thoughts," she said.

He turned his head and held her glance. "I'm not sure where to start." He lifted her hand and pressed her palm to his lips. "I love you too, you know. When you told your brother how you felt about me, I wanted to kiss you." He grinned. "Obviously, the time wasn't right then."

"But it is now," she murmured as he pulled her close.

His lips were warm and tender. The scent of his breath was pleasing and slightly minty. She wrapped her arms around his neck and kissed him back with every bit of love in her heart. She'd never felt this way before, not ever. Ian had never made her feel like Curtis—safe, protected, and cherished.

He finally lifted his head and smiled down at her. "I never

thought to find someone like you, Amy. I love you. We're going to be so good together. I want a lifetime with you and our kids."

His head lowered again, but she put her hand on his chest and pushed. A cold chill swept up her spine. He had to know something before this went any further.

"I—I have to tell you something." Her throat was tight and her eyes burned. She swallowed hard.

His eyes darkened. "You sound serious. Or scared. I can't tell which."

"Both," she admitted. "I realize now that I should have said something sooner, before both of our feelings were involved."

His eyes crinkled in a smile. "I was a goner from the first day."

She wanted to smile, but it was too serious. Would he walk away too? Her lips were dry, and she wet them. "I—I can't have children, Curtis. I had a hysterectomy two years ago. It was ovarian cancer." She hated saying the word. It made her feel unworthy, unclean.

He sobered at once. "Cancer? Are you all right?"

She nodded. "The doctor was sure he got it all, and I had a round of chemo to be sure." She touched her curls. "That's why this is so short. It takes awhile to grow out."

"How'd they find it?"

"I had some routine blood tests run, and a CA-125 was accidentally marked. It's usually not done in a physical. Mine came back high, so they did an ultrasound and found it. Stage one. I was lucky. So many women aren't."

Instead of pushing her away, he pulled her close, close enough that she could hear his heart thudding under her cheek. She let him hold her while she waited to hear him tell her how sorry he was. How he'd pray for her but it was best they found this out now. Her eyes brimmed with tears, and she clutched his shirt for this last embrace before the dream ended. It had always been too good to be true.

"Praise God," he whispered in her hair. "I couldn't bear to lose you, not now that I've found the love of my life."

She swallowed hard. His heart beat strongly against her ear so maybe she hadn't heard him right. "Did you hear what I said, Curtis? No children. Not ever. You're a man who was made to be a father." She couldn't lift her head, couldn't look him in the eye to see pity there where once she'd seen tenderness.

His big hands gripped her shoulders, and he pulled her away to stare in her face. His eyes were tender and earnest. "It's a good thing we have Raine then, isn't it? Because I can see that mothering spirit in you. And we could always adopt if we want more. There are lots of children in the world who need a home."

Her mouth trembled. "But what about the cancer? What if it comes back?"

He drew her close and rested his chin on her head. "Honey, we have *this* day, this hour. And that's enough. None of us can predict how long we have. I could die before you. We take what God gives us."

She pulled away and stared into his face. "You still want me? Even barren?" She blinked at the burning moisture in her eyes. "I was engaged once. He was from a well-known family and was expected to produce an heir. He broke the engagement the day after my surgery."

His fingers convulsed on her arms. "The scumbag." His voice was tight. "His loss is my gain though."

He bent his head and kissed her again. His lips held a sweet promise. She was breathless when he lifted his head. "Convinced?" His eyes were teasing.

"I'm not sure," she murmured. "Maybe you'd better try that one more time."

But as he bent his head, Tom exited the door of the house, shouting, "They've found Raine! Heather remembered something and rescued her. Let's go!"

Adrenaline kicked Amy into action, and together they ran for the Jeep. "Thank you, God."

Only one small house light twinkled in the dark landscape below. The chopper swooped down to land, and Curtis gripped Amy's hand. In a few minutes, he'd have Raine back in his arms. "They said she was fine. I can't believe it."

"And Heather rescued her." Amy shook her head. "I can't wrap my head around that part. She's just a kid herself, you know."

On the flight, Tom had told them that the cocaine had been traced to Grant. He'd used Gina's empty apartment for pickup after he'd gotten hooked on the drug himself. Ben had given him the key for a cut of the profit and some of the stash as well. At least Gina hadn't been part of that. Preston had also been taken into custody for questioning about his part in Raine's kidnapping.

The helicopter began to descend. Several people were on the porch of the house, and he strained to identify his niece, but it was too dark to make out more than just outlines. When the rails touched the ground and the rotor began to whir slower, he pushed open the door and jumped out, then turned to help Amy.

"Watch your head!" he shouted over the rotor noise.

Bent almost double, the two of them ran for the house. Emerging into the wash of light from the porch lamp, he stared at the figures on the porch. Edith held Raine.

Her face red and blotchy from happy tears, Edith lifted the little girl toward him. "She's fine, Curtis, just fine!"

"Raine!" Curtis barely managed to whisper her name.

The little girl reached for him. His eyes stung as he stepped onto the porch and took her in his arms. Her small hands patted his face, and she kissed him. He inhaled the sweet scent of her, the feel of her in his arms, and his eyes welled. "Oh, honey, are you okay?"

She babbled something he couldn't understand and gave him a grin that melted him into a puddle right there. His throat closed, and he looked at Amy, who was weeping unabashedly. "Look who's here to see you." He turned Raine so she saw Amy.

The little one reached for Amy. "Mom." She hesitated and clutched him again as though she couldn't bear to let go of him. Which was fine with him.

Amy smiled through her tears. "She's clean and looks well cared for, Curtis. God heard our prayers." She reached out and caressed Raine's silky dark curls. "We're so glad to see you, honey."

The baby babbled something again, then offered Amy the small doll clutched in her hand. Amy took it and put the doll on her shoulder. Raine smiled wider, then reached again for Amy, who quickly leaned over to brush her lips against the baby's soft cheek.

Amy pulled away, and Raine clutched Curtis's shirt again. Amy's smile was wide. "I don't think she's leaving your arms. I know I never plan to."

He put one arm around her and turned to speak with his aunt. "I wouldn't let you anyway."

Edith was still crying. "She's home, Curtis. God took care of her."

He wished he had another arm to hug his aunt. "I know, I know." Amy's eyes were smiling, and he knew she wanted Edith to know their good news. "Um, there are going to be changes at the house. But we don't want you going anywhere."

Edith's eyes went wide and scared. "Changes?"

"A move is in our future."

"Move?" Edith's voice was careful.

"You've always loved Rosemary Cottage. How'd you like to live there? Well, as soon as we can arrange a wedding. And we're both going to finalize Raine's adoption."

Edith's hand flew to her mouth. "Oh my stars," she said, punctuating every word.

"I couldn't have said it better myself." He scooped Amy closer.

Raine put her hand on Amy's arm. "Stay," she said in a contented voice.

DEAR READER,

I'm so excited to share *Rosemary Cottage* with you! The story has been a real labor of love. You may not know this, but I lost one of my brothers in a terrible lightning accident in 1990. My life was forever changed that day, and I still miss him. I often find myself daydreaming about him walking in the door, still alive. But I know Randy *is* still alive in heaven, more alive than he's ever been.

I loved how Amy struggled with being real in her life. That's such a common thing in our society, isn't it? I struggle with it myself. I'm a positive person and hate to complain or bring someone else down. But being real is how we're supposed to behave. I'll work on it if you will, okay?

I'm a bit of a "healer" myself and am always trying to solve health problems for my friends. I'm very interested in natural medicine, and it was fun to put some of my obsessions into Amy's character—like Bulletproof Coffee made with Toomer's infrared roasted coffee. That's coffee with MCT oil and butter whipped in the blender. I know it sounds terrible, but it tastes a lot like coffee with cream, and it's so good for you. I drink it every day. And I've recently discovered the benefits of cold immersion (thanks to Dr. Jack Kruse) so I had to have Edith surfing in cold water. I tell everyone that nothing is sacred when it comes to writing. Anything my family does or I do ends up making its way into the pages of one of my books!

As always, I love to hear from you! E-mail me anytime at colleen@colleencoble.com.

Your friend,
Colleen

READING GROUP GUIDE

1. What is your favorite part of the Hope Beach setting?

2. How well do you think you know your siblings or other people close to you? What would shock you?

3. Is there someplace from your childhood where you would want to go to find solace? What is special about it?

4. What did you think of Curtis's decision to keep Raine's parentage to himself?

5. Have you ever kept something to yourself because it was too painful to talk about? What helped you get past the pain?

6. Do you know a midwife or have you had any experience with home birth?

7. Amy was a natural healer. Have you ever known anyone like that, or are *you* like that?

8. Heather was taken in by Grant's smooth talk and good looks. Why do you think she was so easily persuaded?

Acknowledgments

My team at Thomas Nelson is a dream to work with. I can't imagine writing without my editor, Ami McConnell. I crave her analytical eye and love her heart. Ames, you are truly like a daughter to me. Our fiction publisher, Daisy Hutton, is a gale-force wind of fresh air. Love her already! Marketing manager Katie Bond is always willing to listen to my harebrained ideas and has been completely supportive for years. I wouldn't get far without you, friend! Fabulous cover guru Kristen Vasgaard works hard to create the perfect cover—and does. You rock, Kristen! And, of course, I can't forget my other friends who are all part of my amazing fiction family: Amanda Bostic, Becky Monds, Jodi Hughes, Kerri Potts, Ruthie Dean, Heather McCulloch, and Laura Dickerson. You are all such a big part of my life. I wish I could name all the great folks at Thomas Nelson who work on selling my books through different venues. I'm truly blessed!

Julee Schwarzburg is a dream editor to work with. She totally gets romantic suspense, and our partnership is a joy. Thanks for all your hard work to make this book so much better!

My agent, Karen Solem, has helped shape my career in many ways, and that includes kicking an idea to the curb when necessary. Thanks, Karen, you're the best!

Writing can be a lonely business, but God has blessed me with great writing friends and critique partners. Hannah Alexander (Cheryl Hodde), Kristin Billerbeck, Diann Hunt, and Denise Hunter make up the Girls Write Out squad (www.GirlsWriteOut .blogspot.com). I couldn't make it through a day without my peeps! Thanks to all of you for the work you do on my behalf and for your friendship. Thank you, friends!

I'm so grateful for my husband, Dave, who carts me around from city to city, washes towels, and chases down dinner without complaint. As I type this, he has been free of prostate cancer for nearly two years, and we're so thankful! My kids—Dave and Kara (and now Donna and Mark)—and my grandsons, James and Jorden Packer, love and support me in every way possible. Love you guys! Donna and Dave brought me the delight of my life—our little granddaughter, Alexa! She's talking like a grown-up now, and having her spend the night is more fun than I can tell you.

Most important, I give my thanks to God, who has opened such amazing doors for me and makes the journey a golden one.

THE ROCK HARBOR MYSTERY SERIES

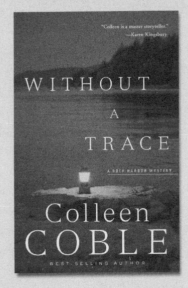

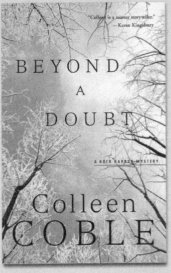

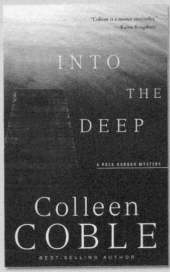

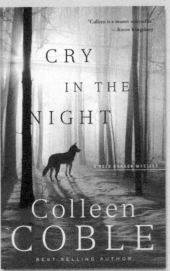

AVAILABLE IN PRINT AND E-BOOK FORMATS

THOMAS NELSON
Since 1798

An Excerpt from *Without a Trace*

It was days like this, when the sun bounced off Lake Superior with an eye-squinting brilliance, that Bree Nicholls forgot all her qualms about living where the Snow King ruled nine months of the year. There was no other place on earth like the U.P.—Michigan's Upper Peninsula. With Keweenaw Peninsula to the north and Ottawa National Forest to the south, there could be no more beautiful spot in the world. The cold, crystal-clear waters of the northernmost Great Lake stretched to the horizon as far as she could see.

But she'd never find those kids by focusing on the seascape. Pressing her foot to the accelerator, she left the lake behind as she urged her old Jeep Cherokee forward along the rutted dirt track. Bree's best friend, Naomi Heinonen, steadied herself against the door's armrest and looked over her shoulder at the two dogs still safely confined in their kennels. The Kitchigami Wilderness Preserve lay to the east, past Miser, a drive of only fifteen miles or so, but on this washboard road, it took longer than Bree liked.

"Don't kill us getting there," Naomi shouted above the road noise.

Bree didn't reply. These lost children weren't some vacationers without ties; they were residents of Rock Harbor, two of their own. And night would be here soon. If Naomi were driving, her foot would be heavy on the accelerator too. The preserve was a formidable tract that could swallow up two kids without a trace.

The wind churned autumn's red and gold leaves in eddies

and blew them across the road like brightly colored tumbleweeds. Equally colorful trees crowded the hills like giant banks of mums. The U.P. in autumn was Bree's favorite time, except when ever-shorter days put strangleholds on their search efforts.

M-18 headed on east, but Bree made a sharp turn onto Pakkala Road, which would take them into a heavily forested area. In the spring, motor homes and SUVs pulling campers plied the road on their way to experience some of the last wilderness left in the Midwest. Today the road was practically empty.

"Fill me in on what we know," Bree said.

"Donovan O'Reilly reported Emily and Timmy missing three hours ago. They were on some outdoor nature thing with their school," Naomi said.

Bree knew Donovan O'Reilly—he owned the local Ace Hardware store. His wife had left him and the kids nearly two years ago, and now his eyes had a haunted look, as though he wondered what fate would hand him next. Bree often stopped by Ace to pick up supplies for the ongoing renovation of her lighthouse home, and a friendship of sorts had developed between them.

"One of the students said she heard Emily talk about seeing a raccoon," Naomi continued, "so that might be what caused the kids to wander off. It's not much to go on, but they've started searching." She chewed on her lip. "You remember Timmy has diabetes? I wonder when his shot is due."

"I was thinking about that." Bree imagined Donovan was out of his mind with worry. "Donovan asked me out last week; did I tell you that?" she asked. She'd been tempted to tell him yes. Her lighthouse echoed with silence, but she had realized it wasn't fair to use someone like Donovan to ward off her loneliness. "I said no, of course."

Naomi didn't reply, and Bree looked at her curiously. "What? You don't like him? Didn't he used to be your brother's best friend? You probably know him and the kids pretty well."

A flush moved to Naomi's cheeks, and she looked out the

window. "That was a long time ago. I only see him at the hardware store now, and I like him fine. Why did you say no?"

"I'm not ready. Maybe I never will be." Bree tapped the steering wheel with impatient fingers, wishing the Jeep could go faster over the bumpy, rutted road. Instead, she slowed and turned onto the access road that would take her back to the campground parking lot.

As she pulled in, Bree saw people fanning out in a search grid. There was an assortment of searchers, ranging from teenagers like Tommy Lempinen to professional types like Inetta Harris, who was still dressed in her business suit. When one of their own was threatened, Rock Harbor residents pulled together.

Bree and Naomi got out, attached leashes to the dogs, and shrugged their arms into their ready-kit backpacks, fully outfitted with first-aid kit, small plastic tarp, energy bars, flashlight, flares, bug repellant, towelettes, compass, Swiss pocketknife, radio, topographic map of the area, canteen, sunglasses, sunscreen, and every other item one was likely to need on a search. A young woman in a brown National Park Service uniform was Bree's first target.

"We're the Kitchigami K-9 Search and Rescue team," Bree told her, though that much was printed on the bright orange vests that both the women and the dogs wore. "I'm Bree Nicholls. Who's in charge?"

The young woman pointed toward a group of people nearly hidden by a stand of sycamore. "The lead ranger is over there." Bree looked and recognized Donovan's ink-dark hair among them.

Bree and Naomi headed toward the group. Donovan saw Bree and broke away. Pain contorted his handsome features. With his black hair and dark blue eyes, Bree had always thought he looked a bit like Pierce Brosnan, though today he was too upset and pale to carry off the James Bond sangfroid.

"Please, you've got to find the kids!" His hands trembled as he thrust two small jackets toward her. "They don't even have their jackets on, and it's supposed to get to near freezing tonight." The torment in his eyes spoke of his fear of loss more clearly than his words. "Timmy's shot is overdue now."

His voice quavered, and Bree put a comforting hand on his arm. She knew the anxiety he felt. "We'll find them, Donovan. The dogs are well trained, and Samson has a special radar for children."

His head snapped up as if mounted on a spring. A dawning hope filled his face. "I'll come with you."

How well Bree remembered that overwhelming desire to help. The waiting was the hard part. When her husband's plane went down, taking their son and all her hopes for their future with it, she had felt a crushing need to do something. In her case, there had been nothing to do but try to move on. With any luck, Donovan probably would not be in that situation.

She shook her head as she took the jackets from his hand. "You have to stay close to base, Donovan. The kids will be scared when we find them, and you'll need to be in a position to get to them quickly when they're found. Try to stay calm. We still have several hours before sunset. We'll find them."

Donovan nodded, but his gaze flickered from Bree to Naomi with a naked appeal in his eyes. "I want to do something."

"Pray," Naomi advised.

His eyes squeezed shut. "I started that as soon as I learned they were gone," he whispered.

Naomi's answer to everything was prayer. Prayer had done little for Bree's own desperate pleas. What use was a God like that?

"Let's go," Bree said.

As they approached the tree line, a slim, feminine figure stepped out of a stand of jack pine and came toward them. Bree lifted a hand in greeting. She should have known her sister-in-law wouldn't be far from the action. She craved media attention the way the mine owners craved cheap workers.

Hilary Kaleva pushed aside the branches barring her way into the clearing as though they were a personal affront. Hilary, Rock Harbor's mayor, was having the mother of all bad-hair days. Her hair, blond like her brother Rob's, was swept up in a formerly elegant French roll, but strands loosened by tree branches now clung damply to her neck. Streaks of mud marred her navy suit, and bits of pine needles clung to the fabric.

"It's the poodle," Naomi muttered to Bree. "I'm out of here. I'll wait with the rangers."

"Coward," Bree murmured. She wished she could laugh. Rob used to call Hilary his "poodle sister," which Hilary found less than amusing, but Bree and Naomi had always thought the description apt. Hilary could be sweet and loving one moment then turn and bite without provocation. And she talked until Bree grew weary of listening. But she could be just as endearing as a poodle when she wanted to be. From the expression on her face, today wasn't one of those days.

Samson woofed at Hilary in greeting and strained at the leash to meet her. The mayor flinched at the sniffing dog, pulling away with a moue of distaste. As if sensing Hilary's animosity, Samson lurched toward Hilary then came alongside Bree and rubbed his nose against her knee. Bree tugged him farther away from her sister-in-law. No sense in upsetting her.

Hilary's scowl eased when Bree pulled the dog a safe distance away. "What are you doing here? I thought you were searching the northeast quadrant today."

Bree's smile faltered. Hilary always managed to drain her confidence with a relentless determination to bend her to her will. "I was home when the call came in. The brick is crumbling on the tower, and it seemed like a good day to repoint it. I was just about to mix the mortar when Mason called." Bree stopped and chided herself for babbling like a kid caught playing hooky. Maybe it was time they both realized Rob's plane might never be found. Not in the northeast quadrant or any other. The forest had swallowed the Bonanza Beechcraft like Superior could swallow a sinking ship.

Hilary's eyes flashed. "You have more important things to do than to repoint the brick on your lighthouse. Let a professional do it."

"The last time I checked, my bank balance was screaming for mercy, Hilary."

Hilary sighed, and she gave a smile that seemed forced. "I'll pay for it. You promised you'd find them, Bree. It's been nearly a year. Rob's birthday is the day after Thanksgiving. I'm counting on giving him a decent burial by then."

Bree wanted to run away from the admonishment. The graves at Rock Harbor Cemetery were as empty as her heart. Even if she found the bodies to fill those graves, it wouldn't change things, but at least maybe then she could bring herself to go there to mourn. Besides, Bree was tiring of Hilary's constant harping on her failure to find them.

"Samson and I are doing the best we can, Hilary. But they could be anywhere. Here in the Kitchigami or maybe even down in Ottawa."

"My patience is running out."

Bree had trained her temper to stay on its leash when she was around Hilary, but some days were harder than others. "I want to find them just as much as you do, Hilary. But I'm not Superwoman." A muscle in Bree's jaw jerked. Hilary didn't understand how hard a task Bree had set up for herself. At least there was still a chance for Donovan's kids. "Look," she finally said, "I need to get on with the search for the O'Reilly children."

She turned and rushed into the woods then hurried along the pine-needle path toward Naomi and the group of rangers under the trees. The rush of cool air soothed her hot cheeks. Would she never find them? Never, never, her footsteps answered.

A dark-haired man was giving directions. About six feet tall and stocky, he gestured with broad hands that looked tanned and capable. When Bree approached, he stopped talking, and his gaze settled on her. Bree smiled and nodded a hello as she stepped forward with an outstretched hand.

"You look like the man I need to see," she said. He looked vaguely familiar, and she wondered if she'd seen him around town. His brown park service uniform matched his hair, and his blue eyes were as keen and intelligent as an Australian shepherd's. She guessed him to be in his early thirties. "I'm Bree Nicholls with my dog, Samson, and this is Naomi Heinonen and her dog, Charley."

The blue eyes narrowed when they saw the dogs. "Who called in the SAR?"

"The sheriff did," one of the men said.

The man pressed his lips together then nodded with obvious reluctance. "I'm Ranger Kade Matthews. I wouldn't have called you in yet, but since you're here we'll try to use you."

Kade Matthews. Bree had heard talk of him at the coffee shop. Rumor said he'd given up a promotion that would have taken him to California when his mother died and left him as guardian of his sixteen-year-old sister. It was to his credit that he'd followed his mother's wishes to have his sister finish school here, though Bree pitied the poor girl. Who would want him as a guardian? She'd run into his kind before, law-enforcer types who wanted to run the show their way even if it cost lives.

"Has anyone found a trail yet?" Bree's gaze wandered toward the gloom of the thickly wooded forest, and she shuffled her feet. The setup always took too long, in her opinion. While people stood around discussing where to start and how to begin, Samson could be homing in on the scent. She knew organization was important, but there was a limit.

Ranger Matthews shook his head. "Not a hint of one. But we're down to the wire here. The little boy's diabetes is a bad case. I've divided the search area into quadrants. The board is over there." He pointed to the trailer set up as a command post. "You and your team can take quadrant two."

"We find our dogs more effective if they're allowed to scent on an article of the victim's then follow where the scent leads. Donovan already gave us—"

The ranger interrupted with another shake of his head. "It's not an efficient way to search. I need to know who's where."

Bree hunched her shoulders and gave Naomi a helpless look. Why did she find it so impossible anymore to speak her mind? When she had first met Rob, her nickname at school was "Brassy Bree" because she had the nerve to do anything she was dared to do. Now she wavered when asked what she wanted to drink. She wanted to argue, but her mouth refused to open.

"We've only got a few more hours of daylight left," Ranger Matthews said. "The sheriff is in the camper briefing the searchers. Please join them."

Thank goodness Mason was here. Bree left the arrogant ranger and went to find her brother-in-law in the camp. Naomi trailed behind her, pausing to say something to Donovan, and Bree wondered at her friend's reluctance to leave him.

The camper sat along the side of the parking lot. It hadn't been leveled and tilted heavily to the right. The silver siding bore scratches and gouges from its many brushes with tree branches and thorny shrubs. The door to the camper opened as Bree approached and Mason stepped out.

"Oh good, you're here," Mason said. Sheriff of Kitchigami County, Mason was thickly built and good-natured, a mellow, golden retriever sort of man instead of the pit bull some in Kitchigami County thought a sheriff ought to be.

"Who's Attila the Hun?" Bree asked.

Mason frowned. "Who?"

"The ranger honcho. Kade Matthews."

"He's a good man. You have a problem with him?"

"He's insisting on a grid search. That will take forever," Bree said. Naomi joined her finally, and Bree thought she looked a little flushed.

Mason shook his head. "I'll handle Kade. You two take this insulin for the boy and find those kids." He handed Bree a syringe.

Bree took the insulin and tucked it into her ready-pack. The hormone was a stark reminder of the urgency of the search. Tomorrow wouldn't be good enough—they had to find those kids tonight. She knelt beside Samson and Charley and held the jackets Donovan had given her under their noses. The jackets had been contaminated with other scents, but Samson had worked under these kinds of adverse circumstances before, and she had confidence in her dog. To help the dogs, she had them sniff the insides of the jackets where there was a greater likelihood of strong scent untainted by handling.

Samson whined and strained at the leash. Bree released his lead and dropped her arm. "Search!" she commanded.

Samson bounded toward the trees. Charley plunged his nose into the jacket again then raised his muzzle and whined. Naomi unclipped Charley's leash, and he raced after Samson. Both dogs ran back and forth, their muzzles in the air. The dogs weren't bloodhounds but air scenters. They worked in a "Z" pattern, scenting the air until they could catch a hint of the one scent they sought. Samson's tail stiffened, and he turned and raced toward the creek.

"He's caught it!" Bree said, running after her dog. Naomi followed Charley. Bree heard the ranger shout as he realized they were disobeying his instructions, but then the sounds of people and cars fell away as though they had slipped into another world. The forest engulfed them, and the rustling of the wind through the trees, the muffled sounds of insects and small animals, and the whispering scent of wet mud and leaf mold all welcomed Bree as though she'd never been away. In spite of their familiarity, Bree knew the welcome was just a facade. The North Woods still guarded its secrets from her.

⌒

After nearly two hours, Bree was hot and itchy. She started to sit on a fallen log, then the drone of honeybees inside alerted her, and she avoided it, choosing instead to rest on a tree stump to catch her breath. Though the bees were sluggish this time of year, she didn't want to take any chances. Naomi thrashed her way through the vegetation as she rushed to catch up with Bree and the dogs.

Samson had lost the scent about ten minutes ago, and he criss-crossed the clearing, searching for the lost trail with his muzzle in the air. Bree unfastened a canteen from her belt and took a gulp of water. Though warm, the water washed the bitter taste of insect repellant from her tongue. She dropped her backpack onto the ground and pulled out a small bag of pistachios. Cracking the nuts, she tossed the shells onto the ground. She munched the salty nutmeats and took another swig of water.

Naomi came up behind her, short of breath. "Anything?" She pushed away a lock of hair that had escaped her braid. Naomi was like a cocker spaniel with her soft brown hair and compassion-ate eyes—and like a spaniel, just as persistent. Her spirit never flagged, and she always managed to transfer her optimism to Bree.

Bree shook her head and held out the bag of nuts to Naomi. "Want some?"

Naomi wrinkled her nose. "I don't know how you can stand to eat those things. Give me walnuts or pecans, not those funny green things. You eat so many of them, we'd never need search dogs to find you; we'd just follow the shell trails."

Bree grinned and put the bag of nuts back in her bag. She screwed the lid back onto the canteen and fastened it to the belt around her waist. "Time to get moving again."

"Charley's lost the trail," Naomi said. Charley nosed aimlessly among a patch of wildflowers while Samson thrust his head into the stream running to their right.

"Maybe the other searchers are having better luck." Bree snapped her fingers, and Samson came to her. He shook himself, and droplets of water sprayed her jeans. She knelt and took his shaggy head in her hands and stared into his dark eyes. "I know you're trying, buddy," she whispered. "But can you try just a little harder?" Samson's curly tail swished the air, and he licked her chin as if to say he'd do what he could. And Bree knew he would. As a search dog, Samson was in a class by himself.

Bree knew dogs. From the time she could barely toddle, she'd had a dog. When she and Rob had lived in Oregon, she'd been introduced to K-9 Search and Rescue, and she knew it was what she was meant to do. Margie, her first dog, had been a pro too, but she'd had a stroke three years ago, about six months after Samson had come along.

She'd never seen a dog with as much heart as Samson. His markings and size betrayed his German shepherd lineage, but his curly coat was all chow. Since the day she'd found him in a box by the river, barely alive and not yet four weeks old, his gaze had spoken to her more clearly than any human words could. When he'd turned his head that day and tried to lick her hand, she lost her heart. There was a special bond between her and Samson, and he loved search and rescue as much as she did. Together they'd been on search missions all over the country as part of the FEMA team.

He whined and sniffed the air as if determined not to let her down.

"If Samson can't find the kids, we might as well all go home," Naomi muttered. "He could find a flea in a hay field."

Bree grinned. "The fleas seem to find him." But she knew Naomi was right. Samson was special. She wanted him to prove it today.

Up ahead, Samson began to bark and then raced away. Bree's adrenaline kicked into overdrive. "He's found the scent again." Her fatigue forgotten, she followed the dogs.

Libby arrives at the Tidewater Inn hoping to
discover clues about her friend's disappearance.
There she finds an unexpected inheritance and
a love beyond her wildest dreams.

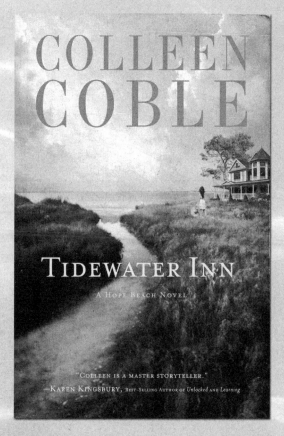

The first novel in the Hope Beach Series

AVAILABLE IN PRINT AND E-BOOK

THOMAS NELSON
Since 1798

9781595547828-A

Love is on the way

Available in print and e-book

9781401687007-B

"*The Lightkeeper's Bride* is a wonderful story filled with mystery, intrigue, and romance. I loved every minute of it."

— CINDY WOODSMALL,
New York Times best-selling author of *The Hope of Refuge*

THE BEST-SELLING MERCY FALLS SERIES.

AVAILABLE IN PRINT AND E-BOOK

ABOUT THE AUTHOR

Photo by Clik Chick Photography

RITA finalist Colleen Coble is the author of several best-selling romantic suspense novels, including *Tidewater Inn*, and the Mercy Falls, Lonestar, and Rock Harbor series.